The Way Things Should Be

Carrie Carr

Yellow Rose Books

Nederland, Texas

Copyright © 2005 by Carrie Carr

All rights reserved. No part of this publication may be reproduced, transmitted in any form or by any means, electronic or mechanical, including photocopy, recording, or any information storage and retrieval system, without permission in writing from the publisher. The characters, incidents and dialogue herein are fictional and any resemblance to actual events or persons, living or dead, is purely coincidental.

ISBN 1-932300-39-2

First Printing 2005

9 8 7 6 5 4 3 2 1

Cover design by Donna Pawlowski

Published by:

Yellow Rose Books
PMB 210, 8691 9th Avenue
Port Arthur, Texas 77642-8025

Find us on the World Wide Web at
http://www.regalcrest.biz

Printed in the United States of America

Acknowledgments

I want to thank Lori L. Lake for her tireless editing and good humor; the folks on my email list for their continued support; my wonderful wife AJ for always cheering me on; and for my publisher Cathy, who still allows me to live my dreams through my books.

Dedication

To my Mom, who showed more strength this year through trying times — you're my hero.

And to my wife, AJ, the woman of my dreams and the keeper of my heart. Forever and always, my love.

Chapter One

HANDS, WRINKLED WITH age, gently patted the leather-bound picture album before tucking it away into a cardboard box. A quick glance around the room showed Travis Edwards that it was the final book to pack, so he climbed to his feet and dusted his hands across the thighs of his faded jeans. Still slender and active, and with his thick silver hair and neatly trimmed mustache, he looked closer to sixty-five than a man who had just celebrated his eightieth birthday. He placed the palms of his hands against his lower back and stretched his tall frame as a woman with faded blonde hair entered the room.

The middle-aged woman handed him a large glass of iced tea, condensation already making the outside of the tumbler slippery. "Mr. Edwards, why don't you let me finish up in here?"

"Thank you, Nancy, but that's really not necessary. You've had enough to handle with the other parts of the house. The least I can do is finish putting away old pictures for the move."

Travis had recently returned to Dallas to pack up his personal belongings so that he could move back to Somerville to be with his family. His granddaughter Lexington had offered him a room at her home, but Travis's pride wouldn't allow that. Instead, he enlisted Lexington's partner Amanda to find him just the perfect house in town, which she did. It was a few short blocks away from Amanda's grandparents' home, and the four-bedroom house would be perfect for him and his housekeeper, who had agreed to make the move with him.

He took a deep draw from the glass and sighed in relief. The look he received from his long-time housekeeper brought a smile to his face. "I know, I know. You're going to tell me *again* how I should have just paid for someone to do all of this, right?"

Nancy shook her head. "Of course not, Mr. Edwards. That would be rude." She smirked with the familiarity of their years together. "But I did promise your granddaughter that I'd keep an eye on you and not let you overdo it." She waited until he drained the glass, and then took it from his hand. "If you'll go upstairs and rest for a little while, I'll make sure that these boxes are properly marked."

Travis knew when he'd been beaten. "That sounds like a good idea. I'll just—" The ringing of the doorbell interrupted him. Before the housekeeper could take a step, he waved her off. "I'll take care of it. Probably one of the movers here early." With a smile and a wave, Travis stepped around a pile of boxes and headed for the front door.

He opened the door and looked into eyes that somehow triggered painful memories, rendering him speechless. A moment later, the pain was replaced with confusion. Standing on the front steps of his home was a thin woman who appeared to be in her late thirties, with brown hair and eyes so light brown they were almost golden. Shaking off the eerie feeling, Travis attempted to smile. "May I help you?"

Looking embarrassed, the woman brushed one hand through hair that barely reached her collar. Her clothes were clean, but she was obviously out of her element in the well-to-do neighborhood. A wrinkled denim jacket covered her black tee shirt, which was tucked into faded blue jeans. The scuffed white sneakers on her feet had seen better days, and she was carrying a dark green backpack over one shoulder. "Is this the Edwards' residence?"

"Yes, I'm Travis Edwards. Is there something I can do for you, miss?" Travis felt vaguely unsettled at the woman's presence. Her features were familiar, although he couldn't place where he might have seen her before.

Her face registered surprise at the owner of the grand house answering the door. "I don't know, Mr. Edwards." She let her hand fall to her side and mumbled, "This probably wasn't a very good idea."

"I'm sorry, but if you're trying to sell me something, I'm really not interested. You see, I've got a lot of things to finish up today, and—"

"No, sir, I'm not selling anything. My name's Eleanor Gordon, but everyone calls me Ellie." She reached under the collar of her tee shirt and pulled on a chain, which held a large gold class ring. "My mother is Naomi Gordon."

Travis leaned forward. His heart began to pound when he recognized the ring. "Where did you get that?"

Ellie lifted the chain over her head and handed the jewelry to him for closer inspection. "My mother gave it to me. She said it belonged to my father."

"Your father?" Travis looked inside the gold band and read the engraved initials *W.T.E.* "This was my son's." His eyes met hers. "I think you should come inside so we can talk."

She followed him inside, stepping past boxes and trying to take in the grandeur of the large house. A winding staircase took up much of the marble floored foyer, and neatly labeled boxes were stacked against the walls. As she followed Travis down a carpeted hallway, Ellie noticed the occasional expensive chair, or table, along the way. The farther into the home she got, the more nervous Ellie became. What had started out as a quest to find the other half of her family quickly turned into wanting to run away as fast as she could.

Travis led the silent woman into the sitting room, one of the last areas left to pack. He motioned with one hand to the Victorian divan. Ellie promptly sat down on the edge, as if afraid it would break under her weight. She took the backpack that had been slung over one shoulder and placed it on the floor by her feet. Travis sat on the chair across from her and studied her slender form. Already small in stature, the way her clothes hung on her made Ellie appear as if she was in need of a few good meals. He looked up as Nancy appeared in the doorway.

"Mr. Edwards? Is there something I can bring for you and your…guest?" She cast a dubious glance at the woman seated on the divan, but her years of training wouldn't allow her to be rude. It wasn't in her nature.

Travis looked away from Ellie, who stayed silent. "Oh, yes. Thank you, Nancy. How about bringing us some of those nice sandwiches and more tea? I believe that Miss Gordon and I have a lot of things to discuss." He waited until Nancy left the room, then turned his attention back to the young woman.

Ellie's eyes were fixed on the battered leather encasing her feet. She could feel the older man's gaze upon her, but her nervousness kept her from meeting his eyes. The butterflies in her stomach were dive-bombing the candy bar she'd had for breakfast, and once again Ellie privately questioned her sanity for coming here. She jumped when Travis cleared his throat.

"Miss Gordon, I don't want to appear nosy or rude, but would you mind telling me how you came to receive this?" Travis raised the ring and chain he still held in his hand, fearing if he loosened his hold it would disappear. "It's not that I don't believe you, it's just that—"

"No, I understand." Ellie swallowed hard and forced herself to look into his eyes, which held no censure, only kindness. "A few months ago, I was helping my mother clean out her attic and found a bunch of old letters and pictures." Ellie bent over and unzipped her backpack. Rummaging through its contents, she retrieved a photograph, which she passed over to Travis.

Although he had a good idea of what was coming, nothing could have prepared him for the emotional jolt that the old black-and-white provoked. His son, looking strong and handsome in his Army uniform, shared an intimate smile with the woman standing next to him. Neither one was looking at the camera, but it wasn't hard to see that they were very much in love.

"That was taken the weekend before he shipped out. Mom says that she was already pregnant with me in that picture, although neither of them knew it at the time."

"How long—" Travis's voice cracked. He cleared his throat and tried again. "How long did they know each other?" It wasn't like Billy to hide the fact that he was in love. His son had always worn his heart on his sleeve and usually bragged to the world about his latest "true love."

Ellie was uncomfortable with the fact that her appearance had upset the man in front of her. He seemed very nice, not to mention much too old to be put through such an extreme emotional shock. She mentally cursed herself for not thinking things through and for impetuously racing into the situation before getting all the facts. "I think they'd been dating for about a month before the picture was taken."

Although the woman sitting before him was a carbon copy of his late son, Travis felt he had to ask the next question. "And your mother is completely certain that Billy was your father? Just because he had given her his school ring, doesn't necessarily mean they were in an exclusive relationship."

"She was sixteen, Mr. Edwards. He was her first and her only until she married my stepfather five years later." Ellie pulled out another picture, this one in color. Standing at the beach in their bathing suits was an attractive family: a woman with dark hair and eyes with her arm around the waist of a man who was blond with light eyes, and an eight-year-old Ellie standing behind a toddler with blond hair that was almost white. "That's my brother, William. He's five years younger than me."

"William?"

"Yes, sir. My dad is a great guy, and it was his idea, according to my mom." Ellie accepted the color picture back from Travis, but allowed him to keep the black-and-white. "That one is for you, Mr. Edwards. I thought you might want to have it."

Travis brushed the dampness from his eyes. He was saved from speaking by Nancy, who brought in a tray holding a plate of sandwiches, two glasses of tea, and a pitcher. When she saw how upset her employer was, it took all of Nancy's training not to go into attack mode. She put her hand on his shoulder in a comforting gesture. "Is there anything else I can get for you, Mr. Edwards?"

"No, Nancy. Thank you." After Nancy left the room, Travis addressed his guest once again. "So, your mother never told you about your father? Why wait until now?"

Ellie sighed. She had sometimes asked herself that very question. "Mom told me years ago that my father was killed in Vietnam, and that she didn't know of any living relatives. I never questioned it because Anthony, my stepdad, has always been an excellent father. I had no reason to want to look into my roots. But, like I told you earlier, when we found the old letters that your son had written my mom, I wanted to know more about him. So, here I am. All she knew was that he was from Texas, so I traced the school ring to Dallas." She didn't mention all the phone calls she had to make to find out where William was interred. She visited the cemetery to see the memorial stone, and she found where her grandmother had been buried. The headstone that bore her grandfather's name had no dates, which led her to hope he might still be alive. This was one of four houses left on her list of homes to check, and she was glad she had finally found the right Travis Edwards.

"And you just dropped everything to come find me? What about your family, your job?" Travis held out an empty plate to Ellie, motioning that she should take it and a sandwich. At first she declined, but when she saw he wasn't going to give up, she took the plate and placed half of a sandwich on it.

"Thank you." Ellie picked up one of the glasses and took a long drink, not bothering to sweeten the tea like she normally would. The cold liquid quenched her parched throat, and the shock of it hitting her empty stomach caused her to stifle a gasp. "My family understands my need to learn about my real father, Mr. Edwards. They don't like it, but they understand. They're back in San Diego, where I was born. As for my job, well, let's just say I'm on vacation." She stopped speaking and took several bites of the sandwich, trying to keep from looking like it was her first real food in days, which it was.

Travis leaned back in his chair and watched the woman eat. She didn't gulp her food, but he could tell that she was definitely hungry. Her manners showed a good upbringing, and he could almost hear his beloved wife's voice telling him to quit treating their granddaughter like a stranger. "Eleanor? I'm sorry, may I call you Eleanor?"

She nodded, then swallowed. "Yes, sir. You can call me Eleanor, or Ellie. Whatever you like, Mr. Edwards."

"Excellent. But only if you call me Travis. And, maybe when you're more comfortable, you can call me Grandpa, or Grandfather, whatever you'd like."

Ellie almost choked on her iced tea. She wiped her mouth with the back of her hand. "Thank you, Mister . . . I mean, Travis. I'd really like that."

He smiled and stood up. "I'd like that, too, Ellie. Why don't you let me show you upstairs, where you can get cleaned up and maybe rest? I'm sure your journey from San Diego was a long one." Travis watched as Ellie eyed what was left of the sandwiches. "Why don't I have Nancy bring these up to your room?"

"Thanks." Ellie reached down and grabbed her backpack, then stood up. "I don't want to put you to any trouble. I'm sure I could find someplace nearby to stay." Only she knew how bogus her offer was, since she had less than thirty dollars left in her pocket. But Ellie had made it this far without charity and was too proud to change her ways now.

"Nonsense. I have more than enough room and plenty of places to sleep, at least until the movers get here. What are your plans now?" Travis led Ellie to the staircase in the foyer, where he took the steps slowly so as not to make her nervous. "I hope you plan on staying for a while, so that we can get to know each other."

Ellie hadn't thought that far ahead. Her main goal, which was to meet more of her family, had been attained. *Movers? That figures. I finally find my grandfather, and he's moving away. Seems to be how my luck runs.* Now she was at a loss. She followed Travis up the stairs, all the while wondering where she was to go to from there.

Chapter Two

IN A CLEARING just beyond a deserted gravel road, two men stood in deep conversation. Both were dressed in dark suits, and the taller of the two scrawled notes on a clipboard he held while the other chewed on a thick cigar and looked around. The occasional birdcall and the rustling of golden leaves on the trees were the only sounds around them, often punctuated by the scratching of pen against paper.

Not used to the heat of the Texas fall season, cigar man unbuttoned his suit coat. He pointed through the trees to the north. "You say a spring-fed creek runs about fifty yards away? How much water are we talking about here?"

The tall man looked up from the notes he was taking. "From the geologist's report, the main spring originates about ten miles away, but it's fed by several smaller ones as it travels south." Sweat caused his wire-framed glasses to slide down his nose, and he impatiently pushed them back up with one finger. His short, dark hair was plastered to his head, making him wish that he had left his jacket in the rental car that was parked on the other side of the fence. "Properly dammed, we could have a nice lake to the west of here within a year."

"Good. Our employer has been breathing down my neck for months, Wilson. We need to finish up buying the land around here, no matter what the cost." Cigar man spit a wad of soggy tobacco near the other man's feet and tossed what was left of his cigar to the ground. "We're not going to have any trouble with this, are we?"

Wilson casually took a step forward and crushed the glowing stub under the sole of his imported leather shoe. "Not that I'm aware of, Mr. Billings. Since the owner of the land defaulted on his payments so quickly, not many people know about the upcoming auction. It shouldn't take much of a bid to win."

"See that we do. After that Montana fiasco, my ass is on the line." He took a white handkerchief from his pocket and wiped the perspiration from his face. His bald head gleamed in the morning sun, and he hastily ran the cloth across his crown. "I don't care what it takes. We *have* to get this land. Once we've secured this tract, then the rest of the area should fall into our hands easily." Billings reached inside his coat for another cigar and snipped off its end with a silver cutter. He took his time lighting the rolled tobacco, closing his eyes as the smoke rolled around in his mouth. A long moment later, his eyes reopened and he removed the cigar and pointed it at the man who stood across from him. "Nothing, I repeat, *nothing* better screw this up, Wilson. If my ass gets burned, you can be sure yours will be melted." He spat again, then re-buttoned the dark coat and stalked to the fence.

A LIGHT KNOCK on her door caused Amanda Cauble to look up from her desk and brush dishwater blonde hair away from her face. "Come in." When an older woman entered the room, she stood up and hurried around the desk to embrace her. "Gramma, what a wonderful surprise. What brings you to the office today?"

Anna Leigh Cauble returned her granddaughter's exuberant hug, then allowed herself to be seated in one of the guest chairs while Amanda sat next to her in the other. "Can't I come to see my granddaughter when I want?" Although in her seventies, Anna Leigh was still a beautiful woman, and her slender form rested regally in the chair. Her once reddish-blonde hair was now completely silver and kept short in the latest style, showing the pride she took in her appearance. The expensive red slacks suit fit her well, and her moderate jewelry consisted of a thin wedding band and diamond stud earrings.

"Of course you can. I'm just so glad to see you, that's all." Amanda brushed the wrinkles from her navy skirt. "How about I take you to lunch to make up for my manners?" She watched as Anna Leigh smiled and knew that she'd been forgiven.

"Actually, I was coming to ask *you* to lunch, dearest. But I'm not one to pass on a free meal, especially from the manager of such a fine establishment." Although Anna Leigh owned Sunflower Realty, which Amanda managed for her, she no longer worried about the day-to-day workings of the business.

Knowing she'd been gotten again, Amanda shook her head and stood up. "Let me get my purse, and we'll go down the street to The Crossing. At least they have a good lunch menu."

A short time later, both women were stationed at window

seats in the bustling restaurant, sipping iced tea and waiting for their orders. Amanda watched her grandmother for a moment, then tapped the table. "Okay, spill it."

"Spill what, dear?" Anna Leigh tried her best to appear innocent, but failed miserably.

"Come on, Gramma. Your hands haven't stilled since we sat down, and you keep looking around the room as if you were afraid someone was watching. What's up?"

Anna Leigh took another sip of her tea, then set the glass down on the table. "You are much too smart for your own good, Mandy. I swear, you're as bad as your grandfather." She straightened the knife and fork on the table. "I need your help. I know you're real busy with the office right now, but the girls put me in charge, and well, I'm at a loss."

"In charge? What are you talking about?" Amanda leaned forward to hear her grandmother's muted words. "What girls?"

"From the office, Mandy. Don't tell me you don't know." At that moment, the waitress brought each of them their salads. "Thank you."

"You're welcome, ma'am. Is there anything else you two ladies need?" the waitress asked, even though she was already looking at another table, calculating how long it would be before they needed refills on their drinks.

"No, thank you. We're fine." Amanda dismissed her politely, anxious to hear what Anna Leigh had to say. After the waitress left, she waited for a long beat. "Well?"

Anna Leigh raised a forkful of lettuce to her mouth, but didn't eat. "Well, what?" She put the food into her mouth and chewed daintily.

"Argh!" Amanda threw her hands up in the air in frustration. "What about the girls at the office? Is there something wrong that they asked you to bring up to me?" She looked down at her bowl of salad, suddenly not very hungry.

Feeling bad, Anna Leigh swallowed her food and shook her head. "No, of course not. I was talking about the baby shower." She reached across the table and patted Amanda's hand. "I thought you knew about it."

Amanda rolled her eyes. "All this secrecy is about a baby shower? Good grief." She picked up her glass of tea and swallowed about half its contents.

"Of course, Mandy. You know what a gossip Wanda is. It's almost impossible to keep anything a secret from her, but we're determined to surprise her with a baby shower." Wanda Skimmerly worked at Sunflower Realty with Amanda. After years of marriage, she and her husband Dirk were expecting their first child. It wasn't something that they had planned for, but they were excited just the same. The other women at the office were so happy for them both, they wanted to do something fun for them.

"Well, good luck, Gramma. I bet she figures it out before you get it planned." Amanda started on her salad, relieved that her grandmother's news wasn't of a more serious nature.

Anna Leigh returned her attention to her plate. They concentrated on their salads for several minutes before she cleared her throat. "I was thinking about having the shower at our home next Saturday, Mandy. What do you think?"

"I'm sure it'll be fine, Gramma." A shrill sound to the left of their table caught Amanda's attention. She watched as a woman comforted an infant, rocking and cooing quietly. Intent on the scene, she almost didn't hear her grandmother's next words.

"Excellent. Then I can count on you to help me host it, right?"

Amanda had just taken a drink of tea and almost spewed it all over the table. She hastily swallowed, then coughed and sputtered for several moments before she was able to speak. "Me? Why me?"

Unruffled, Anna Leigh dabbed at her lips with her napkin. "Because you're my granddaughter and the manager of the office. Why not?" She looked up into Amanda's eyes. "Is there a problem, Mandy? I suppose I can always find someone else to help me, if you're too busy."

"No, Gramma, it's not that." Amanda honestly didn't know why the idea of co-hosting a baby shower made her so uncomfortable. But her grandmother had been there for her when no one else was, and she was determined to repay her in this small way. "Next Saturday?"

"That's right. I'm hoping that you and Lexington could maybe stay over Friday night, so we can get an early start on Saturday. What do you think?"

I'm thinking that Lex will probably want to kill me for this. As much as Amanda dreaded a baby shower, she hated to imagine her partner's reaction when she told her they'd been drafted to help with one. She listened politely as her grandmother started talking about plans, colors, and refreshments.

"HAVE YOU COMPLETELY lost your mind?" Lexington Walters yelled, throwing her hat down in disgust. Her dark hair was plastered against her scalp where the hat had been, but she didn't seem to care. She glared at the man standing in front of her, who had the good sense to be looking at the ground and not into her stormy eyes, turned almost violet with anger. "What makes you think I'd go along with this?"

The man being dressed down bit the inside of his cheek to keep from going off on the rancher. This was his first day of work at the ranch, and he thought his previous experience with breaking horses would impress her. Once she had finished her tirade, he looked into her face and shrugged. "It's the way I've always done it, Ms. Walters. I've never had any complaints before."

Lex picked up her hat and dusted it against her leg. "You've obviously worked for some real idiots, then, Roger." She heard his intake of breath, and wasn't surprised at the explosion.

"Look, lady, I've been in this business since before you were in diapers, and I don't appreciate you talking to me like I'm some sort of green kid." Roger stepped closer until they were almost nose to nose, which was a surprise to him, since he was almost six feet tall. "If you don't like my methods, fine. Let me talk to the guy who usually breaks in your horses, and we'll compare notes."

"You want to talk to the 'guy' who breaks our horses?" Lex laughed. "You're looking at her." She looked over at her foreman, Roy, who had been standing nearby in case the new hire got out of hand. "Have the boys bring up a couple of horses to break, Roy. Tomorrow morning I'll be showing Mr. Jenson how we do things at the Rocking W." She turned back to Roger. "Don't be late." Lex walked off, leaving Roger staring at her back, dumbstruck.

Roy patted the newest ranch hand on the back in both in sympathy and amusement, then headed back to the bunkhouse. This wasn't the first time that he'd witnessed a new hire underestimating their boss.

A tall lanky teen, who had been watching from a distance, waited until Lex was far enough away from the other men so that he wouldn't be heard. Ronnie jogged up and fell in step beside Lex, waiting for the right moment to speak.

"Okay, Ronnie. Spill it. You seem to be busting at the seams with something to say." Lex continued to walk, but she slowed her pace slightly so that the teenager could keep up. Although the sixteen-year-old had gone through a recent growth spurt, he was still several inches shorter than she, and because of his gangly build, he moved clumsily at times. He had practically become her shadow since his adoption months earlier by Martha and Charlie, and Lex had to admit to herself that she enjoyed his company.

He shook his head at her perception. It never failed to amaze Ronnie how Lex seemed to know everything that went on at the ranch. He was hoping he'd grow up to be half as good at what he'd decided to do, which was go to school to become a veterinarian. Now if he could just get up the nerve to tell his benefactor. But for now, he was more interested in how Lex ran the ranch. "Did I hear right? Are you going to break some horses tomorrow?"

"Yep." Her anger still bubbling, Lex kept her answers short. If she hadn't caught Jenson with the sadistic bit he was planning on using for breaking horses, she'd have ended up with several animals with ruined mouths. Lex couldn't believe the ignorance of the man, who had come to the ranch with glowing letters of recommendation.

Ronnie could tell that Lex was still fuming over her confrontation with the new hire, but his excitement got the better of him. "I know that I'm supposed to clean out the stables on Saturday morning, but would it be okay if I came up to the corral and watched you break horses first? Maybe I can take care of my chores tonight, after dinner." He held his breath in anticipation of her answer.

The teenager's request caused Lex to stop in her tracks. "Why would you want to waste your time watching something like that?"

"I don't think it's a waste of time at all, Lex. It's another part of how the ranch works, and you promised you'd show me everything."

"I did, didn't I?"

"Yes, ma'am. You told me that as long as my grades stayed up, you'd teach me everything you know about ranching." Ronnie smiled with pride. "I'm on the honor roll this semester, so I've kept my part of the bargain."

Lex nodded, then resumed her trek. "So you have." She couldn't help but admire Ronnie's thirst for knowledge, something that he had shown almost from the moment he arrived at the ranch. "I'll make you a deal. You finish up your homework tonight, and the two of us will take care of the stables after we teach Jenson a thing or two. How's that sound?"

"All right!" Ronnie whooped, pumping his fist in the air and jumping up. At Lex's grin, he put his hands in the back pocket of his jeans and tried to appear nonchalant. "That sounds like a good deal to me, Lex. Thanks."

His exuberance brought the rancher out of her foul mood. She wrapped one arm around the young man's shoulder and pulled him close. "Anytime, buddy." They walked the rest of the way to the ranch house in silence, both thinking about the coming morning.

"OH, MANDY. ISN'T this just the most darling thing?" Anna Leigh held up a garish pink infant dress for her granddaughter's inspection. "I think that Wanda would love it."

Amanda rolled her eyes. For someone with as much class as her grandmother had, the woman had absolutely *no* taste in baby clothes. "Gramma, you've already bought four other pink outfits. What if she doesn't like pink?"

"Nonsense, dear. All baby girls look good in pink." But to her credit, Anna Leigh returned the item to the rack. She turned to see Amanda staring at a young couple nearby.

The man, tall and very nice looking with dark hair and eyes, held a six-month old baby. He bent his head down and kissed the child's head while his wife looked on with a smile. They were about Amanda's age, and she couldn't help but be envious of the cooing bundle as she looked on. It seemed that everywhere she looked lately there was either a pregnant woman or someone with a baby. Even Wanda, who had never expressed a desire for a family, was due in the next few weeks. Her sister Jeannie was also expecting, due in another month.

Concerned at the look on Amanda's face, Anna Leigh touched her arm. "Is everything okay, Mandy? You seem a million miles away."

"Hmm?" Amanda blinked. She pasted a smile on her face and turned around. "I'm sorry, Gramma. What did you say?"

"I asked if anything was wrong. You're not yourself today."

Much to her dismay, tears welled up in Amanda's eyes. "I'm fine, really." She turned away, embarrassed by her emotions. "If you'll excuse me for a moment, I need to go to the ladies room."

Anna Leigh watched in surprise as Amanda rushed away, wiping at her face with her hands. "Now I wonder what all that was about," she murmured. She made a mental note to call the ranch in the next few days and check with Martha, hoping that the housekeeper would have some insight into her granddaughter's strange behavior.

LEX STEPPED OUT of the shower and wrapped a towel around her body. She fluffed her hair dry with another towel, then walked into the bedroom. At no sign of her lover anywhere, Lex frowned.

Amanda had been quiet all through dinner, not even joining

in the teasing when Martha gave Lex a hard time about attending Wanda's baby shower. After the meal, Amanda quietly excused herself, citing her need to make a few phone calls before locking herself in the office.

Worried, Lex glanced at the bedside clock. Almost two hours had gone by since she had last seen Amanda. *I didn't think she'd be that upset with me.* When Amanda told her about the baby shower, Lex had been less than enthused. Of course, the rest of the table enjoyed a nice laugh at her expense, not that she minded. The thought of spending hours with a group of women oohing and ahhing over baby items was not Lex's idea of a good time. Charlie had slapped her on the back and promised the rancher that she'd live through the ordeal, while Martha offered to buy her a dress for the occasion. All she had to do to quiet a giggling Ronnie was glare at him, but Lex figured her lack of enthusiasm for the event had upset her partner more than she'd thought.

She hurriedly dressed in a pair of boxers and a heavy tee shirt, determined to speak to Amanda and find out what was bothering her, once and for all. In her haste, she nearly knocked the object of her search over, when they met at the bedroom door.

"Sorry," Amanda mumbled, putting her hands on Lex's hips to steady herself. She didn't bring her eyes up, instead finding the floor beneath them fascinating.

"No, I'm the one who's sorry." Lex backed into the bedroom, pulling her lover with her. She started to sit them down on the bed, when Amanda broke free of her grasp and headed for the bathroom.

"I'll be back after my shower." Amanda was almost to the bathroom door when she felt Lex's hands on her hips again.

"Want me to scrub your back?"

Not looking at Lex, Amanda disentangled herself. "That's okay. You just got dry." She closed the door in Lex's face. "I'll be out in a little bit."

Lex stood staring at the closed door. She was torn between going in and apologizing or allowing Amanda her space. The way she had been dismissed helped her decide, and Lex dropped her shoulders and went to lie on the bed to wait.

A short time later, Amanda stepped out of the bathroom, wrapped in the flowery terry cloth robe that Lex had given her when they'd first met. She crossed to the dresser and found a long nightshirt, then turned and headed back to the bathroom without speaking. She came back out a few minutes later, her hair still damp from her shower.

"Feel better?" Lex asked, more for something to say than anything else.

Amanda sat on her side of the bed, her back to Lex. "What's that supposed to mean?" She slipped under the covers and lay on her back, looking at the ceiling.

"Nothing. I just—"

"I'm sorry," Amanda interrupted, rolling over to face her lover. "I didn't mean to snap at you like that, Lex."

Lex rolled over until she mirrored Amanda's posture, her head propped on one hand. She used her other hand to brush the damp hair away from the sad eyes across from her. "What's wrong?"

Turning her head, Amanda kissed the palm that caressed her face. She closed her eyes, not certain how to answer the question. "I don't know," she whispered, her voice breaking. "Hold me, please?" An instant later she was cradled in strong arms, her head pillowed on her lover's chest. The soothing motion of Lex's hands stroking her hair and back calmed Amanda somewhat, but she still felt unsettled. *What is wrong with me?* Not wanting to think about it any further, she concentrated on the loving touch, allowing herself to unwind.

The tense body in her arms slowly relaxed, and before Lex could question her anymore, Amanda fell asleep. The rancher lay in the darkness, holding the woman she loved and wondering what she could do to help.

Chapter Three

HAVING BEEN UP half the night worrying, Lex awoke later than normal to find Amanda's side of the bed cold. She got up and went into the bathroom, not surprised to find it empty. On Saturday mornings, Amanda liked to go downstairs and help Martha with breakfast. The compromise worked well for everyone: The housekeeper still fixed the meals, and both households ate together in the main house. On the weekends, Martha allowed Amanda to join in the meal preparation, and the two of them normally did the grocery list together on Sunday. After finishing her morning routine, Lex dressed and hurried downstairs.

"Good morning," Amanda greeted Lex warmly when she stepped into the kitchen. She poured a cup of coffee and set it down on the table before wrapping her arms around her lover for a hug.

Lex returned the embrace, somewhat confused at Amanda's bright disposition, especially considering the evening before. "Good morning to you, too. I guess you slept pretty well?" She allowed herself to be led to the table and pushed into her usual chair.

"I sure did." Amanda bent and kissed Lex on the cheek. "Thanks," she whispered. She patted the rancher on the shoulder and moved back over to the stove, where Martha was putting the finishing touches on breakfast.

At that moment, Ronnie and Martha's husband, Charlie, stepped into the kitchen, the boy excitedly relating something to the sheriff. "You should have seen the look on his face. It was priceless." He stopped when he realized that all eyes were on them. "Morning." Ronnie kissed Martha on the cheek before taking his place at the table.

"From what Ronnie tells me, it sounds like you've got a busy morning ahead, Lex," Charlie drawled, sitting down across from her. Although dressed in the brown uniform of the sheriff's department, the lawman hadn't put on his duty belt, which allowed him more ease at the table. The heavy leather belt that carried the tools of his trade was still at the cottage he shared with Martha. He stretched his long legs beneath the round table as he settled in.

Lex shrugged her shoulders. "Not much different from any other Saturday, Charlie. What's on your agenda for the day?"

Martha and Amanda brought the dishes over to the table and sat down, and the rest of the meal was punctuated by the normal small talk. Lex finished before everyone else and stood up. "If you'll excuse me, I've got to take care of some things down at the barn before I go up to the corral." She kissed Amanda on the cheek. "See you at lunch?"

"Definitely."

"Great." Lex nodded to the others before leaving the room.

Ronnie eyed his half-full plate, then the doorway. He began to shovel forkfuls of food into his mouth at a quicker pace, until Martha halted his hand midway to his mouth.

"Hold on there, Ronnie. Where's the fire?" Even though she hadn't been his guardian for long, Martha was used to the ways of teenagers, having raised Lex. She brushed a loose strand of hair from her face. Still more brown than gray, the bun she wore it in never lasted past breakfast. She often wondered why she continued to pull it back as she had for most of her fifty-plus years.

He chewed hard, then swallowed. "What?"

"You're tossing down that food like you haven't eaten in days. What's the rush?" Martha frowned. "Didn't you get enough to eat at dinner last night?"

"Yes, ma'am, I did. It's just I gotta hurry, or I'll be late." He continued to eat steadily, although at a much more acceptable pace.

Charlie exchanged looks with Amanda, who shrugged. "It's Saturday, son. What on earth would you be late for?"

Ronnie finished his meal and wiped his mouth with a napkin. "They're going to break some horses up at the corral this morning. Lex promised to let me watch." He looked at Martha. "May I be excused?"

"Of course." Martha remembered a similar scene in this very kitchen, probably fifteen years earlier. Lex used to get excited about the same things, and she understood how important it was to Ronnie. "Don't be late for lunch, though. We've got a date with a math book afterwards, too, if I remember correctly." Not only an excellent housekeeper, Martha had been studying for her teaching degree when she came to work at the ranch over twenty-five years ago. She had tutored Lex through many difficult subjects as the young woman grew up, and now was doing the same for Ronnie.

"Yes, ma'am." Ronnie jumped up from the table and kissed the air by Martha's cheek. "Bye!" He raced out of the kitchen, excited.

Charlie leaned back in his chair and shook his head. "I'm about halfway tempted to head up there myself," he mused. "I'd like to see Lex show those men a thing or two."

"Oh? What do you mean?" Amanda asked, raising her fork to her mouth.

"Ronnie told me on the way over that Lex had a run-in with the new hand. She's going to show him the *proper* way to break a horse."

Amanda's fork dropped to her plate. "What?"

"Not again," Martha grumbled. "The last time Lexie did that, she broke two ribs, not the horse." She tossed her napkin down on her plate and stood. "I swear, that girl doesn't have the sense that God gave a goose. She hires those men for a reason, crazy kid." She continued to grumble as she gathered up the empty dishes from the table.

"Are you telling me that Lex plans on getting on one of those wild horses?" Amanda asked, her appetite gone. She pushed away from the table. "She didn't mention anything like that to me last night." *Not that she had the chance*, Amanda's inner voice chastised her. *Your little tantrum saw to that, didn't it?*

Charlie stood up. "Well, she is in charge of the ranch. Ronnie told me that the new man had some sort of homemade bit that he wanted to use on the horses, which would have cut their mouths to pieces. I don't blame her for wanting to clear things up." He barely had time to catch Amanda before she tried to run from the room. "Where are you off to?"

"I'm going to go talk some sense into her, Charlie. There's no reason she should risk injuring herself just because of some jerk at the bunkhouse." Amanda tried to twist out of Charlie's grasp. "Martha, tell him."

Martha shook her head. "No, honey. He's right. Lexie is the head of the ranch, and we can't go racing off and embarrassing her in front of her men. That would just cause more trouble than good."

"Maybe. But you can't just sit around here and wait for something to happen, either." Amanda looked up at Charlie. "Please, take me up there? At least we can watch from a distance, or something."

"Oh, no. You're not going to get me in the middle of this."

He stepped back. "I've got some paperwork I need to finish up at the house." Charlie grabbed his hat. "I'll see you ladies at lunch."

Amanda watched him leave, her arms folded across her chest. "Am I the only one around here who cares what happens to Lex?"

"Of course not, Amanda." Martha walked up and stood beside the distraught woman. "We all care. But Lexie's been doing this since she was a teenager. There's no one better at it than she is, I can guarantee you that."

"You've all lost your minds," Amanda muttered, stomping out of the kitchen.

LEX PARKED THE Jeep next to the bunkhouse. Before she opened the door, she looked at Ronnie. "A lot of the guys like to sit on the top of the corral to watch, but I'd prefer if you'd just stand a few feet back."

"Sure, Lex. But why?"

"Some of the horses like to try to brush the rider off on the corral posts. I've seen men get their legs broken because they weren't fast enough to get out of the way." She climbed out of the vehicle to meet him on the other side. "Do you think I want to face Martha if something like that happened to you?"

He laughed and pulled his gray felt cowboy hat down to a more snug position. It had been a birthday present from Lex, and Ronnie was rarely without it. "I don't blame you there. She's tough."

They walked to the corral where the men were gathered. Several of them hollered a greeting, which Lex acknowledged with a wave. She nodded to Roy, who was inside the corral helping two other men saddle a horse. He had the sinewy build of a man who had worked hard his entire life, and his skin was bronzed by the sun. Having been the foreman at the Rocking W for close to twenty years, Roy had watched Lex grow up and was more than happy to work for the woman she had become.

"Hey, boss. We're almost ready for you." Roy traded looks with Tony, another ranch hand. By unspoken agreement, they kept Roger away from the animal, just to be on the safe side. "I've got this, if you don't mind checking the gate." A large pen was connected to the corral by a long chute where they loaded the animals to tag or vaccinate. Roy wanted to make certain the gate was properly closed since there was another horse already in the chute. The last thing they needed was another animal in the corral while Lex was astride this one.

Tony nodded. "Gotcha." He received a glare from Roger, who had just left the chute area.

The new hire walked over to Roy and roughly grabbed the heavy rope that was to be used as reins, causing the horse the shy away. "What's the matter? Don't trust me?"

Roy attempted to calm the frightened animal, thankful when Lex stepped into the corral and helped him. "We've got this, Roger," the foreman said. "Why don't you go find yourself a good seat?" Once the man was out of earshot, Roy whispered to Lex, "Are you sure this is such a good idea? I swear these are the wildest bunch I've seen in a while, boss."

"What's the matter, Roy? Afraid I can't handle it?" Lex teased, as she carefully ran her hands over the horse's skin. She paused when she saw a raised mark on the animal's stifle, above the hock on its rear leg. "What's this?"

He leaned down and studied the spot. "I'm not sure, but if I didn't know better, I'd swear it was a welt." Their eyes met. "Looks pretty fresh, Lex."

"That's what I was thinking." As much as she tried to give everyone a chance, she was beginning to dislike Roger Jenson. "Would he have had any time alone with the horses since they were brought up from the back pasture?"

"I'm not sure." Roy scratched his chin. "Hell, Lex. I didn't think to keep a continuous eye on him. Do you think he'd do something like this?"

Lex pursed her lips and nodded to where the men were gathered. "I don't know, Roy. But he's looking pretty smug right now." She was well past being angry. "I've half a mind to go over there and knock that damned grin off his face, that's for sure."

"Maybe we should just save this for another time," Roy suggested. "If he whipped these horses to scare them, it would be foolish to try to break them now."

"Are you calling me a fool?" Lex asked. "Never mind. Just cover him up so I can get on." She waited until Roy held a piece of burlap over the horse's face, then hurried into the saddle and grabbed the heavy ropes. Bracing herself, Lex nodded.

Roy stepped out of the way, pulling the burlap down with him. He quickly climbed through the corral beams and said a silent prayer for the stubborn woman who clung to the bucking horse with just the strength in her thighs and her grip on the ropes they used for reins.

Although she should have been terrified, Lex couldn't help but grin at the adrenaline that rushed through her. She had always enjoyed this part of ranching, even though it was one of the more dangerous jobs. As the horse kicked his rear legs in the air, she leaned back and held the ropes taut. The unexpected spin almost caught her off guard, but she was able to stay in the saddle. Not even the loss of her hat tore her concentration away from the animal beneath her, as she continued to hang on.

AMANDA PACED AROUND the house for a whole fifteen minutes before she decided to drive up to the corral and see what was happening. It didn't take very long to navigate the narrow dirt road, and before she knew it, she had parked her Mustang next to Lex's old Jeep. Once she got out of the vehicle, she could see the men hanging off the fencing of the corral, some yelling encouragement to Lex, who was being tossed around like a rag doll. Horrified, Amanda rushed over and climbed up next to them so that she could see.

The horse didn't seem to be tiring. Lex was beginning to think that maybe Roy was right, and that trying to break the animal was a mistake. She was contemplating jumping off when she heard a familiar voice ring out over the din.

"Lex!" Amanda screamed, seeing her lover struggle to control the huge animal.

Turning her head toward the sound, Lex didn't see the horse's head suddenly jerk sideways. Her firm grip on the ropes caused the animal to fall on its side, rolling completely over before jumping up and running to the far end of the corral.

The crumpled form on the ground didn't move. Two men rushed to the horse to keep it back, while Roy and Amanda hurried over to check on Lex. Both landed on their knees next to the still body. Lex was lying on one side, her face turned to the ground. Roy pulled off his gloves and touched the side of her throat, checking for a pulse. A low groan caused him to jerk away. "Lex?"

"Damn," Lex coughed, rolling over onto her back. She looked up into the worried eyes of her wife. "What are you doing here?"

Amanda ran her hands over Lex's body. "Are you hurt?"

Lex sat up, wheezing, and rubbed her midsection. "Nah. Just got the breath knocked out of me." A hard slap to her shoulder caught her off guard. "Ow! What was that for?"

"For scaring me to death!" Amanda stood up as Roy helped Lex to her feet. "Don't you ever do that again, Lexington Walters." She wiped the moisture from her face, her tears of worry now turning to tears of anger. "What were you trying to prove, anyway?"

Roy, for his part, decided that discretion was the better part of valor, and quietly left the two women alone in the middle of the corral. He motioned to the men to take care of the horse, and headed for the bunkhouse for a cup of coffee. *I'll bet she'd rather take her chances with the horse. I know I would.*

Lex followed Amanda out of the corral, picking her hat up on the way and dusting it off against her thigh. She waited until they were away from the men before answering her lover's question. "For your information, Amanda, this is what I do. What are you doing here?"

Amanda stopped and spun around. "No, Lex. What you do is *run* a ranch. What part of that says you have to ride wild animals?"

"I'm not going to ask my men to do anything that I wouldn't do," Lex retorted.

"They all know that. But does that mean you have to risk your life? How do you think that makes them feel? It's their job."

The rancher paused. She had never actually thought about it that way.

Amanda could see that she had Lex's attention. "And what about what we have? Dammit, Lex, we've only been together for a year. Don't you think we deserve more time together than that?" She stepped closer and put her hands on Lex's hips. "I can't bear the thought of losing you so soon after finding you."

"Amanda." Lex took off her gloves and tucked them in her back pocket. She reached up and wiped the tears from her lover's face. "I'm sorry." She was relieved when Amanda leaned forward into her arms. "Please don't cry, sweetheart."

The anguished plea only caused Amanda to cry harder. She buried her face in Lex's dusty shirt and held on tight.

Lex was about to say something else when she heard snickering behind them. She turned her head and saw Roger shaking his head.

"Looks like she's got you on a pretty short tether, Walters. Guess you're too whipped to show me how to break ponies."

"Back off, Jenson."

He either didn't hear the low order, or didn't care. Roger moved closer. "Damned cute, though. Is she any good in the—" His comment was cut short by Lex's fist. She had released her hold on Amanda and punched the obnoxious man square in the face.

Lex stood over Jenson, her hands clenched at her sides. "You've got exactly ten minutes to get off my ranch, asshole." She wanted to pick Roger up and pound on him, but Amanda's hands on her back calmed her.

"Fine." He climbed to his feet and licked his lower lip, tasting blood. "I didn't want to work for a damned woman, anyway."

"Come on, honey." Amanda pulled at Lex's shirt. "Let's go back to the house and get you cleaned up."

She would have rather stayed to make sure Jenson left, but Lex decided that she'd upset Amanda enough for one day. "Sounds good to me. I think I'm wearing most of the corral," she joked, as she crawled into the passenger's seat of Amanda's car and closed the door.

NOT A WORD was spoken as they drove back to the ranch house. Amanda was still trying to calm down after the horrifying scene at the corral. She kept seeing Lex's motionless form lying in the dirt, and the fear of losing what they had was fresh in her mind. She knew that she had overreacted, but didn't know how to voice her apology, so she kept quiet.

For her part, Lex was still fuming over the arrogance of Roger Jenson. She was also irritated with herself for not checking his references more carefully, taking the names he had given at face value. *That'll teach me. Now I've got to put another ad in the paper to replace him, since it's almost time to break some horses to sell.*

It wasn't long before Amanda parked the Mustang in front of the main house. She was out of the car and halfway to the house before she realized that Lex wasn't with her. With one foot on the front porch, Amanda turned around and looked back over her shoulder. Lex was still in the car, staring straight ahead with an angry look on her face. *I really screwed up this time. She's furious.*

Before Amanda could go back to the car, Lex opened her door and climbed out. Lost in her thoughts, she didn't even acknowledge Amanda's presence as she walked by her and into the house. She was through the den and almost to the office when Amanda's quiet voice stopped her.

"Lex?"

"What?" Lex spun around and stood, waiting for the reason her train of thought had been disturbed. She wanted to call the newspaper and place her ad for the Sunday edition and had very little time left to do so.

Amanda understood that her lover was upset, but the curt tone still hurt. "I thought you were going to go upstairs and get cleaned up." The dirt and grime covering Lex's clothes left a light trail behind her, and Amanda knew that Lex normally didn't like to track anything into the house that would cause Martha any undue work.

"I will, but I've got some things to take care of, first." Lex turned back around and went into the office, closing the door behind her.

"But..." Amanda barely got the word out of her mouth before she was alone in the room. She was about to go upstairs alone, when her own anger got the best of her. *I'm not going to allow her to brush me off like that. We need to talk about this.* Her mind made up, Amanda crossed the room and knocked on the office door. When she didn't get an answer, she slowly opened the door and peeked inside.

Lex sat at the desk, typing away at the computer. She had removed her hat, and there were rivulets of mud down the side of her face where she had perspired. Intent on the screen in front of her, Lex didn't hear Amanda step into the room.

"Ahem."

Frowning, Lex looked up from the computer. "Amanda? What's the matter?"

An incredulous look crossed Amanda's face. "What's the matter? You snapped at me and locked yourself in here, and you want to know what's the matter?" Her voice began to rise as she grew more upset. "I know I screwed up back there, but that's no reason to bite my head off and then ignore me."

"What?"

"I'm sorry that I was so concerned about you. I guess just because we're married, I don't have that right." Amanda's temper was in full force, and she had a lot to get off her chest. She pointed her finger at Lex, who had pushed the chair away from the desk and stood up. "I know we're going to disagree on things, but I'll be damned if I'll let you just walk away from me without so much as a word."

"But I—"

Amanda moved around the desk until she was less than a foot away from her lover and waved her left hand in front of Lex's face. "We're partners, Lexington Walters. The day you put this ring on my finger, we agreed to share everything. And, for your information, I'd like more than a year to share with you. Life's too precious to go around doing crazy things like you did today." The look that Lex gave her caused Amanda to pause in her tirade. "Well?"

"Can I talk, now?" Lex asked quietly.

Amanda pursed her lips in thought. "Okay."

Taking hold of Amanda's hands, Lex raised them to her lips and kissed them. She looked into her wife's eyes, upset with herself at causing so much anguish in the woman she loved. "I'm sorry, Amanda. I didn't mean to snap at you, I was running out of time to get the ad placed for Jenson's replacement before the deadline for tomorrow's edition." She leaned forward and kissed Amanda lightly on the lips and then pulled away. "And, I'll do my best to not take stupid chances anymore, okay?"

"Okay." Amanda's ire dissipated almost as quickly as it had flared. She used her thumb to wipe a smudge of dirt from Lex's cheek. "Why don't we go upstairs and get you into the shower? I doubt that Martha will allow you at the lunch table like this." Once Lex emailed her ad, Amanda led her partner from the office, relieved that the misunderstanding was behind them.

Once upstairs, Lex followed Amanda into the bathroom and allowed herself to be undressed. She was enjoying the attention as her shirt was slowly unbuttoned, until Amanda gasped. "What?"

Amanda ran her hands delicately across Lex's torso, where a mottled bruise had started to form. "Does this hurt?"

"Not much," Lex assured her, craning her neck to see. The discoloration covered her lower abdomen just above her hips. "Must be where the saddle got me when that damned horse rolled over." She looked back up into the concerned face of her lover. "Really, sweetheart. I barely feel it." She pulled Amanda close, determined to take the worried look off her face. "Wanna scrub my back?"

The playful tone caused Amanda to grin. "I think that can be arranged." Her own shirt was pulled from her body before she had a chance to say another word. Moments later, her bra joined the shirt on the floor, and Amanda stood in front of Lex, wearing only her jeans and sneakers. Gentle hands traced the contours of her chest. She trembled in anticipation.

"Cold?" Lex asked, a sly look on her face. She didn't wait for an answer, but unbuttoned the faded jeans and slid them down. Looking up from where she knelt, Lex wrapped her arms around Amanda's legs and leaned into her. "I love you, Amanda," she murmured.

"I love you, too." Amanda pulled Lex's head closer to her body and stroked her hair. Once again she was reminded just how precious what they had was, and she vowed to herself to protect their love, no matter what the cost.

Chapter Four

THE PASSING SCENERY held little interest for Ellie as she reclined in the car's leather seat. Fields covered by cattle and the small trees were different from what she was used to seeing, but Ellie was more intrigued by the interior of the limousine, having never been in one before. Although the last few days spent with her grandfather had made her more comfortable with him, she still felt completely out of place in her faded jeans, tee shirt and scuffed sneakers.

She hadn't wanted to abuse his hospitality, but found it continually more difficult to tell him no. Travis, being the sharp businessman he was, proudly used that to his benefit. Since Ellie came to him so late in her life, he was determined to make up for the lost time any way he could. It had taken Travis several hours of gentle persuasion earlier in the morning to convince his granddaughter to call her parents in California.

Travis's question startled her out of her trance and she looked up to meet his kindly face. "How's your family doing, Ellie?"

"They're doing fine, sir. Mom is afraid that I'm making a pest of myself." Actually, Naomi Gordon was furious with her daughter, insisting that they'd done just fine without the Edwards family up to that point and not understanding why her daughter was still in Texas.

Travis couldn't help but laugh. He patted his granddaughter on the knee, pleased when she didn't shy away or flinch. "You've actually been a lot of company to me these past few days. If you'd like, I could talk to your mother and assure her that I practically had to force you to stay with me."

Inwardly cringing at the thought, Ellie shook her head. A proud woman, her mother would probably inadvertently say something that would offend Travis, and that's the last thing she wanted. "No, that's okay. I think that Mom just doesn't understand why I'm still here." She often wondered the same thing herself, since her original goal of finding and meeting her father's family had been achieved.

"You can always lay the blame on me, Ellie. I just thought that since I was going back to Somerville so soon, it would be the perfect opportunity for you to meet your cousin." Travis had to admit privately that it wasn't the only reason he'd asked her to stay. The fact that he hadn't known about Ellie's birth was a mitigating factor in his not being involved in her life, but he still felt pangs of guilt for not seeing another granddaughter grow up. Spying familiar terrain, he pointed out the right-hand window. "Speaking of Lexington, the turnoff for her ranch is up ahead."

The white limousine turned onto a well-graveled road that was almost hidden by oak and cedar trees. Ellie leaned across to get a better view. They had spent the majority of their time talking about her family and his late wife, Melanie, and hadn't really touched on the subject of her cousin. Now she wished she had asked more questions. The covered wooden bridge the car went across seemed well built, if not a little out of place in Texas. "Exactly what kind of ranch are we talking about? Is she some sort of cattle baron or something?"

"A cattle baron? No, not really. Lexington was given this ranch by her father, and she's worked hard to keep it running. But she raises mostly horses on it, now." He could tell Ellie was nervous and wanted to put her mind at ease. "I think you'll really like her, and her partner, Amanda."

Ellie was completely confused. "Partner? I thought you said she owned the ranch alone."

"The ranch is Lexington's, true. But you could say that Amanda has a claim to it by proxy, especially since they've been married. I've never seen two people more in love than those two." Travis smiled fondly in remembrance. "It does my old heart good to see them so happy."

Ellie's eyes widened at this revelation. "Married?" The idea of two women in that sort of relationship was something she hadn't ever thought much about before. She was about to ask more questions when the car pulled into the circular driveway of the ranch house. It was quite different from what she had expected; the brick exterior looked more like a residence in Dallas than a ranch house out in the middle of nowhere. Ellie mentally gave her cousin points for not living in a log cabin, or something like it. She allowed the driver to help her from the car, Travis not far behind.

"Beautiful, isn't it? I think the girls chose well when they had it rebuilt." Travis mistook Ellie's silence for awe as he led her up the steps and onto the porch. He was about to knock on the door when it opened, and a tall, slender woman dressed in boots, jeans and a dark blue tee shirt embraced him.

"Grandpa! You should have called to let us know you were coming in early. We weren't expecting you until later on today." Her eyes tracked to Ellie, and her face wore an expectant smile. "Hello."

Travis put his arm around Ellie in a protective gesture. "Lexington, I'd like for you to meet Eleanor Gordon." When Lex held out her hand to the other woman, he added, "Your cousin."

Cousin? As they shook hands, Lex tried to keep the friendly smile on her face instead of the bewildered expression that was working its way to the surface. "It's a pleasure to meet you, Eleanor." She gave Travis a look that told him he had some explanations to give. Before she could say anything else, another woman came up behind her.

"Lex, are you going to leave them standing on the porch all afternoon, or are you going to let them in the house?" Amanda put her arm around her wife's waist and pulled her out of the doorway. "Hi, Grandpa Travis. You certainly made good time." She waited until everyone was in the hallway before she gave the older man a firm hug. "I've missed you."

"I've missed you, too." Travis held out his hand in Ellie's direction. "This is Eleanor Gordon. Ellie, I'd like to introduce you to my *other* granddaughter, Amanda Cauble."

Ellie shook hands with the younger woman, easily disarmed by Amanda's bright smile. "Hi, Amanda. It's great to meet you. Please call me Ellie."

Lex looked on as her lover charmed their guest. She followed the group into the den, standing back and watching her cousin interact with Amanda and Travis. The woman was obviously older than either she or Amanda, and her pale brown eyes were almost golden. She seemed comfortable with their grandfather, and Lex wondered just how long this mysterious "cousin" had been around. *Ought to be interesting, to say the least.*

For her part, Ellie had trouble believing that Amanda was one of "those women" that she had sometimes heard whispers about. Her cousin Lex, on the other hand, although attractive, radiated a no-nonsense aura that almost scared her. She had no trouble at all putting Lex into that category. The way the woman stared so intently without speaking unnerved her. *This is going to be fun*, she thought to herself. *Not.*

AFTER THE EVENING meal, Lex excused herself to check on the horses down at the barn. It wasn't long after she finished feeding the animals that the barn door opened and a figure stepped inside. Realizing who it was, she continued to brush Thunder's coat, her back to the unwanted guest.

"You don't like me much, do you?" Ellie asked, leaning up against one of the rails. Out of habit, she had her hands in the pockets of her denim jacket.

Lex didn't turn around. "I don't know you."

"That's true, I suppose." Taking her hands out of her pockets, Ellie moved forward and leaned over the stall door. "I'm not some golddigger, if that's what you're worried about." She watched as the brush glided rougher than before across the dark coat of the stallion. "I don't know much about horses, but it looks like you're trying to rub him raw."

Glaring over her shoulder, Lex lightened up on the brush. "You're right. You don't know much about horses." Realizing they were going to have this conversation whether she wanted to or not, she stopped her rough stroking of the animal and turned around. "Why are you here?"

Ellie knew what Lex was asking, and it wasn't about her trip to the barn. "I wanted to know about my family."

"After all these years? Seems a bit out of the blue to me." At dinner, Travis and Ellie had filled them in about who Ellie was and where she came from, but it still bothered the rancher. "From what you've said, you have a good family back in San Diego. Why bother coming halfway across the country to look up people who didn't even know you existed?"

"You're right. I do have a good family," Ellie admitted, picking at a rough spot she found on the board she was leaning over. The look that Lex was giving her made her more than a little uncomfortable, and she knew if she continued to meet her cousin's eyes, she'd say something that she might regret. "But all of my life I've felt like some little part of me was missing. When I read the letters that my father wrote to my mother, it made me realize what that part of me was." Ellie finally raised her head to see an unreadable look on Lex's face. "You're lucky to have Travis for a grandfather. In the few days that I've known him, he's made me feel like family. I just wish I'd found those letters sooner, so that maybe I could have met my grandmother, too."

A pained expression crossed Lex's face at the mention of their grandmother. Because her father and brother kept her in the dark, she had grown up without contact with her grandparents, as well. It had only been in the last year that she rediscovered the love of her grandfather, and the ache that separation caused went bone deep. She didn't trust Ellie, so she decided a subject change was in order. "How long do you plan on being here?" Earlier, and much to Lex's dismay, Amanda had offered Ellie the use of the guest room for as long as she wanted.

"I'm not sure. Why?"

"Just asking." Lex opened the stall door and brushed by her cousin. She decided to try to get her grandfather alone so that she could find out all he knew about Ellie. *Something just doesn't feel right, here. She's up to something.*

Ellie watched as Lex put the brushes away and left the barn, a determined set to her shoulders. "Nice talking to you," she muttered, staring at the back of the retreating woman. "I wonder if all of her kind have chips on their shoulders like that." Shrugging her shoulders, Ellie left the barn as well, contemplating her next move.

AMANDA HEARD THE back door slam, and heavy boot steps stomped down the hallway. She looked up from the table where she and Martha were making up the grocery list for the coming week. Travis had excused himself earlier, and was in the den, reading. Amanda's eyes met the housekeeper's. "I don't think Ellie's visit with Lex went very well."

"Doesn't seem like it, does it?" Martha agreed. She was about to say something else when the back door opened again and the other half of their topic walked into the house. "We're in here, Ellie," she called out, hoping to get some clue as to what had transpired in the barn.

Ellie poked her head into the kitchen and smiled when she saw that Amanda was with the housekeeper. She stepped further into the kitchen and joined them at the table. "Thanks."

"Would you like something to drink?" Martha offered.

Ellie looked at the table, unable to meet their faces. "No, thank you."

Amanda could feel the agitation coming from Lex's cousin. She wasn't sure what had happened in the barn, but she was aware that for some reason Lex didn't like or trust Ellie, and she was determined to find out why. She touched the older woman's arm in concern. "Are you all right?"

Am I? Maybe coming here with Travis was a mistake. It's obvious that my cousin has no use for me. Ellie looked up and tried to smile. "I'll be okay." The consideration given to her by this total stranger was comforting, in a strange sort of way. Amanda didn't fit the stereotype that she had in her mind about lesbians, and she felt more comfortable with her than her tough cousin.

"Is there something I can do to help?" Amanda asked.

Embarrassed, Ellie pulled her arm away. "Not unless you can tell me what I did to make Lex hate me so."

"What has she done? Maybe I should go talk to her." Amanda started to rise, but was stopped when Ellie reached out and grabbed her arm.

"No, wait. I don't want to cause any trouble."

Martha took the opportunity to chime in. "Lexie doesn't hate you, Ellie. She's just got a lot on her mind and tends to come across that way. It takes her a while to get to know people. Don't let her crankiness get to you." The housekeeper's face wore a comical expression, and the other two women couldn't help but laugh.

Outside the doorway, Lex paused. She had been about to go into the kitchen, when she heard she was the topic of discussion. *Crankiness? That's a load of bullshit.* Disgusted, she quietly turned and headed for the master bedroom, deciding to turn in early and keep from having to defend herself to her family.

"WHAT ABOUT THIS one?" Amanda asked her partner. She held up a pale green baby blanket for inspection.

Lex cocked her head to one side with a thoughtful look on her face. "Why green? I thought that girls were supposed to have pink." Surrounded by baby items and maternity clothes, Lex felt entirely out of place. "Besides, I don't know why we're still shopping. We found something for Wanda's baby over twenty minutes ago."

They had waited until Travis and Ellie had gone to meet the movers at his new home before starting out on the shopping trip. Lex hated to waste a work day, but when Anna Leigh called and had to cancel at the last minute, she didn't want Amanda to go on alone. Now, she was having second thoughts.

"Yes, but I want to pick out something for Jeannie and her baby. I can't believe that you of all people would think that way. Most pastels are perfectly suitable for either sex."

"But the baby isn't supposed to be here for another month, right?"

"And due dates aren't set in stone, Lex. Early deliveries run in my family." Amanda handed the blanket to her lover. "Here. Since you're so dead set against me carrying anything heavier than my purse, you can be the pack mule today." Although she loved Lex dearly, Amanda was sometimes aggravated with her overly protective wife. Her exasperation was short-lived when her eyes landed on a blouse several yards away. "Oh, look! Don't you just love that shade of yellow?"

A martyred groan was Lex's only response as she dutifully followed. She silently hoped for a reprieve from the shopping excursion, but had an uneasy feeling that it was just beginning. She made what she hoped was an appropriate sound when Amanda held up the blouse and asked her opinion. *I swear to God, if we can just go home soon, I promise to never curse again.* She accepted the blouse and added it to the growing stack. "Don't you think we should break for lunch? We've been at this for hours."

Amanda glared at her partner. "It's only been forty-five minutes, Lex. You didn't have to come, you know. I was perfectly capable of driving myself."

"I know you are, Amanda. But when your grandmother had to cancel at the last minute, I—"

"You just wanted to come along and babysit, right? Dammit! I'm not helpless, you know." The irritated woman pushed by a confused Lex.

"Where are you going?"

Amanda threw up her hands and stopped. She turned around and wiped tears of frustration from her eyes. "If you must know, I'm going to the ladies room. I'll be back in a few minutes."

"Amanda, wait." Lex started to follow her, but stopped when Amanda continued to walk away, waving her arms over her head. "Damn." She watched helplessly as the woman she loved stomped off. "So much for this being a happy time."

Once Amanda returned from the restroom, she yanked everything out of Lex's hands and silently made her way to the nearest register. Her mood didn't brighten after they left the store.

The drive home was silent as Lex wracked her brain for something to say that would calm her still-seething partner. She took her eyes from the road long enough to glance across the seat of her truck, concerned at the faraway look on Amanda's face. "Penny for your thoughts?"

Feeling guilty over her earlier outburst, Amanda continued to stare through her window at the passing scenery. She wasn't sure why she felt the way she did. Over the past couple of months her nerves were on edge, and she often took out her frustrations by snapping at Lex or crying for no apparent reason. Just remembering the hurt look on her lover's face was enough to bring tears to Amanda's eyes. *She doesn't deserve that. I've got to find a way to make it up to her.*

The extended silence from the other side of the truck

brought renewed pain to Lex's heart. She still wasn't sure what she had done to warrant the silent treatment, and now she was afraid to reach across and touch Amanda. *I don't think I could handle it if she pulled away.* Lex didn't attempt conversation again until after they drove across the bridge that led to the ranch house. A brisk wind jostled the truck as it exited the wooden structure. "Looks like the weather's going to be changing." She mentally cringed at the desperate attempt.

Amanda turned away from her window and met Lex's eyes. "Maybe it'll take my rotten mood with it." The tentative smile she received wasn't much, but it was a start. "I'm sorry, Lex. I don't know what's gotten into me lately." She reached across and grasped Lex's forearm. "Can you forgive me?"

"There's nothing to forgive." Lex pulled the truck in front of the house and shut off the engine. She unfastened her seatbelt and turned to give Amanda her complete attention. "I know something's been bothering you for a while now. Do you want to talk about it?" At the negative shake of her wife's head, Lex looked down at the seat between them. "I can't help you if I don't know what's wrong, Amanda. Talk to me, please."

"I...I can't."

Hurt by the rebuff, Lex pulled back and opened her door. "Fine." She reached into the back seat of the 2500 Quad Cab Dodge to grab the shopping bags, then climbed out of the truck. "I'll take these into the house for you." Before she closed the door, Lex looked into Amanda's eyes. "I'm going to check the back fence. I'll see you sometime this evening." She was thankful that at least she didn't have her cousin to put up with, seeing as how this entire day proceeded to go from bad to worse.

The door closed and Amanda was left staring at Lex's back. She felt fresh tears well up in her eyes and didn't even attempt to stop them.

Hearing the slam of the front door, Martha stepped out of the kitchen, drying her hands on a white dishtowel. She watched as Lex carried several bags into the den, and was surprised to see her storm down the hallway moments later. "Lexie? Where's Amanda?" When the distressed woman was even with her, Martha grabbed her arm to stop her. "What's going on?"

"She's on her way in. I've got to check the far fence this afternoon, so don't wait lunch on me." Lex pulled her arm from the housekeeper's grip and continued down the hall until she passed through the back door, slamming it behind her.

Seconds later, Amanda came in the front door, wiping her face with one hand. She peeked into the den and, not seeing Lex, straightened her back and met Martha mid-way in the hall. "Did you see—"

"Lexie? She took off out the back door like her tail end was on fire. What on earth is going on?" Martha led Amanda back into the den and guided her to the sofa, sitting down next to her. "You two have been touchy for a while now. Do you mind me asking why?"

Amanda looked at the bags Lex had dropped on the coffee table. "I'm not sure, Martha. I mean, I know that I've been out of sorts lately, so I guess that Lex is just picking up on that." She leaned back and closed her eyes. "Maybe we've just been spending too much time together; I don't know."

Martha sat quietly and thought about the tensions that had been running through the house. "I don't think that's it, honey. You two have never had any problem being together before now. This has all been building for months. Ever since you heard that your sister was expecting, you've been a bit prickly."

Amanda turned her head and opened her eyes. "That's not it. I'm very happy for Jeannie and Frank. Why would them having a baby upset me?"

"Maybe it's because you want what they have?"

Amanda's eyes widened at the thought. "I don't think so, Martha. I'm thrilled for them; I can't wait to hold my niece in my arms. But I'm certainly not ready for that drastic a step." A chagrined smile formed on her face. "Besides, Lex doesn't quite have the equipment to be a father."

Martha gave her a playful slap on the leg. "Hush up, child. You know there's other ways to go about it. Have you talked to Lexie?"

"No!" Amanda jumped up from the sofa as if she had been burned. "I mean, well, of course not. I don't know if we're ready for that kind of responsibility. Heck, I don't know if *I'm* ready. That's such a big step." Terrified of the direction the conversation was going, Amanda reached into one of the bags on the table. "Let me show you the things that we picked out for the shower, and for Jeannie and the baby. I think you'll really like them."

ASTRIDE THE LARGE black stallion, the silent figure watched from the copse of cedar and oak trees as two men continued to bicker back and forth. Lex nudged the horse out of the hiding place and stopped when she was a few feet away from the men. She crossed her forearms over the saddle horn and leaned forward. "You fellas lost?"

The shorter of the two men spun around, startled. "Hey,

boss." Roy walked up to Lex's horse and patted its neck. "Didn't think we'd be seeing you out here today. Thought you had business in town." He was relieved to see that Lex bore no outward signs of injury from Saturday's fiasco. But he also knew better than to say anything about it.

"I did, but I'm back." Lex didn't feel like talking about what had transpired earlier. "Thought I'd come out here and check the fence. I didn't know you'd be here." She swung her right leg over the saddle and dismounted, allowing the reins fall to the ground. "What's up?"

Roy turned back to the fence, where he leaned on one of the posts and looked at the property beyond. "I just wanted to come out and see how much fence we'd have to move if you bought the land next to us."

Lex turned and looked at the foreman, then at the other man, Ted, who was loading tools into the back of a truck. "What do you mean, if I bought it? I didn't even know it was for sale."

"You didn't? Aw, hell, boss. I heard that it was going to be auctioned and just figured that you already knew all about it." Roy took Lex's arm and led her away where they could talk more privately. "Ted's girlfriend works at Johnson's Auctioneers, and she told him yesterday that she'll have to work late the next few weekends because of some of the big sales they've got coming up."

Damn. I've been letting too much of the ranch go lately. I used to find out about these important things way in advance. Lex patted her foreman on the back. "Thanks for letting me know, Roy. I'll make a few phone calls and see what's up." She gathered Thunder's reins and pulled herself into the saddle. "You guys better get back. Lester's bound to have supper waiting for you." On her command, the huge animal spun around and took off for the trees at a gallop.

THE SLAM OF the back door roused Amanda from her bout of self-pity. She had spent the better part of the afternoon upstairs in their bedroom, lying on the bed with her face buried in Lex's pillow. She raised her head and listened, hoping to hear boot steps on the stairs. When several minutes passed and there was still no sign of Lex, Amanda curled up around the pillow again and stifled a sob. As distressed as she was with the way things were between them, she didn't know what to do to make them right again.

Downstairs, Lex didn't even realize how quiet the house was as she made her way into her office. She closed the door, then circled around the desk to drop into the leather chair. Rifling through her Rolodex, she found the number she had been searching for and picked up the phone. Several rings passed before a man's voice answered on the other end. "Ed? Lex Walters. How're you doing?"

She leaned back in her chair and propped her dirty boots on the edge of the desk. "Great. Hey, listen. A little birdie told me that the MacGregor land to the north of us is going up for auction in the next couple of weeks. Is that true?" Lex picked at a spot of dried mud on her denim-clad thigh as she listened. "Right. Is it a public auction, or sealed bids? Excellent." She dropped her feet to the floor and grabbed a pen, scribbling on the desk blotter. "Uh-huh. No proxies? Gotcha." Lex tapped the pen against the paper. "Thanks, Ed. I'll see you next Saturday. Bye."

After hanging up the phone, Lex leaned back in her chair again and put her boots back on the desk. She linked her fingers behind her head and smiled. "I've finally got a chance to get that grazing land I've been wanting for so long." The MacGregor property had some of the best grasslands in the area, and she had been trying for years to talk the old man into selling. "I wonder what changed his mind." She had no way of knowing that MacGregor had had a stroke, and after being placed in a nursing home, signed the property over to his grandson, who defaulted on the mortgage and then immediately put it up for auction. Nonetheless, Lex knew she had a good chance of picking up the property the following weekend with a low bid, since not that many people even cared about the property, much less knew about it being up for sale.

LEX STAYED IN her office until Martha called everyone to dinner, and she was concerned at how Amanda looked. Her eyes were red and puffy, and she barely looked up from her plate, which she had hardly touched. Lex was just thankful she didn't have the presence of her cousin to put up with. Travis had called earlier, and he and Ellie were in the middle of unpacking, so they wouldn't be able to make it to dinner.

The silence at the table was uncomfortable, although Ronnie seemed oblivious to it. He swallowed a bite of food and caught Lex's eye. "Roy wanted me to tell you that the horses from Saturday are doing okay. He's got two of them in training saddles and plans to try to ride them again next weekend."

"That's good." Lex was pleased with how Ronnie took an interest in the ranch. She sneaked a peek at Amanda, who continued to play with the food on her plate. The disastrous shopping trip still had Lex on edge, but she wanted to try to bridge the gap it had caused between them. "Amanda? Would you like to take a walk with me after dinner?" she asked, bracing herself for rejection.

Amanda, not sure if she had heard correctly, looked up into Lex's face. Instead of the angry or indifferent look she had expected, all she saw was love and concern. "I'd like that," she said, almost shyly. Finally having something to look forward to, she scooped up a bite of food and placed it in her mouth.

A short time later, the two women stepped out the back door of the house, the light from the stars and moon guiding them. Lex held out her hand and was relieved to feel Amanda's slip into it and squeeze. She led them down by the hay barn, walking slowly to pass the time. Lex wasn't sure what she had done wrong, but she was determined to clear things up between them. "I'm sorry about earlier."

"So am I," Amanda admitted. She stopped and turned to face her lover. "I don't know what's going on with me." Not comfortable with the feelings she had, Amanda tried to make light of her emotional turmoil. "Maybe I'm PMS-ing or something."

The frown on Lex's face grew. "I don't think that's it, and neither do you." She looked down at their joined hands, shadowed by the moonlight. "I want to help, if I can, Amanda. But you've got to talk to me."

"There's nothing wrong! Why can't everyone just leave me alone, and quit badgering me?" Amanda broke free and rushed into the barn, wiping tears of frustration from her cheeks. Leaning against a fragrant bale of hay, she heard boot steps behind her and turned around. The hurt look on her wife's face pushed everything else away, and she took a step to fall into Lex's waiting arms. "I'm sorry," she whimpered, burying her head into the soft denim of Lex's shirt.

"Shh. It's going to be okay, sweetheart," Lex said, holding Amanda with one hand while using the other to stroke her hair. *At least I hope it will be.* She slid down into the hay, pulling Amanda into her lap and trying to offer what comfort she could.

Not much time had passed before Amanda took a cleansing breath and sat up. She patted Lex's chest as she looked up into her eyes. "Thanks. I guess I needed that."

"You're welcome. Feeling better?" Lex removed a strand of hay from Amanda's hair. The gesture reminded her of the first time they were in the barn together, over a year earlier. "Remember the first time we were in here?"

Amanda smiled. "How could I forget? I fell for you, literally and figuratively." After Lex had rescued her from a raging creek, the grateful realtor had spent the next few days helping her around the ranch. While they were in the hay barn, Amanda climbed to the top of the bales, slipped, and fell into Lex's arms, which precipitated their first kiss.

"I had already fallen for you," Lex admitted. "The moment I pulled you out of that creek." She leaned forward and covered Amanda's lips with her own, feeling the familiar thrill when her lover's hands reached under her shirt to caress her skin.

"I felt the same way." Amanda unbuttoned the denim shirt. "But I kept telling myself it was some kind of hero worship." She pushed the shirt out of the way and reached around to unclasp Lex's bra, sliding both garments from her wife's body, then gently pushing Lex onto her back.

Lex's face broke out into a happy grin. "Hero worship, huh?" Her eyes widened as nimble hands unbuckled her belt and opened her jeans. "Uh, Amanda?"

"Hmm?"

"Don't you think we should go back to the house?" Feeling her jeans being pulled down, Lex automatically raised her hips to help.

"Nope." Amanda slid the denim down and then covered Lex's body with her own, which was still clothed. "I want you right here, right now. Got a problem with that?"

"Nope," Lex parroted, extending her arms and quickly relieving Amanda of her own clothes. "As a matter of fact, that's the best offer I've had all day." She wrapped her arms around Amanda and rolled over, causing them both to laugh with joy and relief.

Chapter Five

AMANDA PULLED HER Mustang into the drive at her grandparents' house, several hours early for the baby shower. She couldn't believe how quickly the week had passed. Although Lex had been busy preparing for the property auction, they had still managed to spend quite a bit of quality time together. She dreaded the questions that her partner's absence from the shower would cause, but Lex had explained that if she wanted the property, she had to be at the auction in person for the opening of the bids.

The front door of the house opened and Anna Leigh stepped out, waving. "Mandy! I'm glad you're here." She waited until her granddaughter was on the porch before continuing. "I'm having the hardest time deciding what kind of punch to serve."

Oh, yeah. That's a real emergency. Amanda pasted what she hoped was a convincing smile on her face and followed her grandmother into the house.

Before she knew it, hours had passed and most of the women from the office as well as several of Wanda's friends were seated in the living room. Amanda glanced at her watch and sighed. The only person missing was the guest of honor, and Wanda's sister was in charge of bringing her. The slamming of car doors caused a smile to break out on Amanda's face. She tried not to open the door the moment the bell rang, but wasn't quite successful by the surprised look on the women's faces. "Hi."

"Hi." Wanda frowned, then looked at her sister. Because the other women had parked their cars out of sight, she didn't have a clue as to what was going on. "I didn't know you'd be here, Amanda. Karen told me that your grandmother needed us to stop by for something, but she didn't say what."

Amanda held open the door and stepped back. "Why don't you come in? I think she's in the living room." She struggled to keep the grin off her face as the two women stood in the doorway of the room where the others were "hiding."

"Surprise!" a chorus of voices shouted.

Wanda held her hands to her cheeks. "Oh, goodness! I can't believe this." She turned to look first at her sister, then at Amanda. "I can't believe you kept this a secret from me." Before she could say anything else, she was pulled into the room by the enthusiastic bunch, as voices vied excitedly with one another.

SIX MEN STUDIED one other across a large table; Lex was the only woman in the room. She almost jumped to her feet when Ed Johnson walked into the room carrying a briefcase. Nodding at each of the others before sitting down, he settled at the head of the table.

"Gentlemen. Lex," he added, a slight smirk on his face. "We've opened all the bids, and now have a winner." He opened his briefcase and pulled out large envelope. "There were several close bids, but one was higher by a good two percent. So, our client has agreed to the terms of that bid." He pushed the envelope past two men, one of them Wilson, until it rested in front of Lex. "Congratulations, Lexington Walters. Looks like you've bought yourself some prime grazing land."

"Excellent!" Lex opened the envelope and glanced at the papers inside. She looked up at Johnson. "I'll have the bank draft to you in about an hour," she promised.

Ed Johnson nodded. "Perfect. I'll have the paperwork ready for you by then." He looked around the table. "Gentlemen, thank you for your time."

All but one of the men stood to leave, some of them giving Lex a less than polite look. One man, wearing wire-framed glasses and an expensive suit, waited until the others left before standing before her. "Excuse me, Ms. Walters?"

Lex rose and tucked the envelope under her arm. "Yes?"

"I'd love a chance to talk with you, if you have the time."

Not wishing to be impolite but wanting to surprise Amanda by making an appearance at the baby shower, Lex said, "Depends on how long you want to talk. I've got another appointment."

Wilson wiped his sweaty palm on his pants leg before holding it out. "My name's Andrew Wilson." He was surprised at the firm handshake he received from the attractive woman.

Lex resisted the urge to wipe her hand on her jeans. She couldn't remember the last time she'd be given such a limp, damp handshake, and it immediately put her on edge. "Mr. Wilson, what is it I can do for you?"

He looked around the empty room as if afraid someone might be listening to their conversation. "Could we go someplace private to talk?"

Lex left the room and walked down the hallway to the front door. "Like I said, I've got things to do, Mr. Wilson. But if you want to walk me to my truck, we can talk on the way."

Damn. Billings is going to kill me if I don't get her to listen to reason. He followed her, waiting until they were outside before speaking. "Ms. Walters, I don't know what you paid for that land, but I'd be more than happy to give you double, right here, right now." Wilson almost ran into Lex's back when she stopped suddenly.

"Double?" Lex turned around and glared at the young man. "I don't know what you're up to, mister, but that land's not for sale. Not at any price." The offer made her extremely uneasy, and she reminded herself to talk to Ed about this stranger. "But thanks." Lex opened her truck door and climbed in. She rolled down the window. "I'm sure you can buy some other land around that's just as good, Mr. Wilson." Lex tipped her hat to the man in the suit before rolling up the window and backing the truck out of its parking place. She didn't see him scramble to fish a cellular phone from his coat pocket, or the look on his face when the person on the other end of the line started berating him.

"OOH!" WANDA HELD a tiny ruffled dress up to her chest. "It's adorable, Mrs. Cauble." Although she had worked for Sunflower Realty for years, Wanda couldn't bring herself to call the owner by her given name, no matter how Anna Leigh tried. "Thank you!" She had been opening gifts for what seemed like hours, and the group's enthusiasm hadn't waned a bit.

Amanda felt her smile slip. The constant noise and chatter were beginning to get on her nerves, and more than once she'd found herself making excuses to leave the room. "Let me go check on the coffee," she said, standing and then weaving through the crowd of women.

On her way back from the kitchen, Amanda ran into one of Wanda's friends, who had left the living room earlier to freshen up. The woman, short and heavyset, gave Amanda a curt look. "Where's that good-looking partner of yours? I thought you two were inseparable."

"She had another appointment, Judi. Now if you'll excuse me, I really should get back to the party." Amanda edged by the nosy woman, but not before she heard Judi's parting shot.

"Guess the honeymoon's over. That certainly didn't take long."

Anna Leigh looked up as Amanda sat next to her. She could tell her granddaughter was upset by the way she bit her lower lip and kept from looking at anyone. Quietly she whispered, "Mandy? What's the matter, dearest?"

Amanda shook her head, but didn't answer.

With a quick glance around to be sure they wouldn't be missed, Anna Leigh took Amanda's arm, pulled her out of the room, and led them to the kitchen, where the sounds of the party could barely be heard. Gently pushing Amanda to a chair at the table, Anna Leigh dropped down beside her and tried to look into the younger woman's face. "Now, tell me what's wrong, Mandy. And don't you dare sit there and say 'nothing.'"

"Oh, Gramma." Amanda leaned over and wrapped her arms around her grandmother's neck, finally allowing the tears to fall. "Do you think that Lex is tired of me already?"

"What?" Anna Leigh pulled back until they were looking eye to eye. "Whatever gave you that idea?"

Sniffling, Amanda reached for a paper napkin on the table and wiped her eyes. "We've been arguing a lot lately. Not to mention the fact that she's not even here with me today."

Anna Leigh shook her head at her granddaughter's warped logic. "My dear child, you told me she had a very important private auction to be at this morning. And we both know how well Lexington would fit in at a baby shower."

"I suppose you're right. But what about our arguments? We didn't used to fight all the time."

Thinking for a long moment, Anna Leigh decided to bring up something that had been bothering her for a few weeks. "Mandy, look at me." When the tearful eyes met hers, Anna Leigh's heart almost broke, but she held firm to her resolve. "You've been somewhat, how should I put this—"

"Bitchy?" Amanda offered, a wry smile on her face.

"No, I wouldn't say that, dear. But you've certainly been preoccupied lately. Would you care to talk to me about it?"

Amanda jumped up and started rearranging the plastic drink cups around the punch bowl. "Why does everyone keep asking me to talk? There's nothing wrong, dammit!" She threw a stack of colored napkins across the room, then spun around to find her grandmother's sturdy presence close by. Amanda easily fell into the older woman's arms once again, sobbing uncontrollably. "Why, Gramma? Why is everyone having a baby except me?"

AFTER DROPPING OFF her bank draft and signing a large stack of papers, Lex whistled along with the tune on the radio as she drove toward the Caubles' house. She planned on surprising Amanda by showing up for the end of the baby shower, and nothing could ruin her good mood. When her cell phone rang, Lex snapped it off her belt. "Hello?"

"Ms. Walters?"

Lex frowned. "Yes?" She thought the caller would be Amanda and was disappointed that it wasn't.

"I'm sorry to bother you on a Saturday," the voice continued, "but I'm afraid I have some bad news."

"Oh-kay." Realizing it wouldn't be a short call, Lex turned the truck into a nearby parking lot so that she could give the caller her undivided attention. "Who is this?"

"Oh, yes. I'm terribly sorry, Ms. Walters. This is Rodney Cline, with Edison Investments." The firm that she entrusted with the large majority of her money had recently changed hands, and Lex hadn't had time to get to know the new people involved with the company.

"Right, Mr. Cline. What can I do for you?" Lex pulled down the visor and studied herself in the mirror, double-checking for any gray hair, which she did when no one else was around. It was a secret fear of hers, looking older than she was, and the last thing she needed was any reminder that she was older than Amanda.

The man on the other end of the phone released a heavy sigh. "Ms. Walters, would it be possible for you to come by our offices as soon as possible? As I said before, I have some news that I really don't want to relate over the telephone."

Lex looked at her watch and thought for a moment. *Is he out of his mind? I'm not about to drive all the way to Austin, and on a damned Saturday to boot.* "Do you have any idea where I am, Mr. Cline? I've got an important engagement to keep, and there's no way that I can miss it. Just say what you need to on the phone." Although she didn't know what the man wanted, Lex decided that whatever it was, it couldn't put a damper on her afternoon. She was even looking forward to surprising her wife at the shower, and decided she'd stop off on the way and grab a bouquet of flowers for both Wanda and Amanda.

"All right, if you insist. I'm afraid I have to be the bearer of some rather unfortunate news," he rushed out. "The gentleman handling your account hasn't been to work since Wednesday, and we've discovered some irregularities."

Lex felt the contents of her breakfast begin to churn. "And?"

"It seems that he made some unauthorized transactions with

your funds, Ms. Walters. We're still trying to figure out what, and why."

"Unauthorized? But don't you folks normally just handle things? What's all of this mean?"

"It means, Ms. Walters, that the stocks and cash in your account are gone." Cline cleared his throat, preparing for the worst.

Lex slumped down in the truck seat and rubbed her eyes with one hand. "Gone? What do you mean, gone? How the hell did this happen? Don't you have ways of preventing something like this?"

"Normally, yes, of course. And we'll do a thorough investigation to see exactly what has happened."

"So, you're saying I have nothing left at all? Why the hell did he pick me?"

"We can't figure out why it was just you, but the authorities have been notified. I'm terribly sorry about all of this, Ms. Walters."

"Sorry doesn't bring back the money I trusted you with, Cline." Lex leaned forward and thumped her head on the steering wheel. *Okay, don't panic.* She had enough in the bank to cover buying the new property, and to keep the ranch running for several months. The sale of the next herd of horses should see them through until spring. She just hoped that nothing unexpected came up in the meantime.

"Ms. Walters? Are you all right?"

"Of course I'm not all right, you dipshit. Your stupid firm just lost hundreds of thousands of dollars of mine, and you ask me if I'm all right?" She took a deep breath in an attempt to control her temper. "That pissant better hope the authorities find him before I do, Mr. Cline, because I plan on taking each and every penny out of his worthless hide." Her final words were so quiet he had to strain to hear them. "You'll be hearing from my lawyer."

The broker swallowed hard as the angry woman disconnected the call. He was just glad that she was in Somerville and not in Austin, where he would have had to deal with her temper in person.

THE LARGE TRUCK had been parked behind Amanda's Mustang for over ten minutes, yet the driver still hadn't left the vehicle. Lex leaned on the steering wheel and looked at the neatly-kept two-story house, mentally debating with herself on whether or not to actually go inside. She wasn't sure how she was going to bring up the subject of her lost investments with her lover, especially as touchy as Amanda had been lately. Taking a deep breath, Lex gathered up the three bouquets of flowers she'd picked up on the way and got out of the truck. To make the surprise complete, she decided to ring the doorbell, hoping that one of the Cauble women would answer it. She wasn't disappointed.

Anna Leigh's face lit up when she realized who stood on her front porch. "Lexington! This is a wonderful surprise. But what are you doing ringing the bell?" Her answer was a large bouquet of roses.

"Sorry I'm late, Gramma. I hope y'all saved some ice cream."

"These are exquisite, Lexington. Thank you." Anna Leigh held the flowers up to her nose and inhaled deeply. "Mmm."

Lex stepped inside and looked around. "Is my beautiful better half around?"

Anna Leigh lowered the bouquet and kissed the younger woman on the cheek. "Everyone's in the living room, dear. And I believe we were just about to have cake and ice cream."

"Cool." The rancher mentally prepared herself for the onslaught of women and stepped into the living room.

Amanda looked up in surprise at the figure in the doorway. "Lex?" She watched in amusement as her partner brought a beautiful flower arrangement from behind her back to give to Wanda.

Lex went down on one knee and handed the flowers to the guest of honor, who immediately began to cry. "Wanda, I'm really sorry I'm late, but I hope these will help you forgive me."

"Oh, Lex. These are absolutely beautiful." Wanda looked across the room at Amanda. "Any time you want to trade spouses, I'm more than ready. Dirk never brings me flowers."

The entire room expressed comments of appreciation, and several of the women stood up and crowded around Wanda to get a better look. Lex took the opportunity to sneak away to sit next to Amanda. "Hey there, beautiful." She handed her wife a dozen yellow roses, knowing that they were Amanda's favorites.

"Hey there, yourself," Amanda said. Her grandmother had helped calm her after the earlier outburst, and now she was just tired. She couldn't help but smile at Lex, especially knowing how much her lover disliked large gatherings. "Thanks for coming. Did you win the bid?"

"Uh, yeah. The property is ours. But I'd rather not talk about it right now, okay?" Even though the man she had spoken to earlier at the auction rang all her warning bells, with the new financial developments, Lex was ready to consider selling the newly purchased property to him.

Amanda studied her partner closely. It wasn't like Lex not to be excited about such a big land deal, especially since she had coveted the grazing area for years. A talk was definitely in order once they got home. "I can't believe you're here. I know how much you hate things like this."

"True." Lex leaned over so that no one could overhear her. "But you should also know how much I love you, Amanda. You're worth a hundred of these hen parties." She nodded to the bouquet that Amanda held. "So, am I forgiven?"

"You were never in trouble, you silly thing," Amanda assured her, bumping Lex with her shoulder. "But if you really want to be my hero, you could take me away from all of this."

Lex stood up and bowed, holding out her hand. "You wish is my command, darlin'. Let's sneak out, and I can drive you in on Monday to get your car."

Taking her partner's hand, Amanda allowed herself to be pulled from her seat. "I'll call Gramma later to explain." She followed Lex out of the room, relieved to get away from all the reminders of what she didn't have.

BY THE TIME they were on the road home, a light rain had begun to fall. Amanda peered at the gathering clouds and was thankful that Lex was driving. She looked over at her wife, who seemed completely engrossed in the drive. "Penny for your thoughts?"

"I could probably use all the pennies I can get," Lex grumbled, still upset about the earlier phone call from the broker.

Amanda reached across the truck console and grasped Lex's arm. "What do you mean?"

The rain started falling harder, and a bright flash of lightning lit up the sky in front of them. Lex slowed the truck in deference to the weather, wishing she could slow the conversation as well. "You know that I put my inheritances in investments, while I kept the ranch money in the bank?"

"Yes. I also remember that your investments were doing pretty well. Why?"

After turning the truck onto the gravel road that led to the ranch house, Lex glanced over at Amanda. "They're gone."

"What?"

"The investments, Amanda. They're all gone." Lex stopped the truck before they reached the bridge, and turned in her seat to look Amanda directly in the eyes. "Some punk the investment company had working for them took everything I had. And with the money I just spent on the new land, I'm close to tapped out."

Amanda's eyes widened. Although Lex had never acted like she had a lot of money, she had always seemed comfortable that between her inheritances and investments, the ranch would never go broke. Now, it seemed like that was a definite possibility. "Oh, my God."

"Yeah." Struggling to keep her tears from falling, Lex turned and looked at the bridge, unable to meet Amanda's gaze. "I don't know what I'm going to do, Amanda."

"There's always what I have. We can use that."

Lex shook her head. "That's not an option."

As much as she hated it, Amanda understood what Lex was thinking. Her parents had already accused the rancher of being after her money, and even though that wasn't the case, Amanda knew how proud her partner was. Thinking fast, Amanda blurted, "What about your grandfather? He could—"

"No!" Lex turned back to face her wife. "He's not doing as well as you might think. I mean, sure, he's got enough to live out his life comfortably, but the oil bust hit him really hard." She sighed. "Besides, the last thing I want him to know is that I screwed all this up."

"But Lex, it wasn't you." Amanda unbuckled her seatbelt and raised the console so that she could get closer to her lover. "And I'm sure he'd understand that."

When the strong arms wrapped around her shoulders, Lex was unable to control her emotions any more. She buried her face in Amanda's neck and let the tears that she had held at bay finally fall. Only with Amanda did she feel safe in letting her guard down like this. After a few minutes, she pulled back and sniffled. "He can't know, Amanda. Please. I've got to try to work through this myself."

"*We* will work through this," Amanda amended, placing a kiss on Lex's lips. Her eyes darkened as she frowned in thought. "Do you know why this guy targeted you, of all people?"

"No. I guess he thought because I was a woman, he'd have an easier time getting away with it."

"Maybe. But the guy obviously doesn't know you, or he would have found someone else to mess with."

Lex finally smiled. "You think?"

"Yep." Amanda scooted back across and buckled her seatbelt. "Let's go home."

"Good idea." Lex put the truck back into drive and slowly navigated across the bridge. As she pulled up to the house, she noticed her grandfather's car in the driveway and sighed. "I hope he's alone."

Amanda couldn't figure out why Lex didn't get along with her cousin. The woman seemed nice enough to her. "Let's just get inside and worry about it then, okay?"

"Yeah," Lex grumbled, getting out of the truck and waiting for Amanda to go up the steps to the porch. She didn't trust Ellie any further than she could throw her, and the last thing she wanted to deal with now was some gold-digger trying to swindle Travis out of his money. She followed Amanda into the house and was surprised to hear noise coming from the den.

Hearing the sound also, Amanda walked into the den. Ellie was sitting on the sofa, watching a loud action movie. She touched the other woman's shoulder but pulled it back quickly when Ellie jumped and turned around. "Hey there."

Ellie fumbled for the mute button on the remote, settling for the pause and stopping the movie. "Hi, you two. I wasn't expecting anyone home for a while."

"Obviously," Lex muttered. She frowned when Amanda lightly slapped her on the arm. "What?"

Ignoring her partner, Amanda walked around the sofa and sat next to Ellie. "Have you been alone long?"

"No, not really. Grandpa went to the bunkhouse to talk with Lester, and Martha suggested that I come in here to relax and enjoy the movies." Ellie looked at her cousin, determined to try to get along, if only for Amanda's sake. She wasn't certain why the younger woman's opinion mattered to her, but it did. "Nice collection."

Lex rolled her eyes and dropped down into a nearby chair. "Thanks." She swung one leg over the arm of the chair and crossed her arms over her chest. *Grandpa, huh? Sounds like the little shit already has her hooks into him. I just hope I can figure out what her game is before it's too late.*

Mentally shaking her head at her partner's behavior, Amanda leaned forward and tried to disarm the two women. "I'm afraid it was a lot better before my mother burned Lex's house down."

"Your mother?" Unable to help herself, Ellie gave Lex a peculiar look. "You must have been as nice to her as you are to me."

Sitting up, Lex placed both feet on the floor and glared at her cousin. "Give me a break. At least we knew what Amanda's mother was all about. She didn't just show up one day, expecting to be welcomed into the family with open arms."

"Lex!"

Ellie waved off Amanda's concern. "That's all right. I probably deserved that." She stood and crossed to the doorway. "But some of us weren't born with silver spurs on our feet. My family had to work for every cent it got." She walked out of the room before she could hear Lex's sputtering.

"That bitch!" Lex jumped to her feet and was almost to the door when Amanda grabbed her shirt. "I bet I worked harder when I was ten years old than she has in her entire life!" She tried to twist away, but Amanda held firm. "Damn her to hell!" Her ire released, Lex slid down the wall until she was sitting on the floor. "I've never even owned spurs," she choked out, before her anger turned to tears and she found her lover in her arms for the second time that afternoon.

Chapter Six

IGNORING THE OTHER people in the room, the slender woman smiled at her visitor. "You're such a sweet man," she remarked loudly. "Taking time out of your busy week to come see me like this." Liz had been a model patient, and knew it was only a matter of time before she was released. The testimony of the man in front of her, as well as that of the staff, would work heavily in her favor. Leaning across the table, she spoke more quietly. "Now, give me all the juicy details, and don't leave anything out."

"It went just like you said it would." Terence was so proud of himself that he almost bounced in his seat. "I just wish I could be there when she finds out, so I could share that with you, too."

Struggling to keep a maniacal laugh from escaping her lips, the pale woman tapped her closely trimmed fingernails on the tabletop. "I'm sure the look on her face will be similar to the one she exhibited when her house burned to the ground."

He put his fingers to his lips. "Shhh. No sense in letting everyone else in on the fun." Looking around the room to make certain that no one was in a position to overhear them, he leaned forward also. "The other matter went off well, too. I just can't believe no one's noticed it yet."

"She never cared about the money, the foolish girl. That's why I have to take it away from her, so she'll come to her senses and come back to me, like it's supposed to be."

Terence leaned back in his chair and smoothed his hair back with both hands. "And don't forget about me." He never took the time to think about Liz's reasons for getting the money. She had given him some sob story about how her husband had taken away everything she had, including her daughters, and then had her committed. While the story didn't quite ring true, Terence overlooked the obvious loopholes because of his greed.

"Of course not. You'll get what you deserve," she promised.

If he caught the double meaning behind the words, he didn't

show it. "I guess once this is all over, I'll have to thank Cheryl." His cousin was a nurse at the institution, and it was her phone call several months previously that had brought Terence together with Liz. Befriending the quiet patient, Cheryl had felt sorry for her because Liz's family never visited. No one seemed to care, and Liz gave evidence that she was shrewd with finances, so Cheryl had called Terence to see if he'd be interested in a visitation program. Realizing the patient was a brilliant businesswoman, she thought that her cousin would benefit from the woman's knowledge and practically begged him to meet Liz. Little did she realize how well the two would get along.

After hearing *her* version of why she had been committed, Terence agreed to help Liz—for a cut of the profits, of course. Terence quickly blew each paycheck within a couple of days, and then had to live off what he could scrimp together for the next two weeks. He was tired of helping other people get rich while he drove an old car and lived in a crappy apartment. With Liz's sharp mind and Terence's connections, it all seemed almost too easy. His written testimonial, along with nurse Cheryl's, would help the woman they knew as Liz to be released from the institution, where she had been confined for almost six months.

LEX SPENT THE majority of Monday morning and afternoon on the telephone, trying without success to get more information about the theft of her investments. Tired and with her patience worn down from dealing with unhelpful customer service representatives and telephone menus that she needed a road map to follow, she was about to get up from her desk and head over to Martha's when the phone rang again. Amanda was already over at the cottage, having decided to take the day off to regroup as well. Anxious to join her lover, Lex grumbled and picked up the phone. "What?"

"Ms. Walters?"

"Yes, this is Lexington Walters. Who are you?" Lex leaned back in her chair and stared at the picture of Amanda on her desk. Looking at it would have to do until she could get whoever was bothering her off the phone.

"Um, yes. This is Andrew Wilson. We met Saturday at—"

Not in the mood for niceties, Lex cut him off. "I remember you, Mr. Wilson. Is there a reason you're bothering me today?"

He cleared his throat. "Actually, yes. I wanted to see if you'd had a change of heart where that property is concerned. You see, my boss bought the land north of there, and he'd really like to add more connecting acreage. I'm sure we could come up with a figure that would be more than fair."

"I doubt that. You can come up with figures all day long, Mr. Wilson, and it wouldn't be enough to interest me in selling a property I've just bought." Lex closed her eyes and counted to ten. It didn't help much.

"You have no idea who you're dealing with, Ms. Walters. My employer—"

"Don't you try and threaten me, you little weasel! Even though I had been thinking of selling, I sure wouldn't sell to *you*. Now, quit bothering me, before I hunt you down and show you how we geld troublesome horses!" She slammed down the receiver and got to her feet. "Stupid little pissant." Taking her hat from the rack by the door, Lex stomped through the den, not even noticing her grandfather sitting quietly in the corner, reading the newspaper.

Travis watched his granddaughter leave the room, then raised the paper. "She must have gotten that temper from her father's side of the family," he muttered. Even Travis had no desire to encounter Lex when she was angry.

AMANDA WATCHED AS Martha tried to frame a response to Ellie's latest commentary. Even as good-natured as the housekeeper was, she had been put on the defensive several times during the course of the conversation. Lex's cousin had proven to be an intelligent, if somewhat uninformed individual, and she had extremely strong opinions on the subjects that she brought up. Amanda couldn't believe how close-minded Ellie was on everything.

"But don't you see, Martha? Surely as a teacher yourself, you understand the importance of teaching evolution *and* creationism. Don't students have a right to know everything? Or do you want them to grow up actually thinking that they were descended from apes?" The look on Ellie's face told them how she felt about that.

"I agree that a child's spiritual needs are important," Martha calmly said. "But the place for that kind of teaching is in the church."

Ellie, sitting on the sofa next to Amanda, reminded her of some of the old biddies at her church. Their superior attitude was one of the reasons she didn't always make it to Sunday services. Ellie leaned forward, trying to ignore the sensation of Amanda's hand coming to rest on her leg. She knew that it was there to keep her from getting carried away in the conversation, but for some reason, it only served to distract her. "I suppose the next thing you're going to tell me is that you actually approve of Lex's lifestyle." She felt a sudden loss as the hand quickly disappeared from her leg.

"I've very proud of my girl," Martha said. "I raised her the best I could, and I think she turned out very well."

"Sure. But as a Christian, aren't you disappointed, or even just the tiniest bit disgusted by how her life goes against everything that the Word of God teaches?" She turned slightly to point a finger at Amanda. "I think I know what I'm talking about. My mother was a deeply religious woman, and I was raised in a strict Baptist household. Without Lex's obviously perverted influence, who's to say that Amanda here wouldn't be happily married with children by now?"

"You've got some nerve," Amanda interrupted. "Coming into our home and condemning the way we live, just because it's different than how you think." She took a deep, calming breath, in order to keep from reaching over and slapping the woman next to her. "For your information, I *am* happily married — to the woman I love more than anything in the world. She didn't 'influence' me. As a matter of fact, I pursued her. And I don't appreciate your holier-than-thou attitude, Ellie."

Ellie held up her hands in a defensive posture. "Whoa. Hold on a minute, Amanda. I was just voicing an opinion." She looked over to Martha, who wore an expression on her face that showed that she was trying to control herself, whether from joining in Amanda's tirade, or laughing over it, Ellie wasn't sure. "No offense, Martha. I'm sorry if my mouth overrode my brain."

"No offense taken, Ellie." Although she was steaming mad inside, Martha didn't want such a sensitive topic to ruin the day. She just hoped that the more time Ellie spent with Lex, the more she'd understand that her bigoted views were wrong.

"Thank you." Ellie turned back to Amanda. "I'm sorry if I upset you, too, Amanda. Believe me, it was the last thing I ever wanted to do. It's just that you're young and beautiful and could have your pick of anyone. I guess I just can't see why you chose Lex."

Amanda smiled at the mention of her lover's name. "Because she's the other half of my soul, Ellie. I hope that someday you'll find someone who makes you feel that way. Because believe me, it's the best damn feeling in the world."

"If you say so." Ellie patted herself on the thighs, then stood up. "I think I've irritated you both enough this afternoon. So if you'll excuse me, I'm going to go back over to the main house and see what my grandfather is up to."

Martha watched her leave. "That girl has some real tough

issues to ponder." She looked at Amanda, who frowned. "Don't tell me you didn't notice it."

"What?"

"Never mind, dear." She noticed the way Ellie kept looking at Amanda, but she wasn't surprised that Amanda hadn't noticed since Lex's partner only had eyes for a certain tall brunette. Standing up, Martha gathered up the empty coffee cups from the table. "Let's just say that those that holler the loudest usually have the biggest burr under their saddle blanket."

A FEW FEET from the back door of the ranch house, Lex almost knocked Ellie to the ground. She was still seething over the phone call from Andrew Wilson and hadn't noticed her cousin coming up the path.

Ellie had to turn sideways to keep from being thrown to the dirt. "Hey, watch it."

"Back off, Ellie. I'm not in the mood for your shit," Lex snapped as she stomped to the barn. She didn't realize that her cousin was behind her until the door didn't close after she stepped inside. "What?"

"You know, for someone who's supposed to be *gay*, you sure are cranky all the time." Ellie slipped in the door behind Lex and leaned up against the far wall, watching the emotions race across her cousin's face. After a few quiet moments, she spoke. "I don't get it."

Rolling her eyes, Lex walked over to the stall where the newest horse was stabled. Roy had informed her earlier that the filly was saddle broken and should bring a good price when they decide to put her up for sale. "What is it that you don't get?"

"Why someone as sweet as Amanda would want to be with a grump like you." Ellie concluded that Amanda must not really be gay, because she was a lot nicer than the other lesbians she'd seen on television and movies—especially her cousin. "If she weren't here, she'd probably be married to a nice guy and have a couple of kids right now."

The comment hit Lex in one of her most vulnerable areas. She'd often wondered what Amanda saw in her, but she wasn't about to give Ellie the satisfaction of knowing that. "You don't know Amanda very well, then. Because she's never said a thing to me about wanting children."

Ellie laughed, although it wasn't a happy sound. "Come on, cousin. I haven't been around very long, and even I can tell that she's upset about not having a *real* family." Ellie decided that the arrogant woman in front of her deserved to be brought down a few pegs, and she was glad to be the one to do it. "Have you even discussed children?"

"You are so full of shit," Lex argued, although she didn't sound quite so confident.

"I am, huh? Haven't you noticed how quiet Amanda gets when someone mentions her sister's pregnancy? Or the sad little look on her face when Martha talks about that lady at the office who's expecting?" Ellie started to take a step closer to Lex, but the look on her cousin's face caused her to stop. "Or, since you're obviously the *man* in this relationship, have you just decided that whatever you say is the way things should be?"

Lex crossed the barn and tangled her hands in Ellie's denim jacket, shoving her cousin back against the wall. "Shut the hell up! It's not like that." She was dangerously close to knocking some sense into her cousin when a gasp at the open door caught her attention.

"Lex! What are you doing?" Amanda rushed to stand between the two women. She turned back to look at Ellie. "Are you all right?"

"Oh, yeah, sure. Just trying to have a conversation with Butch, here. But she's, ugh—" Ellie was cut off in mid-sentence by another hard shove against the wall by Lex.

"Shut up." Lex felt herself suddenly pushed away by Amanda. "Hey!"

Amanda put both hands on her lover's chest and looked into her eyes. "Honey, stop. Please." She turned around and pointed a finger at Ellie. "And you, cool it with the name-calling." She moved so that she had both of them in her vision. "I swear, you two are like a couple of kids. You're grown women, so act like it." Amanda grabbed Lex by the front of her shirt and pulled. "Come on. We're going for a walk."

Lex glared at her cousin as she turned to go with Amanda. From the moment that Ellie first appeared at the ranch, she had seemed determined to be on Lex's bad side, and this little confrontation really proved it. As a parting gesture, Ellie sneered at Lex as she was leaving. It was almost enough to stop Lex in her tracks, but Amanda had a firm grip on her clothes and wasn't stopping. "Bitch," Lex muttered under her breath. She allowed herself to be led down a trail behind the barn, and the cool afternoon slowly helped her anger subside.

Not long after they'd left the barn, Amanda traded her grip on Lex's shirt for her lover's hand. She felt the tension drain from Lex and looked over to see a calmer look on her face. "You doing any better now?"

"Yeah."

"What caused you to go off like that? It's not like you, Lex."

Lex looked out at the nearby trees. "It's no use, Amanda. I've been trying all day to see if there was some sort of insurance or something on the money I had invested, but all I get from these so-called experts is that I'm out of luck. No one wants to admit to anything, and all they'll tell me is that they're looking into it, and it could take weeks or months to find out what happened. But for now that money is gone." She turned her head until she could see Amanda's face. "I may have to sell off bits of the ranch in order to keep it afloat, starting with the property I just picked up." Although selling to that obnoxious man who kept bothering her didn't seem like an option. *I'd rather starve. Something just doesn't seem right about all this.*

"Oh, Lex. No." Amanda felt like crying. She knew how much the ranch meant to her lover. "I've got a pretty decent amount in my trust fund. It's not like I ever use it for anything. I could—"

"No! We've already talked about this, Amanda. It's not right."

"Why not? I thought you told me that this was *our* ranch." Stubborn pride or not, Amanda wasn't about to stand by and watch Lex give up her dream.

Shaking her head, Lex pulled away from Amanda and took several steps alone. "That's not the point." Her voice was so quiet, it was almost impossible to hear her. "I can't ask that of you."

Amanda walked toward her and placed her hands on Lex's hips. She could see the tight set of her lover's shoulders and wanted to try to make her understand. "You're not asking, Lex; I'm offering." She used her grip to turn Lex around so that they were facing each other. "Let me contribute, for a change. I love this ranch as much as you do, Lexington Walters. Let me be more a part of it."

There were so many reasons why she needed to say no. Lex didn't want it to look like she married Amanda for her money, which is what Amanda's family had thought when they first got together. She had brought Amanda out to the ranch to live, not asking for a cent. How would Amanda's father feel if he found out that she had accepted a large chunk of change from Amanda? *And her mother — God help me if her mother ever found out, that evil bitch.* She opened her mouth to speak, but found it covered by Amanda's hand.

"Don't answer right now, Lex. Think about it, and we'll discuss it more later. I just want to put the offer on the table, so to speak." Amanda removed her hand and dropped a kiss in its place.

Lex let out a sigh. *Can't hurt to think on it, right?* Wrapping her arms around her lover, she returned Amanda's kiss and once again silently marveled at her luck in finding such a wonderful woman.

FROM HIS SEAT in the living room, Travis heard the back door slam and footsteps pound down the hallway. He turned his head and saw his granddaughter's profile in the door. "Ellie, why don't you come in here and join me?" he asked, patting the vacant spot next to him.

Still seething over her encounter with Lex, Ellie did as she was asked. She glared at the dark television, then turned to look at her grandfather. "Have you been sitting in here by yourself long?"

"For a bit," Travis admitted. "But I enjoy the quiet, to tell you the truth." He had a pretty good idea why Ellie was so upset, and part of him questioned his decision to spend time inside so that his grandchildren could become acquainted. "Are you all right?"

Ellie took the question seriously, thinking for some time before answering. "I'm not sure, Grandpa. For someone who is living against the scriptures, Lex sure is full of herself."

Sitting up in his seat, Travis wasn't sure he heard right. "What?"

"This whole 'lesbian' thing. She's just not normal, Grandpa. And she's obnoxious, to boot."

Travis bit the inside of his mouth. Going off on Ellie wasn't going to make her any less self-righteous and would probably only cause more bad feelings between the two women. "Lexington has been going through quite a rough time this past year, Ellie. Perhaps you'd be less likely to judge her if you knew more about her."

She shook her head. "I doubt it." After the silence lengthened between them, Ellie turned to her grandfather. "How do you do it?"

"Do what?"

"How do you tolerate how she is? I mean, the queer thing and all." Ellie's question came out quietly and without her usual bitterness. She honestly couldn't understand why everyone seemed okay with how Lex lived her life. It completely confused her.

Travis pulled his newfound granddaughter closer to him and waited until her head rested on his shoulder. "To tell you the truth, I don't even think about it. To me, she's just Lexington. And she's happy. That's all I could ever ask for."

"Was she strange as a child?"

"I wouldn't know," he murmured, his voice suddenly sad. "This last year was the first time I'd seen her since she was four years old."

Ellie looked up into Travis's face. "Really? Did you stay away because you didn't like how she was?"

"No, dear. Nothing like that. Her father kept her grandmother and me away from her. It wasn't until last fall that I was able to get back in touch with her."

"Oh? What happened then?"

Travis went on to tell Ellie about the past year and what Lex had been through. About how she had pulled Amanda from the creek, then struggled against cattle rustlers whose leader almost killed Lex by pushing her off a cliff. How his friend, who was the cook for the ranch hands, contacted Travis to let him know, precipitating Travis's rush back to Somerville and the reunion with the granddaughter he'd never stopped loving.

He then went on about Lex's childhood, or lack thereof, and how, even from an early age, she was expected to take care of the ranch, struggling for, but never receiving, her father's approval. He told of the stresses that Lex had been under and of how she finally reconciled with her father just before he died of pancreatic cancer. How Lex's own brother schemed against her to get his hands on her money and her property. And finally, Travis spoke of his own excitement at finding another grandchild, only to have the two at each other's throats every time they got together.

"Wow." Even though she still didn't approve of Lex, Ellie at least had a good idea why her cousin was on such a tight string all the time. "She's been through it, hasn't she?"

"Yes, she has." Travis sat up so that he could look directly into Ellie's eyes. "Don't get me wrong, Ellie, I don't condone Lexington's little temper tantrums. But I at least understand where she's coming from. That young woman has been hit from all sides her entire life. No wonder she's cautious about who she trusts and reacts the way she does. But let me tell you this: she is the most loyal and generous person in the world. And nothing is more important to her than her ranch and her family. She's nearly given her life for them time and again."

"Her family? From what I can tell, that's just you and me, Grandpa. She may be nice to you, but she's clearly doesn't like me."

"You're wrong, Ellie. If you think that only blood relations can be family, you've got a lot to learn."

"Well, if she had a husband, I could understand that, but—"

Travis shook his head at Ellie's narrow-mindedness. "Amanda is Lex's family. She loves Lex with her whole heart, and they are as married and as much family to each other as I was to your grandmother, my sweet Melanie. Martha is Lex's family, too. She's the only mother Lex has ever known. Sheriff Bristol is like an adopted father to Lex. And Amanda's grandparents treat Lex as their own granddaughter.

"I was not in the picture for most of Lex's life, but I'm thankful each and every day that when I turned up here at the ranch, Lex and Amanda welcomed me into their family with open arms. As her family, we all have one very important thing in common—we love Lex and she loves us. And rather than sit in judgment of her 'lifestyle,' we'd rather she know that despite the problems and conflicts in her life, we will stand by her with all the love and support we can give her. She's worth it."

Ellie nodded. "All right. But don't expect me to suddenly forget that she's queer, Grandpa. That's just something I can't overlook. As far as I'm concerned, it's just wrong."

"Just give her a chance. At least try to get to know her, before you sit in judgment on her, Ellie. That's all I ask."

"I'll try." But Ellie didn't think she'd ever understand her cousin or her unnatural ways.

As for Travis, he wondered if Ellie had really heard a single word that he'd said.

Chapter Seven

AMANDA AWAKENED TO light kisses across her throat. She moaned and reached up to wrap her arms around Lex, never opening her eyes. "Now that's my kind of alarm clock." The kisses started to move lower down her chest. "What time is it?"

"A little after seven-thirty," Lex mumbled, intent on her task. She pulled a bit of flesh into her mouth and started to suckle gently.

"Ah. Well, that's not too... seven-thirty?" Amanda sat up in the bed, disengaging the warm lips from her breast. "Why didn't you wake me earlier?" She climbed out of bed, taking her previously discarded nightshirt with her. "I need to be in the office before eight."

Lex rolled over to watch her lover race around the bedroom, gathering clothes and grumbling under her breath. "I thought you needed the sleep, sweetheart. You were tossing and turning half the night."

Stopping in the middle of the room, Amanda tried to keep from yelling at Lex's attempt to help. "It's just that I've got a ton of paperwork with deadlines to get caught up on, and I really didn't want to have to work late tonight." She walked over to the bed and sat down, laying her clothes beside her. "I should have told you last night." Amanda leaned over and kissed her wife before getting up and gathering her clothes again. "Thanks for watching out for me, honey. The extra sleep did help."

Since she'd decided to spend the day riding, Lex skipped her usual shower and got dressed while she waited for Amanda to get out of the shower. She was pulling on her boots when her partner stepped from the bathroom, fully dressed for the day. "Wow. You look great."

And she did. The navy blue two-piece business suit skirt was cut right above the knee, and the white silk top opened at the neck, showing off the heart-shaped diamond necklace that had been a gift from Lex the previous year. Low-heeled navy pumps finished the outfit, which was a lot dressier than Amanda usually wore to the office. "Thanks. It's new."

"Any reason for the fancy outfit?" Lex asked. She couldn't remember any special dates, but that didn't mean that there weren't any.

"No, not really. I just thought that since I'm the office manager, I should dress like it at least part of the time," Amanda admitted. "Do you think it's too much?"

Lex stood up and crossed to where Amanda was standing. She ran her hand across the soft material in a light caress. "Too much clothes? Yes. At least for what I had in mind. But for work, no. I think you look fabulous." She accentuated her final words with a heated kiss.

"Lex," Amanda gasped, trying to get her equilibrium back after the kiss, "that's not fair."

"All's fair in love and horseshoes," Lex said softly biting under Amanda's ear. "Just thought you should know what you missed by getting out of bed."

Swallowing hard, Amanda took a step back. "H— horseshoes?" She shook a finger at her wife, but couldn't keep the grin off her face. "You are so bad."

"Uh-huh. And if I could have kept you in bed a little bit longer, you'd have seen just how bad I can be." Deciding to cut Amanda some slack, Lex put an arm around her shoulders and started to lead her from the room. "But if you're real good, I'll show you tonight," she whispered in Amanda's ear.

"Definitely not fair," Amanda whined. "And I'll hold you to that, Stretch." They both laughed as they walked down the stairs.

After breakfast, Lex walked Amanda out to her car. She stood at the open driver's door while Amanda climbed in the vehicle. "I'm going to spend the day riding over to the new property. You know, check out what we've got, and make sure it's okay to put stock on. So I probably won't be home until around dark."

"Okay. But be careful."

"Aren't I always?" Lex asked, before she leaned in and captured her partner's lips in a lingering kiss.

After Lex pulled back, Amanda reached up and wiped her lipstick off Lex's lips with her thumb. "That's what I'm afraid of." She allowed her wife to close the car door, but she hurriedly rolled down the window before Lex could walk away. "I love you. Oh, and would you take your cell phone with you, please?" she yelled after her.

Lex put her hands on her hips and grinned. "Yes, mother. I

suppose you want me to wear clean underwear, too?" she teased.

"No sense in starting anything new," Amanda retorted, earning an outraged look for her comment. "That's what you get for teasing me, smartass." Her smile faded, and her looked turned serious. "Cell phone, please?"

"Sure thing, sweetheart. I was planning on it, anyway." Before Amanda rolled up the window, she added, "I love you, too." Lex winked at her and stood on the front porch until the Mustang drove out of sight. Once the car was gone, she exhaled heavily. "Mooning over your wife isn't getting the chores done, Lexington. Sooner you leave, the sooner you get back." She turned and walked back into the house, still talking to herself.

MICHAEL CAUBLE BRUSHED a tiny speck of lint from the camera lens, then packed it in a leather case. His photography studio had become very successful in the past few months, and it seemed like he was always running from one appointment to another with little time to spend with his family. If he hadn't talked his father, Jacob, into helping him with the larger jobs, he'd probably never see him, either. He made a mental note to call Amanda for lunch sometime during the week, in order to catch up with her. A quick glance at his calendar showed today as the only open day, and he was just about to call her when his phone rang. "Cauble Photography. Can I help you?"

"Michael? This is Frank." His son-in-law rarely called, but with Jeannie due to deliver their first child next month, Frank called more often, usually to share some little tidbit that happened during the pregnancy or to ask advice on how to handle a cranky mother-to-be.

"Hi there. Is that daughter of mine still giving you a hard time?" Michael sat down at his desk and looked at the photographs in front of him. Jeannie was his oldest, and she and her husband had been trying for years to have children. He kept reminding her of that fact when she'd call him from California, upset at some imagined slight that Frank had done.

"Actually, Michael, she's in the hospital. There's been some complications."

"What kind of complications? Is she all right?"

Frank took a deep breath. "I don't know, Mike. The doctors are talking about doing a Cesarean, but they've got to get her stabilized first." His voice got quiet. "I'm scared, Michael. She's just so damned tiny, and the baby's gotten so big, even this early." Jeannie wasn't due for another six weeks or so, but because of her small frame, she looked enormous. "I can't lose her, Mike. I just can't." The big man started to cry.

Completely out of his element, Michael ran his hand through his hair, trying to think. Hearing his normally cool-headed son-in-law fall apart on the phone wasn't helping, either. His first instinct was to catch the next plane out, but he had a huge wedding to work the next day, and it was too late to cancel. He'd even hired his father as an assistant, due to the size of the ceremony. "What about your parents? Are they there with you?"

"No, I can't reach them. They've been in Europe for an extended vacation. I don't even know what damned country they're in!" Frank's voice rose, then quieted. "I don't think I can handle this, Mike. She's all I've got."

"Shhh. Everything's going to be fine, Frank. I'm sure of it." Michael's eyes rested on the picture he'd taken of Amanda and Lex's commitment ceremony months previously. *Amanda! She's really good with Frank. Maybe she can help. But something like this would be better discussed in person.* "Listen. I'm going to go over to the realty office and talk to Amanda. Are you at the hospital now?"

Frank sniffled, trying to get himself together. "Yeah. Have her call my cell phone, will you? She has the number."

"I sure will, Frank. Hang in there, son. We'll get through this."

"Thanks, Mike. I'm sorry about this, but I just didn't know what to do."

Michael was already grabbing his car keys. "Don't apologize; we're family. Now go get some air or something. Amanda will be calling you in a little bit, okay?" He hung up the phone and hurried out the door, barely taking the time to lock up behind himself.

TERENCE FOUND A parking space close to the building and pulled his new Volvo into the spot. He knew that he shouldn't have spent the money, but he was tired of driving around in the rusted old heap he'd had before. He smiled as he remembered the auto dealer's face when he told the man that he wanted to trade in his 1977 Thunderbird for a new C70 convertible. The disbelieving salesman nearly chased him from the showroom, but the man's attitude changed when Terence offered to pay cash. As he climbed from the vehicle, Terence brushed his hand across the top of the door and grinned. Now if he could just figure out why Liz had asked him to come to the hospital today, he'd be all right. He signed in at the front desk and almost jumped out of his skin when he heard Liz's voice behind him.

"It's about time you showed up; I've been waiting for over an hour." She stood there, dressed in an expensive silk business suit, a young woman beside her. "This is my daughter," Liz said loudly. "She wanted to meet you."

The woman wasn't quite what he'd pictured. She seemed taller and heavier than he had been led to believe. Terence frowned at her, but held out his hand. "It's nice to meet you, uh—"

"Amanda," the woman supplied, in a loud voice also. "Thank you for being such a good friend to my mother while I was away." She picked up a small suitcase and motioned to the door. "I think Mother has spent enough time here, don't you think? I had to take a taxi from the airport, so if you don't mind, we'd appreciate you giving us a ride."

"Oh! Sure." Terence took the bag from the young woman and followed the two of them out of the building. He was about to ask Liz a question when she held up her hand.

"All in good time, Terence. I've already made reservations at the Hyatt Regency, so if you'll just drive, we can talk in the car." Liz scanned the parking lot. "Which one is yours?"

Terence mentally cringed. This wasn't how he wanted Liz to find out he had bought a new car, and an overly expensive one at that. He pointed to the convertible. "It's that one. But I can explain—"

Liz waved him off, before opening the passenger door. "Later. Just get me away from this dreadful place, will you? We can discuss your propensity for spending money on the way." She looked over at the young woman still standing beside Terence. "Well? Are you coming, *daughter* dear?" Liz seemed to find something very funny and was still laughing when the other two finally got into the car with her.

A short time into the drive, Liz pointed to a bank. "Pull in there, Terence. I have to take care of some business." As he did as she asked, Liz turned around to address the woman in the back seat. "Coming, dear?"

The woman smiled back at her. "Yes, *Mother*." As she got out of the car, she tapped Terence on the shoulder. "Nice to meet you, Terry." With a quick wave, both women disappeared into the bank.

Terence spent the next half hour reading his owner's manual for the Volvo. When he heard the click of high heels approaching, he looked up to see Liz, who was alone.

She slid back into the passenger's seat and turned to look at him. "Well? Are you just going to sit there all day, or are you going to take me to the hotel?"

"What about your daughter?" he asked, quickly putting the book back in the glove box. "Shouldn't we wait for her?"

Liz looked at him as if he'd grown another head. "My daughter? Oh, you mean Sara. No, we won't be seeing her again, I'd imagine." She pulled the visor down and looked at herself in the vanity mirror. "Put up the top on this beast, Terence. My hair already looks frightful."

He did as he was told, and after the top was in place, Terence couldn't hold his questions any longer. "I thought your daughter's name was Amanda. Why did she disappear? And how in the world did you get released so soon?"

"You dear, dear boy." Liz patted him on the leg and shook her head. "Sometimes I wonder how you survived before you met me. Drive, and I'll try to answer all your inane questions." Once the car was back en route to the hotel, she settled back into her seat. "Getting released was actually quite easy. As the hospitals have extremely long waiting lists, all it took was the right paperwork. And, of course, affidavits from my doctor, your cousin, and most of all, my daughter." Here she began to chuckle. "The court systems are so overworked, it wasn't hard to get someone to pose as Amanda and get away with it. The right amount of money to the right person, and here I am." Her arms spread wide, Liz laughed. "Freedom is delicious, especially when it's bought."

Terence shivered at the sound of Liz's laughter. "So, what's next on the agenda?"

"A hot bath, room service, and a shopping trip. Not necessarily in that order." She turned her head to study Terence's face. "Don't worry, dear. The fun's just beginning."

That's what I'm afraid of. He worried that this was a whole new side to Liz, and he wasn't too sure he liked it.

LEX SET THE hoof back on the ground gently, although what she really wanted to do was slam it down. Thunder's loose shoe wasn't a tragedy, but it did change Lex's plans for the morning. She patted him on the shoulder and climbed out of the stall. Looking around the stable, she counted three heads: Thunder, Amanda's pony Stormy, and the new filly that had just recently been saddle trained. Obviously the ranch hands had taken the other horses out to work, and this was what she was left with. She eyed the paint pony, and then shook her head. As small and gentle as the mare was, she knew that there was no way she'd survive the kind of riding that Lex liked to do. That left the newest filly, and Lex walked over to her stall. Larger than the paint, she seemed strong and healthy, if a bit high-spirited. "Guess it's you and me, girl."

It took Lex longer than usual to saddle up the filly, but she didn't mind. Fact was, she was looking forward to getting back on the horse, since it was the first one to throw her in a long time. Once outside the barn, she swung herself up in the saddle, prepared for the side dance that the filly performed. "You are a frisky thing, aren't you? Let's just see how well you handle." She spun the frolicsome animal around and headed up the north trail.

The filly kicked up her heels and tossed her head. Lex, ready for the young horse's antics, tightened the grip of her knees, pulled down the brim of her black Stetson, and laughed. "That's it. Show me what you've got."

A short while later, the animal settled down. The fall morning was a bit cool, but Lex's long-sleeved denim shirt was more than warm enough. In order to avoid an argument with Martha, her duster was tied to the back of the saddle, although Lex didn't think she'd need it. She inhaled deeply. The leaves on the trees around her had already begun to change. Lex relished the rich scent of autumn that the fallen vegetation brought. It was one of her favorite times of the year.

A small brown rabbit darted across the path, disturbed from its den by the sound of the horse's hooves. The filly reared in alarm, but Lex tightened her hold on the animal. "You're going to have to do a lot better than that if you want to toss me off this time." Once the horse had settled down a bit, Lex patted the warm neck below her with one gloved hand. "A little rabbit won't hurt you, you big chicken." Satisfied that the animal was calm enough, Lex tapped her heels into the filly's flank and quickened the pace.

The morning flew by during the quiet ride. Finally, they came upon the new opening in the fence that Roy and the hired hands had added the day before. Roy had asked her if she wanted the entire length of fence removed, but since Lex wasn't too sure if she'd even be able to keep the land, she told him to just make an opening large enough for a truck. She'd worry about the rest later.

Once on the new property, Lex headed the filly toward the creek. It surprised her by being quite shallow in several places. Farther downstream, it slowed to a bare trickle. "I wonder what's up with that?" she asked the horse. "It's usually flowing pretty well this time of year." Lex decided that further investigation was in order, so she turned her mount around to head upstream.

AMANDA COULD HAVE sworn that the pile of folders on her desk had grown since she'd last looked at them. She had put off that part of her job for most of the morning, but knew that they wouldn't get done on their own. She sighed and took the next one off the top, opening it and studying the figures before her. "I'm going to have to show Margaret how to use a blasted calculator," she grumbled, marking through one of the lines and writing correct figures to the side. As much as she loved her job, she truly hated paperwork, much preferring to be out showing houses to people. "Geez! Six times two is twelve, not eighteen." She scribbled another notation on the paper. Three more mistakes later, Amanda was on the verge of calling Margaret into her office when her phone buzzed. "Yes?"

"I'm sorry to bother you, Amanda, but you've got a visitor."

"Thanks, Shelly. Send 'em on in." Happy for the temporary reprieve, Amanda closed the folder and returned it to the stack. When the door opened, she stood up and walked around the desk. "Daddy! Wow, what a great surprise."

Michael gladly wrapped his arms around his youngest daughter, needing the emotional support her embrace brought. He continued to hold her until Amanda pulled back to look into his face.

"What's wrong?" When he didn't answer immediately, her eyes widened in alarm. "Is it Grandpa? Gramma?" When he hesitated, she continued her questioning. "Oh, my God. Is it Jeannie? The baby?"

"Shh. I'm sorry, sweetheart. I didn't mean to upset you." Michael led his daughter over to one of the guest chairs in front of her desk and then sat down next to her. "I just got a call from Frank. Jeannie is in the hospital."

"The hospital? What's the matter?"

"She's developed some complications, and it looks like they're going to have to take the baby early." Although obviously distraught, Michael tried to keep his voice even. "They're trying to get her stable before they do a Cesarean, but the surgery could be as early as tomorrow morning."

Amanda looked down at their joined hands, and at how her father kept rubbing her knuckles with his thumb. *A year ago he'd probably be off on one of his "business" trips, and wouldn't even know about Jeannie's pregnancy. I'm so glad to have my father back in my life again.* "Poor Frank. He's probably beside himself." She stood up, breaking the grip that Michael had on her hands. "Looks like we'll be on the next flight to California, huh?"

"Well, that's the problem." Michael ducked his head in shame. "I can't go until tomorrow evening, at the earliest."

"Why?"

Michael finally looked up to meet his daughter's eyes. "I've got that huge wedding to photograph in Austin tomorrow. I even had to hire Dad for extra help." He couldn't have felt worse if someone had punched him in the stomach. "Nothing really changes, does it? I'm still putting work before family," he said, looking back down at the floor.

"Oh, Daddy." Amanda knelt at his feet and looked up into his face. She could see how torn her father was. "This isn't the same, and you know it. Before, you were the head of a company—now you're the only employee." She tried to make light of the situation. "I'm sure you'd hate to fire your photographer for not doing his job, wouldn't you?"

"What did I do to deserve you?" he asked, reaching over and brushing an errant strand of hair away from Amanda's eyes. "If it wasn't so late, I'd try to give it to someone else, but there's just not time."

"I know."

"And I can be on the next flight out of Austin the moment it's over."

Amanda smiled. "I know."

Michael stood up and pulled Amanda up with him. "I guess it'll just be you, Lex, and your grandmother. Dad and I will be there as soon as we can."

"Not a problem. Considering how terrified Lex is of airplanes, you're probably doing the smart thing." Amanda walked back around her desk and picked up the telephone receiver. "Now I get to have the fun of telling her we're flying out today. I'm sure she's going to love that."

THE FURTHER UPSTREAM she rode, the denser the trees became and the more shallow the creek. Lex could see that the creek walls were still muddy, and she couldn't understand the sudden loss of water. They'd had the usual amount of rain, and the flowing water should have been at least knee to waist deep in most places.

Another thing bothering her was the silence. Typically, she'd hear birdcalls and the rustling of animals in the underbrush. But now, the only sounds were of her horse, the squeaking of the leather saddle, and the slight noise made by the slow running creek. Not normally the nervous type, Lex felt the hairs on the back of her neck rise, and she looked around the trees for anything unusual.

Not too far away, under the cover of the heavy trees, a man stood watching the path that Lex took. He pulled out a walkie-talkie and spoke into it, careful to talk quietly so as not to give away his position. It was his job to guard the area from trespassers, and when he received word back on the radio, he couldn't help but smile. Pulling a small notepad from his shirt pocket, he scribbled down the horse's and rider's description, and then faded back into the foliage.

The dense mountain cedar mixed with the changing oak leaves made seeing very far almost impossible. "You're losing it, Lexington." Not even the high-strung filly seemed bothered by the unnatural quiet as she stretched her neck forward and shook her head, causing the bridle to jingle.

Lex stood up in the stirrups to relieve the tightened muscles in her back. Feeling rather foolish, she was glad that no one else was around to see her unusual bout of excitability. She stiffened her legs out front to keep them from cramping and had just ducked under another low-hanging branch when the cellular phone on her belt vibrated. Shifting slightly in the saddle to reach for the phone, she finally worked it free from her waist just as a loud explosion ripped through the quiet.

The noise terrified the skittish filly, and she took off through the trees at a dead run. Lex managed to hold on until another explosion made the horse rear. The top of Lex's head smacked into a thick, low-hanging tree branch. Dazed, she dropped the cell phone and slid semi-conscious from the saddle, her left foot caught in the stirrup. The horse never slowed as Lex hit the ground and was dragged through the underbrush.

LIZ LOOKED AROUND the hotel suite. "I'm so glad to be back in the civilized world," she told Terence. Then she held out her hands, displaying them to him. "Just look at my nails. I'm sure it will take weeks to get them back in shape. And the clothes! May I never see cotton again. No wonder the people in the state hospitals are unbalanced. Not one shred of silk there."

"Uh, okay." Terence had never seen this side of Liz before. Her eyes were glazed, and her speech was almost frantic. "Have you taken your medication today?"

"Medication? You mean that junk they tried to poison me with? Of course not. I quit taking that days ago." Liz looked out through the window. "Lovely view, isn't it?"

Terence imperceptibly shook his head. *That would explain*

why she's acting so strange. Maybe later I can talk her into going back on the meds. She definitely needs them. Deciding it was time to change the subject, he opened his briefcase and found an envelope. "Here's the information for your Swiss bank account, Liz. I thought it would be best to put the funds from California there, instead of your other account." At her previous request, he'd opened up a bank account in her name, with him as just a rider, and deposited the money from the sale of the rancher's stocks. He just hoped she didn't see how much he had taken out for his little "shopping spree" which included new clothes and the Volvo. By the maniacal look in Liz's eyes, Terence didn't think she'd notice.

He was wrong.

Liz took the envelope and opened it, scanning its contents quickly. "That stupid child! She actually had *more* money in her trust than what she started with. Has she not learned anything from me?" She then looked at the bank statement of her other account. After carefully reading each page of the report, Liz threw the papers down and slapped Terence's face. "You fool! I didn't authorize that kind of spending!"

"But, Liz," Terence stammered, holding one hand against his cheek as he tried to back away from her.

"Don't you 'but Liz' me, you little toad." She closed the distance between them again, until she was right up in his face. "You've probably drawn all sorts of attention to yourself. I wouldn't be surprised if the authorities were minutes away." Her face had taken on a frightening shade of red, and spittle flew from her lips as she continued to berate her accomplice. "I had everything planned out perfectly, you jackass!"

Terence held up his hands to protect himself from her ire. "Don't worry, Liz. I bought the car here in Austin. It's a big city, and no one will tie us together."

That seemed to placate her, at least for the moment. She looked thoughtful, tapping her blunt nail against her teeth. "I suppose." She turned and walked away, obviously dismissing her minion.

She sat down next to the telephone and dialed a number. "Yes, front desk? I'd like a manicurist, a pedicurist, and a masseuse sent up to my room immediately. Thank you." She hung up the phone and looked at Terence as if she hadn't seen him there. "Are you still here? Go. I'll contact you when I want you."

"Now wait just a damned minute, Liz. We're partners in this. Don't think you can just—"

"Get out!" she shrieked, picking up the Bible from the

nightstand and throwing at him.

Realizing that he wouldn't be able to talk to her at the moment, Terence decided the smartest thing to do was leave. He could always come back later. He opened the door and was about to close it behind him when he heard her voice again, this time deadly calm.

"And don't you dare spend another penny unless I tell you to, Terence. It wouldn't do to upset me again," she warned, just before the door closed. She waited until she knew he was gone, then picked up the phone again, dialing a number from memory. After several rings, it was answered. "It's me. I have another little job for you. Yes, that's right. I need another little 'accident.'" Elizabeth Cauble kicked off her shoes and stretched out on the bed, listening to the voice on the other end of the line. "Right. Same terms. I'm at the Hyatt Regency, room 842. We can discuss the particulars when you get here." Smiling, she hung up the phone.

"AS USUAL, SHE'S not answering her phone." Amanda hung up the handset and looked at her father. "She was going to ride over to the new property and check it out. I guess she's in a low place or something. Maybe Martha's heard from her." She picked up the phone again and punched in the number.

"Hi, Martha, it's me. Has Lex checked in with you today?"

"Lexie? Checking in? Are we talking about the same person?" the housekeeper asked, amused. "I'm afraid not, Amanda. Was she supposed to?"

Amanda released a heavy breath and sat on the edge of her desk. "No, not really. But I just tried her cell phone, and she wasn't answering."

"And that's news?"

Despite her anxiety, Amanda couldn't help but laugh. Martha knew Lex better than anyone, herself included. "No, I suppose not. But something's come up, and I really need to reach her."

"Is everything okay? I told that stubborn woman to take a radio with her. But no, she said the phone would be more than enough. I ought to—"

"Martha, please. Jeannie's in the hospital, and we're going to have to fly out this evening. Could you please let Lex know, if she shows up?"

Martha's tone immediately changed. "Oh, honey. I'm sorry. Would you like for me to pack your bags for you? That could save some time."

"Yes, please. I'd really appreciate it, Martha." Amanda gave her father a smile to let him know everything would be okay. "I'll be home as soon as I can, all right?"

"Of course, Amanda. You drive careful, and I'll let Lexie know the moment she gets in."

After the call disconnected, Amanda gathered up her purse and briefcase. She eyed the paperwork on the corner of the desk, guilty about the relieved feeling that she'd be able to put it off for a little while longer. *I'll see if Shelly can look over the figures while I'm gone. She's got a good head for numbers.* She met Michael halfway across the room, and with her hands full, gave him an awkward hug. "I'll call you as soon as we get to the hospital."

"Thanks, sweetheart. I really wish I could be going with you. I'll see you tomorrow night, though, right?"

"Right." Amanda kissed his cheek. Before she could leave, her phone rang again. She wasn't going to answer it, but Shelly's voice came over the intercom.

"Amanda? I'm sorry to bother you, but your grandmother is on line two."

Placing her things on her desk, Amanda picked up the phone again. "Thanks, Shelly." Curious, she tapped the button. "Gramma?"

"Mandy dear, how are you?"

"Well, I—"

A voice from a loudspeaker almost drowned out what Anna Leigh said, so she raised her voice to be heard. "Have you seen your father or grandfather? I can't seem to find either one of them."

"Actually, Daddy is right here with me. Where are you?"

Again, the voice echoed through the phone. Anna Leigh had to wait before she could answer. "I'm at the hospital in San Antonio, if you can believe that."

"What? Why a hospital?"

Michael heard what Amanda said, and rushed over to her side. "Is she all right?"

"I don't know. That's what I'm trying to find out." Amanda was beginning to wish that she'd never gotten out of bed this morning. "Gramma, why are you in a hospital in San Antonio? What happened?"

"No dearest. *I'm* not in the hospital. Wanda is."

"Wanda? What's she doing in San Antonio?" Meeting her father's eyes, Amanda could only shrug.

"Her sister wanted her to go shopping, and nothing would do but some shops in San Antonio. I offered to drive them both down here. You know my car's a lot more comfortable than either one of theirs. I'd hate for poor Wanda to be cramped up in one of those little—"

"Gramma, please! Why is she in the hospital? And where is her sister?" Amanda felt like tearing her hair out. Her grandmother did love to tell a story, but often ended up completely off the subject. Seeing that Michael was just as frantic, she asked, "Can I put you on speakerphone? I think it would be easier than trying to relay everything to Daddy."

"Of course, Mandy." Anna Leigh's voice now came through the speaker loud and clear, except for the occasional sound of the hospital's intercom system. "Now, where was I?"

"You were telling us what happened to Wanda," Amanda said, rubbing her face with her hands.

"Oh, yes. That's right. We were shopping, and poor Wanda's water broke, right in the middle of the maternity store. I felt so bad for her, poor dear. She was terribly embarrassed. But the salesclerk assured us that it had happened more often than she could count and calmly called an ambulance."

"Her water broke? But I thought she wasn't due for another few weeks."

"Exactly. But you know how Mother Nature can be. Remember, Michael? We thought that our little Mandy would never come into this world. She was determined to stay right where she was, wasn't she?"

Michael smiled at the memory. He remembered how Elizabeth threatened to sue the doctor, the hospital, and finally her husband, when she went several weeks past her due date. "I remember, Mom. But if Wanda's sister was with you, why are you still in San Antonio?"

"Rita had to take my car back to Somerville to get her children from school and find a baby sitter for them. So, I volunteered to stay here with Wanda until she gets back."

"Damn," Amanda muttered. She had hoped Anna Leigh could go with her and Lex to California.

"What's wrong, Mandy?"

"Oh, nothing." Amanda looked at Michael, who shook his head. Telling Anna Leigh about Jeannie right now would only upset her, and there wasn't any use in that. She thought quickly. "I just lost the office pool on when Wanda would have the baby, that's all."

Anna Leigh laughed. "You girls are something else. Well, I see the doctor coming this way, so I'd better go see what's going on. Michael, please let your father know I may not be home until tomorrow, all right?"

"I sure will, Mom. He's going to help me with that big

wedding in the morning, so maybe I'll just go over and stay with him tonight."

"That sounds great. You boys try to stay out of trouble, and I'll see you when I get back. Mandy, I'll talk to you later, too." Anna Leigh hung up the phone abruptly.

Amanda traded looks with her father. "When it rains, it pours, huh?" She picked up her purse and briefcase again. "Can this day get any worse?"

SHARP BRANCHES AND twigs flayed Lex's head and shoulders as the horse raced through the heavy brush. She tried to reach up and work her boot free from the stirrup but couldn't quite reach. Just as she thought the filly was tiring and slowing down, there was another blast, this one closer. The animal spun and changed direction. Lex used the movement to finally slip out of her boot. She dropped to the ground in a heap, wheezing and gasping for breath.

Still dazed, Lex lay amongst the leaves and brush, trying to figure out whether or not she had any serious injuries. Although her entire body ached, miraculously nothing seemed broken. She sat up and looked around, completely lost. "Damned horse," she muttered, rubbing her forehead. She knew she'd have a definite knot where she'd made contact with the initial tree branch.

It took some time, but Lex finally got her thoughts together. She couldn't stay where she was, and even if she could, her pride wouldn't let her. She tried to get to her feet, only to have her left leg collapse under her. Falling back to the turf, Lex cursed and grabbed her knee. "Shit!" She sat still until the pain was at least a bit more manageable. Some part of the leg that had been stuck in the stirrup was definitely sprained, at the very least. There was no way she'd be able to walk on it without some help.

Disgusted and hurting, Lex lay back on the ground and looked up at the canopy of golden leaves above her. It would be getting dark soon and the cool air would turn much colder. She wished for her coat, which was probably halfway across the property by now, tied to the saddle on the spooked horse. She had no idea where her cell phone was, or if it even worked anymore. "This day just keeps getting worse."

Chapter Eight

TRAVIS HUNG UP the office phone and walked back into the den. He met Ellie halfway and scooped her up in his arms and swung her around.

"Good news, Grandpa?" Ellie asked once her feet were touching the ground again.

"The best. Someone wants to buy my house in Dallas. I've got to go up tomorrow and take care of the paperwork."

Ellie hugged him again, this time more vigorously. "That's great."

"Thank you, sweetheart. Do you want to stay here, or go with me?" Travis hoped that she'd stay and try to get to know her cousin better, but he had a feeling that any friendship between them was a lost cause.

"Well, since Lex doesn't seem to want me around anyway, if you'd like, I could always stay at your house in town and help Nancy unpack things." Ellie leaned against the back of the leather sofa, enjoying the look of excitement on her grandfather's face. She had come to care for Travis very quickly and was glad that she'd made the trip from California, if only to meet him.

The front door opened and quickly slammed shut. From the hallway, Amanda saw Ellie and Travis. She hurried into the den to join them. "Have you seen Lex?"

Ellie could see that Amanda was upset, appearing almost frantic. "Why? What has she done now?" She was hoping it was something bad because in her eyes, Lex didn't deserve a woman as sweet as Amanda.

"She hasn't done anything." Amanda tossed her briefcase onto a nearby chair and ran her hands through her hair. "I was just hoping that she'd come back early from her ride." She walked over to Travis and surprised him by wrapping her arms around him. "I'm glad you're here, though. This has already been one heck of a day."

Travis was glad to hold Amanda and felt her arms tighten around him. "Is there something that I can do to help?"

She sighed before stepping away. "Go with me to California tonight?"

"Tonight?"

"Jeannie's having complications, and I need to get out there as soon as possible."

Put on the spot, Travis didn't say anything right away. "Well, sure, Amanda, but—"

Ellie said, "But Grandpa was going to Dallas tomorrow to sign the papers on his house. Someone wants to buy it. Is that why you're looking for Lex?"

Travis put his hand on Amanda's shoulder. "Don't worry about the house. They can just wait until I get back."

Amanda shook her head. "I couldn't ask that of you." Being in the real estate business, she knew how important time was to a buyer. If Travis hesitated in the slightest, he'd probably lose the opportunity. And considering how the market was, he might not find another one for months. "Besides, I'm sure Lex will be back any time now. It's getting close to dinner time, and she knows how Martha feels about that."

"If you need me to, I'll be glad to go with you," Ellie offered. *It's just like my selfish cousin to not be here when Amanda needs her. Someone ought to knock some sense into that arrogant bitch.* "I've still got the money that I was going to use to get back home." What she really had was the return flight ticket, which she hoped she could trade in at some point since she didn't have much left for her in San Diego, anyway.

Amanda wasn't sure if she wanted to have Ellie along, but she could see that was the only way she could keep Travis from canceling his plans. She hoped that Lex would be home soon, and it would be a moot point. "Thank you, Ellie. But if you go, I'd be glad to pay your way."

"Actually," Travis said, "I'd feel better if you'd let *me* pay for all the tickets. Once you're in Los Angeles, Ellie can fly down to see her family." Since he couldn't get Ellie to call her mother very often, he wanted to somehow make sure she touched base with her. "Then, if you'd like," he told Ellie, "you can fly back here and spend some more time with us."

Ellie hid her shock. These people talked about money like it was nothing to worry about. She had had to sell her car and most of her belongings just to be able to travel to Texas. But she wasn't so proud as to turn down a free flight—and with Amanda, too. "That's very kind of you, Grandpa. I'll pay you back as soon as I can."

He raised his hand to forestall any objections. "Oh, no, you won't, young lady. What good is money if you can't spend it on your grandkids?"

Amanda hugged Travis again. "Thank you, Grandpa Travis. You're just too sweet. Now if Lex would just get home, I'd feel a lot better." Suddenly remembering her brother-in-law, Amanda covered her mouth with one hand. "Frank! I need to call him." She rushed to the office to use the phone, leaving Travis and Ellie looking at each other in confusion.

She sat at the desk and picked up the phone. Flipping through the Rolodex nearby, Amanda found the phone number for Frank and dialed. While she waited for him to pick up, she noticed the day's mail stacked in the inbox. Rifling through it, she found a letter addressed to her, and was about to open it when Frank answered.

"Frank? This is Amanda."

"Oh, God, Mandy, It's so good to hear your voice." His own voice shaky, Frank did his best to stay calm. "They want to take the baby early. And poor Jeannie is so weak."

Amanda took the envelope that was addressed to her and slipped it in her jacket pocket. "Is she doing any better, Frank? Daddy told me that the doctor's were trying to stabilize her."

"I don't know. They keep rushing around, but no one's telling me much. I can't lose her, Mandy, I can't."

"You're not going to. We all know how tough Jeannie is. She's put up with you all these years, hasn't she?" Amanda joked, trying to soothe him.

Frank's laugh evolved into a sob. "I hope so."

"Look, we'll be there as soon as we can, okay?" Amanda was already flipping through the Rolodex again, this time searching for the number of the airline they liked to use. "I'm going to make our reservations as soon as I hang up with you, Frank. Just hold on, and when you see that sister of mine, tell her I said for her to quit scaring you like this."

Still sounding overwhelmed, Frank said, "All right. I will." He hung up.

Amanda held the receiver in her hands, trying to get herself under control. For all her brave talk, she was terrified, not knowing how serious her sister's condition was. It pained her to be so far away at a time like this. She quickly called the airline, and found out that the only flight out that day was in less than three hours. They'd barely have time to pack before they'd have to race for the airport. She made reservations for three and checked her watch, hoping that Lex would be home soon.

DEEP IN THE woods, Lex looked at her watch. It was close to dinnertime, and she knew it would soon be dark. She tried again to move her leg, almost crying out at the pain in her knee. The joint was severely swollen, causing the denim material of her jeans to tighten uncomfortably. As it was, she realized that the cloth would have to be cut away, and she wasn't looking forward to that chore or the pain it would cause.

She rubbed at the small knot on her head. "Sitting here feeling sorry for myself isn't helping. I need to find a way to get out of here." Lex looked around for something to use as a crutch or a cane. Nothing nearby looked useful, and she resigned herself to having to search for a suitable piece of wood. She rolled over onto her right side, careful to not jostle her injured leg too much.

Slow going, Lex pulled herself along the trail where the horse had dragged her. Although her leather gloves protected her hands, she had to pause frequently to catch her breath. Finally, after what seemed like forever, she found a sturdy piece of deadwood and used it to rise to her feet.

Every step on her left leg was agony. "Damned horse, bolting like that." The thought of the filly brought back to her mind the reason it bolted in the first place. "Who on earth would be using explosives out here, and why?" Lex misstepped and almost fell. "Shit!" When she found a fallen tree off to the side of the path, she was able to sit down without too much trouble.

Between the pain and not having had lunch, she was beginning to feel sick to her stomach. Lex looked down at her swollen knee, torn between leaving it like it was and cutting the material to release the pressure around the swelling. She leaned back against another tree and closed her eyes. Her thoughts went back to the explosions that had put her in this predicament. "I'd better tell Charlie about it when I get back to the house." *Yeah, right. At the pace I'm setting, Charlie will be retired from the sheriff's office before I get home.*

MARTHA FOUND AMANDA in the master bedroom, checking the bags that she had packed earlier. Travis had told Martha the latest developments, and she wanted to see if there was anything else she could do to help. She noticed the tight set of Amanda's shoulders, and immediately went over and put her arm around the younger woman. "What can I do, honey?"

The comforting touch was almost Amanda's undoing. She turned around and sank into the housekeeper's embrace. They stood that way for some time, until Amanda pulled herself together and stepped away. "I think I needed that, Martha. Thanks."

"You don't have to thank me, Amanda. Travis said you'll be leaving in a bit. Is there anything I can do for you?"

Amanda zipped up the small suitcase. "Unless you can get Lex here in the next fifteen minutes, no." She lifted the case from the bed and carried it over to the door. "I tried calling her cell phone earlier and didn't get an answer. Where the hell is she? It's nearly dark."

Martha shook her head. "I don't rightly know. Blasted woman told me she didn't need the radio, since she'd have the phone." She sat down on the bed and straightened out her apron. "She was just being stubborn. We all know how lousy the reception is with that stupid thing." For not being available when Amanda needed her, Martha planned on giving Lex a strong talking-to once she got back to the house. "She's going to get a piece of my mind, believe you me."

"Don't do that, Martha. I'm sure the time got away from her, and it's just taking her longer than she expected to get home. But I really wish she was going with me." Amanda knew Lex was going to be upset that she'd missed her, and even more upset when she found out her cousin took her place on the trip. *I don't know what's going on between those two. It's like some sort of competition or something.* "I guess I'd better go downstairs and get Ellie. We can stop off and pick up some of her things on our way to the airport."

"Ellie? Is she going with you?" Martha didn't like the sound of that, not one bit. She recalled how the woman looked at Amanda. *Even with all her self-righteous prattling, that woman's got a hankering for what's on someone else's plate.*

Not understanding the concerned look on Martha's face, Amanda nodded. "It was Grandpa Travis's idea. He didn't want me going alone, and he's got to go up to Dallas first thing tomorrow and sign the papers for the sale of his house. And since Lex isn't here—"

"Would you rather that I went with you? I can be packed in a matter of minutes." Martha didn't want to be around when Lex found out that Ellie went with her partner.

"I appreciate the offer, Martha, really. But you've got Charlie and Ronnie to look after. Ellie's just going to fly with me, then take another plane down to visit her family in San Diego, and Dad will show up tomorrow. I'll be fine."

Martha didn't look so convinced. "Are you sure? Because it's really no trouble for me, you know."

"What about Ronnie? Do you really want to leave him to the

mercy of all these men?" Amanda asked, only halfway joking. It was bad enough he followed Lex around like a lost puppy and emulated her every move. The last thing they needed was for him to end back up in the bunkhouse with the ranch hands.

"I suppose you're right." Martha stood. "At least let me walk you downstairs." When they got to the doorway, she turned to look into Amanda's face. "You watch Ellie, you hear? Don't be afraid to hurt her feelings if you need to."

"Why would I want to do that? She's been pretty nice to me. It's Lex that she has trouble with."

Martha reached out and put her hands on Amanda's shoulders. "Just don't let her get away with anything, that's all." She was afraid she'd said too much, so Martha led Amanda from the room, leaving the other woman more confused than ever.

ELLIE FIDGETED IN her seat, excited to be sitting so close to Amanda, who peered out the small window. She noticed that Amanda's silk blouse was open, and got a glimpse of the part of her breast that wasn't covered by her lacy bra. Intrigued, Ellie watched as the smooth skin rose and fell with every breath that Amanda took. Suddenly Ellie realized what she was doing. *What's wrong with me? Why am I looking down Amanda's shirt?* Embarrassed, she quickly turned away. *Dear Lord in Heaven, could my cousin's tendencies be rubbing off on me? I have spent a lot of time at the ranch.* She closed her eyes and tried to clear her mind, but all that she could think about was how smooth Amanda's skin looked. For reasons she couldn't begin to articulate, she wanted to know if it felt as soft as it appeared.

For her part, Amanda was thinking about Lex. Martha promised to have her call the second she arrived back at the house, but Amanda couldn't help but think that something just wasn't quite right. She turned to say something to Ellie and noticed the look of panic on the other woman's face. *Oh great. Is fear of flying hereditary in this family?* She touched Ellie's arm. "What's the matter?"

"Were you always this way?" Ellie blurted, still trying to make sense of her own hormones, which were running rampant, especially with Amanda touching her arm.

"What way? What are you talking about, Ellie?"

"You know, *this* way. Or did being around Lex cause you to become," Ellie's voice lowered, "queer?"

Amanda began to laugh until she saw that Lex's cousin was completely serious. "Are you asking if I've always been a lesbian?" Not ashamed of who she was, Amanda was amused when Ellie motioned for her to speak more quietly. "Actually, I've always been attracted to women. But even if I had been attracted to men, it wouldn't have mattered the moment I met Lex. I fell head-over-heels in love with her as soon as I saw her on that muddy creek bank in the pouring rain."

Ellie rolled her eyes at the declaration. "Hrumph."

"Haven't you even been in love?"

"Love doesn't really exist, Amanda. It's just something that greeting card companies came up with to make more sales." Ellie crossed her arms over her chest, tired of the conversation. Having been hurt in the past, she had long ago quit believing in something that you couldn't see or touch. She thought that the woman sitting next to her was probably a victim of hero worship, since Lex had pulled her from a creek and saved her life.

"You're wrong, Ellie. Love *is* real. And it's the most wonderful feeling in the world. I pity you for not ever having felt it."

Ellie shook her head. "I know what I need to know. And if love is so great, don't you think you could do better than an ill-mannered redneck like my cousin?"

Fighting the urge to slap the smug look from Ellie's face, Amanda pulled her suit jacket around her and turned back to the window. She might have to fly with the obnoxious woman, but she sure as hell didn't want to have to look at her for the entire flight. "I'll have you know that Lex has much better manners than *some* members of her family. Now if you'll excuse me, I'm going to try and get some rest."

"DAMMIT ALL TO hell!" Lex leaned against a tree, her breath hurried. The sun was almost down, and she had made very little progress. Her denim shirt, once overly warm, was no match for the chilly evening. She slowly rubbed her socked foot against a broken log, trying to remove the bits of leaves and twigs that liberally coated the bottom of the cotton material. If not for the rapidly cooling night, she would have taken it off earlier. She wondered if anyone had actually missed her yet, and then cursed herself for probably worrying Amanda. "Like she doesn't have enough to worry about without me adding to it." Disheartened, Lex started walking again. A soft beeping sound in the brush to the right of her caught her attention. "What the—"

With the leg hampering her progress, it took Lex quite a while to find the source of the repetitive beeping. She used her makeshift crutch to dig through the underbrush and whooped in relief when she finally uncovered her lost cellular phone. Lex picked it up and wiped the device against her shirt, and started to hit the speed dial for the ranch when the familiar "out of area" notice flashed across the screen. "Dammit!" She almost threw it back into the brush, but caught herself and clipped it to her belt.

Following the path along which she had been dragged was taking too long, so Lex changed her plan and decided to work her way back to the creek. It wouldn't be that much faster, but if they started looking for her, it would make her easier to find.

Lex finally broke through the heavy trees. The sun had long since disappeared, and the cool evening breeze brought a damp chill which made her shiver. Her mind flitted again to her duster, which was draped across the back of her saddle. "Probably halfway home by now." The trickling sound of the creek reminded her just how long it had been since she had eaten or had anything to drink, and she hurried as fast as her aching leg would allow. Finally, standing at the top of the creek bank, Lex looked down and tried to figure out the best way to get down to the water without causing further injury.

THE TRAYS CLUTTERING every flat surface in the hotel room attested to the occupant's recent spending. Empty champagne bottles were scattered alongside half-eaten platters of food. On the bed lay scores of hangers filled with clothes in various colors and styles.

Terence stood in the doorway, his mouth open. After being lectured about his excessive spending, this was the last thing he'd expected to see. "What happened to not drawing attention to ourselves?" he asked Liz, who walked out of the bathroom in a silk robe.

"Oh, shut up. I'm staying in the Presidential Suite, Terence. I have an image to uphold." Liz sat down on the edge of the bed and picked up the phone.

"Who are you calling now?"

"Shhh. Hello? May I speak with Amanda Cauble, please?" Liz listened to the voice at the other end of the phone, then frowned. "A family emergency? Really?" She hung up the phone and smiled at her co-conspirator. "She left the office early today. Maybe something has finally happened to the perverted bitch that stole my baby from me." Liz jumped up and clapped her hands together. "Wouldn't that be absolutely delicious?"

The insane sparkle in Liz's eyes scared Terence. *No amount of money is worth putting up with her.* He still had her bank information and didn't think that it would be that hard to take his cut early. Hoping she wouldn't notice, he began to slowly back toward the door.

Still dancing around the bed, Liz saw the slight movement out of the corner of her eye. "Where do you think you're going?" She picked up her purse from the bedside table and pulled out a small, shiny revolver.

"Where did you—"

"Please, Terence. You think that you're the only person I've seen since I got out of that hellhole?" Liz waved the gun at him. "Sit down, you little worm." Once he was seated, she again took her place on the bed and dialed another number. It wasn't long before a voice sounded in her ear.

"Rocking W Ranch, Martha speaking."

"Good evening," Liz drawled, her voice soft, with a thick southern accent. "May I speak with Amanda, if it's not too much trouble?"

"I'm terribly sorry, but she's gone out of town on family business. May I take a message?"

Terence watched as Liz's face contorted into an angry mask, and was surprised that her voice still sounded like a sweet southern belle.

"Oh, goodness, no. That's quite all right. I'll just catch her another time. Thank you so much for your time." Unable to control herself any longer, Liz slammed the receiver down, then picked up the bedside lamp and hurled it across the room. "I *am* her family, damn it! She should be with me!" She started throwing anything she could find, screaming about the unfairness of her daughter living with "that woman," and what she'd like to do to the rancher.

Fearful that her tantrum could get them caught, Terence rushed to Liz's side and wrapped his arms around her in an attempt to calm her. "It's going to be okay, Liz. I'll find out where she's gone, I promise." He sat on the bed and rocked the agitated woman, all the while trying to think of a way to get out of the mess his greed had gotten him into.

RONNIE'S GENTLE HANDS brushed across the filly's lathered coat as his concerned eyes searched the area. He gathered up the dangling reins and led the filthy horse into the barn. Checking the other stalls, he could see that both Thunder and Stormy were standing quietly by, watching him with curious eyes. The other four horses that were used by the ranch hands were watching as well, all with shiny coats and contented looks on their faces. With another glance at the pony, he realized that she carried Lex's saddle. "Lex?" he called out, thinking maybe she had gone into the barn for one reason or another. After looking around and not finding the rancher, he walked over and buzzed the main house on the intercom.

It only took a moment before the buzz was answered by Martha.

"Martha, is Lex up at the house?" he asked, keeping his eye on the filly.

"No, she's not. Why?"

"Because I found the new horse outside the barn, and wanted to know if she needed me to clean her up and feed her." The intercom was silent, and Ronnie wasn't sure if Martha had heard him or not. "Martha?"

"I'll be right there, Ronnie. Leave the horse alone until I get there."

He shrugged his shoulders and looked at the exhausted animal. The filly was covered with mud, and her tail and mane had bits of leaves and twigs tangled throughout. Suddenly the barn door opened, and Martha rushed inside. Ronnie met her at the horse's side and held the reins while the housekeeper looked the animal over. "See? Lex doesn't usually leave her ride looking like this without a reason. I thought maybe she had to stop in at the bathroom or something, so that's why I buzzed you at the house."

"That's fine, Ronnie." Martha ran her hands over the saddle carefully, looking for any clues. One glance at the way the horse was lathered and covered with muck, and Martha knew that something was terribly wrong. Over the top of the animal's back, she tried to smile for Ronnie. "She's a mess, that's for sure." Martha patted the horse and ducked under her neck. "Maybe we can talk this boy of mine into giving you a nice rubdown and some oats."

Knowing the request for what it was, Ronnie wasted no time in removing the saddle. He handed Lex's coat to Martha, who took it and held it to her chest without a word.

"I'm going to run back up to the house. Come in to the kitchen when you get done, and I'll have supper waiting for you."

"Yes, ma'am." Martha's calm demeanor didn't fool Ronnie. He knew that something had happened to Lex, and he just hoped he could show Martha he was old enough to confide in. After she left the barn, he hurried to finish his chore so that he could get back to the house and find out what was going on.

Martha didn't even remember walking back to the house,

but the next thing she knew she was back in the kitchen. She immediately picked up the phone and dialed the bunk house.

"Lester? This is Martha. Is Roy there?"

"And hello to you, Missus. You too good to talk to an old codger like me?" Finding himself extremely funny, the old cook cackled, which progressed into a phlegmy cough.

"Dammit, Lester, this is important. Where's Roy?" As much as Martha usually enjoyed their banter, her nerves were on edge with the thought that Lex was in trouble. *And without her coat. I swear, that woman's going to be the death of me one of these days.*

"Martha, this is Roy. What's wrong?"

Martha leaned against the counter and wiped her face with one hand. "Lexie took out that new horse today, and it just came back. She wasn't on it."

"The filly we just broke? Why would she do that?"

"I don't know why she does what she does, Roy. You should know that by now. But she's out there somewhere, and we can't reach her on the cell phone."

"Why did she take the cell, instead of a radio?"

"Roy!"

"Oh, right. I'll gather up some of the boys and we'll be up there in a few minutes, Martha."

"Thank you." Martha hung up the phone and rolled her eyes to the ceiling. "God give me strength."

Chapter Nine

A CROWD OF people bustled through the airport despite the late hour. Amanda wove her way through them without much thought. She was still angry about Ellie's earlier comments and did her best not to take it out on the innocent people around her. When she saw that she was on the opposite end of the terminal from the car rental agency, she spun around, only to run into Ellie, who had been following close behind her. "Excuse me." She tried to step around the other woman, but found her progress stopped by hands on her shoulders.

"Amanda, please." Ellie didn't know why she wanted Amanda's approval so badly, but the thought that she had upset her was tearing at her heart. "Can I talk to you for just a minute?"

"Can you walk and talk at the same time? Because I'd really like to pick up the rental car and get to the hospital as soon as possible." Amanda twisted out of Ellie's grasp and began the long trek to the car rental counters.

Ellie watched her go, then rushed to catch up. "Look, Amanda," she huffed when she was by Amanda's side, "I'm sorry about upsetting you on the plane. It's just that I get so aggravated by the way Lex treats you."

"What are you talking about?" Amanda didn't slow her pace, but did turn to look at Ellie. "She treats me great. If anything, lately I've been treating her badly."

"That's ridiculous. She lords it over you like some kind of—"

Amanda stopped in her tracks, which caught Ellie off guard. "You don't know us, Ellie. And if you'd taken half the time to get to know your cousin that you've spent cutting her down, you'd realize that Lex has the biggest heart of anyone. But you spent most of your time baiting her and calling her names." Amanda poked Ellie in the chest, not caring what it looked liked to passersby. "So get off your high horse, little miss know-it-all. I don't have time for your childish shit." Amanda stormed off, leaving Ellie gaping at her back.

"Damn." Ellie followed at a more discreet distance and waited until Amanda obtained the keys to a rental car. She hurried to walk beside the angry woman and tried for a lighter approach. "Carry your bags, ma'am?"

Unable to contain the slight smile that broke across her face, Amanda allowed Ellie to grab her bag for her. It was another thing that Lex would have done, and Amanda couldn't help but compare the two women. Although Ellie was shorter and a lot less muscular, she did have similar characteristics. Amanda just wondered if she'd ever realize that. "Thanks."

"You're welcome." Ellie ducked to grin at Amanda. "Listen, I know I've been an ass. But I'd really like to go with you and try to offer any support I can to you and your family, if you'll have me."

"Do you promise to lay off Lex? I'm tired of defending our lifestyle to you, Ellie. And, to tell you the truth, I'm a little tired of you, too."

The words cut through Ellie like a knife. She saw the defeated slump to Amanda's shoulders, and knew that she was one word away from being completely kicked out of the other woman's life. She didn't know why, but the thought of that bothered her more than her cousin's homosexuality. "Truce?"

Amanda's weary look brightened considerably. "Truce." She looked down at the key ring in her hand. "Now, why don't you make yourself useful and help me find a red Buick with this license plate number?"

After locating the car and loading their bags in the trunk, Amanda drove them out of the airport. "Have you been to Los Angeles before, Ellie?" She expertly pulled onto the freeway, not even fazed by the heavy traffic.

"Uh, no. Up until a couple of months ago, I'd never even left the San Diego area. I lived in the suburbs and rarely ventured into the city." Ellie gasped as a car cut in front of them, and she grabbed the overhead handle in fear. "Are these people crazy?"

Laughing at the other woman's discomfort, Amanda reached over and patted Ellie's leg. "Don't worry. I learned to drive with these crazy people. And, at times, I can be just as crazy as they are." She spent the remainder of the trip pointing out attractions and even offered to show Ellie around once her sister was okay.

Due to the late hour, they had no problem finding a parking space at the hospital. Ellie followed Amanda, who acted like she knew exactly where she was going. Several turns and an elevator ride later, they stepped into a hallway where a tall, well-built man was pacing.

Frank saw Amanda and another woman step out of the elevator. He rushed over and scooped his sister-in-law into his arms. "Mandy! I'm so damned glad to see you." He brought Amanda close until the stare of the other woman made him uncomfortable. "Oh. Hi."

"Hi." Ellie didn't like how the man held Amanda, and she stood just out of reach with her arms crossed over her chest. "I take it you're Frank?"

Amanda pulled back and wiped at the tears that had arisen when she spotted Frank. "I'm sorry, my manners seem to have deserted me. Frank, this is Lex's cousin, Eleanor Gordon. Ellie, this is my brother-in-law, and friend, Frank Rivers."

Holding out his hand, Frank was a little surprised when Ellie took her time before grasping it. "Hi, Ellie. It's nice to meet you." He looked behind them. "Where's Lex?"

"That's the question of the day," Ellie muttered. "My cousin seemed to think that riding around playing cowboy was more important than being here."

Amanda glared at the sullen woman. "That's not exactly true." She turned to Frank. "Lex hadn't gotten back from checking out her new property by the time I had to leave for the airport. Ellie graciously offered to fly with me." Her tone spoke of untold stress, and the others remained silent. "How's Jeannie?"

"She's stabilized, and they plan on taking her into surgery in the next couple of hours." Looking years older than when Amanda had last seen him, Frank rubbed his face with his hands. "Jeannie has pre-eclampsia. Her blood pressure has been constantly rising for the past few weeks, and her doctor has been carefully monitoring it. Now it's near the danger level, and it won't come down at all. She's so swollen that you'll hardly recognize her. The doctor said that if we don't take the baby now, we could lose them both. Jeannie is being so brave about this, only thinking of the baby. She made me promise that if anything happens and we have to make a choice, we'd save the baby, but the thought of losing either one of them... I don't know how much more of this I can take, Mandy."

Ignoring Ellie's glare, Amanda put her arm around Frank and led him to the waiting area. "It's going to be fine. We both know how stubborn my sister is."

Frank sat wearily in one of the faded chairs. "This whole thing has drained her, though." He looked up at Amanda. "And she's been asking for you a lot."

"Do you think I can see her before they take her in to

surgery?"

"I don't see why not." Frank started to rise, but was held down by Amanda's hand on his shoulder.

"You sit and rest, Frank. I'll just be a minute."

"Down the hall, second door on the left."

AMANDA SLOWLY PUSHED open the door and peeked inside. When she was certain she had the correct room, she walked in quietly and let the go of the door. The sight in front of her almost destroyed her composure.

Jeannie lay against the white sheets, her dark hair spilling over the pillow. Her normally healthy tan had been replaced by a waxen pallor, and she appeared almost translucent in the muted light. The pregnant, swollen body before Amanda hardly resembled the petite woman that had been her older sister. At the sound of the door clicking shut, she turned her head and opened her eyes. A slight smile crossed her features, and she tried to hold up one hand. "Mandy," she gasped, her hand falling back down to her side. "You came."

"Of course I came, Jeannie Lou," Amanda answered quietly. "I'm just sorry it took so long to get here." She saw Jeannie pat the bed, and accepted the invitation to sit next to her sister. Taking hold of Jeannie's hand, she leaned down to hear her words.

"Look like a beached whale, don't I?" Jeannie quipped in a tired, scratchy voice. She feigned a smile meant to reassure her younger sister, but quickly tired from the effort.

Amanda shook her head as she squeezed her sister's hand.

"I wasn't sure if I could hold on," Jeannie whispered. "I wanted to, though."

"Don't talk like that, Jeannie. You're going to be fine."

"Please, listen." Jeannie pulled their joined hands to her chest. "Frank and I talked a lot about it, and we even had the papers drawn up. We want you and Lex to be the baby's godparents, and her legal guardians if anything happens to us."

"What? But—"

"No, really. I've never known two people who had as much love to give as you two, and we think our baby would be lucky to have you."

Amanda shook her head, scared at all the talk of her sister's mortality. "Nothing's going to happen to you, Jeannie. Don't talk like that."

"Please?"

Her sister looked so fragile. "All right. Whatever you say."

She hoped that agreeing with Jeannie would help her get through the surgery without worry.

Jeannie squeezed Amanda's hand, and her eyes closed.

"I love you, Jeannie." Amanda pulled her hand up and kissed it, then watched as Jeannie's eyes opened again.

"If I don't make it out of surgery—"

"Please don't say that, Jeannie," she begged, struggling to hold back her tears. "You're going to be fine."

Jeannie tightened her grip on her sister's hand. "If I don't make it, please take care of Frank for me. You know how helpless he is."

Amanda's laugh turned into a sob. "God, Jeannie. I don't know—"

"Promise me?"

Realizing that her sister had no breath to spare on an argument, Amanda nodded. "All right. But nothing's going to happen." She leaned down until they were nose to nose. "You're going to be fine, you hear me?"

A discreet throat clearing from the doorway caused Amanda to stand up and turn around. A middle-aged nurse gave her a sympathetic smile. "I'm sorry, Miss. But we have to get Mrs. Rivers ready for surgery. I'm afraid you'll have to leave."

"Okay." Amanda turned back to her sister and kissed her on the forehead. "I'll see you and the baby in a little while."

Jeannie nodded, and closed her eyes again. The conversation had worn her out.

Amanda walked across the room and stopped by the nurse. "Take good care of her. She's the only sister I've got." Her emotions almost escaped her rigid control when the nurse squeezed her arm. The orderlies entered as Amanda edged her way out of the room.

HEARING THE SLAM of a vehicle door, Martha hurried out of the kitchen and through the back door. The white four-door pickup truck bore the ranch brand on the driver's door, and Roy waited with the other two men next to the truck. When Martha stepped up beside him, the four of them went into the barn together.

Ronnie was still brushing down the filly, and he looked up as the group walked inside. "Hey, there. What's going on?"

"That's what we're trying to figure out," Roy said, looking to Martha. "So, you figure Lex took the filly out today?"

Martha nodded. "According to Ronnie, it was her saddle on the animal."

"Where's the saddle now?"

"In the tack room," Ronnie supplied. "I haven't cleaned it yet. I was going to do that once I finished with the horse."

Roy ducked his head slightly in confirmation, then left the group long enough to check out the saddle. When he returned, he removed his hat and shook his head. "I can't see anything wrong with the saddle, other than being dirty." He tried to sound matter-of-fact to keep Martha from worrying too much. "The filly's new to the saddle, so it wouldn't take much for her to try to toss someone off. I'm sure Lex is walking back now, cursing her decision to take a new pony for a ride."

"Maybe. But I'd feel a lot better if you'd go out looking for her. She said something about checking out the new property today, and that's one heck of a long walk. I can't help but think that she would have called."

"All right." Roy turned to one of the men. "Juan, why don't you gather up some flashlights and supplies while Chris saddles up the horses."

"I want to help," Ronnie interjected. "I've finished taking care of the filly, and I can ride as well as anyone else."

Roy looked over at Martha, who sighed, then nodded. The young man had shown a lot of responsibility around the ranch, and another pair of eyes out in the darkness couldn't hurt.

"Okay, Ronnie," Roy said. "I'll need you to run up to the house and get the radios so we can keep in touch." No sooner had the words left his mouth than Ronnie had raced from the barn. Roy put his hat back on. "We'll contact you the minute we find anything," he promised Martha.

"Thank you, Roy." Martha reached over and squeezed the foreman's arm. "Just take care of my boy, and bring my girl home."

"You know I will." Roy waited until the housekeeper left the barn, then turned to help his men get ready for the ride.

"THIS LOOKS LIKE as good a spot as any." Lex had limped around the creek looking for the easiest place to descend, and her best bet seemed to be in front of her. The muddy walls were at less of an angle, and there were several juniper bushes she could hang onto during the descent.

Halfway down, the stick that Lex used as a crutch snapped in two, throwing her headfirst down the embankment. She tumbled through the mud, finally coming to a stop a few feet from the water. "Damn, damn, damn!" She reached down and gripped her knee, struggling to keep from passing out from the pain. She lay there until the stars in her vision disappeared, then sat up and looked around. "Just perfect. I can't even climb down into a creek bed without screwing it up." The sound of the running water re-awakened her thirst, so Lex dragged herself to the edge of the water and scooped some of the clear liquid into her hand.

Once her thirst was slaked, she lay back and looked up at the stars. The night was clear, and she was definitely feeling the chill. The cold water of the creek gave her an idea, and she reached for the utility knife she wore on her belt. Leaning over her leg, Lex cut away the denim material below her knee. She dipped the cloth into the creek, and then wrapped it around her leg. "Shit, that's freezing." But the cold compress would help the sprain. She lay back again and tried to think warm thoughts.

Her injured knee throbbed in time with the beat of her heart, and she once again found herself thinking about Amanda. As strained as their relationship had been lately, she couldn't help but think about the woman she'd vowed to spend the rest of her life with. "I hope she's not too worried." Suddenly remembering her cell phone, Lex tried to use it again, but was still given the "out of area" message. Then the phone beeped twice, and went dark. "Great. Now the stinking battery's dead." She clipped it back to her belt as she fought off a cough.

The cold, damp night air combined with the wet compress caused Lex to shiver, cough, and struggle to stay awake. Against her will, she found her eyes closing. Amanda's face filled her mind, and she thought back to when they'd first met. *I think the moment I saw you lying in the mud next to the creek, I fell in love with you. I tried not to, but there was just something about you, even then.* Lex hadn't been the slightest bit interested in finding love, much less expecting to find it in the most unusual of places. *What did someone like her, see in me? She's beautiful, smart, and could certainly have her pick of lovers. I wonder why she chose me?* Lex had fought her feelings for Amanda, not sure if they'd ever be reciprocated. But every minute they were together opened Lex's heart more and more. And after the kiss in the barn, she knew that she was lost. "And here I am, lost again. But without you," Lex whispered. Lying in the mud, she covered her face with one arm, defeated.

THE HOSPITAL WAS quiet in the late evening hour. Amanda and Frank sat facing the operating room door through which Jeannie had been taken, waiting nervously for any word of Jeannie's progress. Their linked hands drew angry looks from

Ellie, who stood at a nearby window, unable to sit still and watch Amanda take comfort from someone else.

Frank wanted to jump up and rant, scream, and demand to be allowed in the operating room. Having taken all the childbirth classes so that he could be present at the birth, he hated not being with his wife. "What's taking so damned long?"

Before Amanda could answer, several more hospital personnel raced down the hall and through the door, leaving a tense atmosphere in their wake.

Ellie walked over and sat next to Amanda. "Something's up." Although she didn't like the way he and Amanda interacted, she couldn't help but feel sorry for Frank and tried to reassure him. "It's probably something routine."

Frank disentangled his hands from Amanda's and stood to pace the floor. He hands went into his pockets and rattled loose change, and he made a wide circuit around the otherwise empty waiting room. "This is taking too damned long. What's going on in there?" His questions, more to himself than anyone else, went unanswered as they waited.

Jeannie's doctor finally stepped through the door, wearing a serious look on his face. He was almost knocked back by Frank, who rushed over to meet him.

"Well? How is she?"

"Mr. Rivers, you are the father of a beautiful baby girl. Even though she's a little premature, she's doing quite well."

Amanda went over to stand next to Frank, seeing by the look on the doctor's face that wasn't all he had to say. "There's something else, isn't there? What about my sister?"

"I'm afraid we've had some complications." The doctor's voice was quiet, and it seemed as if he were searching for the right words.

"Complications? What kind of complications?" Frank tried to push by the physician. "I want to see my wife."

Putting his arm in front of Frank to block his path, the doctor shook his head. "During the procedure, Mrs. Rivers' blood pressure became elevated and she had several seizures. We—"

Amanda gasped, and words wouldn't come.

"Where is she now," Frank demanded. "I've got to—"

"She's in recovery," the doctor told them. "Listen to me now." He waited until he had their complete attention. "I'm afraid there's no easy way to say this. The seizures caused a stroke, and Mrs. Rivers has slipped into a coma."

Amanda stumbled backward, caught and steadied by Ellie. "Dear God," Amanda choked out.

Frank shook his head slowly, mechanically. "No, that's not possible. It was just a simple Caesarean. Things like this don't happen." He grabbed the doctor by the arm. "She's going to be fine though, right? Tell me she's going to be all right."

"I'm sorry, Mr. Rivers. Although she is stable at the moment, she's unconscious. And, unfortunately, we have no way of knowing when she will wake up." The obstetrician put a steadying hand on Frank's arm before continuing. "Or if she will. And if she does, there is no guarantee as to what her condition will be. We have every hope that she will regain consciousness. The next few hours will tell us a lot."

JERKING AWAKE, LEX sat up and looked around. She didn't remember falling asleep, and wasn't too sure how long she'd been out. Her hands shook as she removed the damp wrap from her knee, but at least the compress had diminished the pain. *Either that, or it's just numb from the cold.* A sound off to her right made her turn her head, and she thought she saw a light in the woods. *Am I hallucinating?*

Men's voices yelled in the distance, and she heard the sound of several horses. *A search party?* Lex almost cried with relief at the realization. "Hey," she tried to yell, but the word came out more like a ragged croak. The mixture of the night air and the dampness had all but taken her voice. The lights were moving parallel to the creek, and it wouldn't be long before they'd be out of sight.

Knowing that her voice wouldn't be any help, Lex tried to stand, hoping to attract their attention. Her injured leg buckled beneath her, and she fell back to the ground, gasping in pain. She could tell that the voices were slowly moving away. Desperate to be found, Lex looked around and found several good sized rocks, and began to toss them into the woods at the lights. *Dammit, over here!*

Ronnie, who was bringing up the rear of the search party, stopped his horse when he thought he heard a noise. To his left, there was a crack, like something hitting a tree. He waited, and heard it again. "Hey, Roy! I think I heard something." The other riders turned their mounts around and backtracked to where the teenager waited.

"What did you hear?" Roy asked.

"Probably his imagination," Chris mumbled. He wasn't too happy about having a kid on a search and had been making rude remarks ever since they'd left the barn. "Maybe he just thinks... Whoa!" His comment was cut short by his horse rearing, when something hit the animal's flank.

Roy tried to keep from laughing. He never had liked Chris very much.

Ronnie pointed to the left, toward the creek. "I kept hearing what sounded like rocks being thrown into the trees."

"Good man," Roy complimented. He waved his hand forward. "Why don't you lead the way?"

"Really?" Ronnie couldn't keep the excitement out of his voice. He tried to look calm by pulling his cowboy hat down lower over his eyes. "This way, fellas."

Lex was beginning to think that the search party had gone on, until she saw the lights coming back through the trees. When the first rider broke through, Lex thought at first she was seeing things. When the beam from one of the lights hit her in the face, she had never in her life been so happy to be temporarily blinded.

Ronnie quickly moved the beam out of her eyes and urged his horse across the slow moving creek. He jumped down to stand a few feet away from Lex, who made no attempt to get to her feet.

"Damn, I'm glad to see you," she croaked.

The other riders soon joined them, and Roy dropped from his saddle next to Ronnie. "Hey, boss. We'd have rode right past you if it wasn't for this guy here." He squatted down and looked at Lex's leg. "Is it broken?"

"Nah, just sprained," she whispered. "But I'd appreciate a little help getting out of here."

"Can you ride?" Roy asked her. When Lex frowned, he almost laughed. Roy looked up at Chris. "You double up with Juan and give the boss your ride."

"Why can't the boy double up?" Chris whined.

"'Cause I told you to, that's why. Or, if you want, you can walk back." Roy winked at Lex, who covered her mouth to keep from laughing. "Ronnie, you get on that side, and I'll take this one." They helped Lex up on her one good leg. It didn't take long for them to get her into a saddle.

Once mounted, Roy leaned over so that no one could hear him. "What happened to you out here?"

Lex was trying to stay in the saddle while fighting off the intense pain. She shook her head and whispered through gritted teeth, "It'd be easier to tell you what didn't."

THE ONLY VISITOR in the room, Amanda watched as her niece slept. The infant lay on its back in the incubator, sucking on a thumb and unaware of the drama that had surrounded her arrival into the world. Tiny wisps of black hair peeked from the stocking cap, and Amanda thought for a moment that this was what a child of hers and Lex's would look like.

Resentment welled up inside her as Amanda realized that her dream was impossible. She and Lex would never be able to have a child together, and the thought hurt. Jeannie had what she never would, and jealousy tore through Amanda.

Remembering her sister's condition, Amanda closed her eyes. Jeannie's prognosis was grim at best. Frank was with the doctors, trying to hang onto anything positive. Feeling sick to her stomach at her uncharitable thoughts, Amanda rushed from the room in tears.

Ellie looked up from her seat in the waiting room as Amanda hurried down the hallway. Concerned, Ellie stood up and was surprised when Amanda fell into her arms. Not desiring to turn down the opportunity to hold Amanda, she pulled the crying woman close. "Shhh. It's okay."

Amanda absorbed the comfort, closing her eyes and wishing it was Lex holding her close. The gentle hand brushing her hair and the strong heartbeat under her ear was different, and she pulled back, a little embarrassed. "I'm sorry about that, Ellie."

"Don't be. I'm glad I was here." Ellie pulled her hand away from Amanda's head and was about to brush the tears away from her eyes when she saw Frank approaching. "Frank."

Engrossed in his own thoughts, Frank didn't pay much attention to the way Ellie was holding Amanda. His eyes were bloodshot, and his suit was wrinkled almost beyond redemption. He had removed his tie earlier, and the end hung out from one of the jacket pockets. "There's been no change," he relayed, rubbing his rough beard with one hand. "There's a specialist with her now, but it doesn't look good."

Amanda turned. "Oh, Frank. She'll make it through this." She took his hands in hers. "Jeannie's tough, and she's got a lot to live for."

"God, I hope so." Frank finally noticed his sister-in-law's wan appearance. "You look worse than I feel, Mandy."

Ellie stepped up and put her arm around Amanda's waist. "I was just going to suggest finding a hotel room so that Amanda could get some rest."

"No. I couldn't." Feeling guilty about her earlier thoughts, Amanda wanted to stay and give Frank her support.

"Mandy, please." Frank pulled her closer and looked down into her tired eyes. "You're not going to be any good to Jeannie if you get sick." He reached into his pocket and pulled out his keys. "Why don't you go to our place?"

"But what about you?"

"I'll be fine. They've offered me a place to rest here so I don't have to leave the hospital." Frank didn't tell her that he'd probably never use the cot. He didn't want to spend any time away from his wife unless he was forced to. "I'll call you if anything changes."

Ellie took the keys from Frank. "Thanks. I'll make sure she gets some rest."

"I'll go, but I won't like it," Amanda muttered. She gave Frank a hug and allowed Ellie to lead her down the hall.

As the two women walked away, Frank couldn't help but feel something wasn't quite right. *That Ellie is a strange woman.* But before he could muse any more on it, a nurse came up to take him back to Jeannie's doctors.

WITH ROY ON one side and Juan on the other, Lex was carried up the steps to the house. Ronnie opened the back door, and the men carefully maneuvered the injured woman inside. Lex hated the helpless feeling, but the pain in trying to use her leg was worse, so she tolerated the attention the best she could. She wasn't looking forward to explaining to Amanda what had happened.

Having heard the back door open, Martha stepped out of the kitchen and gasped at the sight before her. "Goodness! What in heaven's name did you do to yourself, Lexie?"

"It's not as bad as it looks," Lex tried to assure her, as the men carried her into the kitchen and helped her sit in one of the chairs. Her voice was still scratchy from being out in the cold. "Just twisted my knee a bit, that's all."

Martha sat next to her and reached for the denim wrapped around Lex's left knee. "Played doctor a bit, did you?" She slowly unwrapped the material, then tore the leg of the jean higher up so that she could get a better look.

Once the pressure was released, the pain flowed back. "Ow!"

"Quit your hollering, Lexie." Martha looked up at Roy, who was standing in the doorway trying to keep a smile off his face. "Thank you for what you did, Roy. I owe you one."

He shook his head. "Don't thank me, Martha. You'd best be thanking that young man there." Roy pointed to Ronnie, who stood back by the kitchen counter. "If it hadn't been for his sharp ears, we'd probably still be out there searching."

Lex turned to look at a now-blushing Ronnie. "That's right.

Roy said something about that when y'all found me. You're the one who figured it all out."

"Well, sort of. I guess." He scuffed his boot along the floor, unable to meet Lex's eyes. "But I'm sure the others would have heard the noise, too. I just happened to be the first one."

Roy said, "Don't you be making light of it, Ronnie. We were well up the trail by the time you called us back."

Martha beamed. "I'm so proud of you, Ronnie." She looked back down at Lex's leg. "You messed this up pretty well. We'd better have Dr. Anderson check you out in the morning."

"It's just sprained." Lex looked around the room. "Amanda must be pretty upset with me if she's not down here hollering with you." Everyone in the room remained silent. "What's wrong? Where's Amanda?"

"Calm down, Lexie. Amanda's perfectly all right. It's just that she—"

Lex tried to stand, but when she put weight on her injured leg, she immediately dropped back into the chair. "Dammit! She what? Where the hell is she?"

"Jeannie was admitted into the hospital today, and Amanda has flown out there to be with her."

"What? By herself?" Lex slammed her fist down on the table. "I should have been here."

Seeing that Lex was about to have a meltdown, Roy ushered Juan out of the house. He knew that his boss showing such emotion in front of them would embarrass Lex later.

"Stop it. Amanda didn't go alone, and even if she did, she's a grown woman. I'm expecting to hear from her or Ellie any time now." Bracing herself for the explosion, Martha wasn't disappointed.

"Ellie? The woman who keeps bitching about my 'lifestyle,' but can't seem to keep her eyes off my wife, went with Amanda? Whose brilliant idea was that?" Lex stood up on her good leg. "I've got to get out there."

Martha grabbed Lex's arm. "Have you lost your mind? You can't even stand up, much less walk. You have no business going anywhere, except to the doctor."

"I'm not leaving Amanda alone with that woman, Martha. Haven't you seen the way she looks at her?" Lex turned to Ronnie. "Would you mind going upstairs and getting me some clean clothes and my old crutches out of my closet? I need to make a few phone calls."

Not wanting to disappoint his idol, Ronnie dashed off to do Lex's bidding.

"You're not going to be able to get another flight out

tonight," Martha told her. "The one they took earlier was the only flight until tomorrow."

"Then I'll find another way." Lex took one step and almost cried out from the pain. "Would you mind helping me into the office?" When Martha didn't move or say anything, Lex changed her attitude. "Please? I can't just sit here. I've got to go."

With a shake of her head, Martha put her arm around Lex's waist. "Stubborn woman." She took most of Lex's weight on her shoulders and helped her walk down the hall.

Chapter Ten

THE DRIVE FROM the hospital was quiet, except for Amanda giving Ellie directions from time to time. She had gladly handed over the keys to the rental car, knowing that she had no business trying to operate the vehicle in the state she was in. Ellie didn't seem to mind and had actually been very solicitous the entire trip.

"That's it, there on the left." Amanda pointed to a two-story, Spanish-style house. As Ellie pulled the car into the driveway, Amanda thought back to the last time she had been there. It had been a few weeks before she left for Texas to help care for her grandfather who had been in an auto accident. *And not long after, I met the other half of my soul.* She wondered what Lex was doing right now. *I miss her so much.* "I need to call home as soon as we get inside."

"It's kind of late to be calling, isn't it?" Ellie asked, as she got out of the car and grabbed the bags from the trunk. "Wouldn't it be better to wait until morning?"

Amanda closed her door and then took her bag from Ellie. "It already is morning, Ellie. And no, I don't think it would be better to wait. Lex is probably worried sick." She led the way up to the front door and took the keys from Ellie's outstretched hand. "Thanks." After fumbling with the lock, Amanda finally opened the door.

"Whoa." Ellie had followed Amanda inside, and her eyes widened when Amanda flicked on the interior light. The front room was wide, with glossy tile floors and ornate furniture. They dropped their bags just inside the doorway, too tired to care where they landed. "I've only seen places like this on television, or in those fancy magazines at the doctor's office." She chuckled when she thought about what a baby would do to the obviously expensive surroundings.

"What's funny?" Amanda asked in a sour voice.

"Nothing."

Still upset with herself over her own thoughts about Jeannie's baby, Amanda didn't feel like letting Ellie off the hook so easily. "It must have been something, or you wouldn't have laughed. I don't see anything funny about this situation."

"No, really. I think I'm just tired." Ellie didn't want to fight with Amanda over something as silly as what she had been thinking. Deciding a subject change was in order, Ellie made a show of looking around the room. "I bet you'd be living like this, if you had stayed in California and gotten married."

Amanda tossed the keys down on a side table. "I am married. To Lex."

"That's not the same thing, Amanda. I mean, you're an intelligent woman." Ellie stepped closer and touched Amanda's arm. The touch turned into a light caress. "You're beautiful and could undoubtedly have your pick of just about any man you'd want."

Repulsed by Ellie's words, Amanda backed away. "I don't want a man, Ellie. I'm happy with Lex."

"That so-called marriage isn't real, not legally, or in the eyes of God. Everyone answers to Him at some time in their lives."

Amanda reached out and jabbed Ellie in the chest. "Now you listen to me, you holier-than-thou bitch. If I have to 'answer' to your God, believe me, I have a few choice words for Him." She poked Ellie again, causing the other woman to back up against the wall. "And where do you get off being so damned high and mighty, considering how you've been looking at me lately? Do you have a closet to step out of, Eleanor?" Amanda challenged.

"THANKS, ROB. I owe you a big one." Lex shook the hand of the man who helped her off the small plane. "Sorry about the late hour." When Lex couldn't get a commercial flight out, she had called an old high school buddy who owned his own plane.

He helped her with her crutches and then patted Lex on the shoulder. "Not a problem, Lex. If it weren't for you, I wouldn't even have this plane. I am glad to finally be able to return your generosity." When the bank had tried to foreclose on Rob's commercial delivery service, Lex had loaned him the money to stay afloat. He had never forgotten the favor. "Besides, I hear the women out here are hot. I may have to spend a few days down at the beach."

"You're right about that, my friend." Lex allowed him to help her through the terminal. She saw a row of pay telephones and stopped. "Thanks again, Rob. I'll let you go find that beach now."

"Are you sure you don't need a ride? We can always share a cab."

Lex shook her head. "No, that's all right. I'm not too sure where I'm going from here. You go on, and have fun."

"Okay. But if you need anything, give me a call." Rob patted the cell phone in his jacket pocket, then waved and walked out of the terminal.

Finding an available pay phone, Lex reached into her jeans and pulled out the proper change, then fished in her shirt pocket for the slip of paper on which she had written Frank's cell number. She balanced on the crutches while she dialed the phone and was relieved when he answered almost immediately.

"Frank? This is Lex. How's everything going?"

There was a long pause, and then Frank cleared his throat. "Not well, Lex. Has Amanda called you?"

"Uh, no. I just landed in Los Angeles. What's going on?"

"They had to take the baby early. And Jeannie—" His voice broke.

Oh, no. "Are they okay?"

"The baby's fine. She's a little premature, but should only have to stay in the nursery about a week."

"And Jeannie?" Lex dreaded his answer, especially given how the normally stoic ex-football player sounded.

"She's in a coma, Lex. Jeannie had some complications during the C-section, and had a stroke." Frank sniffled. "They don't know if she's going to come out of it or not."

Lex closed her eyes and bent her head. "Damn, Frank. I'm sorry. Is there anything I can do?"

He coughed, then cleared his throat again. "Not right now, but thanks. I'm sure Mandy could use you, though. She and Ellie went to get some rest at our house."

Ellie? That bitch is still with Amanda? I'll kill her. "How long ago did they leave?"

"Just a few minutes ago, actually." Oblivious to the undercurrents of Lex's emotions, Frank gave Lex directions to the house.

Lex wrote down the address. "I'll get on over there. And, Frank?"

"Yeah?"

"Let me know if there's anything you need, okay?"

"Thanks, Lex."

After she hung up the phone, Lex tucked the paper back into her shirt pocket and went out the terminal door in search of a cab. Several vied for her attention, and she took the closest one. She gave him the address, then allowed the driver to help her into the back seat, propping the crutches next to her.

The drive didn't take as long as Lex thought it would, and in no time they pulled up behind the rental car in Frank and Jeannie's driveway. Lex paid the driver, then slowly hobbled her way up the walk.

She stood at the front door, about to ring the bell, when she heard Amanda's raised voice. *What the hell?* Finding the door unlocked, she pushed on it and was surprised by the sight before her.

Ellie was backed against a wall with Amanda in her face. They turned when they heard the front door open.

"Lex?" both women exclaimed at the same time.

"What the hell is going on here?" Lex asked, moving inside. Due to her earlier exposure to the elements, her voice was quiet, but it echoed across the large room. "Amanda, are you all right?"

Amanda moved away from Ellie and met Lex halfway. "I should be asking you the same thing. What happened to you?"

Lex began to explain, but Ellie's attention was still on Amanda's words to her. *Closet? What was she . . . No! I'm not like that! Lex is the pervert, not me.* But Ellie had always been honest, especially with herself. She considered how her feelings for Amanda had grown, and how her cousin's "partner" had intrigued her from their very first meeting. *And my fascination with her breasts isn't quite the "normal" way to feel for another woman. Even I know that.* She looked over and saw Amanda touching Lex, as if to assure herself that she was really there. *I've got to get out of here.*

She decided to take the next flight out to San Diego and worry about her new family later. "I see you're in good hands now, Amanda. If it's all the same to you, I'm going to go visit with my family." Brushing by the couple, Ellie picked up her backpack, went out the door, and jogged down the steps. She spotted the cab pulling out of the driveway and flagged him down. Shaking inside, Ellie climbed into the cab. *A few weeks with my mother ought to clear my head, one way or another.*

HOURS EARLIER, THE sun had made its appearance, but Lex wanted to let Amanda sleep as long as she could. She ran her fingers through the hair that fanned across her chest, and wished that she could have been with her lover sooner. Lex tried to move her left leg and was gratified that the pain wasn't as bad as it had been the night before. *Damned stupid fool. I shouldn't have tried to take a new horse onto unknown property. If I had just stayed close to the house, Amanda wouldn't have had to go through all of this alone.* She thought about the scene that had greeted her the evening before. *Although technically, she wasn't alone. She was with that bitch of a cousin of mine. I'd like to know what went on before I got here. I don't think I've ever seen Amanda that mad.*

"You're thinking pretty hard about something this morning," a quiet voice mumbled. Amanda turned her head so that she could see Lex's face. "Anything you want to share?"

Lex tried to smile, but the dark circles under her lover's eyes almost broke her heart. "Just wishing that I'd been here with you, instead of Ellie." She was also thankful that her voice was back to normal and hoped she wouldn't have to fight off a cold.

With the previous evening's events still fresh in her mind, Amanda couldn't help but grimace. "I wish that you were, too. That cousin of yours has some real issues to work out."

"Like what?"

"Oh, just that I think that she's got more in common with you than she cares to admit."

"In common with me?" Lex sat up slightly, but kept her firm hold on Amanda. "What could she...oh." She couldn't stop the smile that worked its way onto her face. "Bet that was a revelation for her. I always felt that she was a bit *too* friendly with you. But then I thought I was just being unreasonably jealous."

Amanda crawled her way up Lex's body until they were eye to eye. "Martha also mentioned something to me before we left that makes more sense now. Am I the only person who didn't see it?"

"Yep." At her partner's outraged look, Lex leaned forward and kissed Amanda. The light peck quickly turned into a more thorough exploration, until both women had to pull away, breathless.

"Now that's my idea of good morning." Amanda nestled back against Lex's chest. "How's your knee? You never did really tell me what happened to you yesterday."

Checking the limb again by moving her foot, Lex sighed. "It's okay. Not as sore as last night, anyway."

"And?"

"It wasn't that big of a deal, Amanda. I got thrown from that new horse and twisted my knee."

Amanda rose and looked down at Lex. She traced her fingers along Lex's normally smooth face, which was marred by a few scratches that were already healing. After they had undressed for bed the night before, she had found several bruises and scratches along Lex's body, but they had both been too tired to talk about it. "You look a little bit more banged up than if you were just thrown. What really happened?"

This conversation isn't getting any easier. Lex took a deep breath and gathered her thoughts. "Well, I *was* thrown. Sort of. I had taken the new filly out to check the property we had just bought, and she was pretty skittish. There were a couple of explosions off in the distance—"

"Explosions? Where?"

Lex's expression quieted Amanda's questions. "After the second explosion, which sounded further up the creek, the horse reared and pushed me into a tree limb." She rubbed the top of her head, which still sported a painful bump. "My cell phone rang and I was trying to answer it when the horse spooked again and I lost my seat. My boot got caught in the stirrup, and she dragged me for a bit. That's where the scratches came from."

Amanda lowered her head. "That was probably me calling your phone." She raised up and her face was filled with remorse. "I'm so sorry, Lex."

"Hey." Lex cradled Amanda's face with her hands. "I couldn't have stayed on that horse, even with both hands. It wasn't your fault." She kissed the tip of her wife's nose. "Besides, once I *finally* found that damned phone, I couldn't get a signal, anyway. It seemed like things just kept getting worse. Finally Ronnie and Roy found me and brought me back to the house. That's when Martha told me about you and Ellie leaving in such a hurry. So, here I am. And speaking of getting here, what was that little scene I walked in on? You looked like you were about to kick Ellie's ass. Not that I would have minded."

Now it was Amanda's turn to be embarrassed. "I don't know if it would have gotten that far. But then again, I was pretty upset." She looked down at where her hands were stroking Lex's chest in a nervous pattern. "She'd made a few rude comments about you, and with the stress of everything that was going on, I guess I just snapped."

"What kind of comments?" Although she'd never admit it to anyone, Lex was secretly pleased with how Amanda always came to her defense.

"Like our relationship was the result of misplaced hero-worship, and things like that." Amanda knew she would never tell Lex everything, for fear it would only hurt her. *She doesn't have to know that Ellie thought that she "lorded" it over me. Nothing could be further from the truth.*

"Well, she was partly right." Lex pulled Amanda close to her. "Except that she figured the wrong person. You're *my* hero, Amanda."

Unable to find her voice, Amanda snuggled closer to Lex, happy to feel at least part of her life back to normal.

AT THE SMELL of fresh coffee, Liz opened her eyes beneath the sleeping mask she wore. She stretched and yawned, removed the mask, and sat up as Terence handed her a steaming cup of the fragrant brew. "What are you so damned cheerful about this morning? Do you have any idea what time it is?" After a careful sip of her coffee, she muttered, "And how the hell did you get into my room?"

"It's well after nine, Liz. I didn't think you meant to sleep the entire day away. And, I told the maid down the hall that I'd forgotten my key." Terence pulled a chair close to the bed and propped his feet on the coverlet. "Besides, I know you'll be glad to see me when you hear what I have to say."

Still not completely awake, Liz kicked Terence's feet off her bed. "Cretin. Now, tell me what makes you so full of yourself today."

Terence didn't mind the way Liz spoke to him. If anything, he was amused by her grumpy comments. "Be nice, Liz. Or I won't tell you that you're about to become a grandmother."

The coffee that she had just sipped was spewed onto the expensive coverlet, and Liz gasped and sputtered. "I'm what? How is that possible?"

"You have two daughters, don't you? Not just the one who's living with another woman." Terence pulled a piece of paper from his shirt pocket and read from it. "Jeannie Rivers was admitted to a hospital in Los Angeles yesterday morning, pregnant with her first child. Your other daughter, Amanda, and a woman took a flight out yesterday afternoon." He looked up from his paper and felt very proud of himself. He had been up half the night with a friend of his in California, who had relayed the news to him. "So, I think you should be a bit nicer to me, *Grandma*."

Liz was halfway to the bathroom to get dressed when Terence finished his gloating. She turned around and pointed a long finger in his direction. "Don't you dare call me that! I won't allow myself to be that old." When she reached the doorway, she stopped. "Start packing, and then get on the phone and get us the next flight out there. And while you're at it, call room service and get me some decent coffee."

"Yes, *Grandmama*," Terence whispered, unable to contain his glee at finally breaking through Liz's icy demeanor. He picked up several silky items and tossed them into her suitcase, still chuckling at the way she'd spit coffee everywhere.

WHILE LEX FINISHED in the shower, Amanda gathered the clothes they had tossed around the room the night before. She picked up her dress jacket that was partially hidden under the bed, and frowned when an envelope fell from one of the pockets. "Where did that come from? Oh, right. Must be the one that I picked up before we left." Amanda sat on the edge of the bed and opened the envelope, pulling a folded piece of paper from it. She began to read, then gasped in horror, allowing the paper to fall to the floor.

Lex heard Amanda's gasp and limped heavily from the bathroom. "What is it?" She saw the paper on the floor, and bent down to pick it up before landing on the bed next to her wife. After reading a few lines, Lex was still confused. "I don't get it. So you closed out an account."

"No, Lex. This was my trust fund. I never closed out this account." Amanda looked at her lover, willing her to understand. "Someone else has taken it. All of it."

"But who? Maybe it's just some sort of computer error." The argument sounded weak, even to Lex. She had a sneaking suspicion that whoever was the mastermind behind her sudden loss of money was probably behind this, as well. She looked at the return address on the top of the letter. "This is a local bank. Why don't we run over there today and check it out?"

Amanda nodded. "That sounds like a good idea. But I'd like to go by the hospital and check on Jeannie first. Another few hours won't change anything at the bank."

"Whatever you say, love." Lex put her arm around Amanda and kissed the side of her head. "Besides, I'd like to check out this new niece of ours."

THE WARM BREATH on the back of her neck was like a soothing balm as Amanda looked through the glass at the tiny infant, Lex standing behind her. "Isn't she beautiful?"

"It's kind of hard to tell," Lex admitted truthfully. "She's awful little." Although in her eyes, the baby seemed to have Jeannie's nose and her dark hair. *If it were a bit lighter, she could be Amanda's.* A heavy hand squeezed Lex's shoulder, causing her to turn around. "Hey, Frank."

"Lex. Amanda." Still looking rumpled and exhausted, Frank gladly pulled Amanda into a hug. "I'm glad you both are here."

Amanda pulled away from her brother-in-law. "Frank, you

look like you haven't slept at all." She reached up and brushed the hair out of his eyes. "How's Jeannie?"

"The same as she was last night. The doctors aren't holding out much hope, I'm afraid." He peered past the two women and through the glass. "At least Lorrie is doing okay."

"Lorrie?" Both women asked at once.

Frank's face broke out into a tired smile. "Yeah. Jeannie and I..." His voice broke, and it took him a moment to get himself back together. "Before she was born we discussed a name for her. Lorraine Marie, after her two godmother guardians." The names were also Lex and Amanda's middle names.

"That's so sweet, Frank." Oblivious to her partner's confusion, Amanda hugged the big man again.

Lex looked at the baby and then back at the embracing pair. "Godmothers?"

"Sure. Didn't Amanda tell you?" Frank asked, looking over Amanda's shoulder.

"Uh, no," Amanda said, turning around and facing her partner. "We haven't really had time to discuss it. But it's pretty cool, isn't it, Lex?"

Was it? Lex thought about the implications, especially with Jeannie lying comatose. How far did a godmother's responsibility extend? Were there legal implications for a guardian? So much was uncertain about this little child's mother's situation. Could Frank handle Lorrie on his own? Lex's leg ached, and she shifted in pain, wondering what Martha would have to say about it if they ended up taking responsibility for a baby. *She's already raised me, and now has Ronnie to worry about. Would it be fair to her and the rest of the family?* She chose her words carefully. "I don't know, Frank. I'm not sure if I'm ready for that kind of drastic change in my life."

Feeling the serious undercurrents of emotion from the two women, Frank tried to lighten the conversation. "Really, Lex, it's only a formality. Jeannie is a fighter, and she'll come out of this any time. And I'm not going anywhere. Besides, we already designated you two as our first choice in our wills and trust." He tapped Lex on the shoulder lightly and winked.

Lex sighed and turned back to look at the baby again. "If you say so." But she didn't sound very thrilled by the honor.

Beside her, Amanda felt her heart break. If Lex wasn't ready, then she certainly wasn't going to want to be the parent of their own children any time in the near future. She felt her dreams shatter along with her heart.

Chapter Eleven

THE REST OF the week went by quickly, especially since Michael, Anna Leigh and Jacob showed up to offer their support to Frank at the hospital. They had taken rooms at a nearby hotel and took turns sitting with Jeannie, whose condition hadn't changed. Lex and Amanda had continued to stay at Frank and Jeannie's house.

Amanda tied off the end of a crepe streamer, then began to wind it around the banister. Everything was out of order. Amanda and Lex's trip to the bank a few days earlier had been a bust. The banker had been very respectful, and had even shown them the signed papers. Although it didn't look exactly like Amanda's signature, it was close enough to pass. They had also spoken to the clerk who had talked to "Amanda" on the phone several times. He was happy to "finally meet Ms. Cauble in person" and didn't seem to note any difference between the real McCoy and the bogus woman. Even after Lex threatened the bank with a lawsuit, the bank president shrugged his shoulders and apologized, but assured them that, as far at they could tell, everything had been done legally and nothing could be done about it.

She wrapped another bit of the streamer around the banister. They were decorating the house for the baby's homecoming, although her heart wasn't really in it. Frank hadn't wanted to bring the baby home; once their daughter had gained a little weight, he was able to arrange to have her stay in Jeannie's room at least part of the time. He had hoped that the baby's presence might stimulate his wife to wake up. But now, due to a lack of space and available cribs, little Lorrie would have to come home. Amanda looked across the room at her grandmother, who was teasing Jacob about something she couldn't quite make out. *Don't they realize that Jeannie won't be here? How can they be happy?* Disgusted with everyone else's attitudes, Amanda tossed the crepe to the floor and rushed up the stairs.

Sad eyes watched Amanda's retreat. Lex was still nursing her injured knee, and although she hadn't needed the crutches for a couple of days, she still wasn't able to navigate the stairs too easily. She and Amanda had been using the guest bedroom off the formal den, although Frank had asked them to take the master bedroom once the baby was home, since it was across the hall from the baby's room. Before Lex could climb out of the leather recliner that she had been ordered to stay in, Michael sat on the loveseat beside her.

"Is everything all right? You look a little upset." Michael had spent the entire morning watching his daughter and Lex, and he could tell that something was going on between them. He just wished one of them would confide in him so that he could try to help.

An upstairs door slammed, and Lex's eyes closed momentarily. When she opened them and looked at her father-in-law, she couldn't keep the sadness out of her voice. "I'm not sure. Amanda's been quiet lately, and she won't talk to me." She didn't mention that they hadn't really been alone long enough to talk.

"Would you like me to go up and talk to her?" Michael offered.

"No, that's all right." Lex lowered the footrest on the recliner and got to her feet. "I think I'll try my luck with the stairs." She patted Michael on the shoulder and limped across the room.

It took Lex longer than she'd expected, but she finally made her way to the closed door. She tapped lightly on the wood. "Amanda?" An incoherent mumble was the only answer, so Lex opened the door slowly.

Amanda sat on the floor in the middle of the room, which had been decorated as the baby's nursery. Bright yellow walls were accented by pastel stripes of blue, pink, and green. There were butterflies and flowers decoupaged all over the walls, and the white crib, rocker, and changing table looked ready for use. Amanda held an oversized stuffed teddy bear in her arms, and her face was buried in its soft fur. She didn't even look up as Lex limped into the room.

"Amanda?" Lex's knee throbbed from the abuse of climbing the stairs. She gritted her teeth and knelt beside her lover, reaching out and running her hand through Amanda's hair. "Hey."

Finally realizing who was with her, Amanda looked up. "Lex? What are you doing here?"

"Coming to see if you're okay." Lex finally sat down, stretching her legs out in front of her. "Whew."

Amanda put the bear down. "You came up here for me?"

"Yep."

Amanda scooted closer. "You didn't have to do that, you know."

"I know." Lex felt Amanda's arm go around her back, and she countered by putting her arm across her wife's shoulder. "But I hated the thought of you being up here alone, upset."

"Have I told you lately how much I love you?"

Lex grinned, and leaned her head into Amanda's. "You may have mentioned it at one time," she teased. "But I never get tired of hearing it."

THE BEEPING AND the low whoosh of the machinery were the only sounds Frank heard as he stepped into the room. He held Lorrie carefully, still not used to the squirming bundle that was dwarfed by his hands. "Hi, Jeannie. I brought our little girl by." His voice was soft, and he painstakingly placed her in the crook of Jeannie's arm, moving his wife's limp hand to lie across the baby. "She's a lot like her mama, you know. Feisty little thing." He swallowed back his tears and touched Jeannie's face. "She's got my hair, but I think she's going to have your eyes. I wish you'd wake up and see her."

Jeannie remained unresponsive, but Frank continued to talk to her for several minutes. He checked his watch, and knew that the nurse would be coming in soon to attend to Jeannie's needs. He leaned forward and kissed his wife on the forehead. "I'm going to take her home, honey. Your dad and your grandparents are here, and they'll be helping me with her until you get on your feet again. I hope that's soon, because I miss you so damned much, Jean. I love you." His lips quivered against her skin, and he stood back up and wiped his face with a handkerchief, which he stuffed back into his pocket.

Frank gently picked up Lorrie, tucking her blanket around her. "Tell Mama that you love her, Lorrie. You'll be back to visit soon." He cleared his throat and left the room, hating having to leave his wife behind while he took their daughter home.

Almost to the outer doors of the hospital, Frank felt as if someone was watching him. He turned to look over his shoulder and saw someone duck back around a corner. The single glance he was able to get sent shivers down his spine. *That's impossible. She's still locked up in a mental hospital in Texas. I must be imagining things.* Not wanting to take any chances, especially with Lex and

Amanda in town, he decided it would be best to tell Lex what he thought he had seen, just in case.

Outside, Frank walked the short distance to his car, a silver Lexus GS, which he had pulled up close to the hospital exit before going in to get Lorrie. He unlocked one of the back doors and buckled the baby into her car seat, cooing softly at her while his inexperienced hands figured out all the buckles. "Blasted thing is more complicated than it looks," he mumbled. Once his daughter was safely in the center of the rear of the car, he climbed behind the steering wheel and pulled slowly out of the parking lot.

He took the city streets instead of the freeway, thinking back to when Jeannie teased him about that very thing. He hadn't driven them on the highway since he'd found out Jeannie was pregnant, and had also stayed well below the speed limit any time she was in the car with him. As he stopped at a traffic light, he remembered one of the last conversations they'd had about that particular subject.

"Frank, you can drive faster than this, you know," Jeannie had teased her husband. "I'm just pregnant, not made of crystal."

Stopping at the light, Frank turned to look at his wife, who glowed with beauty. "As the mother of my child, you're more precious than crystal. You always have been, Jean." With the traffic light still red, he leaned over and kissed her, love filling his heart. He sat back in his seat, waiting for the light to turn green. "I will love spending the rest of my life with you, Jeannie Rivers. I can't wait to show you how much."

Now Frank's eyes brimmed with tears at that precious memory. He glanced in the rear view mirror, glad that the baby was sleeping peacefully. While he tried to regain his focus, the two cars in front of him proceeded, and he followed them through the light.

He never saw the delivery truck that sped through the intersection from the left, and slammed so hard into the front panel and driver's door of the sedan that the car went into a spin. The car careened onto the sidewalk, barely missing several pedestrians before crashing through a plate glass window of a closed restaurant. The car came to a rest, the only sounds the falling of broken glass, the hissing of the car's engine, and the wail of a baby.

IT HAD TAKEN some doing, but Lex was able to talk

Amanda into going back downstairs. She used the excuse that she needed help, which got her a doubtful look, but Amanda went along with her. Now they stood by the foot of the stairs, listening to Michael's comments about the baby gifts which covered the formal dining room table.

"That's not what I mean at all, Mom. I just said that I've never seen this many packages the last few holidays combined." He yelped when Anna Leigh walked behind him and swatted his rear.

"This baby is the first great-grandchild, Michael. Of course she's going to be showered with gifts." Anna Leigh pointed to the couple standing in the entryway. "Although I think those two should shoulder some of the blame."

Lex limped into the living area, then took her seat in the recliner when her partner gave her a gentle shove in that direction. "Don't blame me. Amanda is the one who kept going shopping all the time." She raised the footrest on the recliner and accepted the pillow that Amanda placed beneath her leg. "Thanks."

"You're welcome." Amanda turned and put her hands on her hips. "I don't suppose that you bought anything at all, did you, Daddy?"

"Well, maybe a small little something," Michael blustered.

"Mmm-hmm," Amanda teased, on her way to the kitchen. When the phone rang, she changed direction and picked up the cordless phone on a nearby table. "Rivers' residence." She listened for a moment, then paled and fell back against the wall, the phone falling from her hand.

Lex saw her wife collapse and jumped up from the chair to rush across the room, heedless of the pain in her injured leg. She caught Amanda before she could completely fall to the floor. "Amanda? What's the matter, sweetheart?" Her heart pounded in her chest, even as she heard the anguished answer.

"Frank. He's..." As the family gathered around them, Amanda couldn't stop her tears. She turned and buried her face in Lex's shirt.

"Hold on, Lex. Let me check this out." Michael picked up the phone from the floor. "I'm sorry, who is this, please? I'm Michael Cauble, and this is my daughter and son-in-law's home." He nodded slowly as the person on the other end of the line continued to speak. Finally, Michael uttered a low "thank you" and replaced the phone on its cradle. He cleared his throat in a fruitless effort to control the desolation in his voice. "There was an accident. We need to, ah..." His voice cracked. "The baby is okay. We need to get Lorrie. Frank is..." Michael couldn't continue.

Jacob stepped forward and put his arm around his son, trying to offer what comfort he could, even as his own heart broke. His wife took a position on the other side of Michael, rubbing her son's back as silent tears tracked down her face.

With her arms wrapped around Amanda's body, Lex held her close and watched as Michael leaned into his parents, sobbing as if he were a small boy. As she gazed at the uncomprehending and heartbroken faces in the room, Lex knew with a quiet certainty that none of their lives would ever be the same again.

THE OVERWORKED NURSE went about her duties briskly, knowing that she had an entire floor of patients yet left to attend. Her tasks complete, she was about to turn and leave when the patient's eyes blinked open. "Mrs. Rivers? Can you hear me?" When the eyes blinked in confusion, the nurse patted her arm. "It's all right. Let me get the doctor, dear. I'm sure he'll be happy to know you're awake." She picked up the phone and dialed the nurses' desk, asking for the doctor on call to come to the room.

Soon afterward, the doctor hurried into the room. "Mrs. Rivers. It's so nice to see you awake." He pulled out a small penlight and aimed it into her eyes. "Let's just see how you're doing, then we'll get rid of that nasty tube."

It didn't take long for them to take the breathing apparatus away, along with the heart monitor. The nurse placed a few ice chips on Jeannie's lips while the doctor watched.

He leaned in and smiled. "Now, Mrs. Rivers, can you tell me what your first name is?"

THE ROOM, WHICH had been festive only a short time earlier, was now quiet, except for the sounds of Amanda's crying and Lex's attempted words of comfort. Michael, Jacob, and Anna Leigh had left for the hospital to pick up Lorrie, where she had been taken as a precaution after the accident.

Lex sat stretched out on the leather sofa with Amanda pulled up against her. They hadn't moved since the family left, and Lex was beginning to worry about her wife.

"It's all my fault," Amanda hiccuped, her face still nestled against Lex's chest. "All my fault."

"No, sweetheart. It was an accident. You had nothing to do with it."

Amanda rolled away so that she was sitting on the next cushion. "You don't know that," she snapped.

Lex reached for her, but Amanda scooted farther away. "Yes, I do. You didn't kill Frank, Amanda. It was a car accident."

"But maybe I did. I wanted what they have, Lex. Jeannie's comatose, and Frank's dead. It's all my fault!" Amanda jumped up and would have run from the room, but Lex grabbed her arm. "Let me go!"

"No."

"Dammit, Lex," Amanda struggled to break free. "Let go!"

Lex stood up and faced her irate lover. "I'm not going to let you run away again. What did you mean when you said that you wanted what they have? Are you talking about a baby?"

The phone rang, saving Amanda from answering. Lex limped over to the phone, taking Amanda with her. She used her free hand to pick up the receiver. "Hello?" She paused for a moment, listening. "No, that's great. Thank you." Lex set the phone down, her face registering disbelief.

"What?"

"That was the hospital. Jeannie woke up."

The shock of the situation was almost more than Amanda could bear. Her anger spent, she collapsed into Lex's arms.

NOT TOO FAR from Jeannie's hospital room, a man dressed in scrubs swiped at the floor with a damp mop. He spent more time looking around than actually mopping, but lowered his head as two nurses walked by.

"Isn't it tragic? Poor Mrs. Rivers practically came out of her coma the instant her husband was killed in that car accident," one nurse related to the other.

"Oh, I know. It's just by some miracle that the baby survived. Why, the entire floor was shocked when they heard the news." They continued on their way, not paying any attention to the surprised look on the janitor's face.

Terence dropped his mop. *I need to tell Liz.* He waited until the two nurses were out of sight, then hurriedly picked up his supplies and hid them in a closet.

Doing a floor-by-floor search, Terence finally found Liz in the hospital gift shop. He looked around to make certain no one else noticed him, then, from another aisle, whispered loudly to get her attention. "Liz!"

The distinguished woman set down the delicate crystal figurine she was looking at and spun around. "Excuse me, do I know you?"

He hurried around the greeting cards and grabbed her arm. "Cut it out, Liz. This is important." Not even bothering to be discreet, Terence pulled Liz from the store, and into the hallway

"This had better be good. I was trying to find a gift for my daughter, you ass."

Terence looked around to make sure no one was looking at them. "Your son-in-law is dead," he whispered.

"Oh, really? Well, isn't that nice."

"Didn't you hear me?" Terence asked, shocked at her attitude.

Liz smiled. "Of course I did. But you're a little late with the news. I heard it about ten minutes ago." She brushed an imaginary speck of lint from her slacks. "It changes nothing, other than making things even easier for me. Now I should have no problem in getting both my daughters, *and* my granddaughter, back. I just wish that damned redneck bitch had been in the car with him."

Although he shouldn't have been surprised, it still struck Terence as extremely cold-blooded, even for Liz. "But he was the baby's father. Doesn't that mean anything to you?"

"My dear boy, you should know," Liz leaned in closer, "that *all* men are expendable."

THE ENTIRE FAMILY stood outside Jeannie's hospital room, including the newly arrived Lex and Amanda. The doctor had just come out to speak to them about Jeannie's condition, and they all waited anxiously for what he was going to say.

"Amazingly, Mrs. Rivers came out of her coma fairly alert. Her speech was affected by the stroke, as were her motor skills." He looked at the concerned faces around him. "She'll need extensive therapy, but she's young and strong. Mrs. Rivers' prognosis is very good. I'm confident that she will make a full recovery over time. Are there any questions?"

Jacob, who had been standing with Anna Leigh, held out his hand. "I think you covered it pretty well, Doctor. Is she up to visitors?"

Nodding, the doctor shook Jacob's hand. "Certainly. Just don't all go barging in there at once. She's still a bit groggy." He adjusted his lab coat. "Now, if you'll excuse me, I have other patients to check on. Just have me paged if you need anything."

They all watched him go, then Anna Leigh leaned back into her husband's embrace. "What will we tell Jeannie when she asks about Frank?"

"I think I should go in and see how she's doing first,"

Michael volunteered. "I'm her father, and if she asks, I think it would be best coming from me."

Amanda, who hadn't left Lex's arms, reached out for her father. "Are you sure, Daddy? I can come in with you, if you need me to." She talked bravely, but the last thing Amanda wanted to do was see her sister being told that her husband was dead. *I know what I would feel if it were me. I couldn't go on without Lex. Poor Jeannie.*

"No, Amanda. That's okay." Knowing the offer for the sacrifice that it was, Michael kissed his daughter's cheek, then squared his shoulders and went into Jeannie's room, closing the door behind him. He was heartened to see all the machines were gone and his daughter appeared to be resting peacefully. Walking slowly to the bed, Michael sat down on the edge and picked up Jeannie's hand. "Hi, sweetie."

Jeannie's eyes opened. Although she seemed happy to see her father, she strained to look past him. "Wher's Fwan?" she slurred.

It took Michael a moment to figure out what Jeannie had said. He used his free hand to touch her face. "We're so glad you're awake, Jeannie. The whole family has been worried about you. And, you've got a beautiful little girl."

Her eyes moistened. Although Jeannie's speech and motor skills were damaged by the stroke, her mind wasn't. "Fwan?"

Michael swallowed hard, his eyes filling with tears, also. "There was a car accident, baby." She looked at him, puzzled. "Honey, I don't know how to tell you this. He..."

Her hand came up and clutched at his arm as she made a strangled sound, her eyes wide. "Wha — wha!"

"Jeannie, Frank didn't make it. I'm afraid he's —"

"Noooo!"

Jeannie's wail could be heard out in the hallway where the gathered family bowed their heads as they wept in shared pain.

AFTER HEARING JEANNIE'S cry, Anna Leigh took her husband by his arm and led him away from Lex and Amanda. Once they were in the elevator, she leaned against him. "That poor child. We need to do something to help Jeannie through this, dearest."

"Such as?" Jacob hurt for their granddaughter also, but he didn't know what his wife was up to.

The doors opened, and Anna Leigh took him by the hand. "Maybe seeing her daughter will help." They stepped out onto the pediatric unit, and she ushered Jacob to the glassed-in room.

The head nurse, who remembered them well from their earlier visits, met them outside. "Mr. and Mrs. Cauble. I'm so sorry to hear about your loss." She reached out and grasped Anna Leigh's hands. "We've been watching Lorraine for any signs of injury or distress, but she seems to have come through all of this just fine."

"Thank you, Serena. It means a lot to us that you've taken such fine care of our great-granddaughter." Anna Leigh had gotten to know the head pediatric nurse during her frequent visits to the hospital, and felt a bond with the woman who also had her share of grandchildren. Her head turned when another nurse brought Lorrie out and handed her to Jacob.

"You just let us know if we can do anything else, Mrs. Cauble. We'll all be praying for your family." Nurse Serena stood next to the other nurse as the couple walked back to the elevator. "What a horrible thing to happen to a nice family. I hope they come out of it okay."

BACK ON JEANNIE'S floor, Anna Leigh and Jacob returned with Lorrie. They spied Lex and Amanda sitting quietly in the waiting area and walked over to join them. Jacob handed the baby to Amanda, who accepted her niece in silence.

Wanting to make sure she was okay, Amanda carefully inspected the small bundle for any signs of harm. "Hey there, sweetie. How are you doing?" The baby squeaked, but was otherwise silent. "You're so beautiful."

Lex leaned over until her head touched Amanda's. "She's all right, isn't she?"

"It looks like it," Amanda assured her. "She's just so tiny. I can't believe that she survived, much less without a scratch on her." She teared up again at the thought of Frank. "This is just so surreal."

"I know, love." Lex put her arm around Amanda, and was about to say more when Michael finally came out of Jeannie's room. He saw the family in the waiting area and headed over to talk to them.

Jacob immediately put his arm around his son. "How's she doing?"

"Not good, Dad. She's completely shut down."

"What do you mean, dear?" Anna Leigh asked.

Michael looked at his mother's kind face. "She threw me out of her room." He rubbed his face with his hands, then looked down at the floor. "She hates me."

"I'm sure that's not true." Jacob escorted Michael to a chair.

"She's understandably upset. But once she has some time to grieve, she'll be able to handle everything a little better."

"Maybe if she sees Lorrie," Anna Leigh suggested. "Holding her daughter could help."

"She doesn't want to see her, or anyone, right now." Michael didn't tell the family the way Jeannie glared at him after he broke the news of her husband's death. Telling his daughter that she was a mother, and a widow, was one of the hardest things he'd ever had to do. Being thrown out of her room broke his heart, even though he understood why Jeannie wanted to be alone. "Let's follow her wishes, at least for now. She needs time to sort things out in her mind."

Anna Leigh dusted her hands together. "I don't like it. We shouldn't leave her here all alone. She needs her family with her at a time like this."

Jacob put his arm around his wife's shoulders. "I don't like it either, Anna. But she's a grown woman, and we need to respect her feelings."

"Mom, please. Let's just go back to the house for now, and we'll try again later. Arguing about it isn't good for anyone."

"All right. But I still don't like it." Anna Leigh followed the group to the elevator, looking over her shoulder once at Jeannie's door. "I don't like it at all."

ONCE BACK AT the house, Anna Leigh took Lex by the arm and led her away from Amanda, who had carried the baby into the living room. "Let's go in the kitchen and gather some refreshments for everyone, Lexington."

"Okay," Lex agreed, somewhat confused. She limped behind the older woman, and was barely into the kitchen when her arm was grabbed and she was practically dragged over to the breakfast area to sit down. "I have the feeling this isn't about getting drinks for everyone."

"No, it isn't. I thought about it all the way over here, and I think that you're the perfect person to talk to Jeannie."

Lex laughed, although it wasn't a cheerful sound. "Yeah, right. I'm such an expert on losing husbands." She started to stand. "I don't think so, Anna Leigh."

"Wait, please." Anna Leigh watched the doorway, and when she was certain that they were alone, she leaned over closer to Lex. "You've had a loss in your family recently, Lexington. I think that would give you more insight than any of us, at least in Jeannie's eyes." She reached across the table and touched Lex's hand. "Dearest, who better than you for Jeannie to share her loss with?"

When it was put to her that way, Lex couldn't argue. The loss of her father was still fresh in her mind, although talking about it again would most likely bring all the pain back to the surface. But she'd do anything for Amanda, and that included doing anything for Amanda's family, as well. "I'll try. But I'm not going to promise anything." She thought about how Amanda looked holding Lorrie, and tried to imagine her wife holding *their* child. Lex now realized how much having a child meant to Amanda, but she still wasn't certain if she was ready for such a drastic change in their lives.

Anna Leigh watched as Lex thought silently. "Is there something else on your mind, Lexington?"

Is there? Just how selfish will she think I am when I tell her my worries about starting a family with her granddaughter? "There is, but I doubt you'll want to hear it."

The woman across from her looked as if she had the weight of the world on her shoulders, and Anna Leigh hated that she had added to that burden with her request. "What is it?"

"I think Amanda wants to have a baby." Once she'd said the words, Lex knew that she couldn't pull them back. "And I don't think I do." She rolled up the placemat in front of her with nervous hands.

Struggling to keep her surprise from showing on her face, Anna Leigh nodded. "I see. Why don't you, Lexington?"

Lex looked up. "I'm not quite the mothering type. Hell, my mother died when I was little. What kind of role model would I be?"

"Are you saying that Martha has been *just* your housekeeper, all these years?" Although she knew that most of what Lex said came from fear, Anna Leigh wasn't about to let her get away with the feeble excuse. "What a shame."

"No! Of course not!" Lex got up in a hurry, which caused the chair she was in to slide across the kitchen floor. "You know that's not what I meant. It's just that—"

Anna Leigh stood up with her, using both hands to grasp Lex's arms and keep her from leaving the room. "You're scared." One of her hands touched Lex's cheek tenderly. "Dearest, we're all scared from time to time. But you can't let fear dictate your life."

"It's not just that," Lex whispered. "My mother died giving birth. Jeannie nearly died giving birth." Her voice lowered even more. "I can't lose Amanda like that, Anna Leigh. I can't."

Although the idea of another one of her grandchildren suffering concerned her, too, Anna Leigh put her arms around

Lex and brought her close. "I understand your worry, Lexington. But would you rather see her sad and upset for the rest of her life? Because I can tell you right now, the desire to have a child isn't something that just goes away."

The thought sobered Lex. Would she lose Amanda over that? Could their relationship survive such a difference in what the other wanted? She definitely had a lot of thinking to do concerning the subject. Lex put her arms around Anna Leigh and squeezed. "Thanks. I'll go see Jeannie in the morning."

LATER THAT EVENING, Lex stood at the door of the master bedroom and watched Amanda in the rocker holding Lorrie. Earlier, Michael and Jacob had brought the chair and the crib from the nursery into the room so that Lex and Amanda could watch over Lorrie. Getting a preview of the maternal side of her partner was something that Lex had not expected to see so soon, and she was pleasantly surprised by her own reaction. Her heart swelled with love at the picture Amanda and the baby made.

"They look good together, don't they?" Jacob whispered from behind Lex. While downstairs, his wife had briefed him on Lex's worries, and he wanted to see if there was anything that he could do to help alleviate her concerns. "Amanda would make a good mother, I bet."

"I'm sure she would," Lex whispered, so as not to disturb the scene. She turned to face Jacob. "Thanks for helping get everything brought over to our room. I'm afraid that Amanda would have ended up sleeping in the nursery if you hadn't." *And of course I'd end up there with her, with the two of us napping on the floor. Bringing the crib and rocker into the master bedroom makes a lot more sense.*

He chuckled, then patted Lex on the shoulder. "She's a mite protective of that little one, isn't she?"

Turning back to look into the room, Lex couldn't help but agree. Amanda hadn't put the baby down since they got back from the hospital. "I think we're all going to be."

"Probably so." Jacob noticed the dark circles under Lex's eyes. "Why don't you go on in there, and you three get some rest? Michael's still trying to track down Frank's parents, so there's really not much more that can be done right now."

"That's probably the best suggestion I've heard in days." Lex gave Jacob a firm hug, then watched as he went down the hallway toward the stairs. She walked slowly into the bedroom, hoping that Amanda would not be startled by her sudden appearance.

Sensing someone else in the room, Amanda looked up and smiled at her partner. "Hi," she whispered, not wanting to wake the baby. She could tell by the way that Lex limped that her leg was bothering her. "Could you come here?"

Lex nodded and moved to stand in front of the rocker. "How's she doing?"

"Good." Amanda shifted the baby so that she could raise the small bundle. "Could you take her so that I can get up? I'm afraid my leg has fallen asleep." Although it wasn't a lie, Amanda knew she'd have no problem rising. She just wanted to give Lex an opportunity to hold Lorrie, which she'd avoided doing so far.

"Me? Hold her?" Lex took a step back. "Do you really think that's a good idea? I've never held a baby before." The closest she'd ever come to holding a baby was when she had been a teenager, and one of her friend's cats had kittens. She'd held one of the blind, mewing tufts of fur, terrified the entire time that she'd crush it in her hands. *Lorrie's not much bigger than one of those kittens. I can't do this!*

Amanda barely lifted the baby. "Come here, Lex. I'll show you how."

Breaking wild horses didn't scare her as much as taking that step forward and putting her hands under the sleeping infant. "God, she's tiny," Lex marveled. She let Amanda place her hands in the correct position, and then she was holding Lorrie. "I bet one of my boots weighs more than she does."

"I'm sure they do." Amanda gently guided the baby in Lex's hands until her wife was holding Lorrie correctly. "See? There's nothing to it."

Lex looked down at the sleeping child, her eyes almost tearing up with emotion. "She's beautiful, Amanda." Holding the baby in her arms, with her lover by her side, made Lex realize what Amanda had been wanting. She didn't know if she was quite ready for such a step, but she vowed to herself to seriously consider it, if not for Amanda's sake, then for her own. "We're going to take good care of you, Lil' Bit," she promised the baby, "and your mama, too." She looked up into Amanda's eyes. "Aren't we?"

"We sure are." Amanda leaned forward and kissed the top of the baby's head, then kissed Lex on the lips.

Chapter Twelve

MICHAEL STORMED OUT of the formal den where he had been on the phone. "Those obnoxious, self-involved, arrogant assholes!" He almost ran over his father, who held out a hand to stop his progress.

"What's the matter, son?"

Still fuming, Michael willed himself to calm down, although all he wanted to do was tear a couple of choice heads from their bodies. "They acted like it wasn't that big of a deal, Dad. I told them their son was dead, and all they seemed to be worried about was missing the next leg of their vacation." He paced around the living room, shaking his head. "Now I know why we never got along. The Rivers have a wine tasting to attend in France, then they'll head home. It'll probably be late next week, though." He leaned against the back of a heavy leather sofa. "Please tell me I never got *that* bad."

Jacob placed his hands in his pockets while he appeared to give the question a lot of consideration. "You were there for the birth of both your daughters, weren't you? And for their high school and college graduations?"

"Yeah. But you know the girls. Do you think I would have been able to miss something as important as their graduations?"

"True." Jacob agreed with his son on that one. "And, before you say it, I know there were a lot of things you *did* miss. I'm not condoning that, but I do understand it. You were the head of your own company, Michael. There were times when you couldn't drop everything and run off to a piano recital."

Although he knew his father was right, Michael also acknowledged there were more times than he could count where he *could* have adjusted his schedule for his children. But at the time, he thought that work was more important. *And just look at me now. I'm struggling to make ends meet as a photographer, but I've never been happier in my entire life.* "Thanks, Dad." Something, no, someone, was missing. "Where's Mom?"

"She drove Lex, Amanda, and the baby up to the hospital this morning. I thought I'd stay behind and see if I could help you with the arrangements for Frank."

Michael nodded. "I know we need to decide something soon, but I was hoping to see what Jeannie wanted." In spite of the fact that he was thrilled that his daughter had come out of her coma, he didn't look forward to the conversation concerning the disposition of her husband's remains. "Do you think that she'll be ready to talk today? I hate upsetting her."

"Your mother is supposed to call and let me know." Jacob put an arm around Michael's shoulders and guided him into the kitchen. "How about I whip up some breakfast for the two of us while we wait? Or some coffee, at the very least."

"SITTING THERE IGNORING me isn't going to make me go away," Amanda stated softly. She stood at her sister's bedside, trying to get some sort of reaction out of Jeannie.

For her part, Jeannie continued to look at the opposite wall. She had heard Amanda come into the room earlier, but just didn't feel like talking with anyone. Buffeted by a wave of despair that threatened to engulf her, she longed to disappear back into the nothingness of her coma. There, she wouldn't have to feel the pain of losing her husband. She wouldn't have to be aware of how helpless she was following her stroke. She wouldn't have to face the challenge of raising a child who would never know her father. Or of struggling for every movement and for every word.

Jeannie finally spoke. "Go 'way, Manda. Weave me wone." Fresh tears sprang into her eyes at the garbled words that came out of her mouth. *I sound like such an idiot. Why didn't I die, too?* She hoped that if she ignored her sister long enough, Amanda would get the hint and leave.

Amanda rubbed her hand across Jeannie's arm, trying to soothe her any way she could. "Do you think that Frank would want you to feel this way? I understand it's painful, but—"

"Shud up!" Jeannie turned her head to glare at her sister. "You don' know ow I beel. You couldnd!" Her eyes conveyed all the anger that her words could not. "Go back do your berfec wuber, an' your berfec widdle wife. Dus weave me be." Jeannie turned her head away to face the wall. "Go 'way," she finished in an anguished voice.

"I love you, Jeannie," Amanda murmured, right before she gave her sister's arm one last squeeze. She left the room and stumbled down the hall to the waiting area, where Lex was watching Anna Leigh talk nonsense to the baby. Amanda sat beside her grandmother and tried to wipe the tears of hurt from her eyes.

Lex put one hand on Amanda's shoulder and leaned down to make eye contact with her. "I take it that it didn't go too well in there, huh?"

"That's putting it mildly." Scrubbing her face with her hands, Amanda inhaled deeply then released the breath slowly. "She's in such pain that she is alternating between self-pity and anger. I tried to talk to her, but she told me that I couldn't know how she felt and ordered me to leave the room."

Anna Leigh looked up at Lex expectantly. She didn't have to speak, her eyes conveyed all she wanted to say.

Lex stood up tall and stretched. "Well, I guess it's my turn then." The last thing she wanted to do was go into that hospital room, but she'd given her word and she never went back on that. She held out her hands to Anna Leigh, who handed the baby to her. "Come on, Lil' Bit. Let's go see your Mama."

Anna Leigh and Amanda watched as Lex carried the infant down the hallway, then disappeared into Jeannie's room. "She certainly looks a lot more comfortable with Lorrie this morning," Anna Leigh commented.

Amanda couldn't help but smile. "She should. I think Lex took as many turns as I did getting up with her last night. When I woke up this morning, Lex was propped up on pillows in the bed with the baby sprawled on her chest, both of them sound asleep. If Lorrie wasn't so young, I'd almost be jealous," she tried to joke, but her heart just wasn't in it.

Pushing the door open slowly, Lex peeked inside. She saw Jeannie lay still in the bed, her face turned toward the wall. She must have heard the door open, because her head turned slightly, then returned to its previous position.

"Hi, Jeannie. I brought you another visitor," Lex explained quietly. Hospitals always gave her the creeps, and this one was no exception.

"Go 'way," Jeannie grumbled, not bothering to turn her head.

Lex ignored the plea, instead sitting in the chair next to the bed. "I'm afraid I can't do that just yet. At least not until we talk for a bit."

"I don' wan' 'alk. I can'. Wisen me. I soun' wike iiod." Jeannie began to cry softly. "Pwese go 'way, Wex."

Lex moved to the edge of the bed. She held the baby in one arm, while she used her free hand to touch Jeannie's shoulder. "I'm afraid I can't do that, Jeannie. There are a lot of folks who care about you, and we all want to do what we can to help you get through this terrible time."

Jeannie shook her head and squeezed her eyes tightly shut, wanting to escape—wanting to be anywhere but where she was, who she was, and how she felt.

"I wish there was something that we could say or do to make everything better for you. This has got to be the hardest thing you've ever had to face." Lex patted the baby, who had started to stir in her arms. She gazed into the baby's eyes. Lorrie was watching her intently. Lex smiled down at her and stroked the tiny cheek with her fingertips. When she raised her eyes again, she saw Jeannie turn her head away. All of the losses in Lex's life surfaced, along with the realization of her deep protective feelings for Jeannie's child. Lex's heart demanded to be expressed. Jeannie's loss became her loss, and the words she spoke next were for the both of them.

"This isn't how it's supposed to be. Frank should be here holding his daughter. You shouldn't have had a stroke. You should be together. You, Frank, and Lorrie. You should be a family. This isn't fair. It isn't right. You shouldn't have to have people standing over you telling you that everything is going to be all right when it's not. When you know deep in your heart that nothing will ever take away the hurt. When all you can hope for is to find a way to live with the pain. This isn't the way it's supposed to be," Lex repeated.

Jeannie turned her head back toward Lex and raised her opened hand to her as if making a plea. Then she shut her eyes again in one last attempt to stem the flow of tears and sorrow that threatened to sweep her away in their intensity.

Lex shifted her hold on the baby and took Jeannie's hand. "I can't make it stop, Jeannie. I can't wake you up from this nightmare." Lex's voice got even quieter and her eyes clouded as her own grief rose to the surface. "It wasn't that long ago I lost my father. Even though we had our differences, I worshipped the ground that man walked on. My entire life was spent trying to be good enough for him, and it took him dying before we reconciled that." Lex realized she'd said more than she should have and cleared her throat to cover her embarrassment. "Anyway, after he was gone, I spent a lot of time brooding over things I couldn't change. All my chances to be a daughter to him were gone. I hated that. I resented that I had to grow up not knowing my mother, and then lose my father just as I found out that he really didn't hate me. Don't do that to Lorrie."

She placed Lorrie in the crook of Jeannie's arm, then drew it up so it cradled the baby. "There's a little girl here who needs her mama. That means you've got a lot to live for. You've got to love her for both you and Frank."

Jeannie's head turned and she looked down at the infant beside her. "God Fwank's hair," she marveled as fresh tears tracked down her face. Then her eyes glanced up and met Lex's. Emotionally spent, all she could do was nod.

"SHE LOOKS SO melancholy. Probably due to living with *that* woman," Liz snarled. Her view of her daughter was eclipsed by Lex leaving Jeannie's room and walking over to stand in front of Amanda. She pulled her head back around the corner, not wanting to be seen. Yet. Turning around, she crossed her arms over her chest. "So?" she demanded of Terence. "Tell me you have some good news, for a change."

He scratched at the base of his neck, wishing once again that he could get into his expensive suits and leave the hospital wear behind. "From what I've gathered, your daughter's condition has improved quite a bit. As a matter of fact, they may want to release her in the next few days." A quick slap against his arm caused Terence to cry out. "Ow! What was that for?"

Liz grabbed a fistful of his shirt and pulled him close. "You imbecile. I wanted to know about Amanda! I already know my other daughter's *condition*. She's a half-crippled, barely intelligible mess. Lord knows what I'll be able to do with her."

"But Liz."

"Don't whine to me, you mealy-mouthed little idiot. I need to know what that hick has done to my little girl to make her so upset. If we can figure that out, it should give me just what I need to take Amanda away from her for good." Liz released his shirt, then wiped her hand on it as if soiled. "One way or another, I'm taking my daughter back."

His eyes wide, Terence watched as Liz retreated down the hall. "That woman is completely crazy." He brushed at the creases in the front of his uniform before taking a different route through the hospital. "I guess that makes me just as nuts, since I'm working for her," he muttered. No matter how hard he tried, Terence couldn't figure out how to get away from Liz without risking her retaliation. *But,* he reminded himself, *at least the pay is good.*

AFTER A LONG morning at the hospital, the family was just about to sit down to a late lunch when the phone rang. Michael, being the closest, answered the call. He waited for several moments, then a smile broke out onto his face. "It's good to hear from you, Charlie. Yes, thank you very much. Sure, hold on a moment." He held the receiver out. "Lex, it's for you."

Lex walked around the kitchen table and took the phone. "Thanks." She held the receiver up to her ear and unconsciously turned away from everyone. "Charlie?"

"Martha told me the news. How are you girls holding up?"

Before going to bed the night before, Lex had spent a long time on the phone with Martha, telling the housekeeper everything that had happened. Since she had to be the support for Amanda, she needed someone to talk to that could be her support. "About as good as can be expected, I suppose," Lex murmured into the phone. "It's really rough around here."

"I can just imagine, kiddo." Charlie was quiet for a moment, then cleared his throat. "I checked out those explosions you said you heard. Seems like whoever owns the property north of you was blowing some rock to make a dam on the creek. They've also cleared a bunch of the land nearby, but I don't know what for. I've got deputies trying to find out more."

"I thought the creek had been dammed. The water was too low for it to have happened naturally." Lex leaned against the counter top, watching as the rest of the family passed plates at the table and tried not to listen in to her conversation. "Since the creek is a source of water for several properties, they can't legally dam it, can they?" With the running of the ranch in her hands for so many years, Lex tried to keep up with all the laws and statutes that affected the ranch. It had saved her many times in the past.

"They couldn't, *if* they dammed it completely. But as it is, water is getting through, albeit slowly," Charlie answered apologetically. "We're not even sure who owns the property, yet."

Lex reflected on the events of recent weeks. At the bidding, Andrew Wilson had seemed a little too anxious to buy the property she had just acquired. Now she just needed to find out who he worked for. "He certainly wasn't smart enough to be working on his own," she mumbled.

"What was that?"

"Oh, sorry about that. I was just thinking about the other bidders there the day I picked up the new property. Some guy was pretty hot about buying it from me."

"Did you get his name?" Charlie asked, still in lawman mode. "I can try checking him out."

"Yeah. He said his name was Andrew Wilson, for all the good that'll do you. I have a feeling this is a lot bigger than we think, Charlie." Lex rubbed her forehead to stave off the headache that was coming on.

"You're probably right. I think while I'm at it, I'll check the tax records for the entire area. Could be someone's up to something."

"All right."

Charlie's voice changed to a quieter tone. "Are you okay, Lex?"

"Sure, Charlie. I'm just fine." She didn't feel fine, though. The gravity of the situation, as well as everything else that had happened, was weighing heavily on her mind. She knew that it was going to get a lot worse before it got better.

"Uh-huh." Not convinced, Charlie let the question drop. "I know you're probably busy out there, so I'll let you go. Give us a ring if you need anything, all right?"

"I sure will. Thank you." Lex hung up the phone, feeling more worn out than before. She turned around and her eyes sought out her partner's. "If everyone will excuse me, I'm not very hungry right now." Lex left the room, and Amanda stood up as well.

"I think I'll go—" Amanda gestured to the doorway where Lex had just made her exit.

Anna Leigh spoke for everyone else in the room. "You go right ahead, dearest. We'll listen for the baby." Lorrie had fallen asleep on the way back from the hospital, and Michael had placed her in the bassinet in the living room. "Let us know if you or Lexington need anything."

"Thanks, Gramma." Amanda rushed out of the room in search of her partner. Not finding Lex on the main floor, she was about to ascend the stairs when she noticed the front door slightly ajar.

Lex sat on the front steps, her elbows on her knees and her head in her hands. She heard the door open and wasn't surprised when she felt someone sit beside her. Her mind was spinning with what Charlie had told her. Lex wondered if whoever bought and dammed the property was involved with her losing her money. She didn't think so, but stranger things had happened. Now there was the added burden of Frank's death and what they were going to do about Jeannie and the baby.

"Lex?" Amanda put her hand on her lover's arm. "Is everything okay at home?"

Raising her head, Lex turned and looked into Amanda's face. "Yeah, things are okay there. Charlie just wanted to let me know that whoever owns the property north of ours has cleared the land and partially dammed the creek. He's still trying to find out who and why." She tried to force a smile onto her face, but wasn't very successful. "Sorry for running out on lunch like that."

Amanda scooted closer and put her arm around Lex's waist. "You don't have to apologize, Lex. I just want to help if I can."

"That's what I want to do," Lex whispered. "I want to help you, and your family. There's just so much going on." She tilted her head to the side until it touched Amanda's. The contact made Lex feel better, but she knew there was a lot they still had to talk about.

LATER THAT DAY, Michael stormed out of Jeannie's hospital room. He nearly ran over the man who was mopping the floors. "Excuse me. I didn't mean to—"

"No, that's all right. It happens all the time," the janitor assured him. He picked up his mop and dropped the head back into the rolling bucket. "No problem." Not bothering to take his orange caution cone with him, the man wheeled the bucket around the corner and out of sight.

Michael watched the man leave, then shook his head. "Strange. I swear that guy is here all the time, cleaning the floor." He went in search of his mother and father, who had made the trip to the hospital with him. Finding them in the waiting area, Michael sat down beside his mother and leaned back in the chair. "How did I manage to have two daughters that were so damned stubborn?"

"I'd have to say it was hereditary," Jacob said with a pointed glance at his wife. "But you always said you wanted children who could speak their mind. What did Jeannie say to upset you?"

"I hated to bring it up to her, but I had to ask what she wanted to do about Frank."

Anna Leigh, who was still glaring at her husband over his earlier remark, touched her son's knee. "I know that had to be hard on both of you. What did she decide?"

Michael stood up so that he could pace around the small area. "She wants him cremated!"

"So? What's so wrong with that?" Anna Leigh asked.

"You don't get it, Mom," Michael tried to explain. "She told me she wanted him cremated so that she could keep him with her! That can't be a healthy thing."

Jacob stood up also, and stopped his son's movement. "I agree, son. But it's also so soon after his death. Maybe, in time—"

"And what do I tell his parents? As much as I dislike them, this won't be easy. I'm sure they'd rather have a grave that they can place flowers on, and things like that." Michael dropped back into a chair. "As a parent, I know I would want some kind of closure."

A tall man in a lab coat stopped when he saw Michael in the waiting area. "Mr. Cauble? I'm Doctor Webster. I've been checking in on your daughter."

Michael stood up and shook the doctor's hand. "Oh, that's right. How is she doing, Doctor? Have there been any problems?"

"No, she's actually progressing quite well. I was just going to talk to you about her care after she's released." Dr. Webster flipped through a folder, then looked back up at Michael. "If she keeps getting better, I'll release her in the next couple of days."

"That's great." Michael looked to his parents for support. "Is there anything special we'll need to do for her?"

The doctor nodded. "I have a list of nursing homes and rehab centers nearby." He didn't see the pair of women who walked into the area. "These nursing homes are all fully capable of handling a case such as hers. If you like, I can—"

"Nursing home?" Amanda asked. "Are you suggesting that we put Jeannie into a home?"

The doctor turned to address the newcomers. "Well, yes. It would be the best thing for her. She's going to need therapy and twenty-four-hour assistance for the next few months. A nursing home would be the best thing for her, and for all of you."

Lex stood next to Amanda, placing her hand on her wife's shoulder. "How could locking her away from her family be good for her? Isn't there another option?"

"Do you plan on taking care of her? Feeding, bathing, and helping her with all her needs?" Dr. Webster hated to sound so harsh, but he had seen so many well-intentioned families ruined by a loved one's illness. "You'd also have to arrange for physical therapy and speech and occupational therapy as well. It would be costly and difficult. Are you prepared for that?"

Seeing the anguished faces around her, Lex said the only thing she could. "Yes. We'll take her back to Texas with us, and her *family* will see to Jeannie's needs." When Amanda turned and looked adoringly into her eyes, Lex knew it was exactly the right answer.

"That's right, Dr. Webster," Anna Leigh added. "You don't know our family very well. When can we start making arrangements for Jeannie's trip home?"

He shook his head and sighed. "I'll have the duty nurse

come talk to you." Dr. Webster walked away, hoping that this family would be able to handle the extreme stress to which it was about to be subjected.

Chapter Thirteen

THE DARKENED HOSPITAL chapel was filled to capacity, all eyes on the gray, polished metal urn that sat on the table at the front of the room. The minister had just finished the short ceremony and leaned down to speak a few quiet words to the woman in the wheelchair in the front row.

Only able to use one side of her body, Jeannie refused to relinquish the grip she had on the strong hand in her lap. She turned her head and appealed to the owner of the appendage, who sat next to her.

"That was a fine service, Reverend," Lex said, understanding that Jeannie didn't feel comfortable talking to anyone outside of the family, due to her speech problems. "I'm sure Mrs. Rivers appreciates your kind words."

Jeannie nodded, still not wanting to speak. After the clergyman left, Jeannie turned to look at the urn, and then back at Lex. For some reason she had developed an attachment to her sister-in-law, and only wanted Lex around her. She looked up into Lex's eyes. "Pwease? My woom?"

"What?" Lex felt the hand in hers tighten. "You want to take the urn back to your room?"

"Mmm-hmm." Jeannie started to cry again, and Lex pulled out a handkerchief and wiped her face.

"Shhh. It's okay. I'll take care of it," Lex promised. There was just something about the Cauble women that she couldn't say no to. "How about if Amanda takes you back to your room, and I'll bring," she looked at the urn, unsure of what to call it, "that back."

"No." Jeannie pulled Lex's hand closer. "Don' weave me."

Lex sighed. "I can't carry that *and* push your chair, Jeannie." She turned to Amanda, who was sitting on the other side of her. Frank and Amanda had been friends since high school, and it was Amanda who had introduced Jeannie to Frank. Lex knew her lover was taking Frank's death almost as hard as Jeannie was.

There's no way in hell I'm going to ask Amanda to carry what's left of her best friend back to Jeannie's room. There's got to be another way.

Before she could figure out what to do, Anna Leigh, who had overheard the conversation, handed Lorrie to Amanda. "Mandy, I think someone is missing their auntie." She winked at Lex, then squatted next to Jeannie's chair. "Would it be all right if I carried the urn for you, Jeannie?"

God bless you, Anna Leigh. Lex waited until Jeannie nodded, then leaned down to release the brakes on the wheelchair. "Let's get you back to your room." She wheeled Jeannie through the throng of well-wishers, remembering far too well how hard it was to be polite to people when all you really wanted to do was hide somewhere and cry.

It didn't take long for Lex, Jeannie, Amanda, and Anna Leigh to return to the hospital room. The cheery atmosphere of flowers and balloons was more than Jeannie could handle, and she leaned forward in her chair and sobbed.

Amanda, holding the baby, bit her lip to keep from joining her sister. She allowed her grandmother to guide her to a nearby chair, where she sat and began to rock Lorrie.

Lex was torn. She wanted to go to Amanda, but seeing Jeannie in such a vulnerable state broke her heart. With Anna Leigh's help, it didn't take long for them to get Jeannie back into her bed. Trying to be of some comfort, Lex sat on the edge of the bed. Jeannie immediately reached for her with her one good arm, and Lex pulled the crying woman close. She gently rocked the grieving Jeannie, who clung to her as if her life depended on it.

The door opened and Michael stepped in, followed by Jeannie's doctor and a nurse. The doctor had been present at the services, and he thought that his patient would do better after a sedative. "Mrs. Rivers, I've prescribed something to help you rest."

"Nooo," Jeannie wailed, clinging tighter to Lex.

"I'm sorry, but it's for your own good," Dr. Webster explained, nodding to the nurse.

Lex turned to block their access to Jeannie with her own body. "Is drugging her into oblivion absolutely necessary? Can't you damned people just leave the woman alone to grieve?" She held Jeannie's head to her chest, trying to keep her calm.

"I think that as her physician I know what's best for Mrs. Rivers. Now if you'll just move out of the way—"

"Back off," Lex snapped. She'd had all she could stand of the pompous doctor. "If you don't want that shot to become an enema, I'd suggest you both get out of here."

Dr. Webster turned to look at Anna Leigh, who had one

hand over her mouth to keep from laughing at his expression. "Did you hear her threaten me?"

"Actually," Anna Leigh chortled, "I believe it was more of a promise than a threat." She got herself under control and began to lead the doctor from the room. "Please, let our family take care of Jeannie. She just needs a little time, not more medication."

"Very well. I'll send a nurse back in to check on her later. If she's still hysterical, I'm going to have to sedate her." He left, followed by his nurse, who was grinning.

Anna Leigh turned back around to face the women on the bed. "Lexington, that wasn't nice."

"But it was well-deserved," Amanda added. "I never have liked that man's attitude."

Jeannie pulled back from Lex's grasp, her shoulders shaking, but she was no longer crying. "E'ema?" she asked slowly, then burst into laughter. "Dat a good un."

"Well, he was a jackass," Lex defended herself, glad to see Jeannie in better spirits. She knew it wasn't the end of the tears, but she was happy to see some healing begin. When Jeannie tried to lean back, Lex helped her lie down on the bed. "Are you going to be okay?"

"Yeah. Wan' some 'ime awone," Jeannie admitted. "You, back oonigh'?"

Lex nodded, combing the hair out of Jeannie's face with her fingers. "Sure. We'll come back tonight." She leaned down and kissed her sister-in-law's forehead. "Have them call if you want us back sooner."

" 'kay." Jeannie closed her eyes, exhausted by the emotional ordeal.

WHEN LEX PULLED the rental car onto their street, she noticed a black limousine parked in front of Jeannie's house. She turned to Anna Leigh, who was in the seat beside her. "Do you have any idea who that is?"

"No, I surely don't," Anna Leigh answered. She turned slightly to speak to Amanda, who was in the back next to the baby's carseat. "Mandy? Do you know anything about a limousine?"

Amanda shook her head. "Nope."

They stayed silent until Lex pulled into the driveway. Not long after, Michael and Jacob drove in beside them.

Lex had already gotten out of the car and was on her way up to the house, where a man and woman stood on the steps. Both middle-aged, the man was dressed in an expensive black suit, while the woman wore a gray linen skirt and matching top. "Excuse me, can we help you with something?" she asked them.

The man walked over to her, the woman trailing behind. "Who the hell are you?"

"Hello, Harrison, Veronica. I wasn't expecting you for a few days," Michael said, moving past Lex and holding out his hand. "I'd like for you to meet my daughter-in-law, Lexington Walters. Lex, this is Harrison and Veronica Rivers, Frank's parents."

Lex offered her hand, surprised when she was ignored. "I'm sorry for your loss, Mr.—"

"Daughter-in-law? How's that possible?" Harrison boomed. He looked back at Amanda, who held Lorrie. "You can't mean? That's ludicrous, Cauble." He put his hands on his hips. "Where have you been, anyway? We've just come from the airport and expected someone to be here."

Michael took a step back, confused by the man's ire. He and Harrison Rivers weren't friends, but they had always been at least civil to each other. "I'm sorry about that, Harrison. We were at the hospital chapel, attending the service for Frank. Had we known you were on the way, we'd have postponed it so that you could—"

"What the hell do you mean, Frank's service? And why at the hospital?"

Jacob moved to stand behind his son. "Mr. Rivers, Jeannie wasn't well enough to travel to a large service, so we had a small gathering at the chapel, where she would be able to attend. As a matter of fact, the urn—"

"Now wait just a goddamned minute! Did you say urn?" Harrison leaned into Michael's face. "You had my son *cremated*? Who the hell made that decision?"

"It was Jeannie's decision, Harrison. After all, she was his wife," Michael explained, getting angrier by the moment. "Not like you seemed to care, traipsing all over Europe."

Harrison glared at his in-law. "Where's the urn now?"

"In Jeannie's hospital room. She wanted it with her."

"What? Is that some sort of sick joke?" Harrison made a point of glaring at Amanda. "One of your daughters is a queer, and the other one's some sort of necrophiliac?"

He was about to say something more when Jacob reached for his arm. "Mr. Rivers, please, I think we all need to calm down."

Harrison jerked his arm away, almost causing Jacob to fall. "This is none of your concern, old man!"

Michael lunged for Harrison. "Hey!" He felt arms grab him from behind and struggled wildly to break free. When his elbow connected with something solid, he was quickly released.

"Ugh," Lex groaned, falling back away from the melee. She had thought she was helping to keep Michael out of trouble until his elbow slammed into her nose, causing it to bleed. She landed on her rear, a few feet away.

"You son of a bitch!" Michael yelled. He was about to punch the larger man in the face when they were both hit with a stream of water.

Anna Leigh trained the hose on her son. "If you're going to act like children, then perhaps it's best we treat you that way," she yelled over their shouts. Once she was convinced that the would-be fight was over, she turned off the hose.

"Are you all right, Lex?" Amanda knelt beside her wife, who was trying to control her bleeding nose. She would have tried to help, but she was still holding Lorrie, who slept through the entire scene.

Michael turned and saw Lex sitting on the ground. "Oh, no. Not again," he said, referring to a time in the past that he punched Lex in the face, thinking that she was after Amanda's money. He ignored a sputtering Harrison and joined his daughter. "I'm sorry, Lex. I guess that's two you owe me now, isn't it?" He pulled out a clean handkerchief and handed it to his daughter-in-law. "Is it broken?"

"I don't think so. Just caught me at the right angle." Lex accepted the handkerchief and held it to her face. "If you keep this up," she joked, "I'll start to think you don't like me." She looked over his shoulder at Anna Leigh. "Nice shot with the garden hose."

"Thank you." Anna Leigh swatted Michael on the arm. "Take Mr. and Mrs. Rivers inside, and the two of you get dried off. I'll expect you to be a good host."

"Yes, ma'am." Michael trudged back to the house, gesturing for Frank's parents to follow him.

"And as for you two," Anna Leigh told the two women, "Mandy, give me the baby, and then take Lexington upstairs to get cleaned up. I'm sure it's not as bad as it looks, but you really need to get that shirt soaking before the stain sets." She referred to Lex's pale gray shirt, which was now liberally stained with blood.

"Yes, ma'am." Amanda did as she was told, then helped Lex to her feet. They both saluted the older woman and hiked into the house.

"OW!"

"Hold still, you big baby." Amanda grabbed Lex's chin to keep her head from moving away. "I thought you said it didn't hurt." They were in the master bathroom, where she stood over Lex, who sat on the edge of the tub.

Lex tried to twist out of her lover's grasp. "It didn't, until you started scrubbing it so damned hard." She reached out and took hold of Amanda's hands. "What are you so pissed off about? It wasn't my fault."

"I know that. And I'm not pissed off, I'm just trying—" Amanda stopped. She *had* been scrubbing the blood from Lex's face harder than necessary. "I'm sorry." She leaned over and placed a light kiss on the tip of her wife's nose. "Forgive me?"

Pulling Amanda's hands to her lips, Lex kissed them. "Nothing to forgive. But you want to tell me what's got your britches all in a twist?"

Amanda laughed. Sometimes the little things that Lex said were just too cute. "Frank's dad."

"We've heard worse from folks before. Why now?"

"He's always been a bit pompous, but he's never been actually mean before." Amanda started to open the snaps on Lex's western shirt. "He usually just said hello, and then went along and took care of his business. He didn't go out of his way to be hurtful."

Lex sat quietly while Amanda removed her shirt, and watched as she placed it in the sink to soak. "Maybe it's because he's hurting, too. The man just lost his only son, then flew halfway across the world, only to find out the funeral was over." She gingerly touched her nose and was thankful it had stopped bleeding.

"Maybe." Amanda picked up the tee shirt she had brought in from the bedroom. "Arms up."

Although she was more than capable of dressing herself, Lex allowed Amanda to slip the shirt over her head and pull it down her body. She knew that her lover needed something to do while she talked or she'd get even more upset. Once the shirt was on to Amanda's satisfaction, Lex stood up. "Thanks."

"You're welcome." Amanda felt a little ridiculous over her earlier behavior, but was heartened when she was enveloped in a strong hug. "Can we just stay like this forever?"

"I wish." But with a final squeeze, Lex pulled away. She bent her head forward and captured Amanda's lips, prolonging the kiss as long as possible. When they at last broke apart, she held one of her lover's hands and led her through the bedroom and into the hallway. "But I think we better get downstairs, just in case your grandmother needs to break out the garden hose again."

Hearing voices, they followed the sound into the formal living room. There they found the Rivers sharing a loveseat with Harrison wearing a towel around his neck and his suit coat and tie missing. At a right angle to the loveseat, Michael sat in a matching chair, similarly clad.

"I understand that, Harrison, believe me. But that's still no reason to go off like you did." Michael noticed the two women standing in the doorway, and he stood up. "Lex, Amanda. Come in and sit down."

Amanda led the way, but made it a point to not look at Harrison as she and Lex sat on the leather sofa directly across from their guests. "I'm sorry it took us so long."

"That's fine, sweetheart." Michael waited until Lex was seated before he addressed her. "How's the nose? Should I be expecting a lawsuit?"

Lex laughed, even though the motion caused her face to ache. "Not this time, Michael. But if I were you, I'd be careful the next time you let me saddle your horse."

Jacob and Anna Leigh entered the room at that moment, each carrying a tray. His held the coffee carafe and mugs, while hers contained stacks of small sandwiches. "That sounds like a good trade-off," Jacob teased, placing his tray on the wide coffee table in front of their guests. He winked at Lex. "Just make sure you take pictures when my son slides off the horse, and I'll be happy."

"Dad!" Michael shrugged his shoulders at Harrison and his wife. "Honestly, she'd never do anything like that." He turned back to Lex. "Would you?"

"Of course not, Michael." Lex accepted a cup of coffee from Jacob, nodding her thanks. "That could be dangerous for my horses." But her smile showed she was joking, and she looked across the room to make eye contact with each of the Rivers. Lex was determined not to let Harrison get away with his obnoxious attitude, if only to put him in his place because he'd upset Amanda. "Mr. Rivers, my *wife* tells me that you're an attorney. What area of law do you specialize in?"

Harrison almost spat out the bite of sandwich he had taken. "Your, ah, well, my firm handles corporate litigation, Ms. Walters. Did I understand correctly that you're a farmer?"

"Rancher, actually. We have a modest spread outside of Austin," Lex said as she took hold of Amanda's hand and pulled it into her lap.

Anna Leigh knew what Lex was doing. And even though she

enjoyed watching the pompous man squirm, she didn't want a repeat of what had happened outside earlier. "Veronica, that's a lovely outfit you're wearing. You must tell me where you got it."

"Oh, this?" The meek woman brushed her hands down the linen suit. "There's this quaint little shop right off Rodeo Drive, and—"

"For God's sake, woman," Harrison complained. "No one really gives a damn where you shop. We have more important issues to discuss. Like our granddaughter."

Michael leaned forward. He had a pretty good idea what Harrison was about to say, but was not prepared for the words that left the attorney's mouth.

"I'm sure Jeanne will be leaving the hospital soon, since there's not much else they can do for her. Am I correct?" At Michael's nod, Harrison continued, "Have you decided which nursing home you'll have your daughter placed in?"

"What? Why?" Michael asked, completely confused.

"Well, you all have lives back in Texas, and I'm sure you need to get back to them. It's obvious that in her present condition, Jeanne cannot stay in this house. It'll be much easier for us to take care of our granddaughter if her mother is placed in a home nearby."

Amanda didn't like where the conversation was going, and she really didn't care for the tone in Harrison's voice. "And what makes you think that *you'll* be taking care of Lorrie?"

He looked at her as if she were an idiot. "You don't think your sister can, do you? We're the only family here that the baby has that's capable of taking care of her."

"I hate to break this to you, Mr. Rivers, but Amanda and I are legally responsible for Lorrie's well-being, at least until Jeannie gets back on her feet." Lex released Amanda's hand and placed her arm across her lover's shoulders. "We're her guardians."

"What? Impossible!"

Jacob piped up and said, "It's all legal, Harrison. Lex is right."

"Just exactly what kind of idiot would set up something like that?" Harrison yelled, his face turning red.

"Your son," Michael explained. "He and Jeannie took care of all the paperwork months ago, once they found out she was expecting. They knew that Lex and Amanda would give their child all the love and protection she needed, should anything happen to them."

Jacob said, "I'd like to remind you that my granddaughter is fully capable of making decisions. Just because she's physically incapacitated at this time doesn't mean she can't make decisions for her child. She's the mother, and she decides."

Harrison stood up, pulling his wife up with him. "We'll just see about that. There's no way in hell I plan on letting a grandchild of mine be raised by the likes of them! Come along, Veronica." He practically dragged her behind as he stormed from the room.

"Thank you for having us. I'm sorry," Veronica whispered to Anna Leigh right before the front door closed behind them.

Michael stood and removed the towel from around his neck. "That went well, didn't it?" When he didn't get an answer from anyone else in the room, Michael tossed the towel on the chair he had vacated. "I'm sorry you had to listen to Harrison's bullshit. The man has obviously got his priorities out of whack." His in-law's words haunted Michael. *It wasn't that long ago that I would have been agreeing with him. Am I that much better than he is, just because I've finally had my eyes opened?* "If you'll excuse me, I've got some arrangements to make so that we can bring Jeannie home."

"Speaking of arrangements," Lex said, "I think we need to talk about where Jeannie will be staying." Lex had her own ideas, but she wanted to give Jeannie's family a chance to talk about all the options. "I don't think she should be put into a nursing home, just because of her condition."

Jacob traded glances with his wife. "We talked about that in the kitchen, and we agree with you, Lex. We think that she'd be better off with family. I suppose we could have the downstairs living room at our home renovated into a bedroom."

"You could, or we could have the office cleared out in the ranch house and turn it into a bedroom. It wouldn't take as much work, and—"

Amanda cut in, "And I could take a leave of absence from the real estate office and take care of her." Her guilt over being jealous of Jeannie's new baby made her want to do something to help.

Lex turned to look at her wife. "We can also hire a nurse and a physical therapist. Jeannie's going to need more than what we can give her, you know."

"Maybe. But I think she'd feel a lot better with her family taking care of her than some stranger." Amanda didn't know why her partner was being so stubborn about this. Didn't she understand why Amanda had to take care of her sister? It was as if Lex was determined to undermine her efforts to do penance.

Standing up, Lex dusted off her slacks, even though there was nothing on them. She knew there was no sense in arguing with Amanda over this. They'd have plenty of time later to do that. "If it's okay with you, I'll call Martha and have her start clearing out the ranch office. Unless you'd like me to have her organize the revamping of your living room?"

"No, Lex," Jacob said. "I think that the ranch would be a better place for Jeannie. She seems to have bonded with you during this time, and being closer to you might be just the thing she needs. That is, if you don't mind," Jacob admitted. "It would take longer to change our living room into a bedroom for her than we have time for, I'm afraid."

"All right, then. I'll just go upstairs and get my cell phone and let you know what Martha says." Hurt by her partner's attitude, Lex left the room, leaving a quizzical Amanda behind.

"Is it just me, or did she just practically ignore my offer to take care of Jeannie?" Amanda asked her grandparents, who sat across from her on the loveseat. For some reason, she thought about what Ellie had said about Lex. *"She lords it over you like some kind of—"* *No, she doesn't. She's just concerned about Jeannie, and is trying to help the family out any way she can. I should be grateful that Lex is so caring.*

The distraught look on Amanda's face caused Anna Leigh to clear her throat. "Mandy? Is everything all right?"

"What? Oh, right." Amanda straightened up in her seat and brushed the hair out of her eyes. "I'm sorry. I guess I was just thinking about what Lex said. I don't know why she seemed so dead set against me taking care of my own sister. I guess she's afraid that if I do, I won't have enough time for her."

"I don't think that's the case at all." Jacob took both of Anna Leigh's hands in his and held them close. "Being a nurse for someone full-time, even if you love them dearly, can take a lot out of a person. I wasn't as incapacitated after my auto accident as Jeannie is now, yet your poor grandmother nearly killed herself by taking care of me. I believe that Lex is just afraid that you'll do the same thing and is trying to prevent that."

"Oh." Amanda had the decency to be embarrassed by her uncharitable thoughts. "I didn't think of it that way, Grandpa." *Guess I have an apology to make.* She was about to get up and go find Lex when she heard the baby's cries. "Sounds like someone is ready for a meal." She stood and started out of the room. "I'll take care of Lorrie, if you two want to sit and relax for a bit."

Anna Leigh snuggled closer to her husband. "We have the room to ourselves for a change, handsome. Got any ideas?"

"I've got several, but most of them would embarrass the kids," Jacob murmured, leaning over and covering her lips with his.

Chapter Fourteen

TIRED OF SWINGING the mop over the impeccably clean floors, Terence locked it away in the janitorial closet. He knew that Liz wanted him to keep an eye on her daughter's hospital room, but he was afraid that someone would start to notice if he kept cleaning the floor nearby. On his way back from the closet, he thought he heard a sound, and stopped outside of her door. He heard the sound again, and opened the door and peered inside.

The woman lying on the bed was trying to write. There was a notepad on the rollaway table in front of her, but it kept sliding away every time she put her pen on the page. She cried out in frustration, then threw the pen to the corner of the room.

Terence felt sorry for her. Given the way she moved, she was obviously partially paralyzed. Looking around to make sure no one was watching, he stepped into the room. "Excuse me, miss?"

Jeannie turned her head and glared at the interruption. "Go 'way," she slurred.

"I'm sorry, it's just that I heard you and wanted to make sure you were okay." Terence took a few more steps into the room, but stayed far enough away that he wouldn't frighten the woman. *Liz never told me her daughter was so beautiful. I can't believe the way she spoke about her, like she didn't matter anymore just because she was ill.* "Is there something I can do to help you?"

"No." Feeling bad because of her inability to speak clearly, Jeannie didn't want to talk any more than was necessary, especially to someone she didn't know.

With a few more steps, Terence moved around the bed and picked up the pen. "Are you sure? I mean, if you need something written, I'll be glad to help you."

Jeannie shook her head the best she could. She watched as he carefully placed the pen on top of the paper. His kindness to a virtual stranger surprised her, but she was unable to articulate her appreciation.

"Well, if there's nothing I can do for you, I guess I'll be going." Terence picked up the call button and placed it in the hand he had seen throw the pen. "If you need anything, just buzz the nurse. That's what they get paid for." With a wink, he slipped out of the room, closing the door behind him.

Outside the door, Terence heard voices coming down the hall. He hurried the other direction until he was safely in the emergency stairwell. "I can't do this." He sank to the top step and buried his head in his hands. "Liz is a lunatic, and I've been helping her ruin the lives of good people. Lord knows what she's going to do to that lovely woman in there, just because she doesn't fit into her plans." The more he learned of Liz's dementia, the more he wanted as far away from her as possible. When he first met her at the asylum, he thought that the older woman was just a pawn in someone else's game, and would be easy to control. As soon as she was out, Liz proved to be a lot smarter, and scarier, than he ever considered. The lure of money no longer held any interest for him. He lifted his head and took a deep breath. It was bad enough that the young woman he'd seen was partially paralyzed, but knowing that she'd just lost her husband and her own mother didn't care made Terence realize that he'd been on the wrong side all along. "I've got to get away from her, and I have to try to make things right."

MOVING JEANNIE AND Lorrie back to the ranch in Texas wasn't quite as difficult as Lex had thought it would be. The only problem had been a vicious argument between Michael and Frank's parents, who accused them all of trying to steal their only grandchild. Showing more diplomacy than anyone expected, Lex promised the Rivers that they would have ample opportunity to visit the infant, and she extended an open invitation for them to come out to the ranch any time they wanted. That seemed to appease them, and the rest of the transfer went off uneventfully.

When they reached Somerville, the family learned that Martha had done her usual flawless planning. Lex's office was now a small bedroom, complete with an electric hospital bed, a recliner to be used as a visitor's chair, and a remote-controlled television on a rack hanging from the ceiling in one corner of the room. The office desk had been relegated to the front corner of the den near the windows, and the computer and telephone jacks had been professionally moved.

After speaking to Lex before she left California, Martha also removed some of the furnishings from the sitting area of the master bedroom, put the extra furniture in storage, and made the space into a miniature nursery. She had left one of the chairs and a table with a lamp so that when Lorrie needed feeding in the middle of the night there would be a comfortable place to take care of her. Martha and Lex had agreed that Amanda would most likely balk at putting the baby in a separate room since she rarely relinquished control of Lorrie's care.

That's something that we're going to have to talk about. Lex stood on the front porch next to Martha while the ambulance attendants wheeled Jeannie into the ranch house. Amanda was already upstairs, ostensibly to put Lorrie down for a nap, but Lex thought that she just wanted to be alone with the baby. Michael was in Jeannie's room, and Jacob and Anna Leigh had just arrived and were getting out of their vehicle.

Martha couldn't help but notice the distance between Lex and Amanda since they'd returned, not to mention the dark circles underneath the eyes of the woman next to her. "You look like you have the world's troubles on your shoulders, Lexie. Is there something you'd like to talk about?"

The smile that Lex forced onto her face never reached those eyes. "To tell you the truth, I'm not too sure where to start." Lex nodded a greeting at Jacob and Anna Leigh, who passed them on the porch and went into the house. "I'm worried about Jeannie. She won't let the urn with Frank's ashes out of her sight. Do you think that's normal?"

Martha put her arm around Lex's waist, and the two of them looked off into the distance. The winter rye was already up, and the blanket of green in the wide field was a beautiful sight to behold. "Normal? No. Understandable, yes." She paused for a moment to gather the words that she thought Lex needed to hear. "Grief does strange things to folks, Lexie. You probably don't remember, but after your mama passed away, your father wouldn't let me change their bed linens. In the mornings, when I would come in to make the bed, I could tell by the way it was mussed that he'd slept on her side, hugging her pillow. Then, over a month later, he made me box up anything and everything that had to do with Mrs. Walters and store it away."

"Really?" Lex tried to remember, but her memories were vague. "The only thing I can remember is being angry at her for leaving, and then thinking that Dad put all her pictures and other things away to punish me for thinking like that." The old familiar hurt was coming back, something that she still couldn't fight. Lex rubbed her tired eyes with one hand. *Enough of that. Dredging up the past isn't going to help things now.* "Were you able to hire a nurse? I know Amanda said that she wanted to take of

Jeannie herself, but I think she's going to have her hands full with the baby."

Understanding the non sequitur, Martha said, "I sure did. I talked to Doc Anderson, and he suggested that I call the hospital. They gave me the name and number of a nurse who had recently retired, although she's only about my age."

Lex turned to face the housekeeper. "Are you hinting that you'd like to retire? Because if you are, I've...ow!" She rubbed her arm where Martha pinched her. "What?"

"For such a smart woman, you can be as dense as a forest sometimes. No, I'm not about to retire and let this beautiful house fall down. I have all the respect in the world for Amanda, but I also know that *you* wouldn't know what to do without me," Martha huffed. "What I meant was she was a little young to have retired. I've had her out to the house, and she'll gladly take the guest room and live out here full-time until Jeannie's condition has improved. Then she'll move back to town."

"That *is* good news. When does she start?"

"I told her next week. With all that's happened, I thought Jeannie would need a little time to get settled before meeting someone new."

Lex pulled Martha into a hug. "Thank you for taking care of all of this for us." She kissed the older woman on the cheek. "You're right, you know."

"About what?"

"We'd definitely not know what to do without you."

THERE WAS A knock on her hotel room door, and Liz looked up from her magazine. She was reclining on the bed, her legs daintily crossed and with nary a wrinkle in the expensive slacks suit she was wearing. When the knock sounded a second time, she took off her reading glasses and set them on the nightstand. With a final grumble about hotel security, she stood and crossed the room to answer the door. "Terence. What do you mean by disturbing me at this time of night?"

He checked his watch. *Two o'clock in the afternoon? What's up with her?* "I'm sorry, Liz, but I thought you might want to know—"

"You fool." She grabbed him by the front of his shirt and yanked him into her room, slamming the door behind them. "What have I told you about being discreet?"

Terence struggled out of her grasp. "Like you've been? Spending God knows how much a day on this room and all its perks?" The slap on his face wasn't expected, but he wasn't surprised, either. He backed away from Liz. "That wasn't necessary."

"Perhaps." Liz ignored his outraged look as she crossed the room to the bar and poured herself a drink from a crystal decanter. "Now that you've disturbed me, what is it that you want?" She sipped the caramel-colored liquid, enjoying how it burned its way down her throat.

"It's about your daughter."

"Amanda? What has that worthless clod Lexington Walters done with my baby this time?" Her calm demeanor broken, Liz's face turned red. "If she's hurt her in any way, I'll—"

"No!" Afraid that she might throw the glass in her hand, Terence hurried over and took the drink from Liz. He placed it back on the bar and attempted to lead her to a chair. "No, not her. Your other daughter. They've taken her from the hospital."

"Who has?" Liz's voice rose in pitch. "Where is she?"

"The family took the other daughter back to Texas. At least that's what the nurse on duty told me this morning when I happened by her empty room." Terence decided that he needed a drink. He was almost to the bar when something hit him in the back of the head. He turned around and picked up the magazine that Liz had tossed at him. "What is your problem?"

"This morning? Why wasn't I notified? My granddaughter, what about her? I need details, you worthless idiot!" She pushed by Terence on her way back to the bar. She picked up her glass and drained it in one swallow.

Terence poured himself a similar drink and tossed it back quickly. "Aren't you concerned about your daughter Jeannie?"

"Who cares about her? She's ruined and worth nothing to me now. But the baby, yes, the baby." Liz filled her glass again and moved to the window to look outside. "I can raise her in my own image, just as I wanted to do with my girls. But that spineless husband of mine kept interfering." With her back to Terence, her voice became softer. "We'll just see about who raises that child."

ELLIE THANKED THE cab driver, then turned and stared at the house she had grown up in. With the plain stucco exterior and red tiled roof, it looked like just about any other house on the block. They had moved there after her mother married her stepfather, so it was the only home she could really remember. She supposed that she had been happy growing up. Anthony treated her like his own, and even after William was born, he doted on his step-daughter. But still, Ellie had always felt that there was something missing from her life, and after the trip to Texas, she knew what it was. The family that she had found was more than she could have expected, and even her cranky cousin couldn't change the way she felt. *This isn't home anymore.*

Rolling her shoulders to relieve the tightness, Ellie strengthened the grip she had on her backpack and walked up the steps and back into her mother's house, perhaps for the last time. She was just glad she had spent the night in a motel and rested up before making the final leg of her journey.

"Tony, is that you?" a voice called from the rear of the house. "I thought you were out in the garage. I haven't—" Naomi Gordon almost dropped the plate she had been drying when she saw who stood in her living room. "Well. The prodigal returns."

The biting comment stung, but Ellie tried to ignore it. "Hi, Mom."

Naomi glared at her daughter, then turned and walked back into the kitchen. She didn't wait for Ellie to follow her because she knew her daughter. As expected, Ellie was only a few steps behind her. "Is that all you have to say? 'Hi, Mom'? I get only one phone call from you the entire time you're gone, and you show up in my house and 'hi, Mom,' me? I ought to kick you out of here like I did before," she carped, referring to when her daughter turned twenty-one and was struggling through college. Tired of supporting both children and a husband who rarely listened to her, Naomi had asked her daughter to leave. Only when Ellie was thirty-two and lost her job did Naomi allow her back into the house.

"Actually, that's one of the things I came back to talk to you about." Not certain how her mother would react, she stood by the kitchen entryway, far out of the woman's reach. "I've decided to move to Texas. I've just come back to get my things."

"Your things? Are you talking about those ratty old clothes and other junk? I threw them out when I didn't hear from you." Life's disappointments had worn Naomi down, and she took out her frustrations on anyone and everyone within her reach. Losing the only man she'd ever loved, she'd only married Anthony because he wanted a family and she had a daughter. He hadn't even cared whose child Ellie was, and Naomi had always considered Anthony weak because of it. She turned away from the sink and met her daughter's angry eyes. "I decided to turn your room into a sewing room, and your junk was just in my way."

Ellie fought the urge to knock some sense into her mother. "You didn't throw away my books, too, did you? I need those."

Her hands dropped to her sides and she clenched her fists. "Please tell me you at least saved my textbooks." Although it had taken her longer than most, Ellie had finished college when she was twenty-eight and had had a good job until she had been laid off. Now in between jobs, she hoped the market was better in Texas.

"Your father saved most of your stuff. We had a big fight over it, as a matter of fact." Bored with the conversation, Naomi returned to washing dishes. "He went through the trash and put your junk in the garage, not that I care."

Thank you, Dad. Ellie was going to miss her stepfather. He was the only reason she'd stayed around as long as she had. *Maybe I can talk him into coming to Texas to visit. I bet he'd like the ranch and my grandfather.* "I guess that this is goodbye then."

"I doubt it. You'll come running back home in no time, mark my words. But don't think I'll be taking you back into my house again. I've done my job raising you." Smug in her assumption, Naomi returned to her household chores, doing her best to ignore her daughter.

Even though she should have been used to her mother's attitude, the words still hurt. As she made her way to the garage, Ellie couldn't resist a parting shot. "Oh, by the way, Mother. I thought you should know that I'm gay." The gasp and the sound of a dropped dish breaking on the floor gave Ellie some wicked sense of satisfaction. *That felt better than I thought it would.*

She took her time in the garage, going through the boxes of things that were labeled with her name. When the door from the house opened, Ellie was surprised to see her stepfather. "Dad? It's early for you, isn't it?"

"Your mother called me at work and demanded that I take an early lunch and come home." Anthony met his daughter halfway, and they embraced in the cluttered garage. "Is what she said true?"

"Which part? About me leaving, or my being gay?"

"Either, I guess. Or both." He led her over to his "sitting area" by the workbench, where he had a small television and two lawn chairs so that he could enjoy sports programs without his wife's constant griping. Anthony reached under the workbench and opened a tiny refrigerator. "Want a beer?"

Ellie sat down and leaned back in the chair. "That would be great. Especially after talking with Mom."

They sat for several minutes, neither one of them speaking, and sipped from the cans of beer. Ellie studied her stepfather's profile in the dim light of the garage. At fifty-seven, his blond surfer looks and perpetual tan made him a handsome man. Not realizing she spoke aloud, Ellie asked, "Why have you stayed married to her for so long?"

"Your mom?" Anthony looked down at his feet and couldn't stop the smile that broke out on his face. "Because from that first moment I saw her, I was in love. And, no matter what she does or says, I can't help but love her still. Your mother was devastated by your father's death, El. The only reason she went on living was because she had you to take care of."

"And she throws that little fact in my face every chance she gets," Ellie mumbled. For as long as she could remember, her mother complained about having to raise children when she'd much rather have been doing something—anything—else.

Anthony touched her shoulder. "Please try to understand, sweetheart. Naomi was just a girl when she became pregnant with you. Her own parents disowned her and threw her out of their house. And when your father was killed, well, it was more than she could take. I'm not condoning her behavior toward you, El, but we're all adults now. Let the hurt stay in the past, where it belongs."

It would take more than a few words to heal the gash in Ellie's heart, where her mother continued to get in little digs every chance she got. But with a new life waiting for her in Texas, she knew that it would be a perfect opportunity to let her mother stew in the tiny cage of hate that she'd lived in for so many years. "I'll try. But that's a lot of years of pain." But she knew if she were ever going to live her own life, she'd have to do just that. Ellie wasn't sure why she was being so open with her dad. *Maybe it's the beer. I haven't eaten anything lately.* "She hates me for sure, now."

"Are you talking about you being gay?"

"Yeah. I'm sure her church has a lot of things to say about that." Ellie finished her beer and crumpled the can. She accepted another from Anthony with a nod. "Thanks. I can't believe you're out here talking to me."

He took a small sip of his beer. "Why? You're my daughter, aren't you? Yeah, maybe not of blood, but you know I love you like my own. You've always made me proud, Ellie, and I'm glad to get a chance to talk without any interference." Anthony leaned back in his chair, holding the beer between his hands on his stomach. "To tell you the truth, I was wondering when you'd figure it out."

"What?" Her head was spinning from what hat her stepfather had just said so casually.

"El, I'm not stupid, and I'm certainly not blind. I've lived in California my entire life; I went to college here. I know a gay or lesbian when I see one." He turned his head so that he could look at his daughter. "Are *you* okay with it?"

The conversation was getting too weird for Ellie. She quickly drained her beer, then threw the can into the recycling bin nearby. "I'm not sure, Dad. I really just figured it out in the last couple of days." *Nothing like a crush on a woman to wake up the hormones. I feel like such an idiot. I hope that Amanda can forgive me.* She stood and gestured to the stack of boxes. "If I give you an address, would you mind having these shipped to Texas for me?"

"Of course, El. I'll be glad to." Anthony stood, leaving his half-empty can on the workbench. "Most of your clothes are in a duffel bag in my closet. Let's go inside and get them."

"They are? Mom said she threw them out." Ellie embraced her stepfather. "Thanks, Dad."

When they pulled apart, Anthony reached into his back pocket and came up with an envelope. "You're welcome, El. Just remember that I'll always be here for you, no matter what."

She accepted the envelope and looked inside. "This looks like a lot of money. I can't take this." Ellie tried to hand it back to her father.

"Sure you can. It's yours, anyway." Anthony pushed the money to Ellie again. "Let's just say it's an advance on your inheritance, before you mother can spend it on her church."

Ellie fought back tears at her stepfather's generosity. As long as she could remember, Anthony had been like this. Kind and charitable, he was the opposite of his wife. "I'll pay you back, I promise."

"Just enjoy your life, El. That's all I ask."

When they walked into the house, they were met by Naomi who stood in the kitchen with her arms crossed over her chest. "It's about time you two got back in here. What were you doing out there for so long?"

"Getting drunk," Ellie sniped. She sighed. "I'm sorry, Mom. I was just going through my things."

"You were never this disrespectful before, Eleanor. I think those people corrupted you."

Ellie moved past her mother and into the living room. Wanting to hurt her mother as much as she'd been hurt, she turned around. "Actually, I'm more myself now than I ever was. They've shown me nothing but love and acceptance, something that's always been lacking in your house. And you want to know the sad thing? My grandfather sends his love to you, too."

"I have no use for those people," Naomi ground out, ignoring her husband's hand on her arm. "They made no effort to find me after William was killed. I was left alone, with a child to raise. Do you have any idea how hard that was?"

"Of course I do, Mom. You've never let me forget it. And as for being left alone, it's not their fault. They didn't even know you existed, much less that you were pregnant with their son's child. Do you know how hard it was on Grandpa Travis when I showed up at his door? You've blamed them, and me, my entire life, when you were the only one who had all the information."

Ellie started to say more, but another round of her mother's version of martyrdom wasn't going to get her to where she needed to be. Ellie wearily shook her head and sighed. Then she went into her parents' bedroom and took from the closet the duffel that her father had packed for her. She opened it and was able to fit her backpack inside so that she only had the one bag to carry. "Thanks again, Dad." Her eyes softened when she saw the regret and love on her stepfather's face. She took one last look at her mother, straightened her posture, and turned defiantly away from her mother's accusing eyes.

When Ellie started for the front door, her mother twisted out of Anthony's grasp. "If you go back to that Gomorra, don't you dare come back!" When her daughter ignored her, she yelled, "Where do you think you're going?"

"Home." Ellie walked out of the house and out of her mother's life. She knew that she'd never come back, and her only regret was that she'd probably never see her father again.

AFTER ONLY TWO days, Jeannie was getting used to the ranch. Although she enjoyed Martha's company, she lived for when Lex took time off during the day to come and visit. The sound of boots on the hardwood floor signaled her sister-in-law's arrival, and Jeannie wished that she had a mirror so that she could see how she looked before Lex came into the room. Feeling a presence at the door, she turned her head and broke into a lopsided smile.

"Now isn't that a beautiful sight?" Lex walked in and sat on the edge of Jeannie's bed. She removed her black western hat and tossed it in the chair next to them. "How are you feeling?"

"Pine," Jeannie managed. She held out her hand and was happy when Lex accepted it. "You?"

Lex squeezed Jeannie's hand. She had to admit that the several trips a day she made into the house were worth it. The bedridden woman had really made remarkable progress, and she hoped that she'd had a little bit to do with it. "Tired, but okay. We're filling the barn with hay, and I don't remember it being this much work before." It also felt good to talk to someone about her day. Amanda was so busy with the baby, they barely spoke two words to each other, and Lex was beginning to feel the loss. But she felt that Lorrie needed Amanda more than she did, so she kept quiet about her feelings. "As a matter of fact, I've got a contractor coming out tomorrow, and he's going to pour a concrete walkway between here, the barns, and Martha's house. I thought you might want to get out of the house sometime."

"Weally?" Although half of her face was misshapen, it couldn't disguise the joy on Jeannie's face.

"Really." Getting the reaction she was hoping for, Lex was proud of her decision. She had been meaning to have some sort of sidewalk poured to Martha's house for a long time, but had never gotten around to it. Jeannie's condition provided her with the motivation, and she was glad. "We got a call from your new nurse this morning. She asked if she could come out to meet you before she starts to work. Would that be all right with you?"

Jeannie nodded. She was nervous about the nurse, but didn't want Martha to wear herself out taking care of her. "Wiwl ew?"

It took Lex a moment to figure out what Jeannie meant. "Do you want me to be here too?" When Jeannie nodded, Lex smiled. "Of course I will. I need to make sure she's up to standards, don't I?"

GETTING OFF THE plane in Los Angeles, Ellie weighed her options. She could book the next available flight back to Texas, or she could do what she really wanted. After a brief uncertainty, the small-framed woman hoisted her duffel bag over her shoulder and pushed through the heavy crowd.

Once she reached her destination, Ellie struggled through another moment of indecision. Before she rapped her knuckles on the faded wooden door, she looked around her. The thirty-year-old apartment complex had never been much to look at from the outside, but since her last visit almost eight years prior, it had definitely fallen into a state of disrepair. Steeling herself for another disappointment, she knocked.

It wasn't long before the door opened and a young man with blond, spiked hair answered. The several piercings in his eyebrows and nose couldn't obviate the fact that he was handsome, and the torn blue tee shirt and multicolored board shorts he wore looked good on him. He stared at the woman standing in his doorway for a long moment, then smiled. "El?"

"Hey there, snotface." The old familiar nickname came unbidden to Ellie's lips, and she hoped that her coming hadn't been a mistake. The last time she'd seen her brother, harsh words were spoken that she had regretted almost from the moment they left her mouth. They hadn't spoken since.

He pulled her into the apartment, then hugged Ellie as if his life depended on it. "Damn, Sis, I don't think I've ever been so happy to see anyone in my life." William "Billy" Gordon continued to rock with his sister in his arms, then he pulled back and looked at her closely. "Where's your Bible? I thought you and Mom didn't leave home without one."

"I guess I probably deserved that." Ellie dropped her duffel and reached up to touch her brother's eyebrow. "Just how many holes *do* you have in your head?"

His bright eyes sparkled. "No more than you need, probably." Billy hugged her again, then drew Ellie into his living room. The furniture, while not new, was in good taste, much different from what the outside of the building led one to believe. A black leather sofa and chairs were surrounded by chrome and glass tables, and the focal point of the room was a state of the art sound system and video center. He waited until Ellie sat on one end of the sofa and then took the other. "What brings you to, I think you called it, 'the bastions of hell'? Did you get so bored in San Diego that you had to travel all the way to L.A.?"

"No, Billy. Nothing like that." Ellie stared down at her denim-covered knee and picked at a loose thread. "I just came by to tell you that I'm moving."

"Really? Did your transfer to the Southern Baptist Convention go through?"

The retort hurt, and Ellie bit down a scathing reply. When she and her mother last visited Billy, they were shocked at his appearance and the fact that he'd quit his job as a manager of a restaurant to open a surfboard shop with his best friend. It was bad enough that he'd moved away from where they influenced his decisions, but when they found out his best friend was a woman, and that they lived together "in sin," it was more than the two self-righteous women could stand. "I'm sorry, Billy. For then, and for all the other times." Raising her head, Ellie wanted to take back the last fifteen years, time she spent under her mother's shadow, and wished that she could just wave a magic wand and remove the hurt and pain she'd caused the man beside her.

He must have heard the remorse in her voice, because Billy let the shield of anger that he used to protect himself fall. He sighed. "Peggy left last year. I was sure that would make you and Mom very happy." They had warned him that not being married would allow his "friend" to leave whenever she wanted, and he'd only be hurt in the long run.

"No, it doesn't. It doesn't make me happy at all." Looking around the clean room, Ellie spoke very quietly. "At least you had the guts to face up to Mom and live your own life. I'm so damned proud of you, little brother. Prouder than you'll probably ever realize."

Billy leaned over and peered into his sister's eyes. "Who are you, and what have you done with my sister?" He fell back when she playfully pushed him away.

"Wise guy." She took a deep breath, and prayed that what she was about to say wouldn't get her thrown out. "I found my birth father's family, Billy. Or, I guess you could say, *my* family." His nod gave her the courage to go on. "My grandfather is about the nicest guy you'd ever want to meet. And my cousin..." She paused, thinking about Lex. The woman absolutely infuriated her, but she thought that was more because of how Amanda felt about her than Lex's personality or actions. "My cousin owns a ranch, if you can believe that. She's tall, dark, and extremely full of herself." Here Ellie grinned. "But she's also loyal and loving."

"Sounds like a great lady." Intrigued by the look on his sister's face, Billy tapped her on the leg. "And?"

"What do you mean, and?"

"Come on, El. Don't forget I've known you forever. What else aren't you telling me?"

"She's gay." Ellie retreated to the furthest point of the sofa, afraid of her brother's reaction. "Lex lives on the ranch with her partner, Amanda." When her brother was silent for too long, Ellie stood up. "Aren't you going to say anything? I just told you that my cousin is a lesbian."

Billy met his sister's eyes, a small smile forming on his lips. "What am I supposed to say, El? I think the important thing here is, how do *you* feel about it?"

"What?"

"I bet that threw your little world into a tailspin, didn't it? You and Mom, always preaching against something, whether it was marriage before sex, say no to drugs, or may all the queers rot in hell." He jumped to his feet also. "Actually, the reason that Peggy left was because I asked her to. I found her shooting up in the kitchen one morning. Nothing I said or did mattered to her, because she had her drugs." Billy walked over to the entertainment center and picked up a framed photograph. The two people smiling back at him were covered with seaweed and sand, and couldn't have looked happier. "She wouldn't stop, El. I found out that her boyfriend was also her supplier, and when I confronted her with it, she moved in with him."

Ellie stepped up behind Billy and put her arms around him. "I'm sorry."

He put the frame back where it came from and turned around. "So, I did the marriage before sex, and said no to drugs. And now you're telling me that your cousin is gay? That's pretty funny."

"Want to hear something even funnier?"

"I could use a good laugh about now." Billy fingered the rings in his eyebrow. "Think I'd look good with purple hair?"

"Maybe. How 'bout me?" Ellie waited until she had his full attention. "Think I look good as a lesbian?"

Chapter Fifteen

BULLDOZERS SHOVED LOADS of dirt and upturned trees, while two men in business suits stood by and watched. Billings chewed on his cigar and gestured to the ongoing construction. "Just how long is this supposed to take, Wilson? We're so far behind schedule now that we've already lost hundreds of thousands of dollars."

"I'm sorry, sir. Things just haven't gone our way. There was a problem with the permits, and then with the zoning. It cost more than I expected."

"I'm not asking for excuses, Wilson; I'm expecting results. This could be the deal that gets me, I mean, us, the recognition in the organization that we deserve." The ring of his cell phone cut off any other ravings. He reached into his coat pocket and took out the device. "Billings here."

Wilson watched as his boss' face lost all color. *This isn't good.*

"No, sir. It's just taking a little bit longer than we anticipated. I'm sure that if we're given a little bit more time, we can pick up the adjacent land that we need. Yes, I understand that. You're right, sir. This area just screams for a resort. No, I don't. The land south of here is perfect, but—" Billings closed his phone. "I'm sure you guessed who that was."

"Yes, Mr. Billings. I have a pretty good idea." Only the head of the organization could instill such fear into a man like Billings. Andrew felt his own blood run cold at what could have caused the reaction.

Billings looked around until he was certain that all the construction workers were out of earshot. "We need that land. No later than next week."

"I don't see how, sir. That woman doesn't want to sell. And to tell you the truth, she scares me a little." Andrew hated the admission, but there was something about the fire in the rancher's eyes that disturbed him.

"Bullshit! She's a woman, you twit." Billings spit a soggy

chunk of cigar between Andrew's shoes. "If she won't sell, then maybe her next of kin will. Get on it, or we'll be contacting *your* next of kin." He flicked what was left of the cold tobacco at his assistant and stomped away.

AMANDA SAT IN the dark den, the solitude almost more than she could handle. Earlier, Martha had found her upstairs and relieved her of Lorrie so that Jeannie could spend some quality time with her baby, leaving Amanda with nothing to do. She debated barging into her sister's room and taking Lorrie back, but immediately felt guilty at her thoughts. Hearing someone come up onto the front porch, she rose to see who it could be. Opening the door, she was surprised to see a sheepish Michael.

"Hello, sweetheart. I thought I'd stop by and see how everything was going." When he saw the sad expression on Amanda's face, Michael moved into the entry and enveloped her in a hug. "What's the matter?"

"It's stupid." The loss that Amanda felt any time Lorrie wasn't in her arms was something that she was ashamed of, and she certainly didn't want to try to explain it to her father. "I thought that you had a full day scheduled."

Michael had an idea as to his daughter's problem, especially seeing her without the baby. But he accepted the subject change amicably, and the two of them moved into the den and got comfortable on the sofa. "I was supposed to work all day, but they called and asked to have it rescheduled for next week." He had been retained by the Somerville school district to take the children's individual pictures, but a last-minute field trip caused them to cancel. "Is that Martha's voice I hear?"

"Yes. She told me that I needed a break, so she's in Jeannie's room with Lorrie." Amanda's tone spoke volumes of her opinion on the matter. "I guess now I have the afternoon free."

"Excellent! I came out to see how your sister is doing, but I think that can wait. How about taking a ride with me?" Although Michael had gotten better at riding, he'd promised Lex that he wouldn't go out alone, and he was itching to get back into the saddle.

Having become an accomplished horsewoman in the past year herself, Amanda understood her father's excitement where riding was concerned. "That's the best offer I've had all day." She stood and gestured at her simple skirt and top. "Just let me go get changed."

A short time later, Amanda was back downstairs, and the

pair was about to leave the house when the phone rang. After the third ring, it stopped, and Martha came out of Jeannie's room in search of Amanda.

"Hello, Michael. It's nice to see you here." Martha turned to Amanda. "I'm sorry to bother you, but you have a call from some bank in Los Angeles. I thought you might want to take it."

"Thanks, Martha." Amanda kissed the older woman on the cheek before going over to sit at the desk in the corner of the den. She picked up the line on the phone that was flashing. "Hello? This is Amanda Cauble. Really? No, I...yes. Thank you. Of course, I understand." She placed the handset back on the cradle and turned the chair around. "They've decided to launch an investigation into my missing funds. I wonder why now, instead of when we were there."

"That's wonderful. And they didn't mention why?"

Amanda shook her head. "He didn't say, only that he was sorry about the earlier misunderstanding."

"Excuse me." Michael looked first at his daughter and then at Martha. "What's this about 'missing funds'?"

The two women exchanged looks, then Amanda took the lead. "I'll explain while we're riding, if that's okay. I really need to get out of the house for a while." She watched as her father thought about arguing, then resigned himself to waiting. "Thanks, Daddy."

"Don't thank me just yet, young lady. I'm not giving up, just postponing the inevitable."

Once they were out on the trail, Michael turned a bit sideways in his saddle so he could easily see Amanda's face as she rode beside him. "I think I've been more than patient, Amanda. Would you kindly explain to me these so-called missing funds?" He listened patiently as she related all the recent goings-on.

After swearing her father to secrecy, Amanda also recounted Lex's problems, and how it all seemed to happen close to the same time. "So, now you know. But please don't let Lex find out that I told you. She's upset enough."

"Don't worry, I'll keep quiet." Michael's sharp business mind raced, even as he tried to appear nonchalant about the matter.

The horses plodded along quietly for a time, their presence not even disturbing the birds or other animals along the path. Finally, Michael spoke again. "If I didn't know any better, I'd swear that this sounded like something your mother might pull."

"I hate to admit it, but I thought so, too. I suppose it's a good thing she's locked up in that hospital." Amanda didn't like feeling that way about her mother, but she slept better at night knowing that Elizabeth could do no harm where she was.

LEX RETURNED FROM unloading hay, only to find the baby with Jeannie, and Amanda nowhere to be found. She couldn't find Martha either and was about to head upstairs for a shower when there was a knock at the front door. Looking down at her dusty, hay-covered appearance, Lex cursed as she went to see who it could be. She was taken aback by a short, balding man in an expensive suit, wearing dark shades and chewing on an unlit cigar. "Yes?"

"You Lexington Walters?"

"That's right." Already Lex had formed an intense dislike for the toad-like man. "And you are?"

He pulled a handkerchief from his jacket and wiped at his perspiring head, even though the outside temperature was moderate. "My name's not important, but my business with you is. Do you have someplace we can speak privately?"

Lex sighed. She didn't have the time or the inclination to play games. Hot and dirty, all she wanted was a shower, and then maybe a little one-on-one time with her partner, if she could find her. Stepping out onto the porch and closing the front door behind her, Lex leaned against the doorframe. "So, talk."

Wilson was right. This bitch is obnoxious. If we didn't need that land so bad, I'd love to teach her a few manners. Billings had decided to make a visit to the rancher himself, since his associate was too much of a weakling to handle the job to his satisfaction. He removed a checkbook from his interior jacket pocket. "Let me get right to the point, then. I've come about the property you recently acquired, and am prepared to pay you three hundred percent over what you invested. That's quite an offer, don't you think?"

"It would be, if I were interested in selling." Lex pushed her hat further back onto her head. "Why the sudden interest in that piece of land? It's mostly trees, scrub brush, and creek. Not really worth farming or ranching." She knew that it also had good grazing, but only someone who had been deep on the property would know that.

"Then I'm doing you a favor by offering to take it off your hands, aren't I?"

"Nope. You're just annoying me and keeping me from a nice long shower." She reached for the doorknob, but her progress was halted when the man grabbed her arm.

"Listen to me, lady. I'm only making this offer once."

Jerking her arm free, Lex glared at him. "Good. Then I'll only have to turn you down once." She stepped closer, until there was very little space between them. "If you touch me again, I'll rip your arm off and shove it up your ass."

"Don't you dare threaten me, woman. Take what we're offering or you won't like the consequences." Billings took the cigar from his mouth and used it to point at Lex. "I'm not someone you want to mess with."

"That makes two of us." Lex grabbed him by the lapels of his coat and shoved him off the porch. "Get off my land before I shoot you as a trespasser."

Billings backed to his car, never taking his eyes off the rancher. "You've just made a very big mistake, Walters." He got into his luxurious rental car and then spun away, the vehicle kicking up gravel and dust in its wake.

Lex took a final look and then went into the house. She assumed he was working for the man she had met at the auction and wasn't too worried. She hated pushy brokers, and couldn't understand the appeal of the property that she wasn't even certain she was going to keep.

ONCE EVERYONE HAD settled down for bed, Amanda stepped out of the bathroom, drying her hair with a towel. Lorrie must have become fussy while she showered, because Lex was stretched out on the bed with the infant snuggled on her chest. The sight almost brought tears to Amanda's eyes, and she stood in the doorway, not wanting to break the spell. For a moment, she imagined that the child her lover held was theirs, and she knew more than anything that was what she wanted, even though Lex wasn't ready.

Lex turned her head to make eye contact with her partner. "Did you have a good shower?"

Shaken from her reverie, Amanda tried to push down the hurt her previous thoughts had brought. "I sure did. At least I won't have to worry about you making me sleep on the sofa tonight."

"Nah, I'd never do that." Lorrie was asleep, so Lex carefully extended one arm out to her partner. "You've always been real good about letting me stay, no matter what."

The comment drew Amanda out of her sad mood, and she moved across the room to sit on the edge of the bed. "I have, huh? Are you saying that you've come to bed less than clean?"

"More times than I care to admit." Although her attention

was focused on Amanda, Lex continued to run one hand gently down Lorrie's back, soothing not only the sleeping infant, but herself. "Did you have a good ride with your dad today?" Lex had been downstairs in the kitchen bothering Martha when the two had come in, hugging and laughing, and Lex had been a bit jealous that it wasn't her with Amanda instead of Michael.

"We sure did. That reminds me, the bank in L.A. called back this afternoon. They've had a change of heart and plan on doing a full investigation into what happened to my trust."

Lex couldn't help but grin. "Imagine that." She had spent hours on the phone, both in California and back home, complaining and threatening not only the bank president, but several different people in the chain of command. *I guess something finally worked.*

Scooting closer to her lover, Amanda brushed her hand down Lex's face. "What's that look supposed to mean?"

"Hmm?"

"You don't seem very surprised by the news, that's all."

"Oh." *Come clean, or dance around the subject?* "I, uh, kind of made a few phone calls in the last few days. That's all." The look on Amanda's face wasn't what Lex had been expecting.

"You what?" Amanda snapped off sharply, causing Lorrie, along with Lex, to flinch. "What did you do? Threaten someone?"

Lorrie started to cry, and Lex sat up and began to bounce her gently. "Shh. It's okay, little one." She raised her face to meet Amanda's angry glare. "Not so loud, Amanda. You're upsetting the baby."

Amanda rose to her feet and paced around the room. "It's okay that I'm upset, but you don't want me to upset the baby, is that it?" When Lex didn't answer, her pace quickened and her voice rose. "Dammit, Lex. I'm not some helpless little thing, you know. I'm perfectly capable of taking care of my own problems! You're always butting into my business. 'Poor little Amanda' can't do anything without her macho lover stepping in. Do you honestly think I couldn't have handled this?"

"Amanda, wait. It's not like that at all. I just—"

"You just wanted to ride in to the rescue, like you always do," Amanda snapped. Months of disappointments and days of stress had finally caught up to her. "Goddamn it! Let me live my life!" She stomped to the window and looked outside. "All my life, someone has tried to protect me. Well, it doesn't always work, does it?"

Lex put Lorrie into her crib before she stepped quietly behind Amanda, afraid to touch her. "I—"

"First, my father, then my grandfather!" Spinning around, Amanda was poised for a battle. "When I got older, I thought, 'Finally! Now I'll be in charge of my own life.' Then Frank came along when I was in high school, and he was even more protective than the two of them together." Her chest heaved from the exertion of her tantrum and Amanda used both hands to push Lex away from her. "He left me! Who's next? Grandpa? My father?" Her anger dissipated as quickly as it had flared, and then Amanda collapsed into her partner's arms as her voice cracked and she started to sob. "You?"

As she held Amanda, relief flowed through Lex. She had been worried that her lover didn't seem to be grieving for Frank as Lex thought she would. They stood in front of the window, Lex never loosening her grasp while Amanda let her emotions pour out.

A TINY SQUEAK awakened Lex, and she had to look around the room for a moment before she realized that it came from the crib. Moving quietly so as not to wake Amanda, she slid out of bed and made her way over to where Lorrie was fussing. "Hey there, lil' bit." Noting that the baby's diaper needed changing, she handled the chore without thinking, then picked Lorrie up to kiss her on the cheek. "I bet you're hungry, too." She took the squirming infant downstairs, hoping that Amanda would stay asleep.

In the kitchen, Lex kept up a running commentary while she prepared Lorrie's formula. Since Jeannie had been comatose after the baby's birth, the doctor had given her shots to dry up her breast milk, not knowing when she'd awaken. Now it was easier on everyone to feed Lorrie with a bottle, and it didn't put as much of a strain on Jeannie. She had already helped with the nightly feedings often, not wanting Amanda to have to be up all night long when she was more than capable of sharing the duties.

Lex sat at the kitchen table, telling Lorrie about her day while the baby fed. "And then that idiot tossed the bale of hay right out the upper window. The damned, I mean, the darned thing nearly hit me." She looked down into the gray-green eyes. "You're going to be as pretty as your mama, Lorrie. Must be something about those Cauble women."

"Thanks."

The voice from the doorway startled Lex, and she looked up sheepishly to see Amanda smiling at her. "I was trying not to wake you."

"You didn't." Amanda moved into the room and stood by Lex, running her fingers through her lover's hair. "I rolled over and the bed was cold. That's what woke me up." She knelt down and looked into Lex's eyes. "I was afraid that I had scared you off."

"No chance of that, love." Lex stretched over until she could place her lips on Amanda's cheek. "Someone was wet and hungry, and I didn't see any sense in bothering you." Seeing that Lorrie was finished with her formula, Lex lifted her to her shoulder, helped the infant burp, then cradled her in her arms. "Want to go back to bed?"

Amanda stood and stretched. She thought about asking for Lorrie, but didn't want Lex to think that she didn't trust her. "That sounds great. I'm exhausted." Amanda was about to leave the kitchen when Lex offered her the baby.

"Here. I think she missed you." Lex hadn't overlooked the look on her partner's face and understood that Lorrie was a connection to Frank that Amanda needed at the moment. She just hoped that Jeannie would feel the same, and soon. So far, even though they would bring the baby in and leave her in Jeannie's arms, she hadn't expressed any desire to try to bond with her daughter, and that worried Lex.

"Thanks." Amanda took Lorrie and kissed Lex, then the baby. She left the kitchen with her lover right behind her, feeling better with every step.

Once upstairs, Amanda was about to put Lorrie in her crib when Lex touched her shoulder. "Let's put her in bed with us tonight. It's late, and I'm exhausted. I don't want to miss hearing her if she wakes up again." Not completely a true statement, but Lex hoped Amanda wouldn't catch her at it.

"Sure." Amanda didn't feel like calling Lex on the little lie. She thought it was incredibly sweet that her partner wanted to make her more comfortable, and had no problem being surrounded by those she loved.

It wasn't long before Amanda and Lorrie were sound asleep, while Lex lay looking at the ceiling in the dark room. She could feel her lover's hand on her arm, as well as the small bundle that slept between them. The evening had shaken Lex more than she had realized. Amanda's meltdown wasn't unexpected, but she was glad in a way that they were alone when it happened. The baby stirred slightly, and Lex rolled over onto her side to watch Lorrie sleep. The sight made her feel something that she'd never thought she'd feel — maternal. She could almost believe that the three of them were a family, and suddenly Lex knew exactly what she wanted. Now all she had to do was tell Amanda.

Chapter Sixteen

Parking her car behind a pale blue Mustang, Natalie Haverly stared at the two-story house before she got out of her vehicle. She hoped that her new employers hadn't checked her references too closely, as she hadn't left her job at the hospital voluntarily. A private duty nursing position was exactly what she needed to pad her resume, and Natalie was determined to make a good impression.

She knocked on the front door and barely had a chance to look around the expansive porch before the door opened and a woman holding a fussy infant greeted her.

"You must be Ms. Haverly. Please, come in." Amanda stepped back to allow the nurse to enter. She was impressed by the woman's neat appearance, from her short blonde hair to her two-piece blue slacks suit. Lorrie continued to cry and Amanda rubbed her back soothingly. "I'm sorry, Mrs. Haverly, but I was on my way upstairs to change her when you knocked."

Natalie smiled in understanding. "Please, call me Natalie. And there's really no need to apologize, Mrs...?"

"Oh! Forgive my manners. I'm Amanda, and this sweet little girl is Lorrie." Amanda led her through the hallway to the stairs. "If you'd like, we can talk on the way, and I can give you a mini-tour of the house at the same time."

"That would be fine. I'll bring my bags in later, if that's all right." On their way to the steps, Natalie couldn't help but notice the ring on Amanda's hand. "That's quite a lovely ring you have. How long have you been married?"

Amanda pointed to the wall opposite the stairs at the framed photograph of her and Lex on their wedding day, a gift from her father. "Lex and I have been together for a year, but our ceremony was only about five months ago." She led the way to the second floor, trying to figure out the look of shock that crossed the nurse's face. At the top of the stairway, Amanda gestured to the nearest room. "Let us know if this room is to your liking, Natalie. It has a private bath, and if there's anything you might need, Lex and I are right across the hall." She walked into the master bedroom and placed Lorrie in the crib to change her. "I hope that being this close to the baby won't disturb you," she continued, still oblivious to Natalie's wide eyes as the nurse continued to look around.

For her part, Natalie had never been so close to one of "those people," and especially had never expected to sleep within steps of where their unnatural acts were committed. *That Bristol woman neglected to mention there were* queers *here.* She tried to clamp down on the fear and disgust that raced through her.

Natalie fought the urge to wipe her hands on her slacks. One of the reasons she had been retired from the hospital was her intolerance to anyone who was different from herself. She had been caught making caustic comments about a gay co-worker, and her dislike for her Hispanic supervisor had been the final nail in her coffin. The hospital board had given her the option to leave quietly on her own before they had to handle her dismissal in a more public manner.

While Amanda showed the nurse around upstairs, Lex came in to pay a visit to her sister-in-law. She had been overseeing the design of the new walkways and was pleased by the contractor's attention to detail. Lex removed her hat and tossed it in the guest chair in Jeannie's room and took her usual place on the edge of the bed. "Good morning, beautiful."

Jeannie leaned into the kiss that Lex placed on her head. "Monin'." She blushed under the attention, but enjoyed every minute of it. *No wonder Mandy walks around with that goofy grin on her face all the time. She sure is lucky to have found someone like Lex, just like I was lucky to have found Frank.* At the thought of her late husband, Jeannie closed her eyes and willed herself not to cry. *Will I ever not miss him?*

Lex noted the change in Jeannie's demeanor and had a good idea what she was thinking about. Honoring her sister-in-law's privacy, she decided a change of subject was in order. "I saw a strange car out in the drive. Have you met your new nurse yet?" When Jeannie shook her head, Lex patted her on the leg. "That's okay by me. It just means that I get you to myself for a bit."

"Aw, Wex."

The rancher ignored her sister-in-law's embarrassment. "You know, it's still nice outside. Would you like to spend a little time on the front porch with me?" At Jeannie's nod, Lex scooped her up out of the bed and placed Jeannie in the wheelchair that was parked near the recliner. As she wheeled Jeannie from the room, she stopped in the den. "I've been thinking about putting a pool table in here, that is if Amanda would let me. What do you think?"

"Poow?"

"Yeah. You know, right over there." Lex pointed to a space near the fireplace. "I think it would look pretty good in that spot."

"Why?"

Lex knelt down so that Jeannie could see her face. "I want a rematch of our last game. You cheated, you know." She referred to the first time Amanda took her to California, and Jeannie and Frank took them out to play pool and have fun. Lex bet Jeannie that she couldn't be distracted, and she soon found out she was wrong. Amanda's sister had pinched her on the rear, causing Lex to lose the game.

The lopsided smile on Jeannie's face never faltered. "You thooudn' have thuch a pinchable butt."

"Oh, yeah?" Pushing the chair out onto the front porch, Lex leaned down to whisper into the other woman's ear. "Don't let my wife hear you talk like that or we'll both get in trouble." Lex enjoyed hearing Jeannie laugh, and hoped that the new nurse would be able to keep her spirits up as well.

SLAMMING THE DOOR behind him, Billings stomped into his hotel room. Although the door was clearly marked "No Smoking," he proceeded to light his cigar as he paced. Before he was able to get even one full drag of the tobacco, his cell phone rang. "What?" His demeanor quickly changed as he identified the caller. "Oh, I'm terribly sorry, sir." He listened for over a full minute as the voice on the other end of the phone yelled. "You're absolutely right, sir. It won't happen again." At his superior's question, he swallowed hard, not wanting to share the next bit of information. "No, sir. I couldn't get her to sell. She's a very nasty woman, even manhandled me." He continued to try to assure his employer that their plans were going well, except for not being able to buy the last piece of property they needed.

Andrew Wilson approached the hotel room he shared with his boss. He couldn't understand why, with as much money as their employer threw around, they had to share a room in a one-star establishment. He could hear his boss's voice through the door and opened it quietly. He noticed the desperate way Billings spoke into the cellular phone and knew that it wasn't a pleasant call.

"Yes, sir. Of course. I agree, whatever it takes." Billings looked up, saw his associate, and frantically waved him into the room. "Do you want me to... You're right." The smile he gave Wilson was not a friendly one. "He wants to talk to you."

Shit. Wilson accepted the phone, then turned away from Billings. "H...hello? Yes, sir. This is Wilson."

Billings enjoyed watching his younger colleague squirm for a change. *Better him than me.*

"Yes, sir. But are you sure that's really necessary?" Wilson paled. "Maybe if we just explain... No. And you want me to? But what about Billings? No, sir, I'm not questioning your authority." He started to walk around the room nervously. "Of course, sir. Yes, I understand." He handed the phone back to Billings. "He wants to talk to you again." Pushing past the heavier man, Wilson went into the bathroom and shut the door behind him.

"Sir? Yes, I'll see to it." Closing the phone, he almost laughed out loud when he heard the retching that came from behind the bathroom door. *Amateur. Serves him right.*

LEX WHEELED JEANNIE into her room, both of them laughing. She'd forgotten what a wicked sense of humor her sister-in-law had. "Back to your room, madam, as promised," Lex intoned regally, stopping the chair just inside the office door. "Oh, hi."

"I was wondering where you two had gotten off to." Amanda was standing at the window, holding a relaxed Lorrie, while another woman sat in the recliner. "Ms. Natalie Haverly, I'd like for you to meet my sister, Jeannie Rivers, and my partner, Lex Walters." She gestured to the nurse, who had risen. "Natalie is the live-in nurse that Martha hired."

The venomous look on the caregiver's face caused Jeannie to recoil. She knew that it wasn't aimed at her, but it made her extremely uneasy. "Hi."

"Mrs. Rivers." Natalie stood up, ignoring Lex's outstretched hand. "I'm sure we'll get along just fine." She turned back to Amanda. "If it's all right with you, I'd like to get my bags and get settled in before I get started."

Confused, Amanda could only nod. "Of course. Lex, would you—"

"No, that's quite all right." Natalie brushed by Lex, who turned to watch her leave. "I can find my way out and back to my room."

"That woman's got a burr under her blanket about something." Lex pushed Jeannie back over to the bed, and knelt beside her to set the brakes. "Are you okay?"

Jeannie gave a short nod. She hoped that the new nurse was just tired, or nervous, and not what she feared. "Tiwer."

Getting her arms under the small woman, it took little effort for Lex to pick up Jeannie and place her back in the bed. "I'm sorry, Jeannie. I shouldn't have kept you out there so long." She pulled the covers up around Jeannie's waist and was about to step back when her hand was grasped.

"No, i' wa' pun."

Amanda moved around the foot of the bed and sat beside Jeannie, looking up to where Lex was standing. "Did you get the same vibe as I did?" When her sister nodded, Amanda turned back to her lover. "I don't think Natalie likes 'our kind' very much."

"Our kind? What the hell is that supposed to mean?" Lex looked back and forth between the two sisters. "What did I miss?"

Handing the baby to Lex, Amanda stood up and walked to the door, then closed it. "Gays. She about swallowed her tongue when she saw our wedding picture."

Lex looked down at the baby in her arms, then up at Jeannie. Seeing an interest there, she reclined so that the baby was resting more on the bed than in her hold. "With all due respect, sweetheart, Somerville is a small town, and we are in the Bible Belt. We're lucky that we're accepted by as many people as we are."

"I suppose that's possible, but did you notice how she ignored you when I made introductions?" Amanda was not to be deterred, and she could see by Jeannie's face that she wasn't alone in her assumptions.

"Maybe she just wanted to focus on Jeannie, since that's who she's here to help." Lex didn't like to make snap judgments about anyone, especially someone they were trusting to aid in Jeannie's recovery.

Amanda threw up her hands. "Come on, Lex. The woman is a homophobe." Much as she would have denied it, the lack of sleep was beginning to wear on her, and her patience was wearing thin.

Having been on the receiving end of judgmental people for most of her life, Lex didn't feel she'd be too comfortable around the new hire either, but she wasn't the one the woman was there to help. "Let's just give her a chance, all right? What could it hurt?"

"I guess." Amanda walked to the bed and sat next to her partner, so that they could both see Jeannie and the baby. "So, what kind of things did the two of you get into today?"

"Get into things? What makes you say that?" Trying to look outraged but failing miserably, Lex tipped back so that she was touching Amanda. "Actually, we just spent some time out on the front porch, didn't we, Jeannie?" Her words were ignored, and she couldn't have been happier about it.

Jeannie was watching Lorrie, who had closed her eyes and dozed off once she was placed next to her mother. She didn't hear the conversation around her, drinking in the infant's features. *I think she's got Frank's eyes. At least they look like the same shape. And her nose!* The only comfort she could take was that he had been able to see his daughter before he was taken away from them so suddenly. *Don't worry, my love. She'll never forget who her father was, I can promise you that.* The earlier activities had tired her more than she wanted to admit, and Jeannie struggled to hold back a yawn.

Hearing the front door slam, Lex stood up. "I think I'll go ahead and make sure Ms. Haverly has everything she needs. Maybe she's just shy." She kissed Amanda, straightened, then bent again, making the next kiss last longer. "I love you."

"I love you, too." Glad that her sister was focused on the baby, Amanda brushed the back of one hand across Lex's cheek. "Come in early tonight?"

"Definitely." After another quick kiss, Lex gathered up her hat and sauntered out the door, her heart lighter than it had been in weeks.

Natalie shifted the strap of her small clothing bag on her shoulder and almost gasped aloud in surprise when Lex met her in the hallway. The woman made her extremely nervous. She wasn't sure if it was the way she dressed: the denim jeans hugged her curves better than they should, and the gray tee shirt accentuated her broad shoulders and slender hips. Maybe it was the bedraggled black hat that she wore, which was pulled low over her eyes. All Natalie understood was that had she known about the number of "those people" who lived in the house, she would have never taken the job.

"Ms. Haverly, would you like me to help you up to your room?" Lex could tell that the bags were more than the nurse could handle, and she was determined to make the woman as comfortable as possible.

"No!" At her curt reply, Natalie could see the confusion on her employer's face, but she didn't care. "I'm perfectly capable of doing this myself," she snapped, hoisting the bag's strap higher on her shoulder.

Lex shrugged and quietly followed behind the nurse until they reached the foot of the steps. The woman was teetering from one foot to the other, and the heavy suitcase she dragged behind her looked almost as big as she was. *I'm not going to let her stubborn pride cause her to fall down our stairs. I'll just stay back and catch her if she needs me to.* She didn't know how soon her silent support would be called upon, as Natalie only made it halfway up the landing before she lost her balance and began to tumble backward.

Back in the converted office, Amanda wanted to pick Lorrie up and hold her, but she wasn't about to disturb the quiet balance between mother and daughter. For the first time since Jeannie had regained consciousness, she was showing a genuine interest in her baby. The peaceful moment was shattered when they heard a scream come from somewhere else in the house. Getting quickly to her feet, Amanda was torn between checking out the noise and staying with her sister. "Will you be all right while I see what that was?"

"'kay." Jeannie hated that she was confined to the bed, because her curiosity was getting the best of her, as well. She watched her sister leave, and wished again that she was mobile.

Rounding the door in the den, Amanda was shocked at what she saw. In the middle of the floor at the foot of the stairs was a jumble of arms, legs and luggage.

"Get your filthy hands off me!" Natalie demanded, her voice shrill and hard. She was smacking Lex in the head with her purse, even though she was lying on top of the hapless rancher. "Pervert!"

Amanda hurried over to rescue her partner. She reached for the nurse and was almost knocked to the floor when the woman redirected her ire at the newcomer. Fending off a violent swing, Amanda yelled, "Watch it!"

"Dammit, lady, calm down." Lex held one arm over her head in a defensive gesture, while she tried to scoot out from under Natalie. "It's not my fault you fell."

Even though she straddled Lex's hips, Natalie continued to attack. "You grabbed me in an inappropriate manner, you sick woman." Her arms were tiring, and the purse she swung moved in a slower arc. "You've been looking at me ever since I showed up." One of her blows finally landed, nearly knocking Lex senseless.

"That's it!" Amanda, tired of the game, got a handful of Natalie's hair and pulled the hysterical woman away from her lover. Once the woman was a few feet away, she knelt and started checking Lex for injuries. "Are you hurt?"

Lex rose to her elbows and shook her head to clear it. "I don't think so. We didn't fall that far." She looked past Amanda to Natalie, who had stood and was adjusting her clothes. "How about you, Ms. Haverly? Anything broken?"

The nurse glared at the two women on the floor. "Just my sensibilities, I believe." She crossed to where they were and picked up her bags, causing Lex to flinch. "I don't think this is going to work out very well."

"Really? What ever gave you that idea?" Lex asked dryly. Tired of the woman's attitude, she decided to tweak the nurse, at least a little. "What's the matter? Did you enjoy lying on me more than you care to admit?"

Natalie's eyes grew round and her face flushed darkly. "Why, I never!"

"Maybe you should. You might like it." Lex ignored the look her lover gave her. "But I think you're right, Ms. Haverly that it won't work out. I'm sorry we wasted your day." She got a morbid satisfaction over the gasp of shock that came from the nurse's mouth. "If you'll tell me where to send it, I'll be glad to give you a day's pay for your trouble."

"No, thank you." Natalie walked to the door, trying to maintain her dignity carting off all her bags in a hasty exit. "Good day." She left the house without looking back.

"ARE YOU SURE you have to leave tomorrow?" Billy asked Ellie. "We really haven't had much time together." Between his job and both of them sleeping in late, Billy had not seen as much of his sister as he had wanted. He was stretched out on one end of the sofa, with a can of beer balanced on his stomach. An empty pizza box sat in the center of the coffee table. His sister was in a similar position at the opposite end a few feet away.

Ellie plucked a runaway piece of pepperoni from her shirt and popped it into her mouth. "I'd really like to get back and mend some fences." Slightly drunk herself, she giggled at her terminology. "Mend fences. Get it?"

"That's bad." Once Ellie's mirth had died down, Billy changed the subject. "You keep telling me all about this 'Amanda' person, El, but what's your cousin like? You've hardly mentioned her." His sister's crush on the woman was evident, and Billy hoped that when she got her heart broken, it would heal quickly.

Giving the question serious thought, Ellie finished off her beer, then belched. What would be the best way to describe the person who seemed to take Amanda's love for granted? She still thought that Lex wasn't good enough for Amanda, but wasn't about to get into that with her brother. "Well, for starters, she's about your age, although she seems older than me most of the time." Ellie couldn't get over how serious her cousin was. She assumed it was because of the huge responsibility of running the ranch, but she thought that Lex needed to lighten up. A lot. "She has dark hair which looks kind of reddish in the sunlight, and her eyes are such a deep blue, they're almost purple."

"No, not the physical stuff." Billy couldn't keep the lecherous grin from his face. Once he had gotten over his shock at Ellie's announcement, he found the whole thing incredibly funny. "But then again, she sounds pretty hot." He got off the sofa and padded barefoot into the kitchen. "Want another beer?" he hollered. Not waiting for an answer, he brought two more cans and handed one to his sister before resuming his reclining position. "So, are you sure that this hottie cousin of yours is gay? Maybe she just hasn't met the right guy."

Ellie drained her beer, put the empty can on the coffee table, and then popped the top on the new one. Her cousin wasn't some swaggering butch, but it was very evident in how Lex carried herself that she was more than comfortable in her sexuality. "Trust me, little brother, there's not a guy alive that could change Lex. Besides, like I told you before, she's happy with Amanda." She hated to admit it, even to herself, but Ellie felt very plain compared to Lex. Given her mousy brown hair and slight build, she knew that she was no match in the looks department.

"Well, you can't blame me for thinking it." He tipped the can to his lips and took several deep swallows. "Will you come back and visit? I'd hate to think that I'd never see you again."

"Of course I will. And, planes go both ways, you know."

Billy shrugged. "Maybe." Then he brightened, and sat up a bit straighter. "Want to go out and pick up a couple of chicks? I promise not to give you leftovers."

"Leftovers? Give me a break. I'd probably have to get two and share." Ellie kicked at her brother, who kicked back in response. "And no, we're not going anywhere. I can't even remember how many beers I've had."

"I guess you're right." He fingered the rings in his eyebrow. "You never said anything about how I looked. Didn't you notice?"

Ellie sat up shakily and made a point of staring at Billy's face. "Of course I noticed. I didn't say anything because I knew you expected me to. But now that you mention it, you do look a little different." She found herself on her back with her brother leaning over her. "Hey, get off, you big ape." When he started tickling her ribs, she squirmed. "Stop it, snotface!"

"Different? That's all you can say?" Billy continued to tickle his sister. Once the air had been cleared, they'd easily reverted back to the old camaraderie they had when they were much younger.

"Yeah," Ellie forced out between gales of laughter. "Did you cut your hair?"

"Watch out, prickly butt." Billy used to tease his sister with that name when she'd do something to make him mad. The nickname would upset her and their mother mainly because it hit too close to home. Now he'd used it just to see what would happen. "I'll take you downtown and get you a tattoo."

Finally able to kick her brother off, Ellie sat up and straightened her shirt. "You wouldn't dare."

Billy's wicked smirk was the only answer he gave.

SNUGGLED UP BEHIND Amanda, Lex slept much later than usual. As per her wife's request, she had come back to the house early the previous night, and after a quick dinner, the two of them retired upstairs. Sated and relaxed in sleep, she didn't hear the back door to the house slam or the racing boots that hit the stairs. The pounding on their door *did* wake her up, and Lex rolled over and grabbed her sleep shirt from the floor. "Come in."

"Lex! I think—" Ronnie paused, suddenly realizing where he was. His face turned scarlet, and he turned to face away from the bed. "You need to get down to the stables, quick. I think that new filly is sick or something."

"Give me a second, and I'll be right there." She wasn't worried about Ronnie turning around, so she swung the covers from her legs and climbed out of bed.

The commotion finally caused Amanda to stir. "What's the matter?" she asked, partially sitting up and rubbing her eyes, before she realized that Ronnie was standing in the door. Her nightgown was lying across the room, so she pulled the sheet up over her breasts.

Ronnie heard the rustling on the bed and was afraid he was going to hyperventilate. "I'll meet you downstairs." He was out of the room before either woman could say another word.

"He's so cute." Amanda watched Lex dress. "Did I hear him say something about the stables?"

"Yeah. Evidently the horse that threw me is sick. Probably just colicky or something, but I'd better check it out." Lex had put Ronnie in charge of the stables, and she had never regretted the decision. More than once his vigilance had kept a problem from getting out of control. "I'll see you for breakfast in a bit." She met Amanda halfway and shared a long, heart-pounding kiss. "Whoa."

Amanda grinned. "Are you sure you wouldn't rather have breakfast in bed?" Before she could be answered, a soft squeak was heard from the crib.

"No, but I'm thinking that someone else is ready for breakfast. I love you." Lex kissed Amanda again before leaving the room in a hurry.

Ronnie stood at the foot of the stairs, still embarrassed. "I'm sorry about bothering you this morning." He took his work at the ranch seriously, and didn't want her to think he couldn't handle it. "But I wasn't too sure what to do."

"Don't worry about it." Hoping to ease the boy's discomfort, Lex put one arm around his shoulders while they moved to the back door. Once outside, the cool morning made her wish that she'd put on more than just a tee shirt with her jeans and boots. She quickened her pace, wanting to be in out of the chill quickly. It wasn't long before they were inside the barn, and without even a closer examination, Lex knew something was seriously wrong. In the stall, the filly was on her side with her head away from the door. She wasn't moving, and Lex knew without a doubt she was dead. "Did you go inside?"

"No, ma'am. I saw her lying there and went right up to get you."

Lex nodded. "Good man." She unhitched the stable door. "Would you mind going back up to the house and asking Martha to call the vet? She's got the number by the phone."

"Okay. Then do you want me to come back here?" Ronnie didn't mention to Lex that he could have just called from the barn. He figured that she had a reason for what she said, and he wasn't about to question it.

"Yeah. Call the bunkhouse while you're there and have the men come down. We'll move the rest of the horses up there." She knelt by the filly and ran her hand across the animal's neck. "I want them all in separate stalls until we find out what caused this."

Ronnie's eyes widened. "She's dead, isn't she?" He felt the weight of failure weigh heavily on his shoulders. "Maybe I should have stayed with her and just called you from here." *My first real responsibility on the ranch, and I screwed it up. Lex is never going to trust me again.*

Turning her head at the catch in his voice, Lex realized what Ronnie must have been thinking. "You did exactly the right thing, son. She's been dead for at least a few hours as far as I can tell. There wasn't anything you could have done different. You understand?"

"Yes, ma'am." He raced from the barn, still upset.

Lex continued to study the dead animal for any traces of what may have caused her death. The filly's head was partially obscured by the straw that covered the bottom of the stall, so she gently brushed it away, only to pull her hand back in surprise. A wire was pulled taut around the dead animal's throat, just under the jaw and behind the ears. She could see a narrow band of blood beneath the wire, and the horse's tongue was swollen and protruding from its mouth.

"Sonofabitch." The sound of the phone on the stable wall ringing startled Lex, and she got to her feet and crossed the building to answer it.

Martha's exasperated tone came through the line. "Lexie, I was trying to get Dr. Hernandez on the phone, when this other call came in. The man says it's important, and he won't take no for an answer."

"That's okay. Put him through, and I'll see what he wants. Probably just an overly obnoxious salesman." Even Lex didn't believe what she said, and she waited patiently while Martha conferenced the two lines. "This is Lex Walters."

A gravelly voice spoke, so low that Lex had to strain to hear. "How's business?"

"Who the hell is this?"

"It's a shame about that little horse. But that's how things are in the ranching business, isn't it, Walters? You just never know what's going to happen."

Her suspicions confirmed, Lex turned to face the door to keep an eye out for Ronnie's return. "Now you listen to me, you bastard. I don't know why—"

"You know exactly why." He laughed, an eerie sound that was anything but friendly. "You've got something we want. But since you've been so stubborn, all I'll give you is what you paid for the property, nothing more."

"Go to hell." Lex slammed the phone down so hard it almost knocked the unit off the wall. She honestly didn't even want the land anymore, but she sure as hell wasn't going to let someone extort it from her. "Asshole."

Chapter Seventeen

ELLIE WATCHED THROUGH the window as Los Angeles grew smaller. She couldn't help but sigh. She hated that she had spent so many years estranged from her younger brother, who had turned out to be a lot better person than she ever hoped to be. Although his clothing, hair and appearance weren't quite what she had expected, Ellie was proud of the man Billy had become. She looked down at her own clothes. Her jeans and gray tee shirt were old but clean. The white sneakers on her feet were scuffed and could stand to be replaced. The first thing she'd have to do once she was back in Somerville was ask her grandfather or Amanda where she could buy some decent clothes. *I need to get a job, but I'll never be hired dressed like this.* She didn't want to spend the rest of her life sponging off her family, no matter what her mother said.

Before Billy had taken her to the airport, Ellie tried once again to reason with her mother. The short argument had hurt, especially when Naomi insinuated that the only reason Ellie was going back to Texas was so that she wouldn't have to go back to work. Even Billy's voice on the line couldn't calm Naomi, and Ellie boarded the plane with the dread that she'd never see her family again.

She thought about what kind of employment she might be able to get in Somerville, since she didn't think there would be very many job openings in her line of work. Waiting tables was out, since she had never been very coordinated and could never remember what anyone's order was. She had spent an entire summer mowing yards to help put herself through school, but the thought of doing that again at her age wasn't exactly heartening. "I could always see if Lex has any openings out at the ranch that I can handle." But the thought of asking her hard-nosed cousin for a job was even more humiliating than listening to her mother rant about her failures.

The plane touched down before Ellie could make any type of decision, and she was leaving the terminal when a man not much taller than she stopped her. "Excuse me, Miss Gordon?" He was dressed casually in khaki slacks and a white short-sleeved shirt, but there was something familiar about him.

"Yes?"

"I'm Mr. Edwards' driver. He sent me inside for you." The man reached up to tip his hat, before realizing he wasn't wearing one. "Sorry. I'm not quite used to the new 'uniform.'"

Ellie smiled. "My grandfather is here? How did he know I'd be coming in today?" She was about to adjust her duffel bag over her shoulder when the driver took it from her grasp.

"I'm afraid I don't know, Miss. But if you'll follow me, I'll lead you out to the car." The chauffeur wove his way through the crowd like an expert, pausing every so often to make certain he didn't lose his charge. Once outside, he stopped at a white limousine with tinted windows and opened the trunk for Ellie's bag. Before she could get to the door, he was there, holding it open for her.

Not used to the star treatment, Ellie almost shrank back. "Um, thanks." She peered inside the vehicle, then quickly climbed in when she saw the smiling visage of her grandfather in the back seat. "Hi!"

"Hello, there." Travis patted the spot next to him. "Better get in here before Thomas tosses you in." He laughed at the nervous look Ellie gave the driver before she hastily climbed in. "Don't worry, Ellie. I was just kidding."

"You can never be too sure these days," she muttered, slightly embarrassed. It was going to take some getting used to, having a family that actually had a sense of humor. She embraced her grandfather, happy to see him. "Not that I'm complaining, but how did you know I was coming in today?"

Travis leaned back in the seat. "A very nice young gentleman by the name of Billy called me early this morning." He didn't want to tell his granddaughter about the entire conversation, especially the part where Billy made it clear that he would be on the next plane to Texas if he learned of anyone hurting his sister, either physically or emotionally. Once that had been said, the two had found a lot in common and settled down for a long talk about families. "He thought I'd like to be here to meet you, and he was right." Travis watched as several emotions flickered across Ellie's face. "Why didn't you call and tell me yourself?"

"I guess I didn't want to bother you." How else could Ellie explain her reasoning? She didn't know her grandfather well, and the last thing she wanted to do was wear out her welcome in the only home she had. Her mother had seen to that.

"The only way you could bother me would be to *not* let me do things for you. We're family, and that's what family does." Travis didn't know what had transpired in California, but he could tell that Ellie had been through a rough time. "Why don't I get you up to speed on what's been going on here, and then we'll get you settled at the house."

Suddenly feeling very weary, Ellie leaned until she felt her grandfather's arm around her shoulders. "That sounds like the best offer I've had in a long time, Grandpa." She closed her eyes and concentrated on his soothing voice, saddened by the events he was relating that she'd recently missed.

LEX STOOD NEXT to Charlie as her men hauled off the remains of the dead filly. The moment she had gotten off the phone with the mystery man, she went to the cottage and asked the sheriff to follow her over to the stables. He was shocked at what she told him, but took very precise notes the entire time. "This was such a waste, Charlie. What kind of sick bastard would kill a horse just to try to scare someone into selling land? It just doesn't make any sense to me."

"It rarely does. I've been in this job for a lot of years, and I still can't figure out human nature."

"Well, I can guarantee if I find one of those assholes, he's going to wish he'd never heard of me." It took everything that Lex had to control her anger at the loss of such a promising young animal. "Why did they single her out? She was in one of the middle stalls." The rancher was just very thankful that her favorite horse, Thunder, had been at the vet's. An examination during the intended replacement of the thrown shoe had indicated a more serious problem with the hoof, and so she'd had one of her men load the horse in a trailer and take him in to be checked out.

Charlie slid his hat back on his head. "Why do these crazy fools do anything? Maybe they saw you riding her and thought she was yours."

"Maybe. But I haven't ridden her but the one time, when I went over to check—" *The new property. Those bastards must have seen me!* "Damn."

"What?"

Lex turned to face Charlie. "She's the one I was riding when I heard those explosions. Someone must have seen me riding her." Now she was really mad. "The sons of bitches knew I was hurt and just left me there."

The death of the horse took on an entirely different meaning for Charlie. It was more of a personal threat to Lex than a general warning. "Are you sure? You haven't had her out around the house at all?"

"No. Just the once." Lex came to the same conclusion the sheriff had reached and was immediately concerned for Amanda, Martha, Jeannie and the others. "Do you think we're in danger out here?"

As much as he hated to admit it, the sheriff thought they should prepare for the worst. "I think you ought to install a security system for the house, especially with Jeannie and the baby here." What Charlie really wanted to do was have several deputies stay around the clock, but he knew he couldn't justify the cost of that kind of manpower.

The thought of having someone intentionally inflicting harm that close to the house made Lex feel physically ill. "Hell, Charlie, we don't even lock our doors out here." She flinched as she considered what might have happened to Ronnie if he had walked in on the actual killing. "It's for a lousy piece of land, for God's sake. Do you think they'd actually hurt any of us?"

"I don't know. But I do know that I'm going about to go home and get into an argument with my wife."

"An argument?"

"Oh, yeah. Can you imagine what Martha's going to say when I tell her I don't want her walking back and forth alone until this is resolved? She's going to bend my ear, but good." Charlie patted Lex on the shoulder. "We'll get to the bottom of this. I'm not going to let these people get away with what they've done."

Lex pinched the bridge of her nose with her fingertips in an attempt to ward off an impending headache. "Thanks, Charlie. Now I get to do the same thing, but with Amanda." She tried to give him a smile. "I think you have the easier task."

IN JEANNIE'S ROOM, the baby was snuggled up against her mother while Amanda talked of inconsequential things. They both had heard the commotion down at the barn, but all that they'd been told was that the newest horse was dead. For the moment, Amanda could only imagine the anguish her partner was going through, and she wanted to be with her to lend support.

"Mandy?"

"Hmm?"

Jeannie took a deep breath, and pictured what she wanted to say, since it was a lot harder for her to be understood. "Go cho

Wex. W'ill be ochay."

"That's not necessary," a tired voice responded from the doorway. "I'm right here." Lex entered and was soothed when Amanda jumped into her arms. *I needed this so badly.*

Amanda stepped back and looked into her lover's eyes. She could see weariness, but something else was there, too. "Are you all right? We heard about the horse down at the barn."

"Yeah, I'm fine. There are just a few things I need to tell you." Sitting on the bed, Lex waited until Amanda was next to her. "The new filly was killed."

Even though Jeannie's eyes widened, Amanda was the one to speak. "Killed? How?"

Lex took hold of one of her lover's hands, gaining strength from her grip. "They tried to make it look like she was strangled, but the vet thinks she was injected with a drug."

"Wait a minute." Amanda released her hold and stood up, shaking her head. "Why on earth would someone kill one of your horses? What's going on here, Lex?"

Rising, Lex nodded to Jeannie, then escorted Amanda out of the room before she woke Lorrie. "It's kind of a long story."

"So? I don't see us in any hurry here." Amanda put her hands on her hips and glared at her lover. "This isn't more of the 'let's protect Amanda' bullshit, is it?"

"No." Lex looked down at the floor. The conversation wasn't going as she had planned, but the way things had gone lately, she shouldn't have expected anything less. Her partner had been so engrossed in taking care of Lorrie that she had neglected just about everything else, including their relationship. Lex took part of the blame for that, since she was also busy with the ranch. *We've got to make more time for each other. I'm not letting this get away from us.* She rubbed her face with her hands, unable to articulate what was necessary to make Amanda understand her.

Ashamed of her outburst, Amanda saw how her words had affected Lex. *She doesn't deserve this. I'm beginning to sound like my mother.*

"I'm sorry." Both spoke at once, and each smiled bashfully at the other.

"Let's get a bit more comfortable, and you can tell me what's going on," Amanda offered, leading Lex to the sofa.

Gladly accepting the extended olive branch, Lex followed. She was happily surprised when Amanda not only sat next to her, but also wrapped both arms around one of hers and snuggled close. Lex leaned over and kissed her lover's temple. "I love you."

"I love you, too." Amanda kissed the shoulder she was

nestled against, feeling better already. "Now, you said that the filly was poisoned? Do you know who, or why?"

"I have a pretty good idea of both. I've been getting 'offers' from a couple of men to sell the property that I just bought, and they won't take no for an answer."

Amanda nodded. "Okay. So is Charlie going to arrest them?" She turned her head so that she could see Lex's face. She was confused by the expression she saw there. "What?"

"I'm sure he would, if I had any proof. But right now, it's just my word against theirs." The hard part came next. "While I was over at Charlie's, I called an alarm company. They're sending someone out in a little bit to see about installing a security system."

"Why?"

Lex glanced down into her wife's eyes, hoping that she'd never lose the trust she saw there. "Because if they were able to get into the stable that easily, I don't want to take a chance on them doing that in either of the houses."

"You're scared, aren't you?" Amanda had seen Lex worried, mad, upset, happy, and a lot of other things, but never like she was now. "This thing really has you rattled."

"Of course I'm scared!" Lex pulled away and stood, then whirled to face the sofa and her partner. "I may be the primary target, but anyone here could be injured. I have a house full of people to take care of, and if I thought it would do any good, I'd ask you to take Jeannie to town and stay with your grandparents until this thing is resolved." She held up her hand when Amanda opened her mouth to speak. "But since I know you won't do that, then I'd feel better about taking a few extra precautions to keep us safe. All of us."

Amanda bit her tongue to prevent herself from going off on Lex. She understood exactly what Lex meant and wanted to support her, not be sidetracked by her own concerns. Holding out her arms, she beckoned her lover to her. "Come back and sit down, honey. Let's work this out together."

WHEN THE LIMOUSINE approached the outskirts of Somerville, Ellie recognized some of the landmarks. "We're not too far from the ranch, are we?"

"No, I don't think so. Would you rather go there first?" Travis was pleased. He had hoped that his two grandchildren would be able to get along, if not be actual friends.

"I think so. I have a few things to clear up there, and I'd feel better getting it done as soon as possible."

Travis nodded. He picked up the phone and told Thomas about the detour, and then sat back to enjoy the ride. It wasn't long before the long white car pulled up in front of the ranch house, near two vans bearing the logo of a well-known alarm company. Travis accepted Thomas's help from the limousine. Puzzled, he looked around. "I wonder what's going on here?" He waited until Ellie was beside him before making his way up the steps to the front porch. Before he reached the door, it opened, and Martha greeted them both.

"Welcome back, Ellie," she said warmly, enveloping the surprised woman in a fierce hug. "It's good to have you home."

Home? I wonder where that came from? Not one to look a gift horse in the mouth, she returned the embrace. "Thank you."

Waiting until the two women broke apart, Travis gestured to the trucks. "What's with the security? Has something happened?"

The housekeeper led them inside and closed the door. "When does something *not* happen around here? Why don't you let me pour you both a cup of coffee, and I'll bring you up to speed."

After their "debriefing," Travis couldn't help but shake his head. "That nurse sounds like a complete nutcase."

"I feel responsible," Martha lamented. "After all, I was the one who did the initial interview. She never once let on she was a bigot."

Ellie spoke up. "Then you certainly can't take the blame, Martha. I'm sure neither Lex nor Amanda feels that way." Even though she and her cousin hadn't gotten along, Ellie knew deep down inside that Lex was a decent person. It was the only way she could reconcile the fact that Amanda had fallen in love with her.

"She's right. Don't beat yourself up over what's already past." For a moment Travis was quiet, then he chuckled. "Although I would have paid good money to see the woman on top of poor Lex, lying at the foot of the stairs."

Not speaking out loud, Ellie had thought the same thing. *Seeing anyone whacking Lex would be entertaining.*

"It was pretty funny," a new voice piped in. Amanda stood in the doorway, holding Lorrie. "I think the best part was when the nurse realized where she was and couldn't get off Lex fast enough." She headed to the table and sat down between Travis and Martha.

Travis reached out and was rewarded by Amanda handing the infant to him. He said, "She's already grown so much." He took his eyes off Lorrie momentarily. "How's Jeannie?" Not wanting to be a bother, Travis had only been out once to visit, but resolved to rectify that.

"She seems to be doing better, although she's still having a rough time." Amanda was impressed with how her sister was coping. She didn't think she'd be able to go on at all if she lost Lex, no matter how much support her family was willing to give her.

Understanding completely, Travis handed the baby back to Amanda and stood up. "Do you think it would be all right if I went in to see her? I may have some insight." Since his wife had just recently passed away, Travis knew all too well the pain of losing someone so dear.

"I think she'd like that." Amanda watched as he and Martha left the room, then turned to smile at Ellie, who had been quiet since she came into the room. "Welcome back."

For her part, Ellie couldn't get over the vision Amanda was with the infant in her arms. Already a perfect woman in her eyes, seeing her as a maternal figure only enhanced her view of Amanda as ideal. "Thanks." She was even more surprised when Amanda leaned forward and pulled her into a one-armed hug. The sunshine fresh smell of woman and child caused Ellie to close her eyes and dream for a moment that *they* were a family, and her arms went around Amanda's neck to return the embrace

"I'd like a panic button in each bedroom and one in the kitchen," Lex said from the hall by the back door. She had given the four men with her a quick tour of the houses and barns and had been told that they'd have the installation done in record time. Just missing her grandfather's exit, she turned to walk into the kitchen...and stopped dead in her tracks when she saw Amanda and Ellie in each other's arms. "Ahem."

Ellie pulled away and hurried to her feet. "Lex." She watched Amanda's face, but didn't see anything but a friendly smile. Her own guilty thoughts made her nervous, as did the unreadable expression on her cousin's face. "I was just, um, well..."

Lex turned to the men with her. "Do you need anything else to get started?" When she was assured they didn't, Lex brought her attention back to the women in the kitchen. She walked slowly past Amanda and the baby until she was within an arm's length of her cousin. "So, what was it that I was seeing here?"

"We, I mean, I—" Ellie continued to stammer as Lex towered over her. *Oh, God, she's figured it all out and is going to kick my ass. I knew I should have stayed in California.* She closed her eyes as Lex drew nearer. What happened next was something she never would have predicted.

"Welcome back, cousin." Lex put her arms around Ellie's trembling body and pulled her close. Frank's death had given her a certain sense of her own mortality, and she was determined to try to make a go of her family, no matter how hard it might be. "I hope you stay longer this time," she whispered.

Opening her eyes, Ellie saw something she had never seen before: Lex's face in a smile. The expression made the serious woman look younger and more beautiful, and suddenly Ellie saw what Amanda must have seen in her cousin to fall in love with her. "Thanks." She pulled away and took a deep breath. "I need to talk to you, when you have a chance."

"Sure."

Amanda stood up. "I need to take Lorrie upstairs and change her anyway." She kissed Lex on the cheek before leaving the kitchen.

Lex stared after her lover. When Ellie cleared her throat, she tried to keep a blush from her face. "Sorry about that. You said that you wanted to talk to me?"

"Yeah. Is there someplace that we can go where we won't be interrupted?" As much as Ellie enjoyed the rest of the family, she wanted to get some things out in the open between them, without any interference. "If you've got the time, that is."

"How about we take a walk? There's less chance of anyone interrupting us that way." Lex smiled at Ellie. "If you're not afraid to be alone with me."

Ellie shook her head. "I think we're past that."

"I think so, too." Lex led the way out of the kitchen and through the back door, wondering what revelations the rest of the day might bring.

THE QUIET TAPPING of the keyboard was the only sound that could be heard in the room, and the noise Terence was making was beginning to get on Elizabeth's nerves. "Do you have to make that infernal racket?" Citing a headache, she had lain down on the bed earlier with a damp cloth covering her eyes and the lights dimmed.

"I'm sorry, but you wanted me to finish this research for you, and I can't do that without typing." Sitting at a desk on the other side of the room, Terence wasn't really sorry. But the last thing he wanted to do was antagonize Liz, who had become increasingly unstable since they'd returned to Austin.

"Very well. But at least *try* to make less noise. My head is splitting."

Mine would be too if I'd drunk as much Scotch as she did on the plane. She's probably got a hangover that would fell a moose. With an evil glint in his eye, Terence purposely thumped harder on the keys on his laptop. *Take that, you hateful bitch.* He was still upset over their earlier conversation, where Liz demanded that he find a way to get her youngest daughter and grandchild away from "that woman." When he'd asked about her oldest, she'd sneered and told him in no uncertain terms that Jeannie was worthless to her, and that he was to forget about her.

Liz moaned and waved one hand in the air. "Terence, be a dear and order some room service. I'm not going to feel like going out for dinner tonight."

"All right. What would you like? Some soup, maybe?"

She sat up and removed the washcloth from her face. "Are you out of your mind? I can't eat that paltry fare. Have them bring up something decent—perhaps a filet mignon. I'm not well." She was about to lie back again when a thought struck her. "Oh, and don't forget the champagne. That should help with the headache." Her order given, Liz reclined and covered her eyes again.

No shit. If I'd had any idea just how "not well" she was, I'd have never helped the crazy bitch get out of the hospital. Terence reached for the phone and placed the order, adding a sandwich and coffee for himself. His stomach had been upset for several days as well, but for entirely different reasons. Meeting Jeannie had given him insight into what was really happening and had put a face on the innocent people Liz was trying to hurt. On the plane ride back, he decided that he'd do what he could to change things and try to make amends. He just hoped that he could finish what he wanted to do and get away before Liz found out.

Elizabeth peeked from underneath the cloth on her eyes. She wasn't stupid. Terence's attitude had undergone a complete turnaround right before they left California, and she was almost certain she knew what had caused it. Even though he wasn't aware, she'd noticed the look of distaste he gave her whenever they spoke about Jeannie. *I don't know what his problem is. That girl is completely worthless to me now.* She also knew that "research" alone couldn't explain the amount of typing he was doing.

Feeling as if he were being watched, Terence paused and looked over his shoulder. Liz hadn't moved, and the cloth was still covering her eyes. He remonstrated himself over his paranoia and went back to his work.

That's right, little man. Keep your eyes on your back. There's no telling when you might find a knife there. Elizabeth closed her eyes once again, making a mental note to call her local "friend" as soon as she was alone.

THE AUTUMN AFTERNOON sun beat down on them both, and Ellie wished she'd left her denim jacket inside. Part of her realized that her discomfort stemmed not only from the weather, but from the amount of alcohol she had consumed the evening before. Ellie had never been much of a drinker, although the thought of something cold to drink before she faced her cousin sounded pretty good to her at the moment. Looking around, she couldn't help but notice the new concrete walkways that linked the main house with Martha's, as well as with the stables. "What's up with all this?"

"It's been something I'd been meaning to do for a long time, actually. But with Jeannie confined to a wheelchair for the time being, I thought it would be easier for her to get around." Lex studied the ground beneath their feet as they walked. "It's not right for her to be cooped up inside all the time. I just wanted to give her a bit more freedom."

"That's really nice of you."

Lex cleared her throat, uncomfortable with the way the conversation was heading. "She's family." She stopped in her tracks and turned to face Ellie. "And so are you. I'm sorry we got off on the wrong foot."

The apology was something that Ellie hadn't expected, and she stood frozen in surprise for a moment. *She's apologizing to me? What's going on here?* "Actually, that's what I wanted to talk to you about, Lex. I wanted to tell you how sorry I am for being such a self-righteous jerk when we first met." She waited until her words registered and then said, "Not to mention, I found out that we have more in common than I first thought."

"Oh?"

"Uh, yeah." Now it was Ellie's turn to be embarrassed. "Here I am, thirty-six years old, and I finally figure out that I'm gay. The chip on my shoulder came from a lifetime of denial. I guess I was upset with you because you seemed so open and comfortable with yourself."

Whoa. I never saw that one coming. Lex held out her hand and smiled. "How about we start over, then? Hi, cousin. Welcome to the family."

Ellie took the offered hand and pulled Lex into a hug. "Thanks, cousin." She didn't know if she was more relieved at Lex's apparent acceptance of her, or that she was finally able to get it all off her chest. Feeling the arms around her tighten, she decided it didn't matter.

Chapter Eighteen

AS THEY WALKED back to the house, Ellie remembered something from earlier. She didn't know for certain quite how Lex would react to her suggestion, but feeling that their relationship was headed in the right direction, she decided to give it a try. "Lex?"

"Hmm?"

"Have you tried to hire someone to help with Amanda's sister?"

Lex stayed quiet for several minutes while they continued their trek along the recently poured walkway. She watched as two of the alarm installers carried wireless equipment to Martha and Charlie's house, feeling relieved that by the time they went to bed tonight, both houses would be protected. Ellie's question had caught her off guard. "Not yet. I don't want to put Jeannie through any more stress than is necessary, and bringing in a new person every day would probably do just that." Her steps never faltered, but she turned to look Ellie in the face. "Why do you ask?"

"Would you mind introducing me to her? I mean, we're practically family, aren't we?"

"Sure. I've got some work to do inside, so maybe you can spend some time with Amanda and Jeannie."

Just hearing Amanda's name caused Ellie's heart to beat faster. Knowing that it was pointless, she still couldn't help but feel almost giddy at the thought of spending more time with the woman of her dreams. Not wanting to damage the tenuous bond she had formed with Lex, Ellie tried to keep a neutral look on her face. "That would be great."

Still not all that comfortable with the woman walking beside her, Lex tried to make polite conversation. "Are you planning on staying around for a while, or is this just a visit?" They climbed the steps to the porch and she held the back door open for Ellie to precede her. She misinterpreted her cousin's continued silence. "You don't have to tell me if you don't want to."

"Actually, that's something else I wanted to talk to you about. I'd like to help out around here, if you'd let me."

Not sure that she'd heard correctly, Lex stopped abruptly in the hallway. "*You* want to work on the ranch?" She couldn't help comparing Ellie to herself. Older, smaller, and never looking like she'd worked outside a day in her life, Ellie just didn't seem like the type who would be comfortable throwing bales of hay or cleaning out stables. "Just exactly what is it you want to do?"

Embarrassed by Lex's intent perusal, Ellie blushed. "Not what you're thinking, I'm sure." At Lex's confused look, she continued, "In San Diego, I worked for a couple of years as a nurse's assistant. I was just thinking that if Amanda's sister was okay with it, I could help take over some of her care."

"A nurse's assistant? Why not a nurse?" As soon as the words left her mouth, Lex wanted to take them back. She could see that the subject was a touchy one for Ellie. "I'm sorry, I didn't mean anything by that."

"No, that's okay. You just reminded me of my mother for a second." Ellie smiled to take the sting out of her words. "She always complained about me not going to nursing school, even though I didn't have the grades for it. And since I've had to work full-time to get myself through college, it's taken me longer." She looked down at the floor. "A few years ago, I thought I'd fallen in love, and I quit to help put him through law school. As soon as he passed the bar, he found someone else. So, I'm running behind on my education."

Having had her heart shattered by love, Lex knew what Ellie was talking about. She put her hand on her cousin's arm in a comforting gesture. "I'm sorry."

Ellie closed her eyes for a moment. "It was a long time ago, at least it feels like it now." She opened her eyes and looked into Lex's face. "Of course, now I know that he wouldn't have been able to make me very happy in the long run, would he? So, I guess it was all for the best."

"Maybe." Seeing the lost look in the other woman's eyes, Lex pulled Ellie into a hug. "You're with family now. So if there's anything we can do to help you with your studies, let us know."

"Thanks, Lex." For the first time in a very long time, Ellie felt truly at home. And it felt good.

THE NOISY DINER hadn't been his first choice of a place to have a meal, but Billings wanted to stay in town until he was able to finish some business. He had removed his tie and jacket and left them in his car, not wanting to stand out too much in the small town. Now he watched as a man in a dark business suit opened the front glass door to the establishment and stepped inside to look around. Rolling his eyes at his associate's inability to blend in, Billings raised his hand slightly to get Andrew Wilson's attention. "Where the hell have you been?" he whispered roughly.

"Sorry. I got lost." Realizing how alien he looked, Andrew loosened his tie and waved to the waitress. "Excuse me, but can I get a cup of coffee?" At her nod, he turned his attention to Billings. "What's the big deal? I'm only about five minutes late."

"The big deal is that our boss has been on my ass all morning. I talked to that damned rancher earlier, and she—"

"Here you go, hon." The buxom waitress placed a cup of coffee in front of Andrew. Her platinum blonde hair was in disarray and her makeup was smeared, but she was still a lovely woman. "Would you like something to eat?"

Andrew smiled at her friendly tone. "What do you recommend?" He hadn't had any intention of ordering a meal, but she was too nice to rebuff.

"I'd recommend the steakhouse across town," she whispered conspiratorially. "Or a sandwich, if you really want to eat here. Just stay away from the fried foods."

"I think I'll stick with the coffee." Andrew noticed her nametag. "Thank you, Francine."

Once the waitress had left their area, Billings thumped the table with his fist. "Are you through flirting yet, or should I leave you alone with your little friend?"

"I was just being polite."

"Never mind." Billings looked around, then stood up. "Come on. I don't want to discuss business in here. There are too many ears around us." He reached into his pocket and pulled out a ten dollar bill, more than twice what his tab came to, and tossed it on the table. He led the way out of the diner with Wilson right behind him.

They went around the corner of the building to the parking lot and got into Billings' rental car. Once they were safely inside, the older man took a cigar from the console and lit it, enjoying the flavor as it rolled around in his mouth. He turned to look at his companion, who was trying to wave the heavy smoke away from his face. "As I was saying inside, I called the rancher earlier."

"What exactly did you say to her?" Unable to stand the smell any longer, Andrew opened his window to let air into the car.

Billings couldn't keep the smug look from his face. "Oh, I may have mentioned how rough the ranching business is, and of course gave her my condolences on the death of one of her horses."

The sick feeling returned to Andrew's stomach. He knew that they had planned on doing something out at the woman's ranch to discourage her, but he'd never figured them for killing animals. "You killed her horse?"

"I told you we had to do something, you idiot. She wouldn't listen to reason."

Andrew was afraid of the answer he'd get, but he had to ask. "And did it get the results you wanted?"

"No." Billings chewed on his cigar for a few minutes as he thought. He finally rolled down the driver's side window and spat a wad of the tobacco onto the ground outside, then turned back to face Andrew. "I thought I'd give her a while, then call her back. You know, let her think about things for a while." Billings leaned across the seat and opened the glove box, where he had left his cell phone. He turned the device on and hit the redial button.

AFTER INTRODUCING ELLIE to Jeannie, Lex left the small room, not comfortable with all the people in such close quarters. She knew that Amanda would be a good buffer between the two women, and only a tiny part of Lex wanted to stay behind and make certain Ellie kept her distance from her wife. Shaking her head at the jealous thoughts, Lex crossed the den to the desk in the corner and sat down.

Between the new property and the expense of the state of the art alarm system, Lex felt the need to contact the bank and make an appointment to discuss her finances, or lack thereof. She flipped through the Rolodex until she found the number she was looking for, then dialed. It took a minute or so of talking with clerks and waiting, but soon the voice of the bank president came on the line.

"Ms. Walters, what a pleasant surprise. To what do I owe this pleasure?" Mr. Collins was always over-solicitous, and his rapid breathing was a sure sign that he was nervous.

"I'm sure you're aware of my recent expenditures, Mr. Collins." Lex looked around the quiet den, glad that she was alone. "I'd like to come in sometime tomorrow, if you have the time, and talk about getting a loan."

Collins was quiet, not certain if he'd heard her correctly. "A loan?"

"Yes. I'm sure it would only need to be short-term, but because of some recent developments that I don't want to get into over the phone, I'm a little strapped for cash at the moment."

"Oh." The heavy breathing continued as the bank president weighed the options. "Of course, Ms. Walters. I'll be here all day tomorrow, so just come right in whenever it's convenient for you."

"Thank you, Mr. Collins. I appreciate it." Lex hung up, hating the thought of borrowing money. She was about to push the chair away from the desk when the phone rang. Thinking it might be Mr. Collins calling back, she quickly picked up the receiver. "Hello?"

"Walters, have you had time to think some more about my offer?" The low, scratchy voice sounded threatening, even as quiet as it was.

I don't need this. "Look, asshole. I don't know who you think you are, or why you want that piece of land so badly, but you can take your money and shove it up your ass." She sounded a lot braver than she felt, and when she reached for a pencil on the desk, Lex was dismayed to see her hand was shaking.

"Do you remember what I said about the dangers of ranching? That doesn't just mean the animals, you know. Living so far away from town isn't safe, lady. Anything could happen to any one of the people in that house."

"Are you threatening me?"

"Just stating a fact." The voice became even quieter. "I'm tired of jacking around with you, Walters. If I hang up now without results, we'll get that land another way."

Lex took a deep breath, then released it. "Go to hell." She slammed down the phone, trying hard not to throw up. The longer she sat there, the madder she got. "I don't know who that son of a bitch thinks he is, threatening me like that." She got to her feet and stomped across the den, going into Jeannie's room.

"What are you doing?" Amanda asked, seeing her partner go over to the door on the other side of the room. Even though the house had been completed gutted by the fire earlier in the year, the gun safe had suffered only minor damage. When the house was rebuilt after Amanda's mother, in a psychotic fit, burned it down, Lex had the contractor hide the gun safe in a closet in the office.

"Just a precaution." Opening the external door that hid the gun safe, Lex dialed the combination and opened the heavy steel inside door. She pulled out a rifle and checked the bolt, satisfied that it was loaded and ready to go. Putting that gun back into the safe, she repeated the procedure several more times, keeping the last rifle out before locking the safe and closing the outer door.

Amanda put her hand on Lex's arm to keep her from leaving the room. "A precaution? What kind of precaution includes guns?" She looked from Jeannie to Ellie, her own heart starting to pound as her lover remained silent. "Lex? Tell me what's going on."

Not wanting to frighten Amanda, Lex was unsure of what to tell her, so she kept quiet. She allowed the rifle to rest against her shoulder as she left the room, her mind struggling to come up with a way to protect her family in the event that the man carried out his implied threat. She heard footsteps behind her, but didn't stop. She knew that Amanda would follow her.

Once they were upstairs and in the master bedroom, Lex made certain that the safety was on and placed the rifle under her side of the bed. She got up from the floor and looked into her wife's stormy eyes, knowing that she was about to get lambasted for leaving the office without giving an explanation for her actions. "Before you say anything, let me—"

"Oh, so *now* you want to talk?" Amanda put her hands on her hips and glared at Lex. "You couldn't have the decency to tell me downstairs?"

"Amanda, please." Lex sat on the bed and bowed her head, waiting for the rest of the explosion. The silence she received instead surprised her, and she looked up to see tears tracking down Amanda's face. "Hey."

Wiping at her face, Amanda stayed a few steps away. "It hurts that you don't trust me enough to confide in me, Lex. I thought we were partners." Tired of the distance between them, she finally sat next to her wife, but refused to look at her. "I know we've been having difficulties lately, and I know they've mostly been my fault."

"No, sweetheart. It's not—" Lex was silenced by Amanda's hand on her leg. She felt her fear dissipate, leaving behind a heavy weariness. When the hand found hers and squeezed, the weariness was replaced by hope.

"We've got a lot of things to clear up, don't we?"

They did, but Lex didn't know if she could handle going through them at the moment. All she wanted to do was curl up somewhere with Amanda and let the world pass them by, at least for a few days. Lex was tired of everything that had happened, and had a bad feeling in the pit of her stomach that it wasn't over.

DOWNSTAIRS, ELLIE WASN'T too sure what had transpired between Lex and Amanda, but the fussing of the baby demanded her attention. Not wanting to just snatch Lorrie from her mother, she asked, "May I?" At Jeannie's slight nod, Ellie picked up the crying infant. "Someone needs a change." She looked around until she spotted the changing table tucked away in the corner of the room. Once Lorrie's needs had been met, Ellie was about to place her back next to her mother when Jeannie shook her head.

"Oo hol' 'er." The moment the words left Jeannie's mouth, her face turned red. She was tired of sounding so ridiculous and was afraid to look up into Ellie's face for fear of seeing either ridicule or pity.

Ellie rocked the baby in her arms. "You're such a beautiful little girl." She could tell that Jeannie was upset and wanted to try to ease her fears, so she decided to talk to Lorrie, hoping that Jeannie would listen. "When I was about seven, there was a playground about a block from our house. I'd go there with my friends and spend the day swinging, using the slide, and all sorts of fun things." She glanced out of the corner of her eye, and could see that she had Jeannie's undivided attention. "One day, I was pushing my best friend Rhonda in the swing. The seats were made from this heavy plastic, and were suspended by thick chains, so I was pushing as hard as I could to get her high into the air." Ellie stopped the story, reliving the moment.

"Wha' 'appen?"

"At the highest point, Rhonda jumped, and the swing came back and smashed me right in the face." Ellie couldn't remember all of the details, but she did remember the blood and the pain from the broken jaw. "I spent the next two years undergoing reconstructive surgery, not to mention having to learn to talk all over again." She looked Jeannie directly in the eyes. "The more you speak, the better you'll be at it. I'm a nurse's assistant, not a licensed speech therapist, but I can get some books on speech therapy and help you, if you'd like."

"Weally? Bu' why?"

That was the question of the day. *Why, indeed?* At first, Ellie had wanted to help around the house in order to have an excuse to stay, so that she could be near Amanda, and get to know Lex a little better. But when she met Jeannie, she knew that she wanted to help this woman get as much of her life back as possible.

"You're family."

By the look on Jeannie's face, Ellie knew that wasn't a good enough answer. "I like you, Jeannie. You're a good person, and you've tolerated my grumpy cousin." She looked down at

Amanda's sister, finally able to see the resemblance. But what she felt for Jeannie was protective, and she hoped that they'd be able to build a good friendship. "But even if we weren't family, I'd like to be your friend."

Jeannie held out her hand, glad when it was accepted. "I'd wike dat too."

AFTER THAT EVENING'S meal, both households settled down into their own quiet routines. Martha, Charlie and Ronnie went back to the cottage, while the occupants of the main house decided to make it an early night and retire.

In the darkened den, Lex sat quietly thinking about the earlier phone call, while Amanda and Lorrie bade Jeannie goodnight. She knew that the man who had called her was behind the death of the filly, but couldn't understand what was so important about that one parcel of land. The thought that she should just give in rankled her, but keeping the people she loved safe was her top priority. "Maybe I'm just being stubborn."

"That's usually a given," Amanda agreed, standing beside the sofa. She had heard Lex's quiet words as she stepped out of Jeannie's room and couldn't resist answering. "What are you being stubborn about this time?"

"The new property." Lex looked up and could barely make out Amanda's outline, but was comforted by her presence. "Maybe I should just sell it."

Amanda could hear the defeat in her wife's tone, and it concerned her. "Why don't we go upstairs and talk about it there? I think we've all had a long day." She waited until Lex stood up before she started out of the den, then turned when she heard the alarm keypad at the front door beep. Her lover bolted the door and turned around sheepishly.

"Just checking." Satisfied that the alarm was set and the house was secure, Lex followed Amanda upstairs. She couldn't remember the last time she had worried about locking the doors, and the thought saddened her.

After depositing a sleeping Lorrie in her crib, it didn't take long for Lex and Amanda to get ready for bed. They turned off the lights, and snuggled up together in silence. The glow of the alarm display next to the door reminded Lex of the recent troubles, and she couldn't repress a heavy sigh.

Amanda feared the worst when Lex remained quiet for a long time. "I know I'm the last person who should be asking this, but do you want to talk about it?" She felt that it would serve her right if her partner didn't want to confide in her, especially with the way Amanda jumped all over her lately when asked that very same question. She almost didn't hear the softly spoken response.

"I think I've really screwed up this time." Lex continued to look up at the still ceiling fan over the bed, which she could barely make out.

Amanda rolled over onto her side, glad for the small amount of light that came from a nightlight near Lorrie's crib. It illuminated Lex's profile in the otherwise darkened room. "Just what is it that you've supposedly done?"

Lex brought up both of her hands and linked them behind her head. "I didn't take them seriously."

"Who?"

"The guys who keep wanting to buy the new property." Lex turned her head so that she could see Amanda. "What if someone gets hurt just because I'm being stubborn? We've already lost a horse to those assholes, even if I can't prove it."

Reaching across the space between them, Amanda caressed her wife's cheek. "Don't blame yourself for what someone else has done. You can't give in to the demands of others just because they threaten you."

"I don't want anyone to get hurt. There are so many people here depending on me to keep them safe."

Amanda snuggled closer and kissed Lex's chin. "I think you're doing a fine job of that, love."

Tired of her morbid thoughts, Lex pulled Amanda into her arms and kissed the top of her head. "Thanks." She closed her eyes, the love being offered giving her peace like nothing else could.

It seemed to Lex as if she had just closed her eyes when the house alarm sounded. She sat up in bed and glanced at the clock on the nightstand, seeing that it was after three in the morning. Swinging her legs out from under the covers, she pulled on her jeans and hurried over to the keypad by the door, punching in several numbers to silence the alarm.

"What is it?" asked Amanda, as she sat up and rubbed sleepily at her eyes. She turned on the lamp on her side of the bed.

"One of the downstairs windows has been tripped," Lex answered, as she hustled back over to the bed and drew the rifle out from under it. Clad only in her nightshirt and jeans, she started for the door. "Lock up behind me, Amanda. I'll be back as soon as I check this out."

"But—" Amanda's argument was silenced by the door being closed. She was about to get up when the telephone rang.

"Hello? Oh. Hi, Martha." The alarm was wired so that if it was tripped at one house, the other house would also be alerted. Amanda looked over at the crib, where Lorrie continued to sleep. "No. Lex said it was one of the windows downstairs, and she's gone to check on it. Okay, thanks." She hung up the phone, glad to know that Charlie would be joining Lex to check out the house and grounds.

When the alarm company had tried to get Lex to sign a multi-year deal for monitoring, she couldn't help laughing at them. With the county sheriff living less than fifty yards away, she assured them that they didn't need any additional help.

Lex had just closed the door to the master bedroom when she almost ran into Ellie. "What are you doing?"

"I heard the alarm and was going downstairs to check on Jeannie," Ellie said, looking rumpled in a tee shirt that hung to her knees. "Where's Amanda?"

Lex pointed to the door behind her. "She's in our room with Lorrie."

"Maybe I should go with you to where Jeannie is."

"Fine. Follow me downstairs, but stay behind me. Once I've checked the den and Jeannie's room, you can stay in there with the door locked, okay?" Lex started down the stairway, almost jumping out of her skin when Ellie grabbed the back of her nightshirt.

They made it through the hallway and into the den, where Lex carefully checked all the windows. She stepped into the refurbished office and could see the concern on the face of her sister-in-law. "It's okay, Jeannie. Probably just a false alarm." Lex closed the blinds and turned on the light. "I've brought someone to keep you company while I check outside, okay?"

Jeannie nodded as she almost laughed at the way Ellie hung on Lex's shirt.

Ellie sat on the bed next to her. "I hope you don't mind, but I didn't want to be alone," Ellie murmured. "Is it all right if I stay here for a while?"

"Dat's 'ine wi' me."

Lex was relieved. "Great." She was glad that Jeannie wouldn't have to be alone, although she didn't think her cousin Ellie would be much protection. "Close this door and wait until you hear from me. It shouldn't take but a few minutes to check around outside the house."

After inspecting the downstairs windows, Lex turned off the alarm and opened the back door. The cool night air chased the cobwebs from her mind, and she cautiously stepped off the porch and walked around the house to look for intruders. She was almost to the edge of the house when she heard soft footfalls and readied her gun. "Hold it!"

"Dammit, Lex! Put the gun down," Charlie yelled. His hands shook as he quickly lowered his revolver. It scared him to death that he had almost shot someone he loved, but not as much as it seemed to have frightened Lex, who dropped to her knees.

"Oh, God." Placing the gun on the ground, Lex wrapped her arms around herself and began to rock back and forth. "Not again." Her mind flashed back to when she was a teenager, and one of her friends had been killed in a hunting accident. She could smell the blood, and when she closed her eyes, it was Charlie, not her friend, lying in front of her.

Charlie stood nearby, unsure of what to do. He had never seen Lex in such a state. Putting his gun in the holster clipped to his belt, he knelt beside her. "Lex? Honey, it's okay." He put his arm around her shoulders and helped Lex to her feet. "Let's go back inside. It was just a false alarm."

Unable to get past what she had almost done, Lex allowed Charlie to lead her into the house. She didn't even realize when he pushed her down into a chair in the kitchen, and went to lean the rifle—safety on—in the far corner. She was unaware of the footsteps that signaled the arrival of someone else. Lex began to shiver.

Amanda stepped into the room and, and seeing her lover's pale face, took the quilt she had wrapped around herself and hurriedly draped it around Lex instead. "What happened?"

Charlie had the good grace to look embarrassed. "We met at the corner of the porch behind the kitchen; both of us were pointing our guns. When I yelled at Lex, she dropped to the ground and went quiet on me."

"You almost shot her?" Amanda tried to control herself, but her voice rose. "Is that what you're trying to tell me?"

"No! I don't think either one of us would have pulled the trigger without knowing who we were shooting at. She just," Charlie waved at a still silent Lex, "shut down. I've never seen her like this before."

Amanda laid her arm around Lex's shoulder and leaned in close. "Lex? Honey, it's all right. No one was hurt." She continued to talk in low tones for several minutes, trying to get through to her partner.

"Get them out," Lex rasped.

Shocked by the raw tone, Amanda was afraid of what Lex was asking. "What?"

Lex turned her head to face Charlie, who was shocked by the anguish he could see in her eyes. "I want every damned gun out of this house, tonight. Right now." She had to hold her hands together in order to keep them from shaking. "Please."

"Of course, Lex. I'll take care of it." Charlie nodded to Amanda, then quickly left the kitchen.

"I could have killed him, you know." Lex's voice was quiet, but steadier than it had been. "That was too damned close."

Amanda covered Lex's hands with her own. "But you didn't. Everything turned out okay."

Leaning her head against Amanda's shoulder, Lex closed her eyes. "I flashed back to when I was fourteen and Lawrence was killed in that hunting accident. Except I saw Charlie lying dead, not him." She shook her head. "Never again, Amanda. I won't let that happen again."

"I know you won't, love." Amanda pulled Lex close, and gave silent thanks for everyone's safety.

DAWN BROUGHT WITH it a somber morning as the household readied itself for another difficult day. Lex spent extra time at her desk, gathering up the necessary papers to take to the bank. Amanda stood nearby, a frown on her face. She had tried for over an hour to dissuade her partner from leaving the house, especially after what had transpired the evening before. "If you won't listen to reason, then at least let me go with you."

"And who's going to take care of Lorrie?" Lex tucked the remaining papers into a folder and stood up. "I'm fine, Amanda. Really." But she wasn't, and she knew it. After they had gone back to bed, Lex had lain there quietly, afraid to close her eyes and see what her imagination devised. It would take a lot longer than she wanted to let on to get over that image.

Seeing the haunted look in Lex's eyes, Amanda didn't believe a word of what she said. All she wanted to do was take her hurting wife into her arms and never let her go. "We can both go with you."

Lex shook her head. "I'm not going to be gone that long, sweetheart. Just to the bank, then back to the house. Shouldn't take more than an hour or so." She stepped closer and put her hands on Amanda's hips. "Surely you can do without me for that long."

"Smartass." Raising her hands, Amanda linked them behind Lex's neck and pulled her head down for a long kiss. She felt her body tugged closer until there wasn't any space between them, as Lex deepened the kiss. When they finally broke apart, both were breathing heavily. "Kiss me like that again, and you're definitely not going anywhere, Slim."

"Oh, yeah?"

Amanda gave her a quick peck on the lips. "Yeah." She brushed her hands down the front of Lex's dark gray, cotton shirt, loving the feel of the material and the woman beneath it. "An hour or so, huh?"

"Yup." Lex gasped as the wandering hands cupped her breasts. "You're not playing fair, Amanda."

"Who says I'm playing?" Taking a step back, Amanda winked. "Don't be gone too long, honey. I've got plans for you this afternoon."

"Plans. Yeah." Nodding to herself, Lex started out of the room, then heard Amanda call her name. "Huh?"

Taking pity on her flustered wife, Amanda handed Lex the envelope she had left on the desk. "You're forgetting something, love."

"Right." Lex took the papers and leaned over to give Amanda a quick kiss on the cheek. "Back in a flash." She started out the door, then turned around. "I love you."

"Love you, too," Amanda replied. She followed Lex out onto the front porch and watched as her partner made her way into her truck. "Be safe," she whispered, then waved as the truck disappeared down the road and out of sight.

Chapter Nineteen

JEANNIE HEARD THE muted voices in the den, then the closing of the front door as Lex left for the morning. She didn't know all the details about the night before, but after Charlie came in and gathered up the remaining guns, she actually felt more secure. *The thought of sleeping that close to those things made me nervous.* Another thing that worried her was the appearance of her sister-in-law. Lex looked as if she hadn't slept at all, and Jeannie could see the slight tremor in the usually sure hands of the woman she had come to depend on for her quiet strength. A light knock on the door interrupted her musings, and her mood brightened when Ellie stepped into the room, carrying Lorrie. "Hi."

"Good morning. This little one told me that she missed her mommy, so I thought I'd better listen." Ellie placed the infant next to her mother, pleased when Jeannie automatically brought her good arm around to cradle Lorrie. Her own sudden attachment to Lorrie was a surprise. Ellie had never been around infants in a personal setting, so she was completely shocked when she felt almost maternal around Lorrie. When Amanda knocked on her bedroom door earlier in the morning and asked if she'd take care of the baby, Ellie couldn't refuse. Now here she was, with probably the same goofy look on her face as she'd seen on everyone else when they were in the room with the smallest member of the family.

"Danks." Jeannie looked down at her daughter, getting lost for a moment in her eyes. *Oh, Frank. Our daughter is going to be beautiful. I just wish you could be here to see her.*

Ellie watched as Jeannie bonded with her daughter, and it made her think about her own mother. She wondered what she had done wrong in her life to break that precious link. Unlike her brother Billy, she had followed her mother's examples, adhering strictly to the rules and conditions set forth by Naomi. *And look where it got me. Ostracized, and thousands of miles away from home.*

Ellie felt the familiar hurt blossoming inside and turned away from the touching scene of mother and child. "I'll be right back." She stepped out of the room and almost ran into Amanda, who was on her way in. "Excuse me."

"Are you all right?" Amanda put her hand out and caught Ellie's arm as she tried to walk by. "Ellie?"

"Please, just let me go." The last thing Ellie wanted was for Amanda to see her this way. Not wanting her pity, she tried to at least keep from facing her cousin's wife. "Jeannie's holding the baby, so you might want to go in and visit."

Not to be deterred, Amanda refused to let go. "I will, in a bit." She led Ellie to the sofa and sat down, then turned to face the other woman. "Are you still having problems with Lex? Because if that's it, I can talk to her."

"No, we're good." The concern in Amanda's voice brought a lump to Ellie's throat. She had resigned herself to being only family in Amanda's eyes, but the warm hand on her skin was hard to ignore. She swallowed hard, then turned. Seeing compassion and mistaking it for something else, she decided to throw caution to the wind. "Amanda, I need to tell you something."

LEX WALKED ALONG, noticing how the leaves were beginning to fall from the Bradford flowering pear trees that lined the main street in Somerville. She recalled the flak a few years previously when the city council had opposed the cost of planting them, until several private groups came forward with the money. The hardy plants grew quickly, being drought and heat tolerant, and they brightened up the entire downtown area. Finally reaching the bank, she took a moment to watch a pair of sparrows fight over a crumb of something before both of them took flight and hid in the nearest tree. Nervously brushing her hands down the front of her neatly pressed jeans, she entered the building, where she was met by Mr. Collins.

"Ms. Walters, welcome," the bank president said. "It's a pleasure to see you again." Even though it was early in the day, he had removed his jacket and sweat rings could be seen under his arms. He held out his hand and, after an enthusiastic shake, led Lex into his office, and closed the door behind them. "Please, have a seat."

Lex took the chair closest to the door and leaned forward. "I'd like to thank you for seeing me on such short notice, Mr. Collins. I know you're a busy man."

He waved a pudgy hand in the air. "I'm never too busy to

see you. Now, you mentioned something yesterday about needing a short-term loan?"

"Yes." Lex opened the envelope that she had brought with her and handed several papers across the desk. "As you can see, I've had a few unexpected expenditures come up recently, and with winter coming, I don't want to run short."

Collins picked up his glasses and put them on, reading over the documents that Lex had provided. "I see." Reading further, his eyes widened and he looked up. "You're willing to mortgage the land you just acquired? But it's worth several times what you're asking for."

Lex nodded. "Exactly. But the stock we'll be selling in the spring will more than cover the loan, so there shouldn't be a problem. I just wanted to give the bank good collateral."

"It's a more than generous arrangement, Ms. Walters. Are you sure about this?" Although he would have probably given her a loan on her signature alone, Collins wasn't one to turn down a good business opportunity.

"Completely." Lex felt the butterflies in her stomach settle as she watched the bank president get on the phone and talk to one of his clerks about getting the paperwork ready. A timid knock on the door caused her to turn around, and she couldn't help but smile at the woman bearing a tray with coffee and sweet rolls. "Hi, Barbara."

"Good morning, Lex. It's been a while, hasn't it?" Barbara put the tray down on the desk and stole a glance at Collins, who was still on the phone. Barbara had heard through the bank grapevine about Jeannie's stroke and Frank's death, but didn't want to just show up at the ranch uninvited. "How's Amanda? Please tell her how sorry I am about all that's happened lately."

"She's doing as well as she can, thank you. I'll tell her you asked about her." The woman standing before her looked tired. "How are you doing? Is Janna keeping you out too late?"

Barbara checked to see if Collins was listening, but he was still concentrating on arranging the loan papers. "Uh, no. Janna moved back north a month ago to take care of her family."

Damn. Open mouth and insert foot, Lexington. No wonder she looks so ragged. "I'm sorry to hear that."

"It's okay." Barbara jumped as the bank president hung up his phone. "I've got to go." She left the office before Lex could say another word.

Collins stood and gestured toward the door. "If you'll just follow me, we'll get those papers signed so that you can be on your way, Ms. Walters."

"AMANDA, I NEED to tell you something." Ellie took Amanda's hands in hers and scooted closer. Her heartbeat pounded in her ears. "Do you remember when I first came here?"

Not sure where the conversation was heading, Amanda nodded. "I do. Why?"

"The first moment I saw you, I became so confused. All my life, I'd been taught that you had to lead a certain life, and anything else was morally wrong." Looking down at their hands, Ellie whispered, "Meeting you, someone who was obviously a good person, threw everything I'd been taught off kilter. Years and years of listening to my mother, who was, to me, as close to a saint as I'd ever meet, went flying out the window."

"A saint?"

Ellie looked up, her face wearing an embarrassed grin. "Yeah. I'd heard all my life how she sacrificed everything to raise me, all by herself, until my step-dad came along. She went to church, taught Sunday school, helped the poor, worked on all sorts of Christian committees. Everybody acted like she was Christ's righthand woman. So, not knowing any better, I thought she was right about everything." She sighed. "And up until I came here, I continued to think that way." She wasn't about to go into how she'd followed Naomi around, spouting Scriptures and damning everyone who didn't think their way, including Billy. Or how her eyes were finally opened when she had been laid off, and her mother refused to help her. No, those things would stay in the past, just as she hoped that the woman sitting next to her would be a part of her future. Ellie brushed a strand of hair away from Amanda's face. "You have no idea how incredibly wonderful you are, do you?"

"Me?" Amanda scoffed. "I don't think so."

"Yes, you." Releasing her grip on Amanda's hand, Ellie rose and stepped away from the sofa. "I see you, every day, taking care of the people in this house without complaint. And it seems like you never get any thanks for it." Before Amanda could protest, she held up one hand. "No, really. My cousin has no idea the things you've sacrificed for her, does she? I've been watching, and I know."

Amanda stood up also. "It's not like that at all, Ellie. We've compromised, not sacrificed. If you're talking about living out here, it was my idea. I love the peace and quiet the ranch offers, and the short drive from town is perfect to help me unwind when I get off work."

"And what about having a family? Is that one of your compromises, too?" Ellie moved closer, until they were almost touching. "Don't you want children?"

The question hit Amanda in one of her most vulnerable spots, and she felt her composure slip. "Of course I do. And when the time is right, I'm sure Lex and I will talk about it."

"But you already know how she feels about kids, don't you?" Hating to see the hurt she'd put in Amanda's eyes, Ellie ran one of her hands down the other woman's arm. "I'm sorry. I shouldn't have said that."

"But it's true. Lex doesn't want kids." Leaning closer, Amanda allowed herself to be pulled into Ellie's arms, accepting the comfort she so desperately needed.

LEX WALKED OUT of the bank feeling better than she had in weeks. She now had no worries about the ranch surviving the coming winter, and she felt more confident in her ability to take care of her family. As she headed back to where she had parked her truck, she noticed a familiar figure watching her from across the street. When they made eye contact, the man darted into the closest alley. "That little bastard." Looking both ways, Lex waited until it was clear before she jogged across the street, intent on having a visit with her watcher.

She was halfway down the length of the alley when she heard something behind her. Before Lex could turn around, she felt something poke her in the back. She stopped.

"I think we need to talk, Ms. Walters."

Holding her hands up even with her shoulders, Lex turned around slowly. "Wilson, wasn't it?" She nodded at the gun he pointed at her. "Is that really necessary?"

"You've made it that way." He gestured with the gun. "Let's go back a little further. I'd hate for someone to disturb our little chat." Never taking his eyes off Lex, Wilson waited until they passed a trash dumpster, then motioned for Lex to put her back against the wall of a building. "That should be far enough."

Lex could feel the rough brick scratching through her shirt and the sensation somehow calmed her. She thought that if she could just keep him talking, that somehow she'd be able to get out of the alley alive. "What's this all about?"

Andrew glanced around, assuring himself they were still alone. "Don't play stupid with me. You know what we want."

"Why? I'll admit it's a nice patch of land, but you don't look like the ranching type." Lex lowered her hands and crossed her arms over her chest in an attempt to appear nonchalant.

"It's one of the last pieces we need for the resort, and believe me, my employer will do whatever it takes to get it."

Lex pushed off from the wall, which caused Wilson to pull the hammer back on his revolver. "Resort?" Seeing the gun shake in his hand, she held up her own hands again. "Whoa. Easy there."

"I've got a check in my pocket. Sell the property to me, and we can forget this little incident." Andrew was beginning to perspire, and he could feel his stomach begin to knot.

"I can't."

Andrew frowned and stepped closer. "You can't? Dammit, lady, we're not playing around here. If we can't get the property from you, we'll get it from your heirs." He aimed the gun at her chest. "And if not from them, then we'll get it from *their* heirs." He didn't want to shoot Lexington Walters, but it was either the rancher, or him. And Andrew Wilson hadn't gotten as far as he had without a strong sense of self-preservation.

Lex sensed that the man before her wasn't a killer. "You don't want to do this." She spoke quietly and held out one hand. "Give me the gun before someone gets hurt." As Lex reached for the gun, she saw Wilson's finger tighten on the trigger. The loud report from the gun echoed through the alley, and the birds that had been nesting in nearby trees flew away in a panic.

THE SILENCE IN the room was broken only by the sound of rapid keystrokes as Terence, sitting at the dilapidated desk, hurried to complete a personal challenge. He spied the red digital numbers from the clock across the room, and took a calming breath. He assumed he had at least another couple of hours before he was to meet Liz for lunch, but he didn't want to take any chances.

Liz's increasingly bizarre behavior was only one of the reasons for Terence's change of heart. Fearing what would happen in prison to someone as "delicate" as himself, he didn't want to get caught, and some of the things that Liz was doing were sure to bring about their capture.

Coming face to face with one of the people who their actions had damaged had also had a profound effect on his conscience. Hearing Liz constantly complain about how her eldest daughter was "ruined" and of no use to her helped him realize that the woman was completely incompetent, and again he questioned his role in getting her released from the mental hospital. He hoped that what he was doing would help to relieve at least a part of his guilt.

Terence knew that he couldn't return *all* the money that he had taken from the Walters woman, but he was determined to do the best that he could. Using the email addresses he had from the original documents, he wrote Lexington Walters and Liz's youngest daughter, explaining what had happened. He also added a heartfelt apology for his part in the scheme and assured them they would never hear from him again. After clicking the "send" key, Terence felt a huge weight lift from his shoulders.

He sat for several minutes enjoying the freeing of his conscience, then went back to work and removed from his laptop all traces of what he had done. The last thing he needed was for Liz to start snooping around and find out that he had turned against her. Hearing a knock, he closed the lid of the computer and went to the door, wishing it had a peephole. "Who is it?"

"This is the manager. I'm sorry to bother you, sir, but we've had a severe water leak in the room next to yours, and we need to come in and check your lavatory."

Terence unlocked the door and was shoved back several feet by a hulk of a man whose hairy fists grabbed him by the shirt and slammed him into the wall. "Hey! Look, buddy, I think you've made a mistake." His worry turned to abject terror when a small woman stepped inside and closed the door. "Liz?"

"What have you been up to, Terence?" she asked sweetly.

"I don't know what you mean," he stammered, watching as she walked around the room, picking up different things and putting them down. "I was going to meet you for lunch, as we planned. I never expected to see you here."

Elizabeth was standing at the desk. She put her hand on the computer, then pulled it away. "It's still warm; imagine that." She picked up the laptop and threw it across the room, where it crashed against the far wall and fell behind the bed. "Don't play games with me." She nodded to her cohort, and he slammed one hand hard into Terence's stomach.

Gagging at the bile rising in his throat, Terence struggled to catch his breath. "No," he sputtered, just as another beefy hand smashed into his ribcage. He felt the distinct snap of bone. Black spots swam before his eyes as he was jerked to his feet again. "Please, Liz." She came toward him. "Don't."

"My dear boy, you've become a liability to me." Elizabeth patted Terence on the cheek, much as she would a child. "Especially because you're expensive and unpredictable." She turned and headed for the door. "Clean this mess up for me, would you, Eddie? Thanks to our friend here, I've got a long vacation to plan."

"Yes, ma'am," the thug said. His grin showed several gaps where he was missing teeth, and he waited until the door closed behind the petite woman before he removed a gun from beneath his jacket. "Let's take a drive."

TIME SEEMED TO stand still for Ellie; she was enjoying holding Amanda in her arms. They stood in the middle of the den, Amanda softly crying while the older woman comforted her by running one hand over her hair. "Sssh. It's okay," Ellie murmured. She used her other hand to lightly rub Amanda's back, hoping that her touch would help soothe away some of the hurt.

For Amanda, it felt good to finally be able to release some of her pent-up emotions. She didn't know why having a family was so important to her, but hearing Lex's negative thoughts on the subject time and time again was more than she could stand. She took a deep breath to try to get herself back under control and pulled back so that she could look Ellie in the eye. "Thanks."

"No problem," Ellie whispered, her voice husky. She watched as Amanda moistened her lips, and her heart began to race. *This is it.* "Amanda, I—" Ellie leaned forward and closed her eyes.

At that exact moment, Charlie burst into the room with Martha close behind. "Amanda, I'm afraid there's been a problem in town."

Ellie quickly stepped away from Amanda, who had a confused look on her face. *Damn!*

The sheriff stopped and stared at the two women. *I didn't see what I thought I did...or did I?*

Amanda stepped out of Ellie's embrace, not too sure what had just transpired between them. *Was she about to... No. We had cleared all that up.* Then she remembered that they weren't the only two people in the room and that Charlie had said something to her. She turned toward him. "What did you say?" She saw Martha's tear-stained face behind the sheriff, and Amanda felt her heart jump into her throat. "What kind of problem?"

"I don't have many details yet, but there's been a shooting. They've taken Lex to the hospital." Even as he tried to keep a professional demeanor, the lawman's voice shook with emotion. "I'm on my way in now and thought you'd like a ride." He held out a hand to Amanda, who rushed into his arms.

Ellie tried to keep the disgusted look from her face. Although she had recently reconciled with her cousin, she couldn't help but be angry that even when Lex wasn't present, she interfered with Ellie's attempts to profess her true feelings to Amanda.

Amanda wanted nothing more than to rush out and check on her lover, but the sound of Lorrie's cry from Jeannie's room reminded Amanda of other responsibilities. "The baby. Who's going to take care of her?"

"I'll stay," Ellie offered. She was glad to help and felt that she'd just be in the way when they got to town. And she didn't like the look she was getting from Martha, who had witnessed the same scene as Charlie.

Amanda turned and tried to offer a smile. "Thank you." She allowed Charlie and Martha to lead her from the room, hoping her legs wouldn't fail her.

SOMERVILLE WASN'T A large town, but since the local hospital served most of the county, it boasted a well-staffed emergency room. Usually they dealt with car accidents, broken bones, burns, and after-hours stomach aches. So when they were alerted to two blood-covered individuals being brought in with the words "gunshot" and "lots of blood," the staff readied for them quickly.

The doors opened, and two gurneys were wheeled inside. Directed by one of the nurses, the attendants split up and placed the patients in two different rooms. "This one's lost a lot of blood! I can't find a pulse," the attending physician declared when the bed rolled in. He began to bark out orders, which were muffled as the door closed.

Across the hall, another doctor was taking care of his own patient. "Can you hear me?" He noted the glazed look in the victim's eyes and knew it was most likely due to shock. Being extremely gentle, he pulled the blood-soaked shirt away from the patient's body.

While the doctors did their job, a young deputy entered the emergency room, his uniform splashed with blood. Barely out of college, Brett Shields had taken a job with the sheriff's office in hopes that the training would prepare him for a future career as a police officer in some big city. But after what he had witnessed today, he wasn't so sure he was suited to the field of law enforcement. He stepped up to the nurse's station and waited until the head nurse turned around. "Excuse me, ma'am."

Slender and middle-aged, the RN looked as if she'd seen it all. Her gray hair was cut short, and the glasses she wore reflected the florescent lights overhead. "Yes?"

"I'm here about the two people that were just brought in. Is there any word on their condition?" He hoped to have something to report to the sheriff, who had radioed that he was on his way.

The nurse shook her head. "Not yet, I'm afraid. The doctors are busy with them now, but if you'll just have a seat, I'll let you know as soon as I can."

"Thank you." Brett turned to find a place to sit, then looked down at his blood-covered hands, which were shaking. "God." The deputy found his way to a bathroom and scrubbed until his skin was red, knowing that he'd never forget the scene, or the smell. Thinking about what he had witnessed, Brett barely made it to the toilet, where he retched until the dry heaves made him dizzy.

THE RIDE TO town was the longest Amanda could ever remember taking. She sat in the back seat of the sheriff's car, holding Martha's hand and trying to comfort the older woman who was silently trying to comfort her. Several more radio reports came in as they drove, but none could give them any updates or details on exactly what had transpired in the alley across from the bank.

When the hospital came into view, Amanda unbuckled her seat belt and had her door open before the car came to a complete stop. She was halfway to the emergency room door before either Charlie or Martha could climb out of the vehicle.

Once inside, she looked around frantically, trying to find someone who could help her. Several people were seated in chairs that lined the walls, some looking more in need of medical attention than others. A nurse about her own age walked by, and Amanda touched her arm. "Excuse me, I'm looking for some information about my partner."

The nurse stopped and studied the woman before her. "Your partner?"

Exasperated, Amanda tried to keep from slapping the woman. "Yes, my partner. Her name is Lexington Walters, and she was brought in just a little while ago."

"I'm afraid I can't give out any information at this time." The nurse turned to leave, but the sudden grip on her arm stopped her. "I beg your pardon?"

"Please. I have to know where she is, and if she's okay."

Twisting out of Amanda's grasp, the nurse shook her head. "I'm sorry, but you'll have to check with the admitting nurse. I honestly don't know anything." She hurried away, back to pediatrics where she belonged.

Amanda felt a hand on her shoulder and turned around to see Martha's concerned face. "I can't get anyone to help me."

"That's all right, hon. Charlie's going to talk to the head

nurse. Being sheriff has its advantages, you know." Martha escorted Amanda to a quiet spot in the waiting area, where they could watch as Charlie spoke to a woman at the nurse's station. While he was talking, a young man in a deputy's uniform stepped up beside him to speak.

Amanda saw the dark splotches on the deputy's uniform and became lightheaded. She wondered if any of the blood belonged to Lex. Sharp pains ripped through her chest at the thought. Wrapping her arms around herself, Amanda leaned forward until her head rested on her thighs. She didn't see Charlie turn and wave.

Martha saw the signal, and she patted Amanda on the back. "Let's go see what's going on." She stood and helped Amanda to her feet, feeling relief at the smile on her husband's face. *Everything must be all right if he's grinning like that. One of these days, I'm going to move to Florida and retire, so I don't have to be around while that girl of mine takes years off my life. The trouble she gets into would drive anyone into an early grave.* She gladly accepted a hug from Charlie. "She's okay?" Martha asked, as she watched Amanda being led into one of the treatment rooms.

"She's going to be fine," he assured her. "At least until she gets home and gets a piece of Ellie."

Martha looked up at her husband's face. "You saw that, too, did you?"

"Uh-huh. Maybe someone should talk to Ellie and see if she has a death wish."

"That might not be such a bad idea. She and Lexie just now started getting along, and I'd hate for that to change just because Ellie's got a hankering for what Lexie has." Martha hugged Charlie. "Why don't we go get some coffee, and you can tell me what happened to our girl today." They started down the hall, with Charlie explaining the events as best as he knew them.

Amanda opened the treatment room door and stepped inside. She saw the still form on the narrow bed, covered to the chin with a sheet and heavy blanket. Unsure if her lover was awake, she kept her voice low. "Lex?"

Her brain still foggy, Lex wasn't sure if she had heard anything or not. She turned her head toward the sound and saw what she thought was a vision. Opening her mouth to speak, Lex tried to form words, but couldn't seem to remember how. She frowned, confused.

Amanda moved closer. "Honey, can you hear me?" She looked around for a chair and saw lying on a trashcan what was left of the shirt that Lex had worn that morning. It had been cut off her body and was liberally soaked with blood, which confused Amanda. The doctor had told her that Lex had a knot on the side of her head, and was suffering from shock. They planned on keeping her overnight for observation, but she was otherwise fine. *Was he lying, or does he not know what he's doing?*

Lex's frown disappeared, replaced by a slight smile. *She's not a dream.* It was hard to tell, since she'd had some strange ones every time she dozed off. She slipped her hand out from under the blanket and waited until Amanda took it. "Hey."

"Hi." Amanda sat next on the bed to her partner, holding their linked hands to her chest. She doubted if she'd ever be able to let go. "You gave us quite a scare, you know." She could still see traces of dried blood on Lex's neck and in her hair. "What happened?"

"To tell you the truth, I was pretty damned scared, too." Lex closed her eyes and could see the alley again. "It's all pretty blurry." She remembered seeing Andrew Wilson across the street from the bank, and following him between the buildings, and then having a gun pointed at her. The more she struggled to think, the more it hurt. "I can't. Head hurts."

Amanda could tell it pained Lex and tried to put her at ease. "It's okay. Just relax." She stroked Lex's hair until the injured woman's breathing smoothed out. A light knock on the door caused Amanda to turn her head, and she smiled at Charlie and Martha as they stepped inside.

"How's she doing?" Charlie asked, while Martha went to the other side of the bed to see for herself.

Not releasing her hold, Amanda continued to speak quietly. "Her head hurts, and she's a little disoriented. She can't seem to remember much about what happened to her."

"From what the doctor told us outside, that's not too uncommon," Charlie tried to reassure her. "But I'm hoping once the guy across the hall wakes up, he can shed more light on things."

"What guy?" Martha asked. Once she assured herself that Lex was going to be okay, she wanted all the details as to what had transpired.

Charlie backed away from the bed, beckoning them to follow. "The man who had the gun." He didn't want Lex to overhear, both to keep her calm, and to not taint her memory of the incident.

"He's here?" Amanda snapped, clenching her fists at her sides. "The son of a bitch who tried to shoot Lex is still nearby? Are you people crazy?"

"Calm down, Amanda. He's under guard." Charlie moved to block the door so that Amanda couldn't go after the man. "Not to mention that he nearly bled to death on the way to the hospital, so I doubt he's going anywhere for a while."

Now that she knew that Lex was in no immediate danger, Amanda calmed down. At least a bit. She crossed her arms over her chest and glared at the sheriff. "Good. Serves him right."

Martha's eyes widened. Never had she heard Amanda say anything even remotely negative about someone else, much less wish death on them. She stepped closer and began to rub the young woman's back in a soothing pattern. "Do you have any idea what happened?"

"From what I've been told about the evidence at the scene, the two of them were in the alley across from the bank, and he had a gun. There was a struggle, he was shot in the leg, and Lex cracked her head on the building behind her. When the paramedics arrived, she was in shock, but was trying to stem his loss of blood. Otherwise, he'd have died."

"She should have let him," Amanda muttered, still shaken. She couldn't even imagine the terror that Lex had gone through, having a gun pointed at her like that. "Do we know *why* he had a gun? And why Lex?"

Charlie scratched the back of his neck. "Well, we're working on that." Truth was, with the check Wilson had in his coat pocket, he had a pretty good idea as to what the motive had been. He knew he shouldn't discuss the details of the case yet.

"Right." Amanda recognized that look and also knew that she wouldn't be getting any more information out of Charlie. "Do you think it would be okay if I stayed here tonight with Lex? I don't want her waking up alone."

Knowing that he'd been let off the hook, the sheriff nodded. "I don't see why not. Let me go talk to her doctor, and let them know."

"He's not a very good liar," Amanda commented to Martha.

Martha gave Amanda a one-armed hug. "Why do you think I married him? Well, besides the fact that he looks so cute in his uniform." She leaned in close to whisper, "Not to mention, how good he looks *out* of it."

"Eew." Amanda covered her ears. "I didn't need that visual, thank you very much." It was like thinking about her parents having sex: Amanda knew it happened, she just didn't want to know about it. But she was thankful for the distraction, which allowed her emotions time to settle down after the morning's events. She kissed the older woman on the cheek and returned the hug.

Chapter Twenty

IT WASN'T THE weary ache in her bones that woke Lex, or the painful tempo in her head that matched her heartbeat. The last vestiges of an all-too-real nightmare were the culprit, and she struggled to regain her composure as she looked around. The room was unfamiliar, and for a brief period of time she didn't know where she was. Attempting to ward off the headache, Lex's eyes searched the dimly lit room for anything that could jog her memory. When they lit upon a sleeping figure curled up in a beat-up, padded chair, Lex couldn't help but smile. A strangled cry from the restless form was all she needed to move into action. As she sat up, Lex ignored the sudden dizziness and swung her feet over the side of the bed, and fell to her knees next to the chair. "Amanda, sweetheart. Wake up."

The soft plea caused Amanda to jerk upright, and her eyes flew open in alarm. Even in the dim light, she was easily able to make out the features of the woman before her. Amanda raised one hand and shakily traced a pattern across Lex's face. "You're okay," she whispered, her voice cracking.

"Yeah, I'm fine." Lex used the arms of Amanda's chair to push herself into a standing position. The dizziness returned, which caused her to stumble back against the bed.

In an instant, Amanda was up and reaching for Lex. "I don't think so." With her help, Lex was back under the thin covers in no time, and only then did Amanda feel like she could relax. She sat on the edge of the bed, trying to calm her rapidly beating heart. "What were you doing out of bed?" Over and over again, she fiddled with the blanket, more to have something to do with her hands than anything else.

"I woke up and was worried about you." Whether it was the medication or the bump on her head, Lex suddenly felt extremely tired, and had to fight to keep her eyes open. "That chair can't be very comfortable. Why don't you just come up here with me?"

As much as she wanted to comply, Amanda didn't know if that was a good idea. But when her partner scooted to the far edge of the bed and held out her hand, all Amanda's reservations went flying out the window. She slipped off her shoes and crawled in beside Lex and snuggled close to her, fearing if she held her tightly that Lex would shatter.

Comforted at last, Lex said, "Love you," and allowed herself to drift off into a dreamless slumber.

Amanda felt the body she held relax, and knew that Lex had fallen asleep. "I love you, too," she whispered. Lying in the narrow bed, holding Lex's head to her chest, her tears fell into the dark hair as she came to grips with what she had almost lost on this day.

The man who had been in the alley with Lex had not yet regained consciousness, and Lex herself hadn't been much help in clearing up the details of what had happened. All she could remember was the struggle over the gun, then her head being slammed into the brick wall behind her. The paramedics on the scene had reported that Lex was using her shirttail to try to stem the flow of blood from the man's heavily bleeding leg, but she had been non-responsive to their verbal commands, obviously suffering from shock.

Each time Charlie questioned Lex, he was able to get a few more answers, but Amanda had finally put a stop to his interrogation when Lex got upset and her headache became worse. Amanda knew it was only a temporary respite, but she vowed to protect her lover from everyone, including family, for as long as she could.

THE DEPUTY OUTSIDE the closed door stretched his arms over his head in an effort to keep from falling asleep. He hated having to work guard duty, especially on someone who was not only handcuffed to the bed, but was clearly in no shape to attempt to escape. Hearing quiet footfalls coming closer, he jumped to his feet, glad to see a friendly face. "Good evening, Nurse Duggan."

Slender, with brown eyes and short dark hair, the nurse held a Styrofoam cup, which she handed to him. "I thought a cup of coffee might help."

"Thank you, ma'am." Inhaling the strong aroma, Deputy Terry Mardsen thought he could easily fall in love—with the coffee. "Is it always this quiet around here?"

"To tell you the truth, this is the most exciting it's been here in a while." She nodded toward the door. "I need to go in and check on my patient. Why don't you take a quick break? I don't think he's going anywhere."

Deputy Mardsen looked around to see if they were alone, then glanced down at his watch. It was after three in the morning, and he knew the nurse was right. "Thanks. I think I'll go see if there's something good in the snack machine." He took another deep drink of coffee, then left the cup on his chair before moving stiffly down the hall.

It didn't take long for Nurse Duggan to check on Andrew Wilson. She was about to leave the room when his eyes opened, and he reached out for her. She said, "Well, hello there."

He tried to sit up, but was easily held down by the nurse. Turning his head, Wilson noticed that his hand was cuffed to the metal railings on the bed. "Wha—"

"Just stay calm, sir. Let me go get the doctor for you, and he can answer any questions, all right?" She hurried from the room, not even noticing that the deputy hadn't returned to his post.

Around the corner, a pudgy, sweating man watched the goings on with great interest. He took the few steps needed to slip inside the hospital room, then locked the door behind him. "Hello, Wilson. Good to see you awake."

Wilson flinched at the sound of the voice. He reached for the call button, but Billings quickly used his gloved hand to move it out of reach.

"That's no way to say hello, is it?" Billings went to the left side of the bed and dug into his jacket pocket and removed a syringe. "You fucked up, big time. I've been ordered to cut our losses and get the hell out of this hick town."

"But..." Andrew had to clear his throat to continue. Hoarse from lack of use, his voice sounded as if he had swallowed rocks. "What about the land we already have? And the work that's been done?"

Billings took the lid from the empty syringe and held it between his fingers. "We haven't gotten much of the land cleared, so that's not that big of a deal. They'll sell it back to the idiots around here, and take a loss." He opened the plunger wide, then inserted it into the intravenous tube that was taped to Andrew's hand. "What have you told the authorities, Wilson?"

"Nothing, I swear!" Andrew tried to reach the tube to pull it out of his hand, but couldn't. "Let me go, and we can both get out of here, Mr. Billings." His voice continued to rise, until Billings grabbed a pillow with his free hand and held it over Wilson's face.

"I can't. You'd never make it past the door with that leg wound. Sorry about this, kid." Pushing the plunger, Billings watched as the bubble of air made its way through the IV, all the while holding the young man down with his other arm. "Survival of the smartest, boy. Rule number one."

He put the cap back on the syringe and stuffed in into his pocket, then took special care to straighten up the bed. "Too bad, kid. You had some promise. Just a few more things to handle." Unlocking the door, Billings sneaked out of the room and into the night.

CHARLIE SAT AT his desk, staring at the papers strewn about. He had recently returned from the hospital, trying to find a link between the man who tried to kill Lex and whoever was buying up all the land outside of town. They were very good at hiding their corporate tracks, as no two "buyers" were the same. But he had the sneaking suspicion that it was all tied together.

He rubbed his eyes and sighed. The day had already been long, and he figured it would be well into the evening before he left the office. The buzz of his phone caused him to sit up straighter.

"Sheriff, Deputy Mardsen is on the line. There's a situation at the hospital."

Charlie rose and grabbed his hat. On his way out of the office he paused at his secretary's desk. "Did he say what it was about?"

"No, sir, just that it was something you'd better see."

Wasting no time, Charlie was halfway down the hall and had to yell over his shoulder. "Tell him I'm on my way."

THE HALLWAY WAS filled with doctors, nurses, and sheriff's department personnel, all of whom chattered amongst themselves. Sheriff Bristol was in the hospital room with Nurse Duggan, who once again told her story.

"He woke up a little after three, and I immediately went in search of the doctor on call. As far as I could tell, Mr. Wilson didn't appear to be in any discomfort." She watched as the sheriff studied the dead man's wrist. "The chafing wasn't there before I left, but I thought that maybe he just tried to get loose before I came back."

Charlie nodded, and walked around the bed. "Maybe." He squatted and raised the blanket, then shook his head. "If a man is thrashing around enough to bruise his wrist, you'd think that the sheet and blankets would be worked free, wouldn't you?" Standing up, he moved to the foot of the bed, where he once again lifted the blanket, and saw that the sheet kicked loose. "Like this."

Well, I'll be damned. The old country sheriff isn't quite as slow as he acts. Nurse Duggan crossed her arms over her chest. "Are you saying he was murdered?"

"I'm not saying anything until we get an autopsy performed." The idea that someone had walked right into the room and killed Andrew Wilson brought a chill to Charlie's spine. He pushed by the nurse who had found the dead man. She seemed like she was still in shock. "Excuse me. I have some things to take care of." He walked out of the room and beckoned one of the nearby deputies. "After the body has been removed, I want this room blocked off. No one in and no one out." He leaned in closer, so that they wouldn't be overheard. "I also want a twenty-four hour guard on Lexington Walters, until I say differently. But be discreet. I don't want to alarm her, or her family."

"Yes, sir." The deputy stepped away quickly, talking in low tones on his walkie-talkie.

Charlie looked at his watch and decided that a visit upstairs would be in order. *Maybe Lex is up to talking about things now. At the very least, I need to pass along some information to Amanda.* He headed for the elevator, with more than just the dead man on his mind.

The lift's doors opened, and Charlie took in the quiet activity on the floor as he made his way to Lex's room. Just as he was about to lightly knock on the door, it opened, and he stood face to face with Amanda, who held back a startled cry.

"Charlie! You scared me half to death." She looked behind her. Satisfied that Lex was still resting, Amanda pushed the sheriff back into the hall and closed the door. "She's asleep." Her tone was slightly accusatory, almost daring him to try to get by her.

"I'm sorry, I wasn't trying to frighten you. Why don't you let me buy you a cup of coffee?" He saw a deputy standing over by the nurse's station and gave him a slight nod. "I came to talk to you, not to Lex."

Amanda immediately felt sorry for her attitude, but then focused on what he had said. "Why? Is there something the matter?" She noticed the man Charlie had acknowledged. "Wait a minute. What the hell is going on around here?"

"Let's go somewhere quiet, so I can bring you up to speed."

Allowing herself to be led into an empty lounge, Amanda felt her apprehension grow. "Enough of the cloak and dagger routine. What's happening? I saw one of your deputies out there.

Is Lex in some sort of danger?"

"It's just a precaution." Charlie took off his hat and sat on one end of a cot, suddenly feeling his age and wondering if he was getting too old for the stress of the job. "The man we found in the alley with Lex died a couple of hours ago."

"Oh." Amanda paced around the room, absently glancing at the pictures and posters that littered the walls. She turned to look at Charlie. "He was in pretty bad shape, though, right?"

"That's just it. He'd awakened, and the nurse went to get the doctor. When they got back to the room a few minutes later, the man was dead." Seeing the frightened look on Amanda's face, he hurried to reassure her. "It could have been anything, though. We'll have to wait for the autopsy report to be sure."

Amanda crossed her arms over her chest, feeling chilled and sick to her stomach. "But you think he was killed, don't you?" Her voice shook as she asked quietly, "When is this going to end?"

Charlie got to his feet and crossed the room, then pulled the young woman into his arms. "I won't let anything happen to her, I promise." *Now if I could just make myself believe that, maybe we all have a chance.*

THE WARMTH OF the sunlight on her face through the car window was a welcome relief from the confines of the hospital, and Lex closed her eyes in order to absorb as much as possible. Her head still felt as if it was about to explode, but the doctor had assured her that tenderness would diminish over the next few days, as would the nausea that made her keep one hand on the button of the power window. She could almost feel Amanda watching her, which caused a slight grin to form on her lips. "I'm fine."

"How did you know I was going to ask you that?" Although it was true, Amanda hated being so transparent. She kept flicking her eyes between the road and Lex, afraid that the doctors had released her partner from the hospital too soon. "I could have been about to comment on the weather or something."

Lex started to laugh, but the pain in her head quickly made her think better of it. "If you say so." She opened her eyes and faced Amanda. "Thanks for getting me out of there. I was about to go stir crazy. Besides, I've had worse before and survived just fine without staying in a hospital."

"Maybe. But did that include having to face down some idiot with a gun?"

Damn. I hate it when she's right. Lex exhaled heavily and resumed her partially reclined position in the seat. "Can we just drop it for now, please? There's something else I want to do."

"What's that?"

"Go up to where those guys were building their little 'resort.'"

Amanda nearly drove the truck off the road and had to jerk the wheel quickly to keep them from going off into the side ditch. "Are you out of your mind?"

Lex held up one hand. "Hear me out, Amanda. If I'm right, then it'll be as vacant as a ghost town up there."

"And if you're not?"

"Then I hope you can make this truck haul ass in reverse," Lex responded, only half joking.

THE CHURNED-UP MUD and bits of foliage clung to his feet, and more than once he slipped on the debris left by the construction equipment. As far as he could tell, he was the only person in the vicinity, but the silence in the woods around him made him jumpy and nervous. He looked around at the wasted land, where trees were uprooted and everything else just appeared to be uselessly destroyed. The gravel that had been brought in for use as a temporary drive looked almost as bad, and he wondered if the area could be salvaged.

Car tires on the gravel caught his attention, and he quickly hid in the trees until he knew who was there. The familiarity of the vehicle caught him off guard. "They're the last people I'd thought I'd see up here."

Once the truck had come to a complete stop, Lex unfastened her seatbelt. She pointed to the red SUV parked just off the gravel drive. "Whose car do you suppose that is?"

"I don't know, but do you think it's safe to find out?" Amanda's belt was also unbuckled, since she wasn't about to let Lex go anywhere without her. She was just about to suggest calling Charlie when a movement from the woods seized her eye. "Look over there." A not-so-friendly face advanced on the truck, causing both women to cringe.

Lex tried to slide down in the seat, but the insistent tapping on the window told her she had been seen. She sat up and lowered the window. "Hey, Charlie. What are you doing out here?"

"Me? What are the two of you doing? There's no telling what you might have encountered. You could have been putting yourself into danger." He leaned inside the window to look at

Amanda. "I thought that at least *you* would have enough sense to stay away from here."

Amanda raised her hands away from the steering wheel and shrugged her shoulders. "Don't blame me. I figured it would be easier to drive her than for her to take off on her own."

The old lawman laughed. "You're probably right about that." He squeezed Lex's arm. "There's nothing to see here. Whoever those guys were, they're long gone now."

"Yeah. That's what I was afraid of." Lex looked over at the red SUV again. "Where did you get *those* wheels? Something new at the sheriff's office?"

"Hell, no! I knew that the roads out here were going to be nasty, so I borrowed it from one of the guys."

Lex blew out a low whistle. "Seems like you're paying the 'guys' too much. Maybe I'm in the wrong business."

"Nah. His parents gave it to him when he graduated from college." Charlie could see the fatigue on Lex's face. "Why don't you two go on home? I'll do a bit more exploring and tell you all about it tomorrow."

"That's the best suggestion I've heard all day," Amanda agreed, with a pointed look at her partner. She waited until both she and Lex were buckled up, then gave Charlie a tiny salute. "See you at dinner tonight, Sheriff."

He watched as the truck turned around, then he hurried away down the graveled path, knowing it would likely be breakfast before he saw either woman again, if then.

Chapter
Twenty-One

AMANDA CLOSED THE front door behind her, glad to be home from work. A couple of weeks had passed since Lex's close call, but it had reinforced Amanda's realization that nothing was more important to her than the woman she loved. She wanted to spend some quality time with her partner, knowing that the distance between them lately was as much her fault as anyone's. She heard voices coming from Jeannie's room, and walked through the den to investigate.

"Oo don' unnedtand. Did id 'omedin' I need do do." Jeannie was almost in tears, trying her best to convey her wishes. "Id'll be much eadier if I'm in down."

Ellie was heartbroken She considered Jeannie a little sister, and didn't want anything to hurt their budding relationship. "Is it something I've done? I thought we were getting along pretty well."

"No! I jus' dink dat if I'm in a home, rehab would be fasder, and I'd ged well sooner."

Amanda stepped through the door just as Jeannie finished her sentence. "Did I hear right? You want to leave us?" Her sister nodded before turning her head away, embarrassed.

"We've been going round and round on this subject all day. She wants to move into the nursing center in town where she can get more rehabilitation. I told her that I didn't mind driving her in every day, but she's being stubborn." Ellie crossed her arms over her chest, obviously perturbed.

Jeannie turned back to face her sister. "Pwease, Mandy? Id's de only way I'll feel like I'm doin' someding for myself."

Understanding the emotions behind the request, Amanda nodded. "I'll call them in the morning for you, okay? We'll see when we can get you in."

"Danks." Jeannie held out her stronger hand until Amanda grasped it. "Nod jus' for dis, bud for everydin' you've done for me. I wuv you."

"I love you, too." Amanda leaned over and kissed her sister's brow. When she straightened up, she could see tears in Ellie's eyes. "As for you," she pulled Ellie's slight frame into a hug, "thanks for taking such good care of Jeannie. You've really become a vital part of our family." She turned and left the room, leaving behind a shocked Ellie.

ROGER JENSEN SAT in the warm barn, thankful for the protection it gave. The evening brought with it a damp chill that had settled into his weary bones, and he feared he'd never be warm again.

His anger at his present situation had not abated, though. Since being fired from the Rocking W, he had traveled the area, searching and sometimes almost begging for work. The answer was the same everywhere. "Sorry, we're not hiring right now."

He knew better. *That bitch Walters must have blackballed me.* Roger tried to make himself more comfortable in the dusty hay, his face contorting as his mood darkened further. "I'll teach her. A broad that thinks she's a man just needs a little persuading, that's all." He rubbed at his crotch, then reached for the hunting knife that hung on his belt. "And if that doesn't work, I'll teach her a lesson another way."

LEX LOOKED THROUGH the trees at the setting sun, wishing she was already at the ranch house. Knowing it wasn't too much further to the barn, she coaxed Thunder to pick up the pace a little, until he was at a slow trot. The large animal kept up the pace for several minutes until he stumbled and finally stopped altogether.

"What's the matter?" Lex climbed down from the saddle and saw that Thunder was favoring his front left hoof. She bent over, grabbed his leg just above the hoof, and pulled, which caused Thunder to lift the appendage. Lex cursed when the shoe he wore dangled by one nail. It hadn't been that long since the farrier had been to the ranch to replace one of Thunder's other shoes, and Lex was livid. "I don't know why that son of a bitch didn't check all of your hooves, but when I get back to the house, I intend to find out." She gently pulled on the shoe until the remaining nail released. "Looks like we'll both be walking from here."

STANDING AT THE back door, Amanda debated going

upstairs to change her clothes first, but then again, she wanted to look good as part of her surprise. She looked down at the charcoal gray business suit she had worn to the office that morning. The skirt was only an inch or two above the knee, but she knew what a thrill Lex got from running her hands up and down Amanda's stockings. Her mind made up, Amanda stepped out onto the back porch and hurried down the path toward the barn.

The cold wind almost took the barn door out of her hands, but she was able to get the leverage needed, which caused it to slam behind her. The still darkness of the barn unsettled her; she felt as if someone was watching her. "Lex?"

From his hiding space, Jenson smiled. *Oh, this is even better than I had hoped.* What better way to get back at the woman he despised than by doing what he wanted to her girlfriend? He moved stealthily, not wanting to tip off the young woman until he was ready.

Amanda was almost to the tack room door when she felt arms circle her waist. Thinking it was Lex, she was about to snap off a silly remark when she was roughly spun around. Her eyes widened in fear when she recognized Roger Jenson in the dim light. "What—" A leather glove covered her mouth, causing her to bite her lip.

"Shut up, bitch," Roger snapped. He looked around the barn before shoving Amanda into the tack room. "This'll do."

Oh, God. Amanda struggled until his hand pulled away from her mouth and slapped her, hard. She blinked several times to clear the stars in her vision, which beat in time to her pounding heart.

"Don't fucking fight me." He pulled his knife from its sheath and rested the blade along Amanda's reddened cheek where a bruise was already beginning to form. "I don't want to cut that pretty face of yours," he whispered. When Amanda tried to turn her face away from his, he slapped her again, this time letting her fall to the floor.

Amanda screamed and tried to crawl away, but he was too fast for her. Before she knew what had happened, she was lying on her back with one of his gloves stuffed in her mouth. She shook her head, pleading with her eyes.

Jenson enjoyed the feel of the woman writhing beneath him. Seeing the terror in her face was even better than he had anticipated. He placed his left forearm across her chest, just below her throat, and used the knife in his right hand to start slowly cutting away at the buttons on her silk top. "Fun, isn't it?"

Feeling sick, Amanda closed her eyes and thought of Lex. *He may touch my body, but he'll never touch my soul. Oh, Lex, please help me!*

"Damn, woman. You're too pretty to be wasted on that broad. I bet all you need is a real man to teach you." Jenson put the knife in his left hand and used his right hand to touch Amanda's bra. "You sure are breathing hard. Bet you're getting excited too, aren't you?" He squeezed her breast roughly through the fabric. "I'll get back to these later. Got more," he rocked his hips against hers, "pressing matters to attend to."

WITH THE BARN in sight, Lex heaved a sigh of relief. All she wanted to do now was put Thunder up, take a long hot bath, and go to bed. She hoped that Amanda was home, so that they could do two out of those three things together. She immediately picked up her pace.

Once inside the barn, she thought she heard scuffling coming from the tack room. She heard a muffled cry. Trying to be a quiet as she could, Lex dropped Thunder's reins. She hurried inside, and what she saw from the doorway of the tack room almost made her sick. "You're dead, you bastard!" She lunged forward, and though he outweighed her by thirty pounds or more, she managed to knock the man off Amanda and into a bale of hay.

Amanda scooted into a sitting position and wrapped her suit jacket around herself. She pulled the dirty glove out of her mouth and closed her eyes, wanting to be anywhere but where she was.

Lex tried to get her hands around Jenson's neck, but he landed a solid punch to her ribs that left her gasping. He staggered to his feet. She returned his blow with an uppercut to his jaw.

"Is that the best you got, Walters? I think your little girlfriend's tougher than you. At least she was at first." He edged around the room, rubbing his lower cheek. "Then again, she might have started liking it."

Her anger totally out of control, Lex roared and charged Jenson. They pitched over a row of saddles.

Jenson punched her in the face several times, satisfied to see blood appear. "You want to know something else? You may try to act like a man, but you fight like a girl." He used their close proximity to slam his fist into her stomach. Lex crumpled. As her head dropped, he slammed his knee into her face. Lex went down in a silent heap. Confident that he had defeated her, Roger went back to where Amanda cowered and picked up his knife. "Isn't that right, sweetheart? We were having a pretty good time before she came along and messed it up. Maybe we should finish what we started."

Amanda pulled the coat tighter and trembled, never opening her eyes. She tried to shrink back into the rough wood slats of the barn, but the feel of his rough hand on her cheek told her she wasn't successful. "No," she whispered. She thought she had heard Lex's voice, but maybe she had imagined it. He grabbed her jaw, forcing her to open her eyes and look at him.

"I said, we should finish what we'd started." Jenson reached to pull Amanda's jacket from her when an arm wrapped around his neck.

"You *are* finished." Lex dragged him away from Amanda.

Laughing, Jenson twisted from Lex's grip. He sliced at her with his knife. "I don't think so, bitch. It's payback time." He jabbed at her again, enjoying watching the woman try to dodge his advance. When Lex tripped on an overturned saddle and fell onto her back, Jenson stood over her and smiled. A voice from the doorway caused his head to turn, giving Lex the time she needed to get up and tackle him again.

"Hold it right there! Sheriff's department," Charlie yelled, aiming his firearm at the pair grappling along the hay-covered floor.

"You are dead, you son of a bitch! Do you hear me?" Lex screamed, her hands around Jenson's throat. She slammed his head against the ground, time and time again, until he quit struggling. "Dead!"

"Lex, wait!" Charlie holstered his gun and rushed over to stop Lex from killing the unconscious man. When he had trouble prying her hands from around Jenson's throat, he tried another tactic. "Check on Amanda. I'll take care of this scum." His words had the desired effect, as Lex slowly released her grip and looked up at him.

"Amanda?" Her voice caught on the name, and she looked around the tack room, not seeing her partner anywhere. Lex stumbled to her feet and rushed out into the main part of the barn. She searched around frantically until her eyes came upon Amanda, sitting below the intercom. "Oh, sweetheart."

Amanda looked up as she heard Lex's strangled words. Even bruised and bloody, her partner had never looked better to her in her life. She held out her arms, and Lex fell into them, both emotionally spent and unable to speak.

A HULKING DEPUTY escorted Jenson from the barn, politely averting his eyes from the scene in the corner. He tipped his hat to Charlie before dragging the groggy prisoner to the squad car and forcing him into the back seat.

Martha knelt next to Lex, using a clean towel to clean the blood and dirt from her face. "I really think the both of you need to go to the hospital." She had been trying for the past half-hour, unsuccessfully, to talk some sense into the duo. Both were wrapped in quilts that Martha had brought to the barn. Amanda wasn't letting go of Lex, who kept looking at Amanda as if she'd disappear if she so much as turned her eyes away.

Distressed about the shaking body in her arms, Lex knew it would be best if a doctor checked out her partner. Amanda hadn't uttered a word since Charlie had come into the barn, which worried her even more.

"Your beautiful face," Amanda finally whispered, looking at Lex. Several small cuts were still oozing blood, and her face was already sporting different shades of blue and purple.

"It'll heal. I'm more worried about you." Lex reached up, but Amanda pulled away from her touch. The movement almost broke Lex's heart. She started to pull back, when her hand was grabbed by Amanda and her leather riding glove was removed.

"I'm sorry, it's just the smell of the gloves. He—" Remembering the smell, and the taste when Jenson forced the glove into her mouth made Amanda nauseous all over again.

Lex almost started crying at the pitiful tone in Amanda's voice. "Don't you dare apologize." She pulled Amanda close. "But maybe Martha's right, and you should go get looked at by a doctor." She wanted to voice a question, but was terrified of the answer.

Amanda shook her head. "I'll be okay. You got here in time to stop him. He never—" She paused to get her emotions under control. "He wasn't able to—" Amanda started to sob again. "I've never been so frightened in my life. When he started to, you know," she tightened her hold on Lex, "I decided to just close my eyes and think of you, hoping that you'd come to save me."

"I'm so sorry—"

"Don't be. You came, and you *did* save me."

Lex turned away in shame. "Yeah, right. More like I got my ass kicked, and then Charlie came in." She looked around the room until she saw the sheriff. "Charlie?"

He finished up with another one of the deputies and joined the three women in the corner of the barn. "Yes? Can I radio for an ambulance now?"

"No. I think we're all right. But I do have a question for

you." Lex was glad that Charlie knelt beside them, but kept his distance from Amanda. She wasn't sure how her lover would take *any* man's presence at the moment.

"Okay." He tilted his hat back on his head and tried to put a smile on his face. "Shoot."

"How did you end up in the barn? Don't get me wrong, I was never happier to see anyone in my entire life. But you *never* come out here."

Amanda cleared her throat. "While you were fighting with *him*," she couldn't bring herself to say Jenson's name, "I went to the intercom and called the main house. He had that knife, and I was so scared for you. I knew Charlie was there, because I heard him and Martha talking before I came out here to surprise you."

"Surprise me?"

"Mmm-hmm." Surrounded by those she loved, Amanda began to recover. "I thought it would be fun to be in the barn waiting for you when you got home. Stupid idea, huh?"

Lex kissed the top of Amanda's head. "Not at all. I think it was very sweet." She looked around and saw that the barn was now vacant, except for the four of them. "Why don't we head to the house and get cleaned up? I don't know how much longer my old bones can handle being this close to the floor."

That last little comment elicited a laugh from Amanda, who watched in concern as Lex allowed Charlie to help her up. She quickly got to her feet on her own, not wanting Lex to hurt herself by trying to aid her. Wrapping one arm around her wife's hips, she guided them both from the barn. "Bath?"

"Sounds great. Together?"

"Is there any other way?" Amanda asked, causing Charlie to lose his footing when he overheard the conversation. "Trouble there, Sheriff?"

Charlie took his wife's hand and led her away from the pair. "Nope. Not a bit. We'll be in the, umm, kitchen, if you need us." They hurried away, Martha laughing at her husband's discomfort.

THEIR BATH TAKEN, Lex and Amanda headed to bed, neither bothering with nightclothes. Lex crawled under the sheets first, and wasn't surprised when Amanda slid in beside her. Lex wrapped both arms around her lover. "Is this okay?" Her voice almost echoed off the walls in the room, which was eerily quiet since Martha had insisted that Lorrie spend the night over at the cottage.

"Very." Amanda moved until she was on top of Lex, looking

down into her face. "Make love with me?" she asked quietly. She could still feel his touch on her skin and wanted something to erase the horrible memory. "Please?"

Lex raised a shaky hand and brushed the hair away from Amanda's face. "Are you sure? Because if you need me to, I can just hold you."

"Don't," Amanda took a deep breath, "don't you *want* to touch me?"

"Of course! There's never a day, a moment, when I don't." Lex waited until she had Amanda's full attention. "But I also never want to hurt you." The kiss she received effectively silenced Lex's argument, and she lay there quietly and allowed Amanda to take the lead. Although the hands that traced patterns down her chest were incredibly gentle, Lex couldn't help but gasp when Amanda hit a sensitive spot on her ribs.

Amanda stopped immediately. "Did I hurt you?"

"A little." Feeling the loss when Amanda's hands disappeared, Lex caught them and put them back where they had been. "Not enough to stop, though."

Those few little words righted all that had been wrong in her world. Amanda realized with sudden clarity that although it would take her a long time to get over the evening's events, just knowing how Lex felt about her made it easier to move on. "Thank you," Amanda whispered, kissing the hollow of Lex's throat. She knew realistically neither one of was in any shape to go any further and rolled over to snuggle close in order to keep from hurting her wife. "Raincheck?"

"Sure." Lex was grateful that Amanda had changed her mind. Her whole body ached, and she honestly didn't think that lovemaking was in either of their best interests at the moment. A moment later, a soft snore told Lex Amanda had already fallen asleep, but not even total exhaustion was enough to keep Lex from staying awake most of the night. She was afraid the living nightmare she had walked into in the barn would cross over into her dreams, and she didn't want to disturb Amanda. So she kept a quiet vigil until the sun crept into the bedroom the next morning.

"NO! DON'T TOUCH me," Amanda cried, slamming her elbow into Lex's side. "Get away!"

Lex, who had fallen asleep only an hour or so before, jerked awake and looked around the room frantically. "Ow! What?" When she saw that Amanda was having a nightmare, she tried to wake her partner gently. All that got her was another hard jab to the ribs, which sent Lex over the side of the bed and onto the floor. "Damn." Lex had just gotten back on the bed when the door to their room opened and a disheveled-looking Ellie rushed inside.

Ellie didn't even notice Lex's nudity. "What the hell's going on here?" She roughly tried to pull her cousin away from Amanda. When she saw the dark bruise on Amanda's face, Ellie wanted nothing more than to strangle Lex. "Good God, what have you done to her?"

"I didn't do anything to her." Lex struggled out of Ellie's grip. "And it's none of your business, anyway."

Between the noise and the movement around her, Amanda woke up. "Is there a reason the two of you are wrestling on the bed?"

"Ask her," both women answered at once.

Ellie finally took a good look at Lex and blushed. Not only was she nude, but her body was covered in bruises as well. "Have the two of you been fighting?"

The frank appraisal by her cousin made Lex uncomfortable, and she slid back under the covers. "No." She turned to look at Amanda. "Are you okay?"

"Yeah, just a nasty nightmare." Amanda looked between Lex and Ellie. "I'm sorry to have awakened both of you."

Ellie stepped away from the bed, embarrassed. "Sorry about attacking you like that, Lex. I just came in from town, and was on my way to Jeannie's room when I heard Amanda's screams."

Lex couldn't help but be impressed by her cousin's recent change of heart. The Ellie she first met would never have apologized, and more than likely would have gotten in a few good punches before retreating. "That's okay. I'm sure it *did* look pretty strange."

"Now that's a first," Martha commented from the doorway. She had been downstairs handing Lorrie over to Jeannie when she heard the ruckus above them. "You're both behaving this morning? I may just have to sit down before I faint." She crossed the room and sat next to Amanda. "How are you faring this morning?"

"Okay." Amanda was happy to feel Lex take her hand, and she squeezed back. "I had a bad dream a few minutes ago, which caused this whole mess."

Ellie looked at the three women on the bed. "Is anyone going to tell me why Amanda and Lex look like they've gone three rounds in the ring and lost? I thought at first that—"

"I know what you thought," Lex interrupted. "And, believe me, I may be an asshole with a bad temper at times, but I'd die before I *ever* laid a hand on Amanda in anger. Remember that."

Martha saw that Ellie looked like she was about to go on the defensive and decided it was time to defuse the situation before it got out of hand. "Ellie, would you mind going down and keeping Jeannie company until I can get down there to put breakfast on the table?"

"Sure." When she got to the door Ellie looked back at Amanda, who nodded to assure her everything was all right. "I'll see everyone downstairs, I guess."

Amanda waited until she was certain the three of them were alone. "Thanks. I really didn't feel like getting into everything right now."

"That's quite all right, dear. You don't have to tell anyone a thing more than you want, although I think Charlie might have some more questions for you both whenever you feel up to it."

Lex could feel her protective streak kick in. "Why? I thought we told him more than enough yesterday. I don't want Amanda having to relive that nightmare." In truth, it was Lex that didn't want to start thinking about the events of the evening before. Even she knew that they had been lucky that she had gotten to the barn when she did.

Amanda tightened her grip on Lex's hand. "It's okay. I want to make sure he has everything he needs to put that creep away for a long time." She gave Martha a weak smile. "We'll be down for breakfast in a little while so we can just answer everyone's questions at the same time. No sense in going over it more than once."

Lex would have preferred to keep Amanda in bed for the day, if only to protect her from everyone's curiosity and good intentions. "Are you sure?"

"Yes."

Martha stood up. "Do you want me to call your family, and see if they'd like to come out?" At Amanda's shy nod, she dusted her hands together. "Well, then, looks like I'd better get busy fixing up a feast." Before stepping away from the bed, Martha leaned over and gave Amanda a light peck on the forehead. "You just come on down whenever you're ready, and I'll take care of everything."

Grateful for the mothering nature of the housekeeper, Amanda could barely keep her emotions in check. "Thanks, Martha."

Lex watched Martha close the door behind her as she left. "I've got to be the luckiest woman in the world."

"Why's that?"

"Because not only was I raised by her, but I get to spend the rest of my life with you. Pretty good deal, if you ask me."

Amanda sighed and rolled over to snuggle into her lover's arms. "Sounds like we both lucked out, then." She kissed the hollow of Lex's throat. "Think we can sneak in a little nap before breakfast?"

"I don't see why not." Lex pulled the covers up over them both. "I love you."

"Love you, too." Amanda's voice trailed off as she fell asleep, content to have Lex protect her from the bad dreams.

Chapter Twenty-Two

THE NEXT FEW days were rough on Amanda. Her grandmother insisted that she take a leave of absence from the real estate office, and her father made daily trips out to the ranch. As well-intentioned as her family was, their solicitude was beginning to wear on her. The only one who seemed to be giving her any space at all was Lex, and Amanda feared that the ordeal had left its own scars on her wife. She would often wake in the middle of the night to find Lex sitting up, holding Lorrie, and quietly watching their bed and its sole occupant.

It was on one such night that Amanda stirred and rolled over to face where Lex sat in the rocker with Lorrie. The nightlight next to the crib bathed them in a soft glow, showing how tenderly Lex cradled the baby. "Lex?"

The whispered of her name drew Lex from her musings, and she looked up to meet Amanda's gaze. "Hey there. I was trying not to wake you."

"The cold bed woke me." Amanda sat upright and ran one hand through her hair. "I didn't even hear her cry."

Lex glanced down at Lorrie, who had finished her bottle some time ago. She had been burped, but Lex couldn't bring herself to put the infant back to bed. "She gets hungry about the same time every night, so I'm usually prepared for her. I thought you needed your sleep."

"We agreed to take turns." Amanda got out from under the covers and padded over to Lex. "I think you've been doing more than your share lately."

"Well..."

Amanda took the sleeping infant and placed her in the crib. After she was certain that Lorrie was comfortable, she crossed her arms over her chest and looked down into Lex's tired features. "Are you ever going to tell me the real reason you're up all night, every night? And don't even think about lying to me."

Lex couldn't meet Amanda's gaze. "It's just some stuff I'm

trying to work out."

"I'd like to help, but you've got to trust in me enough to talk."

"It's not a matter of trust." Lex stood and walked to the windows, where she quietly watched the night sky for several minutes.

Amanda was afraid she had pushed Lex too far when she heard her partner's ragged whisper.

"I've failed you." Lex turned around, her eyes filled with tears. "Every time I close my eyes, I see what happened in the barn, and I'm so damned terrified that I'll fail you again."

"You can't think that way. Because if you can't get past what happened, how am I supposed to?" Amanda knew she was in dangerous territory, but she had to get Lex to forgive herself before her guilt tore them apart. She closed the distance between them until she could feel the warmth from Lex's body. "I'm a grown woman who is perfectly capable of getting myself in and out of trouble, Lex. I didn't fall in love with you because you took care of me, or saved me from danger." She put her hands on Lex's hips and pulled her closer. "I fell in love with your beautiful heart." Amanda paused and grinned. "Not to mention that sexy smile and gorgeous body. Pretty much a perfect package."

"But—"

Amanda silenced Lex with a kiss. When she pulled back, she saw the look of surprise on Lex's face. "Now, come back to bed and let me hold you, and we'll work through all this stuff together, okay?"

"All right." Lex dutifully followed, her heart lighter than it had been in days.

LEX STOOD AT the foot of the stairs, unsure of which direction she wanted to go. The tantalizing aroma that floated from the kitchen made her mind up, and she proceeded to follow her nose until she was just inside the doorway. "I don't know what's in that pot, but whatever it is, I'd be more than happy to clean it out for you."

Martha turned around and almost dropped her spoon. Lex stood with a clean cloth diaper on her shoulder, while the baby in her arms looked up at her. Her voice caught in her throat at the sight. "If I hadn't seen it with my own eyes, I might never have believed it."

"What? Do I have something on me?" Lex looked down at her plaid shirt. "Looks clean enough to me."

"Brat." Martha turned her attention back to the pot of stew she had simmering on the stove. "Sometimes I don't know how Amanda puts up with you."

"Must be my natural charm." Lex looked down into Lorrie's face before she sat down in a kitchen chair. "Isn't that right, kiddo?"

Martha sighed. "Oh, yeah. Right." She continued to stir the stew. "Speaking of which, where is Amanda?"

"She's in the den, researching the home care facility before she calls them. I swear, that woman is a whiz on the Internet."

Martha brought over a small bit of stew in a mug. "Here, try this and see if it's okay." She knew that Lex would be whining for a taste before lunch, so she decided to surprise her by offering the mug first. "So Jeannie's still set on leaving us? I was hoping she'd change her mind."

"Me, too." Lex took a cautious sip of the hot stew. "Damn, woman."

"What? Too spicy? Not enough spice? Is there something missing?"

"It's fantastic," Lex assured her. "Probably the best you've ever made. As for Jeannie, I know what you mean. Amanda's pretty upset about her leaving, too. That's why she's checking out the care center, hoping that there will be something wrong with it that we can use to keep Jeannie here." She finished what was left in the mug and held it out. "May I have some more, please?" Her attempt at a British accent was flavored by her Texas roots.

Martha shook her head. "You'll have to wait until lunch time, just like everyone else." But secretly she was pleased that her stew was so well received. "How long do you think it'll take Amanda to do her computer search? I want to know when to put the bread in the oven."

"I don't know. She was also going to check her email, since Anna Leigh told her to stay away from the office for the next couple of weeks. I'm hoping she'll be done in the next half hour or so."

A yell from the den caused both women's eyes to widen, and Lex was on her feet instantly. She raced from the kitchen, Lorrie still cradled in her arms.

AMANDA SAT IN the corner of the den where they had set up the computer and desk from Lex's office. She had found nothing but glowing recommendations for the care center where Jeannie wanted to move, and reluctantly, she had to accept that they'd have to let Jeannie go. Before calling the facility to start making arrangements, she had decided to check her email only to find several emails from people she didn't know. This didn't ring any alarm bells. After all, she did run the real estate office and often got letters, both good and bad, either about an employee or a property. The third email elicited a very loud expletive. It gave Amanda the web link to her bank in California, telling her to check her balance. While she waited for the site to upload, she continued to read the letter. In it, the writer apologized for his part in the "temporary" loss of her money, then went on to explain, in detail, what had happened. She let out a yell.

"What the hell's going on in here?" Lex rushed into the room, doing her best not to frighten the baby in her arms. "Are you all right?"

Amanda was too busy looking at the computer screen to turn around. "Come here and see for yourself."

Lex stood behind Amanda and saw the amount of money in the bank account. "Isn't that?"

"Yeah." Amanda opened up the screen of the email. "Now read this."

"Dear Ms. Cauble," Lex murmured, then read silently. *Son of a bitch!* "That's great, sweetheart."

With tears in her eyes, Amanda could only nod. A sudden thought struck her. "I wonder." She closed out her email and quickly switched over to Lex's. "Look. Here's one from him to you, too."

"Go ahead and open it." Lex could feel her heart start to pound in anticipation. The email was similar to what had been sent to Amanda, with the request that Lex check her bank balance as well. At Amanda's questioning glance, she nodded.

"Oh, my God. Was this what your stocks were worth?" Amanda asked, shocked at the amount.

Lex swallowed hard. "I don't know. That's why I had someone handling the investing. But I don't think I'll be making that mistake again. Could you pull up the email, please? I didn't read it all the way through."

Amanda quickly did as she was asked. She had also missed the last half of the letter, and gasped in shock at the revelation. "My mother? How did she get out of the mental institution? She wasn't up for evaluation for another four months."

"I don't know, but I bet you ol' mother is shitting herself over all this. You know how she hates to lose."

"Do you think we're in any danger here? From her, I mean?" The last thing Amanda wanted was for her mother to come back and make their lives miserable again. *Like burning down the house wasn't enough. She had to steal from both of us?* "Family or not, if I ever see her again, I swear I'm going to punch her in the face."

Lex put her free hand on Amanda's shoulder. "Whoa, there. Let's just tell Charlie about this and have the law take care of her. I honestly don't think she's going to hang around here since all this went wrong." She looked down at the computer screen. "I'd sure like to shake that fellow's hand, though. He took an awful risk going against your mother."

Amanda shook her head. "I don't have a mother. That woman was just a vessel that brought two kids into the world." She covered Lex's hand with one of her own. "I wouldn't claim her for any amount of money, and I wouldn't spit on her if she were on fire." She turned back around and closed out the computer programs and shut everything down. "Let me call the care facility, and then we can tell the family about all that's happened, okay?"

"Works for me." Lex stood where she was for a moment. "Mind if we keep you company?"

"I'd love it." Amanda stood and kissed her wife. When she was sure Lex had been thoroughly kissed, she placed her lips on Lorrie's forehead. "Thank goodness you won't have to worry about that woman, sweetie pie. We'll make sure of that."

"Damn right." Lex winked at Amanda, then took a seat in a nearby chair to watch her lover. "Hurry up now. The smell of Martha's stew has my stomach rumbling."

IT TOOK ALMOST a week before a room became available for Jeannie at the care center in town. Jeannie watched as Amanda tearfully packed her meager belongings into a suitcase.

"We're going to have to get you more clothes, Jeannie. I don't want those people thinking we can't afford to dress you." Amanda's voice shook, and she turned her back so that her sister wouldn't see her cry.

"I...habe...enob." Jeannie had been working hard with Ellie on her speech, and she was privately proud of the progress she'd made in such a short time.

Amanda shook her head. "I'd still like to take you shopping, if you'll let me." She placed the last item in the bag and zipped it closed. Unable to look at the urn that took up the space on the four-drawer filing cabinet, Amanda tried to think of a way to ask her sister about it. "What about—"

"I been...tinkin...bout...Fwank." Jeannie wished, at least for this one conversation, she could speak at a normal pace.

"Where's...Wex?"

Oh, boy. This is something I definitely didn't want to bring Lex into if I could help it. "I think she's in the kitchen with Martha, having some coffee before heading over to the bunkhouse. Do you want me to go get her?"

"Pwease."

Amanda left the room, shaking from the emotional toll. *What could she be thinking? Is she going to ask Lex to keep the urn here? Or maybe find some way to place it in her room at the center? God, I hope it's not that.* She stepped into the kitchen, feeling everyone's eyes upon her. "Lex, Jeannie wants to see you. I think it's about, umm, Frank."

Lex frowned. "Frank?" She looked to Martha for help, but the housekeeper just shrugged. Ellie remained conspicuously silent as well. "Okay." Lex stood up and handed Lorrie to Ellie before leaving the room. When she was in the house, Lex was usually holding the baby, a fact everyone but Amanda seemed to have noticed.

Jeannie looked up when Lex stepped into the room. She read the concern on her sister-in-law's face and held out her good hand to try to dispel Lex's anxiety. "I...need...your...elp."

Lex took the offered hand and squatted next to Jeannie's wheelchair. "Name it."

"Fwank."

"Okay." Lex followed Jeannie's gaze to the urn, and nodded. "Do you want the urn to stay here?"

"No."

Wonderful. I get to play Twenty Questions. "Do you want to take it with you? I'm not sure the care center will allow that."

"No." Jeannie exhaled heavily. "Could...ou...buwy im ear?"

What? Did she just ask— "You want him to be buried here on the ranch?"

Jeannie nodded tearfully. "Pwease?"

"Well, sure. If that's what you want. Would it bother you if he was in my family cemetery? My dad's parents are there, and my mother, father and brother, too."

"Dat wud be wondervul." Jeannie pulled Lex's hand to her lips and kissed it before rubbing it against her cheek. "Ou...wudn't...mind?"

Lex brushed the hair away from Jeannie's face in a tender gesture. "I'd be honored. He's family, as are you."

"Tanks."

Amanda stood in the doorway of the room. "Is there something between you two that I should know about?" she asked in a teasing fashion.

"Nah. I think you already know that I love your sister." Lex stood up and kissed Jeannie on the forehead. "Right?"

Jeannie blushed and giggled. Even as serious as the conversation had been, she felt as if a huge weight had been lifted from her shoulders. She watched as Lex picked up her sister and spun her around.

"Lex, you idiot! Put me down!" Amanda instinctively locked her hands behind her wife's head. "You're going to hurt yourself." She couldn't stop the wide grin that broke out on her face at Lex's playful manner. "What's got you so excited?"

"To tell you the truth, I don't really know. But it feels so good to hold you, I don't think I'll ever stop." Lex kissed Amanda soundly.

When they didn't show signs of stopping, Jeannie cleared her throat. "Ged...a...woom."

Lex walked over and set Amanda on Jeannie's bed. "Can we use yours?"

Both Amanda and Jeannie groaned at the suggestion. Amanda was the first to find her voice. "That's just sick."

"Oh. Are you saying I should share?" Lex received the expected slap on the arm for her comment.

"Lexington Marie! You watch your dirty mouth." Martha stood in the doorway wiping her hands on a dishtowel. She had come to the room to tell everyone that lunch was ready and had overhead Lex's last remarks. Although she was secretly glad the three were in a playful mood, she had her own role to play. "You all get cleaned up and get to the kitchen before I feed the stew to the stock."

Jeannie snickered while Amanda fell back onto the bed, laughing loudly.

"Oh, shut up," Lex grumbled, as she released her hold on Amanda and left the room. Her attitude only spurred the other women's mirth, and she could hear their laughter all the way down the hall.

Chapter
Twenty-Three

IT TOOK THEM only two days to get everything ready for the funeral service, although it would take longer than that to make and erect a proper headstone. Lex had called in some favors, as did Charlie, and now all of them were gathered in the Walters' family graveyard.

Although it wasn't that far from the ranch house, due to the weather Lex had insisted that everyone drive. She assured them that she wasn't worried about the land being torn up by the vehicles, and in fact offered to convey anyone who wanted to ride with her in the truck.

The morning brought with it a heavy dew. Across from the grave, Ronnie and Travis stood on one side of Lex, while Amanda and her father stood on the other. The minister's words of sympathy and compassion caused Amanda more than once to seek solace in her partner's arms. Jeannie sat in her wheelchair in front of the grave with Ellie behind her, flanked on either side by Anna Leigh and Jacob. Martha had volunteered to stay at the house with Lorrie, as they all decided that it was too cold and damp for the baby to be out. Amanda watched as Jeannie accepted the condolences of the clergyman, looking much stronger than Amanda felt. The man nodded to Anna Leigh and Jacob before taking his leave, knowing the family needed quiet time alone after the service.

Jeannie looked across the grave to where Amanda stood. She could tell her sister had trouble keeping herself together through the service, and knew that Amanda would have to come to grips with Frank's death in her own way. She believed she was lucky in that respect. *Spending most of my days thinking about nothing else certainly has given me proper perspective. I know I have to get well so that I can raise my daughter and be a contributing part of my family. I hope Amanda finds the peace she so desperately needs.*

Jacob leaned down to whisper in Jeannie's ear, "Do you need more time, or are you ready to go? It's entirely up to you."

"I'm oday. But I wand do 'ome back when de headsdone's here." Jeannie waited until Michael walked to her and then allowed her father to pick her up in his arms. She snuggled against his chest. The heavy grasses and uneven ground made maneuvering her chair almost impossible. "Danks. Id's a wong walk back to de car por me."

Michael kissed her head. "Anytime, sweetheart. And I'll be glad to bring you back out here whenever you want. Just let me know." He could hear the others start to follow them back to where the cars were parked.

Lex kept a firm grip on Amanda's hand, hoping to keep them both emotionally grounded.

The ride back to the house was unnerving Ronnie. He had never been around Lex or Amanda when they were both so quiet, and he looked over to Travis for a clue as to how to handle the situation.

Travis tried to assure Ronnie with a look, but wasn't sure if he had been successful. All he wanted, more than anything, was to take away the pain Lex and Amanda were feeling, but he knew they had to get through it on their own. He waited until the truck was parked beside the house before speaking. "Is there anything I can do to help around the house?"

"Why don't you just come in for coffee," Amanda offered quietly. "Your company would be the best help in the world right now."

"Then that's what I'll do." Travis followed the Lex, Amanda, and Ronnie through the side door and into the kitchen. Seeing Martha trying to make coffee while holding a crying Lorrie, he quickly jumped into action. "Martha, do you want me to take the baby, or the coffee machine?"

The harried housekeeper gave him an exhausted smile. "If you'll finish up the coffee, I'll go check this little one's britches. I'm sure that's what she's so upset about." She patted him on the arm as she left the room with the baby.

Lex waited until her grandfather made quick work of the coffee duties. He had the brew going in no time. "I didn't know you knew how to make coffee."

"Do you think I made my servants do it for me?" Travis asked, thoroughly amused. "I'll have you know I wasn't always well-off, young lady. I worked damned hard for many years to get to where I am today."

"In my kitchen?" Lex teased.

Amanda hastily rose from her seat. "We just buried someone! I don't think it's the time to be so damned flippant." She rushed from the room, tears flowing from her eyes.

"Damn." Lex sighed and rubbed her face. "I screwed that up."

"I don't think so. But it might be a good idea to go find her and calm her down," Travis advised.

Lex hurried out of the room in search of Amanda. Hearing the front door slam, she figured that her wife had gone to sit on the front porch swing, one of Amanda's favorite places to go and think. Lex walked down the hall and cautiously opened the door, peeking outside. "Can I talk to you?"

With her back to the door, Amanda didn't indicate that she had even heard the request. She continued to cry, but wasn't surprised when Lex sat down beside her on the swing.

Lex's voice was quiet. "I'm sorry."

Amanda continued to look down at her hands, which lay clasped in her lap. Her hair fell around her face, and she was hoping that Lex couldn't see how much she had been crying. She felt like a complete fool for making a scene in the kitchen and was thankful that the rest of the family hadn't arrived in time to see her emotional display .

"Please, Amanda, would you look at me?" Lex felt like a first-class jerk, and the longer Amanda went without acknowledging her, the worse she felt. "We all love and miss him, you know. It's just that when I get nervous, I tend to release that pressure by joking." Lex stood, then squatted at Amanda's feet and placed her hands on either side of her partner's legs. "Can't we talk about this?"

The pleading tone in Lex's voice touched Amanda, but she still felt so badly about her own behavior she couldn't, or wouldn't, look up.

"Please forgive me?"

Amanda had no doubts that Lex would continue to beg until she responded, and her guilt over hurting Lex outweighed the embarrassment of her actions in the kitchen. "There's really nothing to forgive," Amanda whispered. "I'm the one who acted like a jerk."

Lex felt her heartbeat slow to its normal speed. Having Amanda upset with her was the last thing she ever wanted. "No, you're grieving. There's nothing wrong with that."

Amanda stood, and helped Lex to her feet as well. She linked her arm with her wife's and guided them both back into the house. "Thanks for coming out to get me."

"Any time, sweetheart." Lex pulled Amanda closer and kissed the side of her head. "But I hope I don't upset you again any time soon. I love you, Amanda Cauble-Walters."

"I love you, too."

With things back to semi-normal, Lex felt herself relax for the first time in days. She just hoped their relationship would weather whatever the next obstacle might be, as well.

LATER THAT AFTERNOON, Lex loaded up Anna Leigh and Jacob's Suburban with all of Jeannie's belongings. She had wanted to drive Jeannie to the care center herself, but Jeannie told her there was no use in her making a special trip into town when her grandparents were going anyway. Although it made perfect sense, Lex didn't like the decision.

Amanda had gone shopping, and now, much to her sister's surprise, Jeannie's worldly belongings included two more large suitcases full of things. Jeannie tried to act upset, but the smile that kept breaking out on her face gave her away.

"Do you need any help with that?" Amanda asked Lex, as she stood next to Jeannie on the porch. "I'm sure we can get Martha to load all that for you, if you can't manage."

"Smart ass." Lex loaded the television and closed the back hatch. She took a deep breath and released it before turning to Jacob. "Now remember, you're not supposed to touch a thing. I've given explicit instructions, and they're getting paid extra to unload your truck and get everything into Jeannie's room. All you have to do is help her unpack her clothes."

"And we'll be more than happy to do just that, Lexington," Anna Leigh assured her. "I can't speak for my husband, but I'm not about to lift some of those boxes. I thought you were going to rupture something yourself."

Lex couldn't help laughing. "I always complain when I work. Just ask Martha. But honestly, don't you dare lift a finger, okay?"

Jacob nodded. "Yes, ma'am. We promise."

Anna Leigh watched as Jeannie held Lorrie, with Amanda and Ellie beside her. "Are you and Amanda going to be all right taking care of the baby until Jeannie is back on her feet? That's a lot of responsibility you're taking on."

"I know." Lex followed Anna Leigh's line of sight and couldn't help but smile at the scene. "We've been doing pretty well so far, and we've had Jeannie to care for, too. So I think we'll be okay. Besides, Ellie's asked to stay here and offered to nanny for us during the day. And of course, we'll be bringing the baby in to visit her mom several times a week."

Anna Leigh clapped her hands. "Excellent. You know, Ellie seems like a very sweet girl."

"You two look to be getting along a lot better, that's for

sure," Jacob commented. "Did you call a truce?"

Lex laughed. "Something like that." She noticed the sad look on Ellie's face, while the others on the porch were all smiles. "I guess it's time to get this show on the road, though. You really want to have her all moved in before dinner time." She walked over to the porch where everyone else was standing. "Miss Jeannie, would you mind if I give you a lift to your chariot?" Lex asked, bowing deeply at the waist.

Unable to contain her mirth at her sister-in-law's antics, Jeannie tittered. She allowed Amanda to lift Lorrie from her lap, and kissed the baby's forehead. "Tanks."

"You're welcome." Amanda did her best to keep from crying at the heart-wrenching separation. "Remember, we'll bring her in every other day, and if that's not enough, give us a call, okay?"

"Otay." Jeannie waved her good hand to Lex. "I'm weady."

Lex bent down and plucked Jeannie from the wheelchair. "I figured for this trip, you'd get the personal touch."

Happy that Lex had been thoughtful enough to put her strong side close to Lex's body, Jeannie hooked her hand around Lex's neck and leaned into the embrace. She understood why her sister was so taken with this woman. Never had she met anyone, her own husband included, who was as sensitive, loving or gentle as the woman who carried her now. She just hoped that Amanda cherished Lex, or she might be in for a fight. *Wouldn't that just freak out the folks!* Jeannie chuckled, which caused Lex to almost drop her.

"What's on your mind?"

No way was Jeannie going to share that little tidbit, ever. "Nuthin'."

Once the wheelchair and all of the passengers were safely loaded into the Suburban, Lex stood on the porch with Ellie, while Martha took Lorrie inside for her nap. Amanda gave last minute instructions to her grandparents in the vehicle, and Lex turned to see tears in Ellie's eyes. "Hey, are you okay?"

"I don't know what it is about those Cauble women that attracts me to them," Ellie admitted quietly. She had become very attached to Jeannie since they'd started working together, and it pained her that Jeannie felt the need to get better care than what she was giving.

Lex, who had heard the quiet comment, put her arm around her cousin's shoulders. "I don't know the answer to that one, El. But if it's any consolation, I think you've got real good taste."

"Thanks." Ellie sighed and walked back into the house, her heart broken once again.

Amanda waved at the Suburban until it was out of sight, then joined Lex up on the porch. "That was harder than I thought it would be."

"I know."

Taking her wife's hand, Amanda led them both over to the swing so they could sit. "It's not going to take Jeannie that long to get better, you know. She's already moving both legs and has limited use of her left hand now."

"I know." Lex knew she sounded like a broken record, but she wanted to hear where Amanda was going with her thoughts.

"I don't know how I'll be able to let Lorrie go once Jeannie is ready for her," Amanda admitted quietly. "She's already such a big part of me."

"Me, too." Lex looked off into the winter rye field that was starting to grow in front of the house. "But you never know. There's really nothing for Jeannie in California anymore. Maybe she'll decide to settle down in Somerville."

Amanda propped both elbows on her knees and placed her chin in her open palms. "That would be great, but—"

"And, I was hoping you and I could discuss giving Lorrie a little cousin or two. It would be tough to be an only child in a family, don't you think?"

It took Amanda a long moment to understand what Lex meant. When she finally figured it out, she almost whooped and jumped off the swing. "Are you sure about this, Lex? You've never expressed a desire to have children of our own. You made it clear in the past that you didn't want any."

"If there's anything these past few weeks have taught me, it's that we can't take one moment of life for granted. I thought I'd have all the time in the world to think about kids, but when that guy pointed his gun in my face, all I could think about was what I still wanted to do and what I'd be leaving behind. You were born to be a mom, Amanda. I can see that, and I want to raise children with you, if you still want to."

Amanda couldn't believe what she had just heard. It was as if Lex had read her mind. She leaned forward and kissed her partner. "I want this for us, too. You and me, having a family. I know that's the way things should be."

"Yup. My thoughts exactly. The way things should be." And she reached over to encircle Amanda in a tight hug, feeling the joy and rightness of the love they shared.

THE END

Other books in this series available from
Yellow Rose Books

Destiny's Bridge

Rancher Lexington (Lex) Walters pulls young Amanda Cauble from a raging creek and the two women quickly develop a strong bond of friendship. Overcoming severe weather, cattle thieves, and their own fears, their friendship deepens into a strong and lasting love.

ISBN 1-932300-11-2

Faith's Crossing

Lexington Walters and Amanda Cauble withstood raging floods, cattle rustlers and other obstacles to be together...but can they handle Amanda's parents? When Amanda decides to move to Texas for good, she goes back to her parents' home in California to get the rest of her things, taking the rancher with her.

ISBN 1-932300-12-0

Hope's Path

In this next look into the lives of Lexington Walters and Amanda Cauble, someone is determined to ruin Lex. Attempts to destroy her ranch lead to attempts on her life. Lex and Amanda desperately try to find out who hates Lex so much that they are willing to ruin the lives of everyone in their path. Can they survive long enough to find out who's responsible? And will their love survive when they find out who it is?

ISBN 1-930928-18-1

Love's Journey

Lex and Amanda embark on a new journey as Lexington rediscovers the love her mother's family has for her, and Amanda begins to build her relationship with her father. Meanwhile, attacks on the two young women grow more violent and deadly as someone tries to tear apart the love they share.

ISBN 1-930928-67-X

Strength of the Heart

In the fifth story of the series, Lex and Amanda are caught up in the planning of their upcoming nuptials while trying to get the ranch house rebuilt. But an arrest, a brush-fire, and the death of someone close to her forces Lex to try and work through feelings of guilt and anger. Is Amanda's love strong enough to help her, or will Lex's own personal demons tear them apart?

ISBN 1-930928-75-0

Also from Carrie Carr
and
Yellow Rose Books

Something To Be Thankful For

Randi Meyers is at a crossroads in her life. She's got no girlfriend, bad knees, and her fill of loneliness. The one thing she does have in her favor is a veterinarian job in Fort Worth, Texas, but even that isn't going as well as she hoped. Her supervisor is cold-hearted and dumps long hours of work on her. Even if she did want a girlfriend, she has little time to look.

When a distant uncle dies, Randi returns to her hometown of Woodbridge, Texas, to attend the funeral. During the graveside services, she wanders away from the crowd and is beseeched by a young boy to follow him into the woods to help his injured sister. After coming upon an unconscious woman, the boy disappears. Randi brings the woman to the hospital and finds out that her name is Kay Newcombe.

Randi is intrigued by Kay. Who is this unusual woman? Where did her little brother disappear to? And why does Randi feel compelled to help her? Despite living in different cities, a tentative friendship forms, but Randi is hesitant. Can she trust her newfound friend? How much of her life and feelings can Randi reveal? And what secrets is Kay keeping from her? Together, Randi and Kay must unravel these questions, trust one another, and find the answers in order to protect themselves from outside threats—and discover what they mean to one another.

ISBN 1-932300-04-X

"An excellent story about two women who've gone through the School of Hard Knocks. You can't help but root for Kay and Randi as they try to make sense of their lives. This is Carrie Carr's best novel yet!"
~Lori L. Lake, author of *Gun Shy* and *Different Dress*

Carrie Carr is a true Texan, having lived in the state her entire life. She makes her home in the Dallas/Ft. Worth metroplex with her wife AJ. She's done everything from wrangling longhorn cattle and buffalo, to programming burglar and fire alarm systems. Her time is spent writing, traveling, and trying to corral their two dogs—a Chihuahua named Nugget, and a Fox Terrier named Cher. Carrie's website is www.carrielcarr.com, for information such as merchandise, personal appearances, and personalized bookplates for her books. She can be reached at cbzeer@comcast.net.

Printed in the United States
29186LVS00002B/57